T. JEFFERSON PARKER
COLD PURSUIT

By T. Jefferson Parker

T. JEFFERSON PARKER

COLD PURSUIT

HARPER

An Imprint of HarperCollins*Publishers*

HARPER

An Imprint of HarperCollins*Publishers*
10 East 53rd Street
New York, New York 10022-5299

Copyright © 2003 by T. Jefferson Parker
Excerpt from *California Girl* copyright © 2004 by T. Jefferson Parker
ISBN 978-0-06-210340-6

First Harper premium printing: January 2012
First HarperTorch mass market printing: October 2004

HarperCollins® and Harper® are registered trademarks of Harper-Collins Publishers.

Printed in the United States of America

Visit Harper paperbacks on the World Wide Web at
www.harpercollins.com

10 9 8 7 6 5 4 3 2 1

For Matt and Trina

COLD
PURSUIT

1

That night the wind came hard off the Pacific, an El Niño event that would blow three inches of rain onto the roofs of San Diego. It was the first big storm of the season, early January and overdue. Palm fronds lifted with a plastic hiss and slapped against the windows of McMichael's apartment. The digitized chirp of his phone sounded ridiculous against the steady wind outside.

"Somebody killed Pete Braga about an hour ago," said McMichael's lieutenant. "You're up on the wheel of fortune, but I'll give it to Team Two if you want."

It was a question McMichael could think about for a long time but didn't.

"We'll take it."

"Somebody bludgeoned Pete in his house, Tommy," said the lieutenant. "Blood and brains all over the place. Patrol's holding the cleaning lady or some such thing."

It took McMichael a moment to transfer Pete

Braga from the roster of the living to the ranks of the dead. Murder was always a surprise. Especially if it was someone like Pete, who seemed like he'd live forever.

"We'll take it," he said again.

A brief pause. "You're sure about this, Tom?"

"I'm sure."

"The Irish are a stubborn people. About as stubborn as the Portuguese. Okay, then. Pete Braga's yours."

Eighty-something years old, thought McMichael. It wouldn't take a gladiator to crush the old man's skull. A local badass hero, done in by the cleaning lady.

"I'll make the calls, Tommy. You get moving. Need the address?"

"I know it."

Pete Braga's estate was on the bay side of Point Loma, right down on the water. Three levels of weathered redwood and plate glass descended to the sand. The glass caught the wind-fractured lights of Shelter Island and the city across the bay.

The driveway gate was open and McMichael could see three San Diego PD patrol cars, two slick-back Fords, a paramedic truck and a red Beetle parked in the sweeping brick drive. A small crowd had gathered at the crime scene tape that ran across the driveway. They looked like carolers between songs, McMichael thought, uncertain and self-conscious, coats and scarves and hair riled by the wind. He lowered a window and badged a uniform. The officer untied one end of the tape and it shot from his hand toward the water.

McMichael followed the walkway to the front door. The path was lined with bronze light fixtures shaped like leaping tuna. Behind the lights a stand of Norfolk Island pines swayed against a faint moon wrapped in clouds.

At the front door an officer T. Sterling handed McMichael an entry log. Before looking at it Mc-Michael studied the outside doorknob, the jamb and frame.

"Shoot," he said, scanning down the log.

"We were first on scene, sir," said the officer. "Slow night, maybe because of the storm coming in. Then the watch commander dropped a possible one-eighty-seven on us. We got here in seven minutes. The nurse who made the nine-one-one call let us in. I noticed substantial amounts of blood on her hands, face and clothing. The old man was in his trophy room, or whatever you'd call it, by the fireplace. His head was caved in. The nurse was upset and not really cooperative, so Traynor took her into the dining room. I ran a warrants check on her and she came back clean."

McMichael signed the log and looked into T. Sterling's eager gray eyes.

"A nurse, not a cleaning lady."

"That's what she said."

McMichael gave the log back to Sterling. "The blood on her clothes, was it smears or spatters?"

"I'm not sure. Mostly smears, I believe."

"What about her face?"

"I think smears, too."

"You didn't let her wash up, did you?"

"I don't think Traynor was going to."

Another officer led the detective to the scene. The trophy room was down a long hallway, then to the right. McMichael felt the coldness of the house in his shins. The hall was wide and well lit by recessed ceiling lights. There were paintings hung museum style, with individual viewing lights fastened above the frames: all ocean scenes—ships and waves in violent moments, the grandeur of catastrophe at sea. One light was trained on nothing, just blank wall with a hanger still nailed to the plaster.

He stepped down into the trophy room, smelling blood and feces and cigar smoke. Two small bundles of firewood lay at his feet. Above him was a cavernous cross-beam ceiling with heavy-duty shop lamps hung in two rows of six. The lamps washed the room in a strong incandescent glow.

McMichael pulled the little tape recorder from the pocket of his bomber's jacket, checked the tape and turned it on. He spoke into it, setting the time and date and location, then narrating what he saw.

Ahead of him was a wall of glass facing the water and the city. Beyond the glass, windblown leaves swirled through the deck lights and a quick blizzard of sand rose toward San Diego Bay. A navy destroyer sat moored to the east, irrationally large amidst the tenders and pleasure craft.

To McMichael's right was a cedar-paneled wall festooned with Pacific trophy fish—tuna, yellowtail, dorado, swordfish, sailfish and sharks. In the lower right corner of the wall hung some of the gear used to catch them—rods, reels, gaffs and fighting belts.

His eye went to the two empty hangers, like he'd

seen in the hallway. One amidst the fish, one in the gear.

The main attraction was a white shark that looked to be three times the length of a man. It was obscenely thick. Rows of teeth glistening, its huge head swung outward in the posture of attack. McMichael noted that the taxidermist had gotten the eyes right, rolled back into the head for protection. He remembered that Pete Braga had made TV and the papers with that one.

To his left was a large fireplace with no fire and two handsome leather chairs facing it. On either side of the hearth stood enormous saltwater aquariums teeming with tropical fish. McMichael stepped past the bundled firewood. Between the chairs was a small table and a lamp with two shades, two bulbs and two brass pull chains. Both bulbs were on. Two half-filled glasses of what looked like red wine sat on the table.

He walked over and looked down on the body of Pete Braga, slouched almost out of the right-hand chair. Braga was wearing a smoke-gray satin robe. He had slid down, legs buckling on the floor, his back and head flat on the chair seat. His arms dangled over the rests, hands relaxed. His head was bathed in blood and the top crushed in the middle—skin and hair and bone seeming to fall in upon themselves. His face was a bloody mask of surprise and confusion, eyes open and still reflecting light. On the hardwood floor to the left of the chair stood a pond of blood littered with pale debris and a short club with a leather loop at the end of the handle. McMichael felt the hair on his neck stand up.

Requiescat in pace, he thought, thirty-plus years of Catholic funeral Latin imprinted in his mind. What a way to get your last ticket punched.

He remembered Braga as a tuna fleet captain, way back in '70. McMichael had been five years old. He remembered him as a Ford and Lincoln Mercury dealer a few years after the tuna industry collapsed—Pete's robust, gray-haired face smiling down at you from freeway billboards on the 5 and the 8, and the 163 and along Clairemont Mesa Boulevard. Remembered him as a mayor and a port commissioner and a city booster, always tossing out the first pitch at a Padres game, smiling while a champagne bottle cracked against a hull, touring the latest opening or disaster.

But easiest of all McMichael remembered Pete as the grandfather of Patricia Braga, the first girl he'd fallen in love with. They were children then, back before they fully understood that the McMichaels and Bragas had spilled each other's blood and that they were supposed to hate each other.

Forensic specialists Bob Harley and Erik Fiore stepped down into the room, toting their bags of tricks. Behind them were the Team Three sergeant Mark Hatter and Detective Barbara Givens.

"Jesus," said Givens.

"Woah," said Harley. "Reminds me of that guy— what, Appleby or something? With the pipe."

Erik whistled low, the sound falling off at the end like something going over a cliff. "Cool aquaria."

Sergeant Hatter said nothing. He was in charge of Homicide Team Three by rank, but McMichael was up for lead on this one, purely a matter of rotation and chance. Wheel of fortune, thought McMichael—whose fortune?

Harley set down his forensic case and brought out a digital still camera, which he looped around his neck, and a Polaroid, which he checked for film.

McMichael told Erik to shoot the video, then start the measurements and sketches. "Get the club first," he said. "Then fish it out of the blood. I want Polaroids of those firewood bundles, close up as you can get. Barbara, do a quick-and-dirty theft check on the rest of the house—see if anything obvious has been lifted. Look for forced entry."

"Got it."

"Then take a look at the VW Beetle out there, but don't go into it yet. After that, I'd like you to handle the press and media. Tell them what we know."

A moment later the medical examiner's team quietly entered. Then Hector Paz, McMichael's closest partner within the team, barreled in behind them like a wrecking ball.

McMichael nodded to Paz and backed away from what used to be Pete Braga and was now San Diego PD case #03-114-M. He checked the trophy wall where the fishing equipment was displayed and found the empty hook between a large gaff and a fighting belt.

"Shoot this hook, Bob."

"There's nothing on it."

"Looks like a good place to hang a club."

2

The nurse was young, dirty blond and tall. She turned from a dining room window when McMichael and Paz walked in: hair up in a loose nest, a blood-smeared cream turtle-neck, a blood-smeared fuchsia cardigan, bloody jeans and short-heeled black boots. McMichael studied her as he approached—blood on her face, neck and hands. Her eyes were very dark brown.

"I'm Detective Tom McMichael. This is Hector Paz."

"I want to wash up."

He looked down at her boots and saw the dark drops in relief against the leather. "Do you mind if we take a few pictures of you first?"

"I mind."

The nurse stared at Paz with a sullen blankness.

"What's your name?" asked McMichael.

"Sally Rainwater."

"What's in the pockets?" asked Paz.

Sally Rainwater looked down and extracted one

black leather glove from each of the cardigan's side pockets.

"You can just set them on the table," said McMichael. "And the cardigan, too, if you don't mind."

She dropped the gloves on the dining table, then unbuttoned the sweater. She dropped it on the table, too, and fixed her dark brown eyes on him. Her pupils looked normal and her eyes were primitively wild, set off by her face and the blood.

"You can wash up," said McMichael. "I'm going to have a female investigator accompany you."

She strode out and McMichael nodded to Traynor. "Get Barbara."

Hector watched them go. "You going to ask her for the boots?"

"I will."

Hector looked at McMichael with his typical expression of suspicion and latent good humor. "She'll clean up nicely."

"I think so."

McMichael then briefed Paz on what Sterling had told him. Paz was a stocky, muscular man about McMichael's age. Like McMichael, he was only three years in Homicide. They were placed on Team Three because of different temperaments. Tom McMichael was tall and quiet and sometimes sly, Hector Paz bullish and aggressive. The homicide captain called them Calm and Heckle. The Team Three case cancellation rate was highest in the unit.

McMichael pulled out two of the dining set chairs, then turned the chandelier lights over the table all the way up. He took the bay view for himself, not for the scenery but to make the nurse look at him while she talked. He used a pen to nudge her gloves a little closer to where she would sit. The blood on them gave off a duller reflection than the leather and left a faint smudge on the cherrywood lacquer.

"Just hover," said McMichael. "Break in when you want to."

"I can hover. Should we Mirandize her?"

"Let's wait. It looked like transfer blood on her. No mist or droplets, except on her boots."

"Except on her boots."

Five minutes later Sally Rainwater walked back in. Barbara looked in at McMichael, shrugged with an undecided arch of eyebrows, then headed back down the hall.

McMichael was writing in a small notebook, which he closed and placed on the table next to his tape recorder. Hector stood in front of a bronze sculpture of a leaping tuna that dominated one corner of the room.

"Please sit down," said McMichael.

She looked at the ready chair, the gloves, then at him. Her face and hands were clean now, her hair in a strict ponytail. No jewelry, no ring. Her clothes were the same blood-splattered mess. She turned the chair toward the picture window and sat so she wouldn't be facing either of them, so all McMichael could see was profile. He studied the high curve of forehead, straight small nose, her good chin and lips.

"You don't mind talking to us, do you, Ms. Rainwater?"

"I'll talk."

"Thank you. I'm going to tape-record this."

She said nothing as McMichael flipped the tape over and turned the machine on. He had her spell her name and give her home address and phone number.

"Tell me what you saw tonight."

"I went out at about nine-twenty for firewood. I came back a few minutes after ten. I went into the fish room and saw Pete dangling over the side of his chair. The sliding door was open and the wind was coming in. Someone was running across the sand toward the bay. He jumped the wall and disappeared. I saw Pete's head and the blood and the Fish Whack'r and called nine-one-one, then tried to bring him back. I couldn't."

Sally Rainwater turned and looked at him, then back to the bay. Hector faced them now, leaning against the picture window.

"Fish Whack'r?" he asked.

"That's what the club is called," she said.

"Describe the person you saw," said McMichael.

"Black running suit, and a dark cap pulled down. It could have been a man or a woman, but it ran like a man. Average build and height. He blended in with the darkness, just jumped the wall and disappeared."

"Just disappeared," said Paz.

McMichael looked at him, then out to where the sand blew across the beach.

Hector found a light switch and hit the outside floodlights. All three of them watched as the wind softened the scores of footprints going all directions in the public sand. McMichael thought of beachcombers, joggers, walkers, swimmers, kayakers, paddleboarders, you name it. Even in winter, San Diegans loved their beaches.

"Was Pete dead when you found him?"

"Yes. I did CPR anyway, until the cops and paramedics got here."

"Did you kill him?" asked Hector.

"No," she said quietly.

McMichael watched her and let the seconds stretch. "Did you move him?"

"Yes." Her voice was soft but clear and, McMichael thought, a little distant now. "He was hanging over the left side when I walked in. I wrestled him up straight and he slid down like that. I figured that was as good a place as any, so I started the CPR."

"But nothing."

"Nothing but blood all over me."

"What work did you do here?"

"I'm a registered nursing aid, but for Pete, most of what I did was just domestic. Cooking, laundry, light cleaning. Some shopping. Sometimes I'd drive him."

"Where?" asked McMichael.

"Errands. He liked to ride."

"How come he didn't go with you for the firewood?" asked Hector.

"The cold weather made him stiff. He liked the fish room when it was cold. Because of the fireplace. But we didn't have any wood."

"We," said Hector. "You two get along pretty good?"

"Yes. Sure. Seven months, I got to like him."

"So you were like, friends."

"We were friends."

"Friends," said Hector with a smile.

McMichael watched her watch Paz. "How was Pete tonight?"

"Fine. He was always fine. Alert. Strong for his age. Healthy."

"Pete ever talk about being in danger, having enemies?"

"He disliked a lot of people. And a lot of people disliked him. I'm sure you know that."

"Any recent threats that you know of?"

"No."

McMichael watched her reflection in the picture window and saw that she was watching his. The first small drops of rain skidded down the glass. "Did that club come from the wall?"

"I think so. It looked like the one that used to be there."

"We'll get prints off the handle," said Paz. "Unless the creep was wearing gloves, or wiped it down."

She stared out at the storm-swept bay, but said nothing.

"Did you wear your gloves when you tried to revive him?" McMichael asked.

She looked at him again and shook her head, a minor motion that seemed intended mostly for herself. "No. Well, at first I touched his head, the sides of his face, to see his eyes. The gloves were on when I did that. Then I went to the phone and took them off to dial. When I straightened him in the chair and tried the CPR, no, I didn't have them on."

"Did you touch the club tonight?"

"No."

"Did you touch it recently?"

"No. Why?" She turned and looked at him, and for the first time he saw confusion in her unhappy brown eyes.

"In case we find two sets of prints on it."

"And what if you find just one?"

"That person is in deep shit," said Hector.

When she turned to look at Paz her ponytail shifted and McMichael saw the tattoo high on her neck, an inch below the hairline, right side, a small red flame with two points lapping at her pale skin. Or maybe it was a red tulip.

"It would help us quite a lot if we could have your boots for blood samples," he said.

"You can take the gloves and sweater, but I'm not walking around tonight in my socks."

"Ms. Rainwater, do you plan to be in town for the next few days?"

She answered yes without looking at him.

"Can I see your driver's license?"

"My purse is in the kitchen. I'll go—"

"I'll get it," said Hector. He was already moving toward the French doors. "Stay put, Ms. Rainwater. You've had a hard night."

Paz came back into the room with a black purse in one hand and a stainless steel derringer in the other. He held the gun between thumb and forefinger, at the bottom of the grip, the short barrel dangling down.

"Sorry, Ms. Rainwater, but the strap snagged, the purse tipped over, and out came your piece. I'll just put it back in. It's yours, isn't it?"

"It's mine and it's registered."

"You got a permit to go with it?"

"Yes. Give me my purse."

She set the purse on the table, dug out a wallet from which she handed McMichael a CDL and a San Diego County Concealed Carry Permit.

He took out his notebook and wrote down her date of birth and the license and CCP numbers.

Hector had glommed Fiore's camera during his purse retrieval, and now used it to shoot pictures of Sally Rainwater's boots.

She took back her documents, slung the purse over her shoulder and started out.

"Ms. Rainwater," said McMichael. "Where did you go for the firewood? Which store?"

"Ralph's on Rosecrans," she said, and kept on walking.

"Did you lock the door when you left?"

"Yes. And it was locked when I came back."

They watched her go, McMichael unable to keep from checking her shape in the jeans. Excellent indeed.

When she was gone, Hector smiled at McMichael and shook his head. "Odds?"

McMichael switched off his tape recorder, hit rewind. "Ninety-ten no. So far, I believe her. And if she did it, she'd bash, grab what she wanted and drive away. She wouldn't call us."

"I got sixty-forty yes. She bashes, stashes the goods in her Beetle out there, calls us, gives a story and sticks to it. Fucking *gloves*, man. Convenient. And she knows the name of that club, but she's never touched it? Come on."

"So she's driving away with stolen property right now?"

"Sixty-forty she is," said Hector.

"Pull her over and ask her if you can look in her car."

"She'd say no. She's not dumb."

"Then beat her home and see what she unloads."

McMichael hit the play button on his little tape recorder, wrote Sally Rainwater's address in his notebook, snapped the sheet out and handed it to Paz.

3

It took McMichael three calls to get Patricia Hansen's home phone number and tell her what had happened to her grandfather. She'd been sleeping and her voice was thick and dull but McMichael recognized it immediately. He could hear her husband, Garland, interrogatively grumbling in the background. She said thirty minutes and hung up.

Besides the painting missing from the hallway, Detective Barbara Givens had found for McMichael two more blank spots—with the lights illuminating nothing—in an upstairs bedroom. And another painting gone from the dining room. Another from one of the downstairs baths.

"Nothing else obvious," she said. "We could use someone who knows the house."

"The granddaughter's coming over."

"Good. The press is out in force. Local celebrity hour."

"Tell them no arrests. I let the nurse go home, Barbara. Leave her out of your statements if you can."

"They already know she made the call," said Givens. She was stout and broad-shouldered, with short blond hair and quick blue eyes that often noticed what others missed. McMichael thought of her as optimistic and he trusted her completely. "Her car looked fine from the outside, Tom. Nothing interesting. Wouldn't mind lifting that trunk, though. And I listened to both the messages on the answering machine in the kitchen—a health insurance solicitation and a call from a man named Victor. No last name and no message."

Victor Braga, thought McMichael: Pete's son. A sixty-three-year-old man with the mind of a ten-year-old. Living proof of the hatred between the McMichaels and the Bragas.

"Try the neighbors on each side, and across the street," he said.

"My next stop. What do you make of the nurse?"

McMichael had to think about that. There was a lot to see but not much to conclude. "Scared, angry. I don't think she did it."

"I'd feel that way, too. Whether I'd bashed him or not."

Back in the trophy room he watched the coroner's team zip Pete Braga into a body bag, one of them cradling the old man's head with a plastic sheet so the pieces wouldn't slide to the floor. McMichael felt bile in his throat and disgust in his heart. But he also felt a confirmation that pleased him in a way he couldn't deny, though he certainly wouldn't confess it to Father Shea.

Because Pete Braga had shot Franklin McMichael, his grandfather, dead in the summer of 1952.

Because Pete Braga said it was self-defense and the district attorney had not filed charges.

Because, in McMichael's book, murder was unforgivable and it always caught up with you in the end, which was part of why he had become a cop in the first place.

Patricia Hansen blew through the front door at twelve-forty in a red hooded raincoat, two steps ahead of Garland. She finished cursing an officer outside, shook out of the coat and hung it on a rack by the door while her husband battled the umbrellas.

McMichael had seen her eight times in the last twenty years, only because they lived in the same city.

"Goddamn Tommy, it's not good to see you but it is."

Flummoxed again, as he had been through the decades by Patricia Braga, McMichael defaulted to a nod. "I'm sorry about this."

"Where is he?"

"They took him to the morgue."

Patricia bit her lip, and for just a moment, standing there in a too-big reindeer sweater and jeans and rubber boots with fur around the top and her riot of dark hair, she looked like the girl he'd first stared at in the fifth grade, which was the moment he had first discovered Planet Female.

McMichael shook Garland's hand and led husband and wife into Grandpa Braga's dining room. He put them at the other end of the table from where he and Sally Rainwater had sat, protecting the latent fingerprints she'd left on her chair and the polished tabletop.

He told the Hansens some of what Sally Rainwater had told him, but not all of it. He left out the man—probably a man—running across the sand into the gathering storm because he wanted the Hansens' unfettered take on the nurse's aid.

"What do you know about the caretaker?" McMichael asked.

"I never liked her," said Garland. "Pete ran an ad in the *Union-Tribune*, said he interviewed half a dozen."

Garland Hansen was a tall, slender man with a chiseled face and hard blue eyes. His Nordic white hair was cut short and brushed back to an appearance of velocity. He was forty-eight, ten years older than his wife and McMichael, an accountant and a former U.S. America's Cup first mate. He was now in middle management at a troubled surf-and-snow sports retail empire known as *Shred!*

"She was probably the prettiest one who applied," said Patricia.

Garland shrugged insincerely.

"Did he check her background?" asked McMichael.

"Of course," said Garland. "She had good enough recommendations. Supposedly putting herself through school, UCSD—biology, I think. Wants to be a surgeon. Pat and I figured if she was smart enough to do that, she could probably handle Pete."

"Handle him?"

Garland looked at Patricia, the silent handoff that married couples perfect.

"He'd fallen several times," she said. "His eyes were going. He kept driving without a license and you guys kept catching him. He hated to cook and clean. And he was lonely. Three children—one almost senseless, as you might remember, and two living out of state. Six grandchildren, including me, but they're hardly around except when they want money."

"What did he pay her?"

"I think it was five hundred a week," said Garland.

"Did she do it?" asked Patricia. Her voice wavered so she punched up the volume, and in this Mc-Michael thought he heard the end of her toughness and the beginning of her grief.

"I don't know."

"Well, is she under arrest?" asked Garland.

"No."

"You didn't let her just walk away, did you?"

"She drove away."

Garland looked to his wife.

"Pretty goddamned funny," said Garland, standing and holding McMichael in his cool blue stare. "Someone murders Pete Braga, and a McMichael is supposed to solve it."

"Drop it," said Patricia.

"I'm afraid that's what *he'll* do," said Garland.

"Mr. and Mrs. Hansen," said McMichael. "Walk this house with me and help me figure out what's been stolen, besides some paintings off the walls."

An hour later McMichael's neatly hand-printed list read:

5 oil paintings by 19th cent. artists—10 to 30K each (hall, bedroom 2nd floor, dining, 1st floor bath #2)

18th century Chinese vase—5K (TV room)

4 a'graphed books by Joseph Conrad—5K per (all books from library, 2nd flr)

a'graphed b'ball gloves: Ruth, Gehrig, Hodges, Williams, Mays, Mantle, Koufax, Rose, Gwynn, etc.—1K to 3K each (office, 2nd flr)

one mounted fish (small to medium)— $100???! (trophy room)

Items named and values estimated by Patricia & Garland, unsure of painter names, book titles, ballplayers, type of fish.

An interesting list, thought McMichael. And almost as interesting were the things not taken: $245 cash still in Pete Braga's wallet on the nightstand, a very good watch, a box full of jewelry in the top drawer of Anna Braga's dresser.

McMichael stood again in the master bedroom and watched the rain pour down on the outside deck, a large wooden platform enclosed for privacy by a waist-high railing but open to the sky. He remembered that Pete had liked to sleep out there, years ago. He remembered the fire pit. He remembered that the bay breeze cooled your skin after making love then the fire warmed you back up and the faint taste of salt and wood smoke on Patricia Braga's neck.

"I spent some good hours on that deck," she said. "Kid stuff."

Garland looked at it, then to his wife. "Looks cold."

"Grandpa slept out there practically every summer night. He used to, anyway."

Garland shook his head. Whether at Pete's sleeping habits or at Patricia was not clear to McMichael.

"What about a safe?" McMichael asked.

"Back to the library," said Patricia.

"You know the combination?"

"He gave it to me when Anna died."

The library was a classic gentleman's room, with floor-to-ceiling walnut bookshelves, ladders to access the volumes, paneled walnut walls, heavy furniture, hunter green carpet. There was a fireplace and a walk-in humidor behind glass doors.

McMichael stepped into the humidor, smelled the sharp sweet scent of tobacco and cedar, felt the air damp on his face. It was about the size of a closet, with shelves on two sides and a humidifier built into the other. He noted Pete Braga's cache: mostly Cuban *maduros*—Romeo & Julieta, Partagas, and Rey del Mundo. But some Dominicans thrown in, and two wooden boxes marked *Libertados*, which McMichael knew well because his sister owned the cigar bar and factory in San Diego's Gaslamp Quarter where they were made. He wondered if the old man went there himself to buy them. And if he'd known his money was going to a McMichael. They were No. 7 pyramids, with dark brown wrappers.

The floor safe was hidden under a brown, brass-nail leather couch. Patricia knelt down and spun the dial.

"I don't know what's in here," she said. "I've never had a reason to open it."

McMichael knelt down beside her. It was a cylinder-type safe, ten inches across and a foot deep.

"Go ahead," he said.

Patricia reached in and lifted a handful of small boxes, which she placed on the carpet. Then another. Some black, some red, some tan, some white. She opened them and lined them up in front of McMichael.

"Grandma Anna's," said Patricia. "This isn't costume jewelry."

McMichael watched her hand as it gently moved across the jewels and gold and silver. He'd always loved the shade of Patricia's Portuguese fingers, especially where the rich dark of the top blended into the paler underside. They were thirty-eight-year-old hands now, leaner and stronger than they had been when McMichael knew her.

"She had a pair of diamond earrings that aren't here," she said. "Big two-carat things Grandpa got in South Africa. But there's got to be some other explanation. I mean—if somebody took them, he'd take all this, too. I mean, if they were even in here to start with. Right?"

"What else?" asked McMichael.

Patricia sighed, picked up a string of pearls, settled it back into the case.

"There's a species of hummingbird named the Anna's hummingbird, so Grandpa had one made for her," said Patricia. "It was life-sized, and there was a stand for it. Wings out, like it was flying. But the feathers were gemstones. It was beautiful, this big splash of red rubies on the throat and neck. Emeralds and diamonds. God knows what he paid for it. That would have been back in 'seventy-five, 'seventy-six. It's not here. It wasn't anywhere else that I saw. I guess you should add it to the list."

"I don't get it," said Garland. "How much do you need to arrest the nurse? Blood all over her? Valuables missing?"

McMichael suppressed an urge to flatten Garland.

"Pete have a will?" he asked.

"Sure. Talk to Hank Grothke."

"Junior or Senior?"

"I think Junior handles the will," said Patricia.

Garland sighed like he'd heard enough. "So, Detective. Someone ripped him off. Someone killed him. My money's on the nurse."

"Noted," said McMichael.

Patricia studied him with her steady dark eyes. "Grandpa was giving her things," she said.

"What things?"

"Paintings and jewelry, I think. I'm not sure, but he let us know—plenty of times—how great she was."

"Maybe he gave her the diamond earrings and the hummingbird," said McMichael.

"No," said Patricia. "He wouldn't give away those things. Those things *were* Anna."

"The nurse took him for a fucking ride, Detective," said Garland.

"Get out of here," said McMichael. "Sign the log on your way out."

* * *

He stood in the trophy room, behind the leather chairs in front of the fireplace, taking in details. Erik was dusting the handle of the sliding glass door for prints. There were yellow stick-ems posted everywhere, numbered to correspond to the lifts. And pink ones identifying the wineglasses, which would be emptied and bagged for the cyanoacrylate chamber back at the lab. Samples of the liquid would travel back to the lab, also, to be worked over by Flagler's forensics people.

Harley stooped over the club, which had been fished from the pool of blood and laid out on a sheet of opaque plastic.

"Superglue for this," he said. "I can *feel* the latents. Flagler will need the hair and brains and whatever else is stuck to it. Here's your firewood portrait."

He slipped the Polaroid from his pocket and handed it to the detective.

"Good," said McMichael, gazing at a potted plant hung near the far corner. Even from here it looked plastic. Its clay pot was supported by a cutesy wooden wall sconce. The top of the sconce flared into a heart shape with what looked like a homily printed on it in chipper, childlike handwriting. Gift from a child or grandchild, he thought—something that might not mean anything to anyone anymore.

"*Yesss!*" said Erik, standing back from the slider. "Whoppin' fingerprints on the handle here, and it looks like blood to me. This joker's toast."

McMichael stood in front of the trophy wall. He looked at the nail from which the club had possibly hung, noting the black fingerprint dust and the yellow tag. He counted twenty-two trophies, not including the missing fish, represented now by a blank space and a small hole. Who'd steal a mounted fish? Up close, he saw the red lip of a plastic screw seat, set in the drywall to keep the screw from pulling out. Something small hung here, he figured, from the size of the space and the single hole.

He looked over at the kitschy potted plant again, then went to one of the two huge aquariums. The tropical fish flitted and swirled through the blue, making their rounds amidst the clams and grass. There was a rock archway, bright yellow and red corals, even a decorative anchor. A tan and black wrasse with neon blue pinstriping glided past. Hermit crabs scurried, their shells impossibly beautiful, their antennae waving.

Lightning cracked through the sky outside and the fish flinched.

He loved his ocean, McMichael thought. And his baseball. And his Fords and his politics and his power. Clobbered dead by a thief for some paintings and baseball mitts and books? How much money is your common creep going to get for things like that? Two cents on the dollar? The guy would need Braga's gate code to pull his car into the driveway, load the loot, get out before the nurse came back with the firewood. It didn't line up as that kind of robbery.

Which left the guy running from the trophy room. Or Sally Rainwater. Or maybe a team, with Sally conveniently out of the picture for the fatal forty minutes and the runner not a runner at all but a guy with a van. *He went that way.*

He looked over again at the potted plastic plant. It had become a brain thorn, which was McMichael's name for something that got into your mind on its own, bothered you and you couldn't get it out. They were usually innocent and mildly annoying, like the names of actors whose shows you never watched, snippets of pop songs you've never really listened to, coaches whose sports you didn't follow. To imagine Joey Fatone humming the latest *NSYNC hit to Bobby Knight over and over again—that was a brain thorn.

So McMichael scratched his itch, walking over to see the plant up close. It was in fact a plastic creeping charlie. The pot was plastic, too; even the heart shape at the top was plastic, molded to look like painted wood. The childlike writing said:

**A HAPPY PLANT
IS A SMILE
FROM
HEAVEN!**

A grandchild's present, thought McMichael, touching the letters, which were raised and painted. Until his fingertip passed over the slick convex center of the O in From.

Odd. And no such thing as a brain thorn at a crime scene, he thought.

Gently, he pried at the sconce. It resisted, then clicked decisively, then swung out on two hinges. A video camera was fit into brackets on the back, allowing it to fit back into a rectangular hole in the wallboard. The lens was aligned with the cutout center of the letter O. The mike had a hole of its own, hidden behind the curve of the pot. A small motion detector was affixed beneath the camera and hardwired into the "record" relay, its sensor partially concealed behind the leaves of the plastic plant. A 120 volt power cord twisted back into the hole and out of sight.

"Hey, guys."

The CSIs crowded in behind him. McMichael swung the hide-a-camera sconce open and shut then open again.

Harley couldn't believe he hadn't noticed it. Erik asked how you tell if a plant is truly happy.

McMichael's heart took a funny little dive when he pushed the eject button and found no cassette inside.

"So much for good luck, serendipity or the existence of God," said Erik.

McMichael concurred on two of the three, good Catholic that he was. He also wondered where the tapes were.

"This crime scene looks like that one two years ago," said Harley. "Applethorpe or something. You remember that, Tom, older guy up in Hillcrest?"

"It's still open. Team One."

"Unusual MO."

McMichael's phone vibrated.

"I'm down in Imperial Beach," said Hector. "Outside a pub called Ye Olde Plank. I really like these little binoculars. I can almost read the bartender's watch. It's about time for last call in there."

"Where's the nurse?"

"Third seat from the end of the bar, drinking at

high speed. And yapping on her cell. She's made three calls in less than an hour, and downed five greyhounds. Least they look like greyhounds."

"She went straight there?"

"No, man. First home, then here."

"Did she take any loot out of her car?"

"Just her purse. But get this—I went around to her front porch, it's right there on the sand, you know? Had a look through the blinds to make sure she was okay. She was sitting on her couch. And over the couch is one of those paintings like Pete had. An old boat in a storm. Same kind of fancy gold frame. It looked like the last painting in the world a babe would hang in her apartment."

"There are five paintings missing from Pete's walls, according to Patricia," said McMichael. "She also said Pete was giving things to the nurse."

"Well, looks like Nurse Sally got at least one painting off the old man," said Hector.

"What did she do while she was home?"

"Cried."

"We'll knock on her door tomorrow morning," said McMichael. "Ask for a tour."

"She'll turn us down flat. But let's get her early, while she's still good and hungover."

"I've got IAD at eight."

Hector was quiet for a beat. "Good luck, man. I forgot about that."

"Wish I could."

Internal Affairs Department was no San Diego cop's idea of a good time. Especially one who liked his job and thought he could make a good captain someday. Especially one who'd worked with Jimmy

Thigpen in Metro/Vice, back before Jimmy got caught in a very expensive hotel room with a prostitute, a Sheriff's Department deputy posing as a prostitute, a big bag of Oaxacan weed and $324,000 in cash.

"Maybe you could run Miss Sally through NCIC while I'm getting grilled about Jimmy."

"Glad to."

4

McMichael made the IAD hearing on three hours' sleep and half a pot of coffee. Being tired strained his patience for men and women he didn't care for anyway. Cops who thought they were better than cops is how McMichael thought of them. And IAD was the incubator of the ambitious, the self-righteous and the power driven, because that was where you could protect the career of a friend or destroy the career of an enemy.

McMichael sat at one end of a long table in a headquarters conference room. No windows. There was a plastic pitcher of water and one glass at his place. At the almost comically faraway other end of the table were Assistant Chief Jerry Bland, IAD director Lieutenant Mitch Huzara, and IAD special investigator Sergeant Andrea Robb. McMichael saw his Human Resources file, positioned squarely in front of Robb. On top of that, a yellow legal pad.

He crossed his hands on the table and stared at his knuckles and thought about Sally Rainwater.

He'd seen her face in a dream. What if she were telling it straight, that she'd come home and tried to resuscitate the old man? He wasn't optimistic about this, human nature being full of mostly disappointing surprises.

Bland and Huzara greeted him when he sat down. Robb positioned a microphone, glancing at him to get the angle right, but not bothering to acknowledge him. Then she fiddled with the recorder controls.

On her way up the ladder, he thought: files handy, blinders in place, ready to cream the opposition. What happened to the idea that cops liked busting dirtbags instead of each other?

"Voice check, McMichael," she said. "Say something."

"It's great to be here this morning."

"Again?"

"It's *great* to be here this morning."

She played it back. "Fine. It even picks up your sarcasm."

She was tall and red-haired and attractive, too, though it rankled him to admit it.

"We may as well get started," said Huzara. He was slight, bigheaded and balding, with a neat gray mustache. "Sergeant McMichael, just to let you know how it works around here, Jerry's representing the chief's office but he's not a part of the IAD. Andrea's going to lead the questions, but Jerry and I will have some, too. You're not being deposed or you'd have counsel here. That may be the next step. Or a polygraph. That's what we're here to determine. This meeting is called an Informal Hearing of Fact and that's exactly what it is. Give us facts, tell us the truth and we can all get to more important things in our lives. Got it?"

"Got it."

Andrea Robb clicked on the recorder and established date, time, participants and purpose of the hearing.

"Sergeant McMichael," she continued, "you worked in our Metro/Vice detail between nineteen ninety-eight and two thousand one, correct?"

"That's right."

"And James Thigpen was on that detail for how many of those years?"

"All of them."

"Did you work directly with him?"

"Yes, it's a small detail."

"What did you think of him?" she asked.

"Smart. High energy. Trustworthy."

"What else?"

"I worried about him because he was young and undercover. We all did."

"You and Officer Thigpen teamed up for a call-girl sting one summer, didn't you—they were working the convention center and the downtown hotels?"

"Yes. We made ten good arrests. Word got out and the rest of them beat it for a while."

"You and Thigpen made ten?" asked Robb.

"Working together. He was mostly trolling. When he got the right approach I'd come out from next door with the cuffs."

"Fun police work?" she asked.

"Humiliating for everybody is more like it."

"You didn't care for Metro/Vice?" she asked.

"Not really."

"Did Thigpen?"

McMichael poured some water and drank. He'd thought about this question almost every day for four weeks, since Jimmy Thigpen had been arrested. Chief Kerr, furious at the arrest, had issued a strict gag on all personnel, so not much was said about Jimmy Thigpen at the Fourteenth Street Headquarters. But that's all you heard in the cop bars—where'd he score the money, who else might have been in on it. Jimmy's lawyers and the district attorney's office had been negotiating for the better part of two weeks. Rumor had it that heads—cops' heads—would roll. Thigpen had been denied bail as a flight risk.

So it was all eyes on Metro/Vice Unit—past and present—and McMichael felt cornered. He couldn't say anything good about Jimmy because Jimmy looked rotten. He couldn't call too loud for Jimmy's head because it might look like he was eager to save his own.

So he went with the truth.

"Jimmy loved Metro/Vice."

"On what do you base that opinion?" asked Andrea Robb, pen poised above her notepad.

"Long hours. Good attitude. Little things, you know. Like he'd use his own car, so the girls wouldn't smell out one of our plainwraps. Or he'd put the wires on everybody if we were taping. Then he'd double- and triple-check them. He was our electronics guy when he was staying back. He took a lot of pride in hiding the wires, on getting good reception. You can tell when somebody likes what they're doing."

Robb looked at him doubtfully. "What about when he was undercover? Same good attitude?"

"Yeah. He played our young-and-innocent john and our desperate junkie or our yuppie businessman if he was out front."

"Played them well?" she asked.

"Jimmy only got blown once. That was his first year."

"Did you notice a change in him the last few months?"

Another question that McMichael had known was coming. This was where they moved then: crosshairs from Thigpen to himself.

"No."

"Right up to the night the sheriffs undercover team took him down in that suite at the Hyatt?" asked Robb, with more than a trace of disbelief in her voice.

"Right up until then."

McMichael watched the silent flourish of eyebrows, glances, shaken heads.

Fuck you all, he thought, if you can't hack the truth.

"So, the new Porsche didn't make you wonder," said Huzara.

"I never saw it."

"And Thigpen's trips to Maui and Aspen and Key West—they didn't make you wonder?"

"I didn't know where he went. He never said."

"What about his moonlighting for Pete Braga?" asked Huzara.

McMichael hated being caught with his pants down. "I didn't know. Tell me."

"Yeah," said Huzara. "Jimmy trucked the new cars down to TJ for budget leather interiors, trucked them back up when they were finished. Saved Pete lots of money. Made some pretty good money himself."

McMichael thought about this, couldn't figure it into what had happened the night before.

"Though a part-time job might not account for over three hundred grand in cash," said Robb.

McMichael sat back and waited.

"Okay," said Huzara. "With all the things that Thigpen never said, didn't *that* make you wonder about him? Most guys, they'd talk about a new car, or a vacation or some easy money on the side."

"He was private. I never suspected a sixty-thousand-dollar car in his garage or those trips you found out about. Or working for Braga. He's a good actor. That's why you put him out there undercover at the age of twenty-one."

Jerry Bland sat back. He was thick, rounded without being fat, and had a face like a steer watching you from a pasture. McMichael knew him to be an accomplished bowler. "So it's our fault Thigpen went bad?"

"I've got no opinion on that, sir," said McMichael. "But I know he had peach fuzz. Literally. And I know he did his six months at the Sheriff's Academy, but almost nothing else before we put him on the street. What, two months at the jail? No patrol. Nothing. On his twenty-second birthday he was behind the Las Flores Hotel getting beaten by four Arellano Felix cartel heavies. That was the one time he got blown. They kicked his balls halfway up his stomach. We had to use a towel to unhook his lips off his front teeth."

"Sure, we know about all that," said Huzara, taking off his glasses to inspect a lens.

"You saw no change in him at all, then?" asked Bland.

"None."

"Tom," said Bland, "did Jimmy ever tell you about any of this? Personal business with the working girls, maybe—dope and cash?"

"No, sir. Not one word."

"Did you ever *overhear* him say anything about those things?" asked Robb.

"No, Andrea."

"Overhear *anyone* talking about those things?"

"Never."

"Ever hear anything about a little group of cops, maybe thought they were extra special, extra cool?"

"Just IAD." Everybody smiled except for Robb.

"You're a funny guy, McMichael."

Silence, then, while Robb checked her tape recorder, Bland leaned back and crossed his hands behind his head, Huzara stared at McMichael.

"I hope Thigpen doesn't start naming other cops," said Bland. "Then we'd have a shitstorm like L.A.'s."

"This isn't L.A.," said Huzara.

There was nothing McMichael could say to that.

"I'm finished for now," said Robb.

"Over and out for me," said Bland, yawning.

"Not for me," said Huzara. "Sergeant, I saw Thigpen last night. He asked me to say hello to you."

"Say hello back when you see him."

"You guys pretty good friends?"

"I already told you we aren't."

"And he never told you about all the money and dope he was stealing?" asked Huzara.

"How many ways can I say no?" asked McMichael.

Robb looked at him, then at the still-running recorder, then back to McMichael. "Anything else, Sergeant McMichael?"

"Nothing."

"Do you realize that your statements here are binding, if not evidentiary?" asked Huzara.

"They're just the truth."

Robb clicked the machine with finality and McMichael stood. There was a long moment when all four of the cops became cops again—McMichael could feel the change in the air.

"So you got Pete Braga?" asked Bland. He often appeared to be chewing on something, then not to be. Department gossips had never been able to figure out what.

McMichael nodded. "Eighty-four, sitting by his fireplace. Bad scene."

"Eighty-four and still pulling strings on the Port Commission. Still selling cars by the million," said Bland.

"Thirty-something years of politics and Fords," said McMichael. "That was news to me about Jimmy working for him."

"I hear things," said Bland. "So, you walked right back into old bad blood."

"That was a long time ago, sir."

"Does it ever really go away?" Bland offered a Wattsaver smile.

"Some of it does."

"I heard there was a nurse involved. Worked for him," said Huzara.

"She says she was out buying firewood when it happened. Ralph's on Rosecrans. I'll check her alibi tonight with the night shift."

McMichael started out.

"So how do you like Homicide compared to Metro/Vice?" asked Robb. She stood and faced him. Her voice was chipper and she had offered Mc-Michael his first smile. It was really something. The whole package was.

"Dead people are honest. You can really turn off your tape recorder now, Andrea."

Andrea Robb colored a little and the smile melted. She reached down as McMichael walked by on his way to the door.

A moment later she caught up with him by the elevator and tugged him into an empty hallway. Mc-Michael was looking forward to her apology.

"Detective," she said, "I've lived on Point Loma for twenty years and there is no Ralph's on Rose-crans. Might save you a lot of driving around."

"Thank you."

"I'm a cop first, no matter who thinks what."

"Good to know."

She nodded and turned the corner for the elevator. McMichael let her go while he dialed the law offices of Grothke, Steiner & Grothke—Pete Braga's counsel.

5

Hector drove to Sally Rainwater's, looping onto Interstate 5 for the short run south. The second storm front had moved in behind the first, holding the city in a noisy gray torrent. The wipers couldn't keep up with the water. McMichael heard the rush of the tires and the roar on the roof and the metal shriek of a minivan that dreamily planed into the guardrail.

Hector finished his briefing on last night's possibilities—a couple of blonde beauties looking for love at the Sevilla bar. He'd gotten one phone number before the captain called him. "How'd IAD go?"

"They can't figure out why I didn't see it coming."

"Maybe because Jimmy's a sneaky little creep. You put somebody that green on the street, put him in with the dope and the girls, you're asking for it. They got to blame somebody. Bland Jerry—he'll pick you."

"How'd NCIC go?"

Hector shrugged. "Eight years ago, Sally Rain-water's boyfriend tried to kill her. Shot her in the throat with a twenty-two but it didn't hit anything too important. This was back in Miami. The boyfriend got out last month, skipped on his P.O. and dropped out. They don't know where he is and he's not supposed to know where she is. Dylan Feder, thirty-five—formerly employed as a life-guard, model, actor, waiter and batterer. Beat her up in 'ninety-four but she didn't press. Stalked and shot her in 'ninety-five. She was twenty."

"Get mugs?"

Hector slipped a twice-folded sheet of paper from the pocket of his coat and handed it to McMichael. Feder was crybaby handsome: curly dark hair, pouty lips, bedroom eyes. Six three, two fifteen.

"I don't understand women like her," said Hector. "Could have any guy she wants, but she connects up with this loser, lets him beat her up. I'll never get that."

"It has to do with a low opinion of yourself."

"I don't get that, either. Total babe like her."

"It's not how you look."

"Yeah, yeah. All right. Mr. Female Insight understands what makes 'em tick but not the savage Hector."

"I've just known a few, they get hurt and think they deserve it. And they always think the guy's going to change. My sister's that way."

"Raegan? Really?"

"Somewhat."

"Whatever. I find that guy in San Diego I'll wrap his balls around his fuckin' neck."

Hector pulled onto the Imperial Beach Pier because he wanted to see the waves. They rolled along, the railings coming slowly past the windows and the rain shooting off the wooden deck in front of them. There were fishermen out, bundled in slickers and hats, staring at their rods. Hector drove halfway to the end and put the car in Park. The waves were huge and disorderly, looming in at competing angles, building on each other. And fast, with big plumes hissing backward off the tops. Walls of pale green water rose up and thundered in at them then passed out of sight under the car, and McMichael felt them explode through the pier caissons and the cement deck and the car tires and into the bones of his feet. Hector didn't surf but he liked the waves, the bigger the better, never drove past a pier in a storm that he didn't roll out and watch. McMichael did surf but not in anything like this. The savage power before him was hypnotic. It miniaturized you. He watched the storm but he thought of Johnny and Steff and wondered how he'd managed to lose so much so fast. Seven years of marriage and a perfect son—one gone forever, the other down to Wednesday nights and weekends.

A different kind of storm.

"McMichael and Paz, Ms. Rainwater. May we come in?"

It was ten-fifteen and the sky was almost black now. A river of water poured from the eaves of the cottage, forcing McMichael and Paz to pick a side or get drenched.

They had moved up close to the barely opened door.

"Go away."

"We'll just be back in an hour with a search warrant."

"Based on what?"

"Missing paintings."

She pulled the door open and stepped back. She was wearing loose quilted Chinese pajamas, black with birds-of-paradise on it. And black Chinese slippers with plastic soles. Her face was pale and puffy and McMichael's eye went straight to the tattoo low and right on her neck. A copy of the one on the other side. He saw that it was neither a flame nor a tulip, but a bird taking flight. The center of its breast almost hid the bullet scar.

She caught him looking, walked away with a shake of her head, and returned a minute later with a faded denim jacket buttoned up high.

McMichael looked at a director's chair that said "Sally R." on it but he didn't sit. Instead he set his tape recorder on the canvas seat and clicked it on.

"Okay?" he asked.

"I don't care," she said.

Hector took one end of the couch. "Got any coffee?"

She stood between them, looking first at Hector then McMichael. Her face looked softer than the night before.

"I'll make another pot."

She walked past Paz and into the kitchen. Hector watched her, then looked at McMichael deadpan.

But McMichael's attention was already on the painting, a schooner tacking into a hard starboard wind. Browns and blacks and chill grays—a seascape in earth tones. The skipper was tiny against the ocean, and far too confident for McMichael. Like he could sail through this or any huge sea, no problem. This attitude reminded McMichael of his father's stories from his days with the tuna fleet, of the arrogance that always seemed to pave the way for tragedy. The schooner captain had it. According to McMichael's father, Gabriel, Pete Braga had it, too. Which was why he'd allegedly cheated Gabriel's father—young Franklin McMichael—out of the first quarter share he ever earned as a purse-seining thirty-three-year-old fisherman aboard Braga's *Cabrillo Star.*

"Cool picture," said Hector, glancing up and behind. "How many missing from Braga's?"

"Five, according to Patricia and the spaces on the walls."

A brain thorn started to form as McMichael's gaze wandered the kitchen, as the tall pretty woman made the coffee, as the rain slowed on the roof. A blue-and-gold vase sat on the kitchenette table to Sally Rainwater's right. It was half hidden by a thick phone book and filled with bright orange paper poppies.

"There's another painting in the study," she said without turning. "To your right off the hall. The hallway bulb burned out so don't bother turning it on. I've got three more in my room, which you are not invited to enter. I'll bring them out if you'd like."

"Thank you," said McMichael. "Be right back, Heck."

The study had an old couch stacked with books, a cheap folding party table with a computer on it, two walls of brick-and-board bookshelves, and one nice glass-fronted lawyer's bookcase by the window. The window faced south, toward the Tijuana Slough and the river mouth and the border. Mc-Michael had surfed the TJ Slough as a youngster because tough guys surfed the slough. It was shark infested and polluted by the Tijuana River and filled with fickle currents that might nudge you with the body of a desperate young man who had dreamed of a job in the Estados Unidos. When you surfed it you were right there on the watery border between a powerful nation and a hungry one. You could sit there on your board, look one way and see neat little Imperial Beach apartments, or look the other and see the decrepit Tijuana shacks and shanties clinging to the hills. After a rain like this, there would be fewer of them. He saw nothing through the window now but a square of gray shot with silver rain.

The painting hung low on the computer table wall, so you could easily look up and see it. It was a small canvas, no more than twelve by twelve inches. A forlorn boat struggled in a violent orange sea while an ice-white moon—or maybe sun—shone down with brilliant disregard. The boat was twisted and stripped down to almost nothing. No sail. No mast. No men. Even with the bright white sun or moon in it, this was the darkest and saddest—and also the most powerful—painting that McMichael had ever seen. It wasn't even signed. Talk about arrogance. It looked like one of Pete's.

He wondered if Rainwater would let him photograph the paintings so he could show them to Patricia. If she'd stolen them, she sure wouldn't, but if she'd stolen them why hang them on her walls and invite the cops in for a look?

And why hang the autographed baseball mitts on the wall opposite, for all the world to see? He touched the leather below Ruth's faded signature.

Sally Rainwater was starting to intrigue him.

He stepped back and scanned the titles on the simple bookshelves: mostly textbooks in the natural sciences—biology, chemistry, anatomy. Several on geography. And a few novels.

The lawyer's bookcase contained only four volumes all on the middle shelf, all held in place by heavy-looking copper bookends shaped like a whale's flukes.

He read the titles: *Heart of Darkness*, *Typhoon*, *The Secret Sharer* and *The Complete Works*, all by Joseph Conrad. All in clear plastic slipcases. And all, if signed by their author, likely boosted from Pete Braga. The windowed doors of the case were locked.

Rainwater was handing Hector a cup of coffee when he walked back in.

"Where did you get the paintings?" McMichael asked.

"Pete gave them to me."

"And the vase on the kitchen table?"

"He gave me that, too. It's Chinese, from the eighteenth century."

Hector deadpanned McMichael again, the coffee cup frozen halfway to his mouth.

"What else did he give you, Ms. Rainwater?"

"Some autographed books and baseball gloves. A mounted calico bass. A necklace of big perfect pearls he bought in Japan for his wife a long time ago. And a pair of pearl-and-sapphire earrings that were hers, too."

She looked down at Hector, then back to McMichael. "That's all."

"What about the Beetle?" asked Hector.

"He gave me the down payment—ten thousand."

"Gave or loaned?"

"Gave."

"Why?" asked McMichael.

Rainwater walked into the kitchen and came back with cups of coffee for McMichael and herself.

"We were good friends."

Her steady dark eyes went from McMichael to Hector and back again, and it struck McMichael that he was no longer running this show.

"You'd only known him seven months," said Hector. "And he gives you diamonds and pearls and half a car and a bunch of pictures and a baseball mitt signed by Babe Ruth?"

"Yes," she said.

"Explain why again," said McMichael.

"He wanted to give me some of his things."

"You having sex with him?" asked Hector.

"That's none of your business."

"They'll ask you in court."

"It's still none of your business."

Hector smiled and McMichael saw the gleam in his partner's eyes.

"I'd arrest her," said Hector. "Possession of stolen property. Murder in the act of committing a robbery, which can get you executed. Throw in prostitution and elder abuse so she'll have to plead down from a mountaintop."

Her dark eyes dismissed Hector and looked to McMichael. "I have proof," she said. "Wait here."

She went past him, down the short dark hallway and into her bedroom. The door shut. McMichael popped the snap on his shoulder holster. Hector slipped his nine from the leather and stretched his gun hand out along the couch back, dipping the weapon behind a cushion.

The bedroom door swung open and the woman came into the dim hallway, pointing toward McMichael something long and round with a hollow end.

He cleared holster and jacket in a short arc. Hector bounded forward with his gun in both hands, exhaling in a loud hiss.

"*Drop it! Drop it goddamnitrightnow!*" yelled McMichael, staring at her over the front sight, his heart pounding hard and a metallic ringing in his ears.

She froze, dropped the thing and raised her hands.

He glanced at the wood floor and saw what looked like a tube of rolled-up white paper. He upped the barrel of his Smith & Wesson toward the ceiling.

"I dropped it!"

"But what the hell else you got?" Hector barreled past, kicking the tube and with his left hand turning Sally Rainwater to the wall. "Hands up and against the wall. *Hands up and against the wall, lady.*"

Hector patted her quickly: hands, coat collar, armpits, back, outside hip and thigh, behind the knees, then moved her around to face him.

"Keep your hands up," he said.

Her voice was not much more than a whisper. "They're up! They're *up!*"

Hector felt around her middle—no higher or lower, McMichael was certain of that—then hips again, then ran his hand over her calves and ankles.

"Okay, I think she's clean."

"Jesus Christ, you guys." Her voice was so faint McMichael could barely make out her words. "Jesus."

"Step back, Heck," he heard himself saying. He thought of the bullet holes in her neck and he saw the cold hard fear in her face. He felt the jittery spike of adrenaline shooting through him and his heart was still banging against his ribs. "It's okay, Ms. Rainwater. Now just come back into the living room here. Move slowly, please, just come back in here and sit on the couch. Okay? Everybody's okay. Everybody's okay."

Hector eased away, gun aimed up, snatching the roll of paper from the floor. He backed past McMichael into the living room.

But Sally Rainwater didn't move. Even in the bad

light he saw that her face had gone white. She opened her mouth and her jaws moved just a little but no words came out.

McMichael heard a faint tapping sound on the wood and saw the puddle between her slippers. Her legs were shaking.

He stepped closer and like a waiter motioned her to her own bathroom. "Clean up. It's okay."

But she still didn't move from the wall. McMichael watched her dark wide eyes find his own. He offered her his hand, palm up. She got his wrist. He had to pull her, gently, to get her moving toward the bathroom. Her hand was cold and electric and strong. She tried to cover her wet pajamas with the other as she walked in and shut the door.

He heard the roar of the shower.

Hector was sitting at the kitchen table, reading. McMichael looked over his shoulder. The sheets were still curved at the tops and bottoms where Rainwater had formed them into a loose cylinder. A rubber band lay beside the blue-and-gold Chinese vase.

To Whom It May Concern,

I gave a painting to Sally Rainwater on December 4 of this year. It's a genuine Albert Pinkham Ryder but he didn't sign it so it's not ever been proven or authenticated but that's not why I bought it in the first place. It's a beauty, about a foot square and it shows a little boat with no sails or crew pretty much

getting the shit kicked out of it by Mother Nature.
It's in a black frame. It's Sally's painting now and
she can do what she wants with it.

Truly,
Peter Augustino Braga

McMichael read Pete Braga's signature, then the
notary stamp and date: San Diego, roughly a month
ago. Witnessed by one Charles Hyams, notary public. The body of the letter was typed in an ordinary
font style and size.

"Hmph," said Hector. "You can fake these."

"Easy enough to find out."

"I'm not good with what just happened, Tom. But,
man, something about her coming out from the
room. Dark hallway. And when I saw you reach . . ."

"Me too. It's just what happens. Better safe."

"Hope she sees it that way."

"We had a right to protect ourselves."

Sheet number two was dated November 11 of
last year and stated that Pete had given Sally Rainwater a baseball glove signed by Babe Ruth. "I saw
him play once at Yankee Stadium. Second best day
of my life, right behind marrying Anna. The ink is
kind of faded out but you can still read his name
under the pocket." Signed by Pete and witnessed by
the same notary.

Sheet three listed four more autographed baseball
gloves given to Rainwater: Williams, Mantle, Mc-
Gwire and Gwynn. "The McGwire and Gwynn
ones are personalized to me, Pete," he wrote. "But

they're property of Sally Jane Rainwater now, just like the rest." Signed and witnessed October 7.

The next four pages accounted for four more paintings, one pearl necklace, one pair of pearl and sapphire earrings, one handmade and hand-painted Chinese vase, four books autographed by Joseph Conrad and one mounted calico bass.

"This now worthless fish weighed six pounds two ounces when I caught it on two-pound test and an anchovy off Pt. Loma about a thousand years ago. It now belongs to Sally Rainwater, freely given to her by me with a clear mind, a mostly shot liver and a full heart."

All signed by Braga and witnessed by Hyams.

McMichael noted that the fish was the first thing he'd given away to his newfound friend—August 19 of last year, a month after she'd come to work for him.

"I almost believe these," said Hector.

"You should," she said quietly, sitting on the couch and staring straight ahead. Her hair was slicked back, her face still white, her eyes dark and distant. She had a faded pink robe pulled up tight to her chin, jeans underneath and fluffy pink slippers.

"Pete had a hummingbird made out of jewels. He'd bought it for his wife. Did he give that to you?" asked McMichael.

"No. He showed it to me once."

"What did you think?" asked Hector.

"It was the most beautiful man-made thing I've ever seen."

"Where did he keep it?" asked Hector.

"I have no idea."

McMichael followed her gaze through the front window to the pier and the heaving gray-black sea. "We found five wall spaces at Pete's house, where paintings used to hang," he said. "Do you know if your paintings are the ones that used to be there?"

"Yes, they are. He was going to put up more, but never got around to it."

"Who'd you call last night from Ye Olde Plank?" asked Hector.

She looked long and hard at him, but McMichael thought he saw the fight going out of her. "Robin, a friend from school."

"How come?" asked Hector.

"You give CPR to a dead man some night, see if you don't feel like talking to someone about it. You can arrest me now or go. I need to start looking for another job."

"We'd like to take these documents with us," said McMichael.

She looked over at McMichael, then to Paz. "Try not to lose them."

Hector stood awkwardly and looked at her. "I apologize for what happened. I was wrong. But don't ever point something like that at a cop."

Hector threw open the door and headed for the car. McMichael hesitated, then pulled the door shut against the weather. "What did you pay for that firewood at Ralph's last night?"

"Four ninety-nine a bundle. Got two."

"Box boy help you out with them?"

"I carried them myself."

"Remember the checker?"

"A handsome Mexican man. Fifty."

"There's no Ralph's Market on Rosecrans in Point Loma."

She nodded but didn't look at him. "Yeah, well—Ralph's, Von's, Albertson's—something like that. I don't pay much attention to the names of markets."

"What was the cross street?"

"Talbot or Canon. Half a mile from Mr. Braga's house, maybe. It's not my neighborhood."

They were still in Imperial Beach when McMichael's cell phone rang.

"Mark and I walked the beach outside Pete's house about an hour ago," said Barbara Givens. "The rain let up for just a minute and we got some decent light. I found a pair of latex gloves and a bloody warm-up jacket stuffed down in a city trash can. About thirty yards from Pete's wall, maybe ten yards shy of the high-water line. They were both jammed down so far the rain didn't really get to them. They've got blood and God knows what else on them. This might be our break, Tom."

"What color on the jacket?"

"Black."

"Nice work, Barbara."

McMichael gave her the Notary information and rang off.

"Bloody latex gloves in the sand by Pete's wall," he said. "Wrapped in a black warm-up jacket."

Hector shook his head. "I still think the nurse had something to do with it. A partner, a boyfriend, something. Maybe that dirtbag with the chick lips and the dreamy eyes."

"Why kill the old man if he's giving her all that cool stuff?"

"Maybe she got herself into his will. Maybe she wants the *really* cool stuff. Like a house at the beach."

6

The law firm of Grothke, Steiner & Grothke had floors nine and ten of the Bay Tower downtown. The detectives rode up in a glass elevator and Mc-Michael watched the rain pour onto the massive aircraft carriers in the harbor. The waterfront was almost deserted now—the tour boats battened down and the tourists driven to shelter by the rain. Scattered car lights eased along the graceful bend of the Coronado Bridge.

Paz talked to the receptionist while McMichael looked past her desk to the suites beyond. Old Grothke, dapper in a vested brown suit, waved at him with a pale hand. McMichael nodded and smiled, surprised that Henry Grothke remembered him. They'd met at a San Diego Symphony fundraiser five years ago, music being one of Stephanie's interests until the life of a cop's wife wore the melodies right out of her.

Old Grothke motioned McMichael toward him and the receptionist buzzed him through with an air of annoyance. Hector tried to smooth her over, mentioning her earrings and something about his birthstone. Her desk plate said Sharona Saddler.

"My fiancé likes them, too. Mr. Grothke Junior's suite is down the hall and to your right, please."

The old man had rolled his wheelchair to the doorway. His hair was downy and white as pillow stuffing. His eyes were blue. A red blanket lay folded over his legs.

"Welcome, welcome," he said.

McMichael bent to shake his hand, which was featherlight and warm. "I'm Detective McMichael. How do you do, sir?"

"Very well. I remember you from somewhere."

"The symphony, at Copley Hall. Are you still going?"

Old Grothke pursed his mouth and frowned. "We saw some wonderful chamber music not long ago. It was . . . oh, well, I'm not exactly sure when."

"That doesn't really matter," said McMichael, looking into Henry Grothke's clear blue eyes.

"There are always vultures in the ice cream," said the lawyer. "You think you know someone and look what happens."

McMichael was formulating a reply.

"*Down the hall and to your right,*" said the receptionist, looking sharply at Old Grothke.

"I'm sure they heard you, Sharona," he said.

"This way, gentlemen," called a sleek man from down the hall. "Dad'll get you talking and send you a bill."

"I'm in the wrong business," said Hector.

"*Down the hall, please,*" said Sharona.

Henry Grothke Jr., arms welcoming and feet together, ushered them into his suite. He was trim, dark-haired and neatly presented, from the cut of his sideburns to the crisp lines of his white shirt. A bashful chin. No ring. McMichael made him for fifty, prosperous and pampered.

The receptionist closed the door behind them and Henry apologized for his father. "Sorry. Dad gets pretty talkative sometimes. He doesn't really need to come in every day, but he likes the human contact."

"Or the receptionist," said Hector.

"We've gone through several." Grothke smiled quickly, then looked down. "I was saddened by what happened to Pete. Just awful in every way. Are you making progress toward an arrest?"

"In fact, we are," said McMichael.

The attorney waited, then sighed. "I know you're interested in Pete Braga's will, so I pulled a copy and read through it. It's a straightforward document, really, and I'm happy to answer any questions about it."

Henry said that Pete Braga's estate was worth a little over twelve million dollars, mostly in real estate and blue-chip stocks. Approximately three million in real estate—homes in Rancho Santa Fe and Mammoth—was in charitable remaindered trusts and would now, with Pete's death, come under control of San Diego's Catholic diocese. Two more homes—in Palm Springs and Mendocino—were also part of charitable trusts, and would now revert to control of the American Tunaboat Foundation, on whose board of directors Pete sat for about four decades. These homes were worth about one million dollars each.

"Typically the trustees will sell the properties to realize cash values more applicable to their needs," said Grothke. "Although, should the San Diego diocese wish to use the home in Mammoth, say, they might choose to hold on to it."

"But up until he died," said McMichael, "Pete was free to use those properties whenever he wanted?"

"And however he wanted. Essentially, he gave the homes to the church and the association, but retained title until his death. And of course he realized some handsome monthly lease revenue from those institutions, and enjoyed a huge reduction in his tax liabilities. It's a very standard arrangement."

"For really rich guys," said Hector.

"Even moderately wealthy individuals can—"

"What about his family," said Hector. "Who gets what?"

Grothke cleared his throat and spread his hands equidistantly upon the desktop. "Mr. Braga has three living children, six grandchildren and eight great-grandchildren. One-half of the remainder of his estate—exclusive of the trusts already mentioned—will be divided evenly between two of his children. That comes to roughly one point seven five million per. The other half will be evenly divided by three of the grandchildren, or approximately one point one million for each. The eight great-grandchildren will receive fifty thousand each. None of Mr. Braga's descendants has shown a desire to take over Pete Braga Ford, except for Patricia, who is only . . . minimally interested in running a car dealership. Her brother,

James Braga, lives in Texas and is not interested in the car business. The franchise of course can be sold. And divided as I just explained."

"What are the terms and conditions?" asked Hector.

"None to speak of. Very straightforward, as I said."

"I'd like the names and telephone numbers of the heirs," said McMichael. "And of the ones he cut out."

Grothke looked at McMichael with a repelled expression. "Normally I wouldn't do that, but I talked to Patricia, who is, practically speaking, the executor here. Patricia told me to cooperate with you in every legal way I can. Mr. Braga's daughter, Elizabeth DeCerra, lives out of state. Son Carl has been disinherited. Son Rex—Patricia's father—died along with his wife, Corrinna, in an automobile accident in nineteen ninety-three. And as you know, Mr. Braga's eldest son, Victor, is not mentally competent to execute a will or much of anything else. Because of his boyhood tragedy."

McMichael bore the accusatory tone with an even stare. He'd been hearing similar versions of it all his life. Victor Braga's beating behind the Waterfront bar fifty years ago was commonly held to be the doing of Gabriel McMichael. Done as payback for his father, Franklin, shot in alleged self-defense by Pete aboard the *Cabrillo Star* a year earlier. Both Victor and Gabriel were just boys then—thirteen. The beating had permanently left Victor with the mental capacity of a ten-year-old. And left Gabriel to maintain his innocence in a world of open hate and secret reverence.

Grothke handed McMichael a printed sheet with the names and phone numbers of Pete Braga's heirs, as well as the descendants not chosen to receive.

"Why did Pete cut one of his sons out of the will?" asked McMichael.

"I won't speculate," said Grothke.

"And half his grandchildren?"

"I have no idea. All I can say is that Peter Braga was a tempestuous man."

"Over the years," said McMichael, "did Pete amend his will?"

"Yes, of course. Fine-tuned, mostly, as the value of his estate changed."

"Did a person named Sally Rainwater come into it?"

"Rainwater? No. None of the married daughters or granddaughters have that name. It's Irish, isn't it? Or American Indian?"

McMichael stared at him and the lawyer looked away. Grothke meant that no Braga would marry a mick because of the history with the McMichaels. Probably true. McMichael would never forget the quick efficiency with which Pete and Patricia's father had ended his fifth-grade friendship with Patricia—changed schools, forbade Patricia from communicating with him in any way, told McMichael's mother that they'd get a restraining order on her son if she couldn't control him. It was odd, the way his world changed so drastically with Patricia banished. It was as if she had disappeared, though he knew she was still living and breathing just a few miles away.

"When was the last time he changed it?" Mc-Michael asked.

" 'Ninety-four."

"What changes did he make?"

Grothke Junior leaned back and shook his head. "With all respect, gentlemen, I don't feel right discussing those specifics. Talk to Patricia. She was very close to him. If she can't tell you, have her call me and with her permission I'll do so. You understand, I hope. Wills are not really about dollars, they're about people."

"Was he planning to change it again?" asked Hector.

"I have no way of knowing that, Detective."

Old Grothke was sitting at the threshold of his suite again when McMichael and Paz walked by. The receptionist buzzed the door open and stood.

"It was April of last year, Detective," said the old lawyer. "The chamber music. I have the old calendar in my drawer."

"That was it," said McMichael, pausing and bending to shake hands again. "Nice to see you again."

"Can I *help* you with something?" asked the receptionist.

"Yeah, validate this." Hector dropped the parking ticket on her desk.

McMichael endured the autopsy in the county medical examiner's office that afternoon. He had never gotten used to the grisly theater, disliked the smell of formalin and alcohol, hated the sound of the saws. The butchered corpses with their yawning Y-sections made him feel queasy and guilty and want to crawl into bed with Stephanie and be forgiven.

Hector was off to court on a parole hearing. Barbara and Hatter were checking the notary, then interviewing Pete's allies and enemies on the Port Commission, of which Pete was a thirty-plus-year commissioner.

So McMichael stood amidst the fumes and the instruments and watched Dr. Arnold Stiles perform the act. With a flat and methodical tone, the doctor narrated his findings into a tape recorder.

"I can see sixteen separate blows," said Stiles. "But there were almost certainly more, lost in the bone shatters on the top of the skull."

"Rage," said McMichael.

"Much of it," said Stiles.

"Can you tell right- or left-handed attack?"

Stiles nodded. "He was hit from behind. The blows are concentrated to the right, so right-handed."

"We figured it from behind."

"That makes sense, with no defense wounds."

McMichael took a deep breath and let it out slowly. For the next few minutes he simply watched Stiles. It was hard for him to tell his revulsion from his anger.

"You look white as Pete here," said Stiles. "Why put yourself through this?"

"It reminds me," McMichael said.

"Rawlings used to watch, too. I'm not convinced it makes a detective any more effective."

"I'm not here to convince you."

Stiles dropped his cranial saw into a bloody tub. There was saw mist stuck to his eyeglasses. He was a short, pudgy man who wore the same lucky necktie for every autopsy he performed in a given year. After Christmas he'd have a new one for the coming year's carnage. The ties were always clip-ons, striped and, McMichael assumed, machine washable.

"Cool down, Tom. I know how you feel. I know what you're doing."

Stiles finally pronounced the cause of death as "repeated blunt force trauma to the head, resulting in nervous system and cardiac failure." The approximate time of death was between seven and ten P.M. on Wednesday, January 8.

McMichael left the building feeling like his soul had been cut out, weighed and thrown away.

* * *

Back at headquarters he waited in Arthur Flagler's office. He felt the pieces of his soul drifting back into place, roughly into place, as he stared out the window and watched the drizzle falling.

He tried to think of something other than Pete. He let his mind go and up came Sally Rainwater and the terror on her face as she took his wrist. McMichael had never been shot, but he figured if he had, and two strangers drew down on him in a dark hallway, he might not like it, either. As he remembered, the fear hadn't stripped her dignity—even standing there in her own pee Sally Rainwater seemed strong and beautiful.

Arthur Flagler breezed in with a package of cookies and a carton of milk.

"The Fish Whack'r was clean," he said. "That's the name of the fish club."

McMichael remembered that Sally Rainwater had known this, too.

"And we didn't get anything promising from inside the house," said Flagler. "Plenty of fingerprints left by Pete and the nurse. But we got prints from the latex gloves. These creeps never think about leaving prints on the *inside*."

"That's good news, Arthur." McMichael took out his notebook and pen.

Flagler bit into a cookie, studied what was left. "It wasn't the nurse. I used her CCP to get a ten-set from the county. You can rule her out, as the basher anyway."

So McMichael thought: Rainwater was telling the truth, or at least part of it. He didn't quite know how he felt. He'd had a suspect and now he didn't. He was pleased that he'd read her better than Hector had, but she could still be an accomplice, even the shot caller. Or she could be an innocent young woman who'd drenched herself in an old man's blood, gotten up close enough to smell the death in his nostrils and still tried to breathe life back into him.

"The prints we got off the latex aren't in any register so far," said Flagler. "We've never printed this guy. Neither has the county. We also got blanked by Cal-ID, the FBI and Western Information Network. I'm trying Interpol and the Naval Investigative Service. Nothing yet."

"Good enough for court?" asked McMichael.

"Six points," said Flagler. "Plenty—*U.S. versus Plaza* or not."

McMichael knew of the recent federal court ruling that prevented fingerprint examiners from testifying that unidentified prints "matched" a suspect's prints. Things were changing in the courtroom, but six points was six points, more than enough to establish a probability beyond question.

"Interestingly, the palm of the right glove had torn out," said Flagler. "Right where you'd expect it to during a beating—all the friction and tension on the palm."

McMichael wondered when. "But no palm prints."

Flagler shook his head. "None that we've found. It might have torn out when he stripped off the glove after."

"That's funny," said McMichael. "A torn-out glove but no prints."

"Maybe he knew it, wiped the club and the door and whatever else he touched."

"He must have known."

Flagler shrugged, then downed the rest of his cookie and took out another. "We got Pete's blood off the warm-up jacket. No surprise. The jacket itself is a common make, available at scores of area stores. A man's extra large. We got an eyelash off it—brown. No flesh attached, so no DNA possibilities. We can determine if it *could* have come from a certain suspect, when we have such a suspect. And we also got two strands of gray nylon/polyester fiber from the floor, where the basher would have stood. Probably from carpet, maybe car carpet. I can match it up with something you bring in, but I can't do much else with them—too common, too many manufacturers, too many dye lots—and no real records or controls on any of them. The floor in that fish room is hardwood, so there were no shoe impressions. But the blood caught some zigzag sole patterns so we're thinking athletic shoe, maybe work boots or some kind of walking shoe. My guys are tracking down a make and model, but that can take time. There were marks—black scuffs—like you'd leave on a basketball court if you wore the wrong kind of shoes."

"Just one set?"

"No evidence of more than one, not in the blood. But this could have been a team thing—I understand there were some fairly large paintings possibly taken. One to do the deed. The other to help with the booty."

McMichael thought about two or even three people pulling off this job. It still made no sense that they'd take art when there were electronics that would fetch a quicker price. And the simple explanation for the blank wall spaces were the gifts to Sally Rainwater.

Flagler took a swig of milk and pressed the last cookie up through the plastic. "Here's the kicker. Erik found a bird feather under the table where the wineglasses were. Yellow, but not dyed. Naturally yellow, like a canary or a parakeet. Funny shape— about an inch long and slender, with kind of a bloom or blossom at the end. Under the scope we got louse sheddings and excrement. So it didn't come from a hat or feather earrings or something like that. It came from a plain old bird. Harley told me Pete didn't have a bird."

"Neither does the nurse," said McMichael.

"Someone does. Maybe he works in a pet store. Patronized a pet store. Eats songbirds for breakfast."

"Why 'he'?"

Flagler smiled. "Possible. The fish billy is weighted aluminum. Really packs a wallop. It could have been a woman. You don't have to be strong, just accurate. A first strike would help, too. It looked to me like Pete never got up from his chair. Maybe he was dozing. Maybe the basher was quiet. But now, thanks to the yellow feather, when you collar this creep you can tell him or her—"

"Don't say it."

"A little birdie told me."

"I thought you would."

"We're still working up the wine to see if Pete's might have been spiked. We've also got a dermal sample for DNA from inside the glove, but that's two days to cook. We'll run an HIV test, mainly to

protect the nurse. Bring me a warm body, Detective—
I've got prints galore."

"Bring me the feather. I'm going to ID it."

"Bob Eilerts out at the zoo is first-rate."

"Thank you, Arthur."

"Tweet-tweet."

McMichael walked into the Homicide area, deserted
now at six on a Thursday night. It was often empty,
in a city of 1.2 million with only four teams to work
murder—everyone out, doing the job. There used to
be seven teams, but budgets were budgets and the
four teams were coming up with good cancellation
rates.

At his desk in the Team Three pen, McMichael
listened to Barbara Givens's message: the notary
said yes, he'd witnessed Pete Braga's several signatures over the last few months, transferring certain
property to Sally Rainwater. Barbara had checked
Rainwater's documents against the notary's log
and everything looked right. The notary himself
was in good standing with the California licensing
board.

McMichael sat back. He'd lost a suspect and a
motive in about half an hour. So, why bash Pete and
run away with little or nothing? Was the creep surprised by the nurse, never getting to finish his job?
A thrill killing? Some kind of vengeance or jeal-
ousy? Did he swipe something they hadn't realized
yet? But in some way, McMichael wasn't surprised:
it hadn't felt like a home invasion from the start.
Bludgeon murders were usually personal. The more

times the victim was hit the more he or she was hated. You looked at the husband, the wife, the lover. Thieves don't take the time to keep on hitting. Strangers don't hate like that. Unless they're just insane.

Patricia Hansen had dropped off a folder containing Sally Rainwater's references. McMichael scanned through the sheets: five previous caretaking jobs for the elderly, three character testimonials from college professors, one from a Methodist minister. They all spoke highly of her competence and personality. She'd moved a little, he saw— Virginia, Florida, Texas and California.

He logged on to his computer and waited for the FBI Violent Criminal Apprehension Program to verify his entry code. While the hourglass icon urged patience, he turned and looked at the pictures of his ex-wife and son at the beach. During their seven years of marriage he and Stephanie had rented an oceanfront bungalow in Oceanside for one week each summer. Every year, McMichael had taken a vertical shot of his wife and son standing on the pier, framed them and lined them up at his work station as a nutshell history. The growing collection had traveled with him from patrol to Metro/Vice to Homicide. He could see how Johnny had grown bigger and stronger, and Stephanie had grown bigger and unhappier. So easy, he thought, to see now what I couldn't see then. Last year's picture was just after the divorce. It showed McMichael and Johnny standing somewhat awkwardly together while a tourist snapped the shot. It had been a rough week.

VICAP finally gave him access and McMichael ran a like-crimes check using residential robbery, bludgeon attacks and Southern California as his parameters. He asked the database to go back ten years.

There were twelve unsolveds, two in San Diego. McMichael remembered both. The first was four years back, an older woman in the Lemon Grove area who was raped, robbed and beaten. She'd survived, but there had not yet been an arrest. Witnesses had placed a "white male, 20–30 years of age, medium height and weight, dressed as a housepainter" near the scene of the attack. McMichael recalled that no one on the block had had painting done that day.

The second was two years ago. Homicide Team One had gotten it. McMichael had heard just bits and pieces over the months, less and less as the case remained open and the leads shrank to nothing. The victim was a seventy-two-year-old white man— Richard Appleton—who was found by his daughter. He'd been beaten with a ten-inch piece of steel pipe that had been discarded near the scene. And robbed of a watch, cash, a handgun.

It had happened in Kensington, east of downtown, late at night, mid-September. The killer had either come through an unlocked door or had a key—no signs of forced entry. No suspect, no warrants issued. Neighbors, friends and family all checked out clean.

But one neighbor reported an unidentified subject loitering outside Appleton's home at approximately nine P.M. that night. *White male, medium build, wearing a dark jogging suit and cap.* Both San Diego homicide detective Ed Drake and the FBI believed that robbery was the motive. Appleton had been sitting in a chair, watching TV.

Boom, thought McMichael.

He went to the Team One pen, found the Appleton murder book and carried it back to his desk.

First he read the witness interview to make sure the Bureau had gotten it right on the VICAP synopsis. It had, word for word.

Next he read the detective-in-charge's crime scene notes, neatly transcribed from his tape recording. Ed Drake had headed up this one and Ed Drake was a detail man. He'd even made a note of the thunderstorms that night over the city. Rain, thought McMichael. Rain in mid-September and rain in early January. Old men sitting in chairs while storms blow through. Hard to hear because of the rain and wind, maybe. Easy to break and enter. Covers tracks. Keeps people inside. Two scenes, two joggers.

Appleton never made it out of his chair. Three of his teeth had landed on a windowsill ten feet across the room. The estimated total value of the watch, cash and gun came to less than five hundred dollars.

No prints. No flesh, blood or fluid samples for DNA.

McMichael flipped forward to the interviews. Neighbors and relatives had said that Appleton was quiet, friendly and often home. He was a widower, a retired machine shop foreman.

No one came up with anything even mildly unusual—except for the jogger. McMichael read the description again, thinking about the time of night and the rain. The neighbor who had seen the jogger was Kyle Zisch, twenty-six, who lived across the street and two houses down. Zisch said he was making tea for his girlfriend when he looked out the kitchen window and saw "a man loitering in front of victim residence." Zisch told the police that he thought it was interesting that the man was in the rain, dressed for jogging, but not really jogging. Zisch said the man finally began running down the sidewalk, slowly, after "appearing to case the house."

McMichael had seen enough die-hard joggers to figure that running in the rain—especially a warm September rain—wasn't that unusual. What caught his eye next was not the jogger, but Kyle Zisch's job and place of employment: "bird handler at San Diego Wild Animal Park."

Boom again.

Maybe Zisch had been the jogger, McMichael thought. It wasn't unusual for a smart young creep to toy with the cops. McMichael wondered if "case" was Zisch's word or the detective's. Maybe the helpful Zisch had a thing for easy marks, late nights, blunt objects, rain. It would be easy enough to pick up a yellow feather on the job, get it caught on a sweater or coat or cap, leave it behind accidentally. Maybe even leave one at the scene on purpose, for the fun of it. There was nothing in the Appleton murder book about feathers.

McMichael ran a records check on Zisch but he came back clean. No prints on file with the PD, the state or FBI, either. McMichael wrote down Zisch's LKA and phone number, and made a note to ID the feather.

* * *

While the VICAP pages printed out, he looked at the pictures of Johnny again and figured the days until he'd see him. Two. Last night, Wednesday, had been a father-son night, but McMichael had dropped Johnny off at home early because his boy wasn't feeling well. The weeknights were pretty brief, anyway: they could bang out the homework then have time for dinner, maybe a walk and a movie or TV. McMichael always tried to do too much on Johnny days, tried to get a week's worth of living into a few waking hours. Johnny was a beautiful boy and the apple of McMichael's eye and his heart broke a little every time he thought of how they had torn his young life in two. Only seven years old.

It was dark outside now but the rain had stopped. A poststorm wind came steady from the west. The lights of downtown were staunch in the darkness before him.

McMichael had grown up just a few blocks from here and had been seeing this view, adjusted for progress but the same in its essentials, for all of his thirty-eight years. He loved the city. Loved the curve of the Coronado Bridge and the hard optics of ocean and glass and concrete, and the stout old downtown buildings and the spikes of the big hotels by the water. He loved the busy muscle of the shipyards and the tremendous vessels of the Fifth Fleet, and the navy installations that claimed so much of the city—cities within the city—closed and self-sufficient and forbidding. He loved the bars and streets of the Gaslamp, so crowded and chaotic with pretty women on warm summer nights. He even loved the huge cemetery out on Point Loma, where his great-great-uncle, killed in France in the Great War, shared a Pacific-side grave with the wife who outlived him by six decades.

But even more than all of that, he loved his son. Johnny was born in this city. He was the city made flesh. Until McMichael had become a father he had no idea that the hugeness of a city could be contained in the smile of a boy. He'd learned that the tremendous, unshaped powers within a man's heart—love, loyalty, gratitude, joy—could become specific with the birth of a child. Everything he had felt, made real.

It was all worth protecting.

8

Spellacy's was quiet when McMichael walked in at six that evening. Hugh stood behind the polished redwood bar, drying glasses. Four men huddled on the stools, conversing with the patient, collegial energy of drunks. McMichael's father was among them. His smile went big when he saw his son. McMichael sat beside Gabe at the end of the bar, by the olives and onions and lemon rinds.

"You've been busy, I bet."

"We got Pete."

"So your sister told me. I hear the nurse was covered in blood."

It always surprised McMichael how much Raegan learned at the *Libertad* Cigar Factory & Lounge. And what Gabe picked up from his stool at Spellacy's Pub. Put them together, you had a CIA for the streets of San Diego.

"It wasn't the nurse," said McMichael.

"I could have told you that, son."

"What else can you tell me, Pop?"

"It was Pete's enemies is who it was. But he had so many, you know, so it's hard to say which."

They took a booth near the back for dinner. Hugh brought them pints and stew and a loaf of bread and butter. Gabe ate like he hadn't had a meal in two days, which was entirely possible. In McMichael's estimation, his father was one step away from being a danger to society, and was already a certifiable danger to himself. McMichael had no idea how his mother had borne his father, other than quietly.

"What I figure is the new airport," said Gabriel, dipping bread into the stew. "Pete was Port Commission, now wasn't he? And Port Commission controls all the bay and the land around it. They control the airport. Every time money changes hands at the airport, Pete's Port Commission gets some of it. But there's people trying to build a *new* airport. Bigger and better and very damned expensive, you can bet. The state makes up this new Airport Authority to *oversee the idea* of a new airport. The city and the business types, they're all for it like you'd figure, but Pete and the Port Commission, they're trying to keep the old airport up and working, right where it is. Then, a few months ago, Pete starts making noises about *letting* the new Airport Authority take over Lindbergh Field, close it down and build the new one. Some of the Port Commission people aren't happy. They think Pete's switching sides and they can't figure out why."

"So, why did he?"

"Because he would have profited from it, mark my words. And I'll tell you this, the Tunaboat Foundation, they were pissed at him, too, because the old airport leases thirteen acres from them. Thirteen expensive acres, right between the terminals and the harbor. That's foundation land. And if the airport moves, they lose a fat and easy paycheck."

McMichael remembered reading just a few weeks ago of the heated debate on the new airport, the way the powerful Port Commission might be coming around to the idea of a new airport that would be outside their immediate control.

"Wasn't Pete on the Tunaboat Foundation board?" McMichael asked.

"He *was* the foundation, Tommy. And he was telling them one thing but planning another."

McMichael thought about it. People were murdered for less substantial reasons than the ones his father was suggesting. Hundreds of millions of dollars were at stake, and if you factored in jobs and power and politics—the stakes went up even higher.

Gabriel's pale blue eyes glimmered as he looked at his son. "Which is exactly what Pete pulled on your grandfather Franklin."

Here we go again, thought McMichael. Thirty-eight years and he knew the speech by heart.

"It's the Portugee way of doing things, Tom. They lie to you. The Irish, we tell you right up front what the deal is. And you can take or leave it. Not the Portugee. They're like gangsters that way."

McMichael nodded along, staring at the poster on the wall that featured a leprechaun cocktail maid. She was offering him a tray of creamy-headed stouts. She was scantily clad, big-eared, exceptionally

pretty and ridiculous. He'd come to believe that the
Irish were their own worst promoters, though he'd
always liked the picture. The cocktail maid became
Sally Rainwater, and he looked away.

"So what if I say the same thing over and over,
Tommy? In case you're curious, I was right here that
night. Ask Hugh, he'll set you straight."

McMichael hadn't thought of his father as a suspect, though Gabriel was passionate, vengeful and
unpredictable. "Who were Pete's partners on the
Tunaboat Foundation?"

"How would I know? But I do know that some of
them like Raegan's cigar club—so says Raegan.
They're regulars. Not Pete, though. Your sister,
she'd throw him right back onto the sidewalk he
came in on."

"Pete's Tunaboat Foundation without Pete."

"Right—the guys he was lying to. Another pint,
son?"

McMichael signaled to Hugh Spellacy, one of
the two brothers who owned the pub. They'd inherited it in 1965 from their father, who had purchased it in 1951 from Franklin McMichael, who
had inherited it from his father in 1939, who had
taken it over for his father in 1901, fourteen years
after it was opened here on Front Street by Dono-
van McMichael, who arrived in San Diego from
County Cork via Ellis Island and wagon train. Just
last year the Spellacy brothers had made news by
refusing to let the city register the pub as an official place of historical interest. This because the city
had declined their applications for four consecutive

years in the early 1980s, when seismic retrofits and code violations were killing them. Historical status would have exempted them from some of it. So they'd paid full retail for the repairs, and just barely survived. Typically Irish, McMichael thought, to carry a grudge of pride so far past its usefulness. The Spellacys had inlaid an old-fashioned bronze plaque near the old cornerstone, designating the pub as a place of "Historical Disinterest" although "still the auldest and finest Irish Public House in the great State of California."

"How's Johnny?"

"He's perfect, Dad."

"You must miss watching him grow. That was one thing I always held on to. Your mother and I never split."

"You were lucky. Mom put up with a lot more hell than Stephanie ever did."

"Stephanie was in it for different things, in my opinion."

"You've said that a million times."

"And she got them. But it's too bad for Johnny and you."

"Anyway, he's perfect. Will Keller be here to walk you home later?"

"Will he be here? He's been here to walk me home for fifty years!"

Keller had been at Gabriel's side since 1953, when they were both thirteen, and Victor Braga was beaten more than half to death behind the Waterfront bar. Logic and uncertain eyewitnesses had brought the police to Gabriel, who had denied knowing anything about it. But Gabe bragged to his Logan Heights Irish friends, a bit too loudly, that Victor had just gotten what Pete deserved. So when the Portuguese boys came after him, they had to deal with Keller, who had knocked out grown men since he was twelve years old.

"When they jumped me down on Ash back in 'fifty-eight, it was Tim Keller who saved my life. Same in 'sixty and 'sixty-four."

Fists and knives, thought McMichael, thirty stitches for his father and a broken jaw for Keller in the 'fifty-eight rumble. "I know, Dad."

Keller and Gabriel had been in more than enough knife and fistfights to land them both in jail, but the Portuguese didn't talk to the cops and the Irish didn't talk to the cops and they both scattered like fleas when the prowl cars came howling to a stop.

McMichael thought how different it had been then. Quaint wasn't quite the word for it. Maybe *proportional*. Now, if young men had a dispute like that it was cars and guns and people died. His father hadn't been attacked in almost thirty years, but Gabe and Keller stuck together anyway—two near-geezers shuffling the downtown streets between the bars and the trolley station and their flophouse hotel rooms downtown.

McMichael hung with his father until Tim Keller came through the door, thin and slope-shouldered as ever, his pale blue eyes a mystery of soul and mischief.

"What's the word, Tommy?"

"You old homies stay out of trouble."

"Trouble keeps a man young—just look at me. Besides, it's all I have left to do. Stay for a pint, Tommy."

"There's work to do."

"Imagine, your son a cop," said Keller, sizing up McMichael, then Gabriel. "After all the trouble you've made in your life."

"That's exactly why he *is* a cop, Tim. Hoping to balance things out."

"The Lord never gets tired of surprises." Keller clamped a hand around McMichael's arm. "And here's some free advice. Pete Braga was mixed up with this new airport thing. There's millions to be made on it, and Pete was after more than his share. See, the airport buys all their cars and trucks from Pete Braga Ford. Been that way for years. What I'm thinking is, Pete might have cut himself a better deal with the new airport. I'd look into that angle, if I were you."

"I'll do that. And what were you up to last night, Tim?"

"Oh, I was right here," he said, eyes cagey and gleeful. "Ask Hugh, he'll set you straight."

On the way out, McMichael leaned across the bar and asked Hugh Spellacy about Gabe and Tim and last night. Hugh set him straight.

For a moment McMichael stood there and watched his father reflected in the mirror behind the bar. Keller sat across from Gabriel in a tableau that McMichael had been seeing for three decades. What was the saying—God invented whiskey to keep the Irish from taking over the world? He shook his head, then caught his own face in the mirror, right below the "e" of Spellacy's. If he squinted a little, which he did, he could look a lot like Gabriel. Just turn his own wavy red-brown hair to gray, bend his smile lines down with age and booze, blanch his alert blue eyes with sun and disappointment, and you'd have Gabe. The McMichael ears, of course, were the kicker—thick-edged and lightly freckled—the ears of County Cork boys who came to America in steerage. His mother had shown him pictures. McMichael wore his hair a little long on the sides, as camouflage and distraction. Ditto Gabe. McMichael could always spot his ancestors in the old photographs: the ones with the tough eyes, the ready smiles, and ears like wing nuts.

He stood in the bright lights of the Von's Market on Rosecrans, comparing his Polaroid of Sally Rainwater's firewood bundle to the ones being offered for sale at $4.99 a throw. The labels were the same—Bear Creek Firewood—though the same supplier might sell bundles to any number of local markets.

He showed a copy of Rainwater's CDL to the manager, who didn't remember seeing her last night. But he was helpful enough to take McMichael to the checkers and box boys and box girls who had been on shift the night before. One box girl was somewhat certain she'd seen the woman between eight and ten P.M. One box boy was almost certain.

One of the checkers, a good-looking fiftyish man named Ricardo, was certain beyond reasonable doubt. "She bought two bundles of firewood and paid cash," he told McMichael. "She did not want any help out."

"Had you noticed her in here before last night?"

"Many times, over the last few months. A very easy face to remember."

He drove out Silver Strand Boulevard toward Imperial Beach. The strand was in fact silver tonight beneath the storm-scrubbed sky, stars close and the moon round and shiny as a hubcap.

McMichael looked out at the liquid mirror of ocean and thought of what he was about to do. *A very easy face to remember.* He listened inward for the soft footsteps of disaster but heard none.

Then he thought of Johnny and Stephanie cozy in their big house in La Jolla, enjoying the nonviolent prosperity of Dr. Clay Blass, oral surgeon. McMichael wondered if they were better off without him. What would he be doing right now, if they'd stayed together? Well, pretty much exactly this, he thought. Steffy would be home feeling alone and worried and be mostly through the first bottle of wine. Johnny would be done with his homework and dinner, maybe watching TV.

And McMichael would get home at nine or so—early, really, because when a case was hot you could work it for a couple of days straight and not come home at all. He'd share a bottle of wine with Steffy and they'd talk and he would try to put the work out of his mind.

But no matter what they talked about, their words would pool over a bedrock of resentment that had begun forming in Stephanie not long after they'd married. It got worse when he made Homicide. At home McMichael would see how genuinely disappointed Stephanie was to realize that his job sometimes took precedence over their marriage, how angry she was becoming, and he'd wonder if he'd somehow misrepresented himself and the work he did. The really surprising thing was that he was doing just fine. It became awkward, then irrelevant to tell her that he was happy here, in the hunt, with her and their son and the little house overlooking Interstate 5 and the harbor. He would sleep poorly if his team was up on the rotation, or sleep like the dead if it wasn't, until early morning when he'd get up and make breakfast and take Johnny to school, then go on to Fourteenth and Broadway and do it again. He liked the hectic velocity of it all, and the feeling of doing something that mattered. Liked making the city just a little better for his wife and son. Didn't mind being on call 24/7—weekends, holidays—every single day of the year except when they were on vacation. Liked putting the pieces together, making sense of hidden things, finally nailing someone to the wall. And the overtime pay really added up. McMichael knew all along he was living a cop's story. He'd known it going in, wanted it. But he'd thought he could rewrite it with a good middle and maybe even a happy ending. Seven years of it and Stephanie had fallen in love with the guy who pulled Johnny's tooth.

He drove past the Imperial Beach Pier and then down Seacoast Drive to the last homes before Mexico. He felt his heart working faster and the damp cold at his temples as he walked to her door. Got the same feeling he had when the pieces of an investigation started to mesh, when he was sure of something he couldn't quite see yet. Felt like he was pursuing the hunch of a lifetime.

Sally Rainwater opened it as far as the chain would go but said nothing.

"I just wanted to thank you for your help," he said. "I'm sorry you had to go through that with Pete, then with us. Your alibi checked at the market and your letters from Pete were legit. You know that already. I apologize for the heavy treatment."

He looked down. He'd thought about what he'd say, hadn't realized it was so little, would be over so quickly.

"I thought you handled yourself with guts and class," he said. "It took a lot to try to save Pete like you did."

"I wouldn't describe the hallway scene as classy."

"It shouldn't have happened."

He couldn't make out much of her face, just eyes and hair and a hand up at her throat holding a cowl or collar tight. "You'll keep looking at me as a possible accomplice, won't you?"

"If you'd like."

"Cute."

"We'll keep looking at you," said McMichael. He now felt as stiff and mirthless as a tax collector. "I'll have some questions and I'll want your help."

"So what are you really doing here? *Looking* at me? Heading off a use-of-force lawsuit? Putting me off guard so you can investigate a murder?"

"I wanted to tell you those things, face-to-face, not over the phone."

"Why?"

McMichael now clearly heard the footsteps of disaster, though they sounded far away and avoidable. The next two seconds became an hour. "I thought you deserved it."

All he could see of her eyes was a glimmer. "Is this a personal call, Detective McMichael?"

"No. Yes."

She didn't move. McMichael prepared his retreat, heard himself trying to explain his side of the Rainwater citizen's complaint to the captain. In the way of most catastrophes, this one had come quietly, then deafeningly. Not until right now did he understand that this was the most asinine and unprofessional thing he'd ever done.

The door closed then swung open and Sally Rainwater stepped aside to let him in.

She was dressed like she was the night before at Pete's, but without the blood and the boots. Pink fluffy slippers again. Even in the slippers she was tall. There was an open textbook and a legal pad and yellow pencil on the kitchen table. A steaming mug by the book.

She shut the door, crossed her arms and looked at him with steady brown eyes. The room shrunk around him.

"I've never done anything like this before," he said. There was a chip of something yellow stuck to her lower lip. McMichael was grateful for it and stared.

"I haven't, either."

"I wondered who you are. You were in my dream."

"I thought about you, too."

Her eyes held a fierce curiosity and McMichael felt pinned. He studied the yellow chip. "I don't know what to say."

"You can sit down."

He sat on the couch under the painting. She made orange tea and brought it to him in a mug with the bag still in it. When she sat in the director's chair she was far away and up higher than him, which only aggravated McMichael's growing sense of incompetence and stupidity.

"Nice place," he said.

"Cheap and on the beach."

"Not many of those left!"

She looked at him and McMichael checked his tea bag.

"I really can't do this," she said.

"Me neither."

She took his mug into the kitchen. Then she came out and pulled him up from the couch and kissed him. Both her hands on his face. It was short but generous and McMichael's heart bounced off the moon. No hiding the physics of things but he turned his waist a little to try.

"Go home now," she said. "Treat me like a regular woman and call me. I'm not a walk-in clinic."

"Roger that."

"Nights are best until I get another job."

"I'm really—"

"If you apologize I'm going to kill you."

"Pleased."

"We might do some good, Detective. Then again, this may be the dumbest thing either of us has ever managed. You got some of my pencil stuck to your lip."

9

"*Psittacidae*," said Dr. Robert Eilerts, chief ornithologist for the San Diego Zoo. It was nine the next morning, a cool and windy forty degrees when McMichael had left home.

Eilerts looked up from the microscope. "One of the parrots. There are over three hundred different species. But if you give me a few hours with the feather I think I can narrow it down."

"I'll pick it up as soon as I get your call."

"Should be before noon. Does this have to do with the Braga murder?"

"I'm sorry, I can't tell you that," said McMichael.

The doctor nodded and colored, then bent back down to his scope.

The Wild Animal Park is northeast of the city, in the dry foothills of Pasqual Valley. McMichael picked up Via Rancho Parkway and steered with one hand through the gentle bends. He could see patches of frost in the shaded swales and the bright glimmer of oaks shivering in the cold inland breeze. He felt giddy and doubtful about the night before, wondering if such cloddish behavior would come back to bite him. All he'd gotten for it so far was a memorable kiss and an invitation to call.

The Wild Animal Park human resources director agreed to show McMichael her personnel mug for Kyle Zisch. "You can find him at the bird show," she said. "He'll come out the exit behind the theater right after the performance—it starts in half an hour."

"Any parrots in the show?"

"Oh yes," she said. "Samson and Delilah. Absolutely beautiful, and huge vocabularies. Be sure to stop by the nursery on your way over. We've got a darling new baby mountain gorilla."

McMichael looked at the baby gorilla in her windowed nursery. Her name was Misty. Diapers and everything. He was surprised how small she was. And how human her eyes were, set in the inhuman face. He wondered if people really could have descended from apes, how things like language and conscience and imagination could flow down one biological streambed and not another. Although, looking into Misty's eyes, McMichael thought he saw his own and Sally Rainwater's, which he made a point not to mention to her. Father Shea had told him once that creation was ongoing and we should all understand that God had made everything to start with.

McMichael bought a disposable camera and a soft drink, then found a bird-show seat third row from the front. The handlers were dressed in safari outfits and kept up a joking banter with the audience. A peregrine falcon tore from the heavens at ninety miles an hour to snag a treat from a young woman on the stage. McMichael stood and snapped some photographs.

Kyle Zisch made his appearance with a flamboyant bird on each arm. He was easy to make from the mug: dark-haired, bearded and bespectacled. His voice was oddly high as he introduced Samson and Delilah. "And I'm Kyle!"

McMichael stood, excused himself rather loudly and took two more shots.

Zisch walked the birds to separate perches and they hopped on. The handler then reached into a waist pouch and set some food on the stands. McMichael could hear the smack of beaks on wood as the birds took their prizes.

"You don't have very good manners, Samson," said Zisch.

"*I learned them from you,*" squawked the bird.

"Delilah," said Zisch, "what's your excuse?"

"*I'm a birdbrain.*"

The audience chuckled and Zisch rewarded them again. He explained that these were macaws, native to South America, and were not known for their talking abilities. But the staff had taken a liking to the two fledglings and had begun building their vocabularies the week they were born. He said they knew over twenty sentences each—and continued to pick up new words and phrases all the time.

"*Clever, aren't we?*" asked Delilah.

The macaws jawboned with Zisch for a few minutes, then the bald eagle glowered and flew, the ostrich strutted and the cassowary rolled a ball with its beak.

After the show, all the trainers came out for a bow and McMichael clapped loudly and took more pictures. A minute later he intercepted Zisch at the exit and asked him for an autograph to go with the pictures he took—for his son Johnny back in Denver. Johnny had been in the hospital lately for tests. Loved birds, mainly birds of prey, but liked parrots, too. Had a parakeet named Sarge.

"Could you write just a little something to my boy?"

"Sure, man."

Zisch wrote in McMichael's notebook with McMichael's pen.

"Hope he'll be okay."

"Thank you," said the detective. "This'll make him happy. Would you mind snapping a picture of me to go with the ones of you and the macaws?"

"No problem."

McMichael traded the camera for the notebook and pen, stood with his back to the theater and smiled. Zisch pushed the button but nothing happened.

"Gotta wind it forward," said the Denver tourist. "There you go. Hey, great show!"

Back at the car McMichael had just put the camera and pen into a paper bag when his phone rang.

"Detective, this is Dr. Eilerts at the zoo. Your feather came from an owl parrot."

"Do they have that species at the Wild Animal Park?"

"They've got four. We have four also. They're very rare and generally don't do well in captivity."

"What else can you tell me about them?"

"They're native to New Zealand's South Island only, and were once thought to be extinct. They've got these extravagant facial feathers that make them appear owl-like. That's what you found. Owl parrots are a large bird."

"Then they're not popular as pets?"

"No—they're very hard to get. And like an owl, they're only active at night, which tends to keep pet owners awake at the wrong hours. Specialty stores or breeders would be a possible source. There are several of them in the city. I've got some numbers for you if you're interested."

He got out his notebook and a spare pen. "I appreciate this, Dr. Eilerts."

Hector, Harley and Erik met him in Fingerprints. McMichael explained that he'd washed both pen and camera with tissues and soap in the bathroom, then used the hand blower to dry them. Then he'd washed his hands with lots of soap and hot water, and tried to touch pen and camera as little as possible before handing them over to the bird trainer.

"The humidity is low today," said Harley. "Was he wearing gloves during the show?"

"No gloves."

"Too bad. That would have brought out the body oils in his hands. Okay—we'll bench laser them first, then the glue chamber."

Harley arranged the pen in the bench laser. "When the monochromatic light vibrates into phase, we'll get coherency. When we turn up the juice, the coherent light will amplify the latents—if there are any latents to amplify."

The bench laser showed a clear partial on the lower part of the pen, where you'd expect the index finger to rest. And a good thumb partial, on the opposite side.

"Grand," said Harley.

"Pure sex," said Erik. "Look at the curves on those ridges."

The upper part of the pen had very small partials.

"Check the top of the clicker, where the thumb would go," said Hector.

The laser light vibrated into phase, but revealed nothing.

Harley photographed the latents as they were amplified under the laser.

The camera contained one nearly full thumbprint on the upper left of the back side, where Zisch had braced the camera in order to advance the film. The thumbprints around the advance wheel were smeared.

"Check the bottom right corner," said McMichael. "I'm hoping for some palm to check against the slider."

Harley rearranged the camera in the laser unit and aimed the light onto the right-side bottom. McMichael watched the partial palm print reveal itself, beautifully bisected by what appeared to be two major lines.

"Line of heart meets line of health, just below the plain of Mars," said Erik. "My college girlfriend minored in palmistry and the other hard sciences, like astrology. That's definitely a right palm, upper right corner, exactly where you'd cradle that camera for a shot."

Harley photographed the prints, then shut down the bench laser.

"Luck of the Irish," said Erik.

"Luck nothing," said Hector. "He's just a good detective."

The cyanoacrylate fuming chamber made the prints visible to the naked eye, chemically hardening them into a nearly permanent record. Erik photographed them with a digital camera fitted with a strong magnifying lens, taking several shots of each print, complete with a ruler for measurement. He came back from the computer printer less than five minutes later with twenty-two large, clear fingerprint images.

Next, they spread out the fingerprint cards taken from Pete Braga's house, and from the inside of the latex gloves found down on the beach.

McMichael had always liked visual fingerprint analysis—trying to match the ridge patterns between two prints. He looked for the telltale bifurcations and endings and furrows that could match one print to another. It was difficult work to do well, very difficult to do well enough for a court of law, which is why the detectives left it to forensic specialists. McMichael reminded himself how easy it was to mistake a blood bridge for a ridge ending, for example, and how too much or too little ink would obscure a minutiae point and lead you to the wrong conclusion.

"No," said Harley after ten seconds. "The left

thumb whorls are miles apart. Ditto the right index loops."

It took McMichael a full minute and a sinking heart to confirm what Harley had seen.

"Nice try," said Erik. "It really was."

"Hey," said Hector. "Not so fast. So this guy leaves one of his bird feathers, but he doesn't leave a fingerprint. He's the brains of the team. He lined up the mark—an old guy just like his neighbor. Made his partner use the club. Just because somebody else's prints were there doesn't mean he wasn't."

"Sure," said Harley, without conviction.

McMichael tried to picture a twosome. A robbery team had made some sense when it looked like the paintings and baseball gloves had been boosted that night. But if you ruled out robbery as motive, that left you with a basher and someone standing around . . . doing what? He wondered if Patricia might have missed some jewelry, besides the South African diamond earrings she'd remembered her grandmother wearing. And the hummingbird. Maybe Pete had cash in there that Patricia never knew about. But why would they close up the floor safe and move that heavy brass-nail sofa back over it? If they'd marched him up there to open it himself, why march him back down to his fish room, sit him down, then start hitting?

Pete was a collector, thought McMichael: baseball gloves, paintings, mounted trophy fish, signed books. And what else was he?

A businessman: sold cars, made investments. A politician: Port Commission, former mayor, city booster.

I'd look to the new airport if I were you.

All I can say is that Peter Braga was a tempestuous man.

McMichael realized he needed to spend a little more time with Pete Braga. Which meant a little more time with Patricia. Which had once been what he wanted more than anything in the world.

Back at his desk he found her number and made the call.

"I'll be aboard the *Cabrillo Star,*" she said. "Meet me at four."

10

Pete Braga's *Cabrillo Star* was berthed in Tuna Harbor, just a few blocks from downtown. Walking up the gangplank McMichael knew that the ship had seen some history. She had been built of wood as a tuna clipper back in the thirties, when they still caught the big fish with poles. She had seen action in World War II along with dozens of other tuna ships requisitioned by the navy to carry food in their freezers. She'd been converted to a seiner—a net boat—after the war. Then retired when the great super-seiners took over the industry and the *Cabrillo Star* became nothing more than a failed tourist venue and a quaint reminder of a time that was gone.

And, in 1952, she'd been the place where McMichael's grandfather, Franklin, had been shot to death by Pete Braga after a dispute over money.

All of this had come to McMichael through Gabriel, who gathered information and gossip about Braga as if it was required by his religion. *So what's*

Pete do with that worthless old tub of leaks he murdered Franklin on? He sells it to the city as a tourist destination and parks it out in Tuna Harbor. And does the city think people will pay to step aboard that stinking rat nest? Of course not. But Pete offered them options on some of his waterfront properties and they saw green—hotels and restaurants and tourist stuff. So what's the city council going to do—buy his rotten old ship for a few hundred grand or lose out on a shot to develop the harborside? Like Pete isn't a millionaire ten times over by now. Like he needs that kind of beer money. Like he's not selling Fords to the city all day every day and offerin' no bargains. Take my word for that.

McMichael called Patricia's name, got no answer, walked the port side past the freezer holds and the converted bait wells. He saw that his father had had it wrong about the *Cabrillo Star*—the hull was clean and true, the decks and bridges were bright white in the cool January sun, hardly a chip on the gunwales or rails, and even the old winches looked ready to handle a couple of hundred feet of nylon net, no problem.

"McMike!"

She came down off the radio bridge in jeans and tennis shoes and a red anorak with fur around the hood. Little oval sunglasses. Her dark curls bounced to her shoulders as she walked toward him and McMichael felt the familiar old tickle in his stomach.

She kissed his cheek and aimed him back toward the bridge. "I'm cleaning out Pete's things," she said. "The city owned this ship for twenty years and never got around to it."

"I thought the city still owned her."

"Pete bought it back when the tourists stayed away by the thousands. The galley's full of old junk."

"What are you going to do with her?"

Patricia started up the ladder. "We've agreed to sell it," she said, looking back down at him. "I got a restaurant guy up in Marina del Rey maybe interested. Three hundred grand he can have it. Sell the Ford dealership, too, though it's worth more."

McMichael waited until she was onto the bridge, then climbed up. "Split five ways?"

"You talked to Hank Grothke."

"Both of them."

Patricia shook her head. "The old man, last month they caught him stalking around the office early one morning, shredding papers. You name it—contracts, wills, magazines from the lobby, even some of those ass gaskets from the bathrooms. Made me think, you know, when I get that old just take me out and shoot me."

"Sure."

"I knew I could count on you."

"I kind of liked him."

"You're still capable of the unexpected."

She grinned at him. He'd never been able to tell if her half smile held joy or something more complicated. Unlike Stephanie, whose face was her heart.

"Never know what you'll find behind enemy lines," he said.

"Fun, wasn't it?" Patricia deployed her half smile again.

"Lots of that."

"Now we're older and duller," she said.

"Yeah," said McMichael. "Wheelchairs and shredders, right around the corner."

Her grin was gone. "What can I do for you, Tom?"

"I can't figure out who'd want to kill your grandfather. The nurse is clean. I don't think she set him up, either. I don't think she was involved at all. Nothing taken from his home, except those earrings you mentioned and maybe the hummingbird. And like you said, why would someone take those and leave the other two pounds of gold and diamonds? Tell me about him, Patricia. What was he doing on the Port Commission with the new airport? How was the car dealership going? And the Tunaboat Foundation—I know it has deep pockets and I hear there were some disagreements on the board. I'm throwing a wide net, but help me if you can."

"Enemies."

"And his state of mind, his clarity."

"Sharpen your little pencil, McMike. Come on down to the galley and we'll get some coffee."

The pot was already made. Patricia poured two mugs black and sat across from him in one of the booths. McMichael looked out the porthole to the south. He could see the navy shipyards and the Coronado Bridge and the cold blue sky. He tapped his pen against his notebook.

"First of all," she said, "Grandpa's state of mind was pretty good. He wasn't particularly forgetful or paranoid or having visions. He was a tough old man. He couldn't see all that well, and he kept driving— like I told you. I think he was a menace to society behind the wheel of a car. But this is the deal, Tom—my grandfather had enemies. He had business enemies, political enemies, personal enemies. You made a crack about dividing his estate by five. Well I don't know if Hank Grothke told you, but Grandpa has three living children and six living grandchildren. He disinherited four out of nine—that's pushing fifty percent."

"Tell me about the disinherited son."

"Carl is gay and Pete disowned him the second he came out of the closet. Carl had just graduated from high school. He's up in San Francisco now. I'll invite him to the funeral but he won't come. He also wouldn't sneak in and kill him. He's a decent and gentle man. One suspect down."

McMichael wrote and considered. "And his daughter?"

"That's my aunt, Liz DeCerra. She's sixty-one now, I think. Lives in Colorado. She's in the will. There, two suspects down."

"What about the grandchildren?"

"There are Cassie, Quentin and Max DeCerra. Pete wrote out Cassie because she ran off with a drug dealer, Quentin because Quentin punched him in the face, and Max because he broke into Pete's place and stole a bunch of cash and Anna's Lady Rolex."

"They sound like nice kids."

"Whatever, Tom. They were his grandchildren. Grandchildren have problems like anybody else."

McMichael wrote. "That leaves you and your brother and sister. Your side of the family stayed in favor."

"We lacked the physical courage of the DeCerras, that's for sure."

McMichael wasn't so sure. Things were about as physical as they could get, back when they were eighteen and seeing each other in secret, and Patricia had always gone straight for the forbidden settings: her parents' shower, her big sister's bed, her grandfather's deck, the living room, the patio chaise longue, the car. There was ample opportunity with her father at sea on one of Pete's boats and her mother a bookkeeper at the cannery. Then there was the beach at night, a picnic bench up on Palomar Mountain, the Regency Hotel by the hour, the sand dunes out toward Yuma, even a sweltering gas station bathroom on the way home.

He smiled and Patricia smiled, too, then she set her sunglasses on the table. Her eyes were dark and clear and McMichael instantly located the golden fleck in her right iris that he'd spotted for the first time when he was ten. And actually written a poem about when he was thirteen, with a rhythm and rhyme pattern based on Joyce Kilmer's "Trees." She'd given a photocopy of it back to him, covered with red lipstick prints and drenched in her perfume, but kept the original.

"What about Quentin or Max?" McMichael asked. "Do you think either of them might club the old man just for spite?"

"No. Those DeCerras are all hot-tempered, but they cool off fast."

McMichael looked up from his notepad. "Victor gets a nice piece of the estate."

She looked at him and shook her head. "And he's nothing but a ten-year-old in a sixty-three-year-old's body. Thanks to Gabe."

"That was never proven."

"He bragged about doing it. We Portuguese aren't exactly deaf, McMichael. And you Irish aren't exactly quiet."

"Is he ever violent?"

"Well, no. But he's a little short on self-control sometimes."

"Did he and Pete get along?"

She stared out the porthole. When she looked back at him he saw the moisture in her near-black eyes. "They loved each other. A man and his first-born son. And with Victor the way he is, it was like Grandpa had a ten-year-old boy forever. Saddest goddamned thing I ever saw—two old men sitting in the Waterfront bar drinking port, one of them talking about fleet rates or whatever and the other showing him his new baseball cards or this new Game Boy gadget or a rock he found. Broke my hard little heart. Victor can blow up in about half a second, but never at Pete. Never. He's Pete's boy all the way, no matter how old he is. Forty, fifty, sixty—always the same."

McMichael had an image of Gabe and Tim Keller shuffling drunk along Kettner while Victor happily jaywalked or checked the newspaper racks for quarters. Living history. Past as present. Learn from or repeat.

"Pat, are you surprised that Pete left so much to the church and foundation? At the expense of his heirs?"

She shrugged and gazed out a porthole. "I wouldn't leave the Catholics three and a half million bucks. But I'm not complaining about my million plus, either. I'd give it up in a heartbeat to have Grandpa alive and complaining and annoying everyone again."

McMichael studied her profile, the elegant lines of neck and jaw framed in the fur of the anorak. Age had made her more beautiful. She turned her dark brown eyes on him.

"How old is your boy now, Tom?"

"Seven."

"Good kid?"

"He's a really good kid. Doesn't understand why Mom and Dad still love each other but don't live together anymore."

"Her decision?"

"Basically."

"But you go with the *we love each other but decided it was best to be apart* story? For his sake?"

McMichael nodded.

"No wonder he doesn't understand. Half of the explanation always sounds like a lie. How's the new hubby, the dentist?"

"Oral surgeon. Tassled loafers, a Testarosa."

"Revolting," she said.

"Yeah, well, she seems happy. Lost thirty pounds, got her face Botoxed and her chest hiked up."

"And you're what, paired up with some young cadet or playing the field?"

McMichael smiled and sat back. "Just working my ass off."

"No sand dunes?"

"Not right now." But damned if he didn't picture Sally Rainwater leaving foot pocks in white sand, looking back at him, a blanket over one shoulder and sandals in her hand.

"You could take the nurse out," said Patricia, somehow reading his mind. "She's pretty enough, but watch for bullet holes."

He cut her with a look but she just smiled.

"Victor still hang at the Waterfront?" asked Mc-Michael.

"His home away from home."

"What about the dealership—was Pete's business going okay?"

"He was grossing a million a year income off of it."

"Arguments with his employees?"

"Every waking second, but nothing serious. They're all making a buck."

"Was Pete a gambler, sports or the tables or the horses?"

"He'd hit Del Mar in the season, drop a few thousand. He was always too tight with a dollar to gamble much."

Tight with a dollar, thought McMichael. He imagined Grandfather Franklin back in the summer of '52—a jovial, failed publican thirty-three years old with a rowdy son, a tubercular daughter, a pregnant wife and very little money. After his first tuna hunt and three bad-luck months aboard the *Cabrillo Star*, he was trying to get his pay out of Pete. *His hat in his hand, Tommy. Your grandfather always so jolly and gentle, even with so much riding on his shoulders. And Pete tells him his quarter share on a bum trip like this one just*

*covers Dad's room and board and fuel for the ship so he
doesn't owe Franklin even a dollar. And Dad tells Pete he
worked as hard as the others but Pete says that's the way it
is with all first-timers on a bum trip, you only get the real
money when you're making a half share on a good trip
where you find the fish quick and don't burn up time and
fuel looking for them.*

"Yeah, I know that fits your father's version of
history," said Patricia. "But tight and dishonest are
two different things. Pete was honest. With his crews
he was generous. Hell, later they bought Fords from
him, so they couldn't have hated him."

McMichael said nothing for a long moment,
thinking instead about the way the past forms the
present, and how impossibly hard it was to change
things once they were set in motion. Fifty years of
hatred and vengeance born from a bad fishing trip
and—most likely—two stubborn and hungry men
who wouldn't back down until one of them was dead.
And their children damaged in different ways, and
their children still bickering over what had happened
and why and who was to blame.

"I'm hearing talk about the old airport and the
new Airport Authority, and Pete maybe switching
sides," he said. "I heard Pete wouldn't let the Tunaboat Foundation sell some of its holdings because
he thought the price would go higher. Sounded
like he was getting the other port commissioners
and foundation guys against him."

"That's all in the papers, McMike. If you want to
know who was on Pete's side and who wasn't, you've
got to talk to the Tuna Foundation and the Port
Commission."

"Give me names. People who lined up with Pete."

"Try Malcolm Case, on the Port Commission. The Tuna Foundation, though, I don't know. But they take over the Cuba Room at Raegan's cigar place on Friday nights. Purely, I think, because it pissed Pete off to see his precious foundation doing business with a McMichael. Maybe Raegan could bug the room for you."

"Good idea."

"Nice seeing you, Tom."

McMichael stood and looked around the galley, wondered what it would have looked like filled with hungry men two months into a journey that might take them halfway around the world. Too tight for me, he thought, too cramped and noisy.

"Franklin was sitting exactly where you were," said Patricia.

"And Pete where you were."

"That's right."

"You always liked the risky places, Pat."

"I always liked what moved my blood."

McMichael guessed the distance between himself and Patricia at about a yard. With your arm out and a gun in it, you were talking maybe six inches between barrel and body. Pete would have been close enough to catch the backspray on his face.

"In my father's version of it," said McMichael, "Pete pulled the gun and Franklin grabbed him."

"In Pete's version, Franklin had a knife. That was also the cops' version—a folding knife with a five-inch blade."

"Gabe said Pete put it there after."

"Pete said it missed his throat by about half an

inch. Took about thirty stitches to fix his arm. Did Gabriel say that cut was part of the setup, too?"

McMichael nodded then smiled. "Of course he did. No wonder it drove them all crazy that we were in love."

"They tried their best to split us up, Tommy."

"They couldn't do it, could they?"

"Never," she said.

"Only you could."

"Yeah. I broke your heart. And I've been apologizing ever since."

"It worked out right. I got Johnny."

"More than I could have given you."

He looked down to where Franklin would have fallen. Right at his feet, probably. Unless he reeled around fighting, like a lot of gunshot victims do. He thought about shooting someone that close up, how you really had to mean it, had to be ready for the blood and the fury. From habit he looked for bloodstains on the floor, but who knew how many times it had been sanded and refinished. He even looked at the paneling behind him for some sign of the exited bullet, but there was nothing.

"It didn't have to happen," he said.

"Most of life's that way."

She walked him abovedecks. "I remembered something that might help. About six months ago Pete told me that twenty grand was missing from his garage. He always kept a little cash out there, in cigar boxes, just-in-case money. Anyway, he said it was gone and I said, damn it, Gramps, the gardener or the nurse or the neighborhood kids or the rats probably made off with it. And he said, no, if it was the gardener he would just take it and go back to Mexico. The rats are too busy chewing into the dog food. And he says it couldn't be the nurse, because she's sweet and he's given her so many nice things, why would she make off with a little bit of cash? That's when he told me about the paintings and some stupid stuffed fish and God knows what else she's fleeced him for."

Twenty grand, thought McMichael. Lots of cash to hide in a garage.

Gifts to Rainwater, he thought. Pete addled? Pete in love?

Then, a brain thorn. But what was it? The cigar boxes? The gardener? The rats? For just a moment he let his mind wander and eddy but he couldn't come up with it. He wrote *BT* in his notebook and put a star beside it.

He wondered why a multimillionaire would stash twenty grand in his garage. Then he wondered why not? "What did you make of Pete's gift giving to his nurse?"

"It frosted my balls," said Patricia. "It still does. And I told him so. But it's not like I could change his mind, or fire her, or make her give the stuff back."

"Did you say anything to her?"

"I told her very calmly—calm, for me—that I thought she was a common prostitute. I threatened legal action, but we both knew Pete could do whatever he wanted. And Pete really liked her. He told me to leave her alone—he'd do what he wanted with her. That was that."

"Why didn't you tell me about the missing cash that night at Pete's?"

"I didn't connect it with a murder two hours old. And you kind of ran us out, because of Garland's big mouth. That was an awfully bad night for me, McMike."

"Yeah, I know it was."

"Did Rainwater bother to tell you about the gifts she took?"

McMichael nodded.

"Well," said Patricia, "now that her sugar daddy's dead, she'll have to hustle along and find a new one."

"I don't think it was like that."

"What was it like?"

"I don't know yet."

"Just ask her—I'm sure she'll tell you nothing but the truth."

McMichael walked down the ramp and onto the dock. It was dark already and the waterfront lights seemed bright and cheerful now that the storm had passed. The tourists were out, bundled and strolling past the *Star of India* and the *Berkeley* and the restaurants. The brain thorn was still in there but he couldn't get a fix on it. Something Patricia had said. It hovered then vanished and then twinkled again, like a small star you only see when you look away.

He walked toward the Gaslamp Quarter and it struck him again how small and useless had been the death of Franklin McMichael, father of almost three, a lousy businessman but a willing quarter-share fisherman at the no-longer-young age of thirty-three. McMichael wondered at the commonplace desperation that had led him to the *Cabrillo Star* in hopes of talking Pete Braga out of a paycheck that he had coming—bum trip or not. McMichael figured—had always figured—that Pete Braga owed Franklin something for his labor and his time. It angered him that Pete had given him only a bullet, then walked. Walked, and gotten respect for killing a man. Of course it was self-defense. You cheat a man out of food for his family, get ready for self-defense. Braga was wrong. And what someone had done to his first-born son just a year later—that was just as wrong. Maybe it was Gabriel, he thought, but maybe it wasn't. His father had sworn upon a Bible that he did not know who beat Victor senseless behind the Waterfront that night. Either way, his father had grown from a haunted boy into a ruined man. Either way, to McMichael it was all just proof of how human beings were dishonest, blind and murderous. Proof of why they needed laws. And cops. Otherwise you just got the same story over and over.

The music and drinkers at Dick's were already loud by the time McMichael walked up Fourth. Some kind of rock bluegrass, heavy on the electric fiddle. Up and down the Gaslamp streets, the restaurant hostesses were setting up their sidewalk easels and the busboys were arranging flatware on the tables outside while the dapper managers ignored them, crossed their arms and surveyed the evening.

He could see Raegan's neon sign from a block away: a cobalt blue cigar wafting tracers of pink smoke, and the pulsing orange word *Libertad*. He found Raegan arranging big-ring *robustos* in a wooden box as one of the cigar makers set them in his finishing bin. She was dressed for Friday night in a black double-breasted suit with a lacy white blouse under it. Her thick red hair was loose and, as always, her skin so pale and smooth it looked like she'd never spent an hour in the sun. She was thirty-three.

"Check *this*, Detective," she said, sliding one of the big cigars past his nose.

"Mmm. Smells illegal."

The cigar roller looked at him matter-of-factly.

"You can't buy a better cigar at anywhere near a hundred a box," said Raegan. "Thanks to this guy."

Enrique shrugged and went on to his next *robusto*. Behind him were three more rolling stations, already shut down for the day. The sound system was playing Cuban music and the lounge smelled of cured tobacco and cedar. There were already some smokers at the bar and the book nook and the magazine table, mostly downtown professionals winding down from the week. The televisions were turned to business and sports. McMichael looked at the big humidors and the glass doors of the private lounges—the Cuba Room, Teofilo's, Papa's Place.

"Can we talk?"

"Well, nice to see you, too, flesh and blood."

"I saw Dad last night. He looks good."

She locked her knowing green eyes on him, then led the way to the Cuba Room. "I can tell when you've got something on your mind, Tom, because you make worthless conversation."

"It's the Pete thing," he said, holding open the heavy glass door for her.

"I heard it was the nurse," she said. "Then it wasn't."

"I ought to just let you and Dad handle this case."

"I couldn't watch the autopsies."

He took a seat on one of the low modern sofas, purple and chrome. Raegan took a swivel recliner and propped her feet up on the ottoman, which gave her a view through the glass doors and into the lounge. McMichael could see the rolling stations and the big common area and the smoke rising into the slow blades of the fans.

"What do you need?" she asked.

"The Tunaboat Foundation still having its Friday-night board meetings here?"

"A few of them get drunk and BS, if you call that a meeting. They've got this room booked from seven to nine, every Friday. Something about Pete?" she asked.

McMichael nodded. "I'd like to listen in. But I wanted to clear it with you."

"Stay cool. Anybody finds out, that would be bad for business."

"Nobody'll know."

McMichael smiled at his pretty little sister. She was a gregarious and street-smart woman who had taken to the nightlife at a young age, liberated by Gabriel's spotty attendance at home and their mother's trust. She'd taken some business classes at State, did an internship at one of the stock-brokerage offices, sold new Porsches, ran the advertising department of a radio station. Just when cigars got popular, she'd hatched the *Libertad*. She'd lucked into a good lease on a prime Gaslamp location, and called on a Cuban ex-boyfriend to gather up some cigar makers in Florida. She'd traveled the Caribbean and Central America in search of her filler and binder tobaccos, and relied upon the time-honored Connecticut shade leaves for wrappers. McMichael had always figured that she got some of Grandfather Franklin's jovial publican's genes. But, hopefully, not his business sense.

She had dangerous taste in men—in McMichael's judgment—fake hard guys who always tried to run the show, then got mad when they saw that she was smarter and less dependent than they were. He'd offered to introduce her to a decent young Fraud detective a couple of years ago, but she'd laughed at the idea of dating a cop. She said she saw enough of those at the *Libertad*, and forbade McMichael to bring any prospective suitors into her store. The Metro/Vice guys had liked Raegan's lounge, back when McMichael was working the unit. Even the chief and some of his people occasionally booked Papa's Place for some smoke, scotch and gossip. McMichael had realized the eavesdropping potential of the attic when he installed the ceiling fans.

"Pete liked your number-seven pyramids," he said. "I saw two boxes of them in his humidor at home."

Raegan's brow furrowed and her plump little lips went tight. "He must have come in on my day off, because I wouldn't have sold to him. I'd have kicked him out."

"Maybe he didn't come in at all," said McMichael. "Maybe they were a present. I was thinking I could look at your customer list."

"What's that going to tell you?"

"Friends, enemies."

"What, buy him a box of pyramids one day, bash him the next?"

"It's connections I'm looking for. That's all. Pete had his fingers in lots of things."

She gave him a doubtful Irish squint, shaking her head. "Why do I have to have a brother who's a cop? Why do I have to love him and sometimes even think he's pretty cool for a nosy gun-slinging detective?"

"I don't sling. I carry. And I owe you."

"You've owed me for a long time."

"Just name it, Rae."

"Don't go sincere on me. Look, I've got all the customers on disc—I use it for my mailings. You can go alphabetical or by date of purchase or name. I've even got cigar preferences and price points. Start with the pyramids—they're not my most popular shape. But remember, if they paid cash, there's no record except of the sale and the product."

"Maybe I could just tinker upstairs in the office while you get ready for your big Friday night."

"So, is the nurse pretty or what?"

"She's pretty."

"Tommy, your face!"

"She's pretty. So what?"

"Oh, my God."

"I haven't done anything completely foolish yet."

"But close to?" Raegan asked eagerly.

"Actually, yes."

"Oh, brother. I'm so happy for you. I was wondering when you'd finally get a life."

McMichael waited for the warmth to leave his face. "Do you have one?"

Her smile outlasted her shrug. "I met a nice guy last week. Local *restaurateur*. Very French. Very handsome, very mysterious."

"Sounds bad."

"He looks to be a little on the bad side," said Raegan. "But in a good way."

"Dad always told me I didn't have the brains I was born with," said McMichael.

"And I don't, either?"

"You don't, either."

"Come on. We'll see. He's a nice guy."

By seven o'clock McMichael was sitting on an overturned bucket in the dark attic over the Cuba Room. He had his head up close to the AC vent and it was not comfortable. But he'd pulled the duct loose from its ceiling fixture so the acoustics were surprisingly good as the voices came up through the grille at him. The San Diego Tunaboat Foundation guys wandered into the Cuba Room one and two at a time.

DEEP BASS: *So I just told the mayor, look, you owe me at least four Super Bowl seats—good ones—or I'm going to get you voted out next time around. He laughs and says what if I get you a booth, and I say you'll be mayor of America's Finest City for as long as I live!*

NASAL WISEGUY: *So he gets another few months.*

DEEP BASS: *Hey, my scan's clean, my PSA's way down and I'm good for another ten.*

McMichael sat still in the cold, dark attic, chin in his hands, listening and looking down at his tape recorder. He figured his chances of getting anything useful were pretty poor, but the murder would be big news here. And the Tunaboat Foundation was now two million richer so it wouldn't hurt to know what they were saying about Pete. It was also Friday night so he didn't have anything better to do. He wondered if this was the life that Raegan had congratulated him on. It was easy to think about Sally Rainwater now, with the mindless chatter going on beneath him, and he was thankful again that last night hadn't blown up in his face. *We might do some good. Then again, this may be the dumbest thing either of us has ever managed.*

Below him, laughter erupted as one of the men likened his wife to a twelve-year-old with a credit card.

NASAL WISEGUY: *Well, just cut her off, Mike.*
DEEP BASS: *That's what she'll do to him.*
YOUNG MAN: *She did that as soon as he married her.*

McMichael wondered if the cops who met here sounded as jocular and retarded as the Tunaboat Foundation, figured they probably did. Something about a roomful of men seemed to drop the collective IQ by about half. Then again, he'd listened in on Steffy and her friends enough to know that women did the same thing, just in a different way. Four women in a room meant four conversations. He thought of the bullet hole in Sally Rainwater's elegant neck and wondered what it would feel like under his finger. He tried to ID the brain thorn that he'd gotten aboard the *Cabrillo Star* with Patricia. Something about the garage, the twenty large, the rats. . . .

He became aware of the silence in the Cuba Room, wondered if the men were passing something around to look at, or maybe just staring at the table, smoking, out of topics for conversation.

Dom, with the big voice, was the one who broke the silence.

DEEP BASS (CONFIDENTIALLY): *I feel terrible about what happened to Pete. It made me think about who I am and how much time I've got left. You never know—eighty-four years of kicking butt then something like that. We didn't agree on hardly anything, but Pete was Pete.*

YOUNG MAN: *They'll catch whoever did it. Give him the injection, like he deserves.*

NASAL WISEGUY: *Fuckin' bash his brains out is what he deserves. I'd do it. I'd volunteer for that one.*

YOUNG MAN: *Me, too. I keep thinking about the way I fought the old guy on just about everything. You know? It makes you realize how short your life is, like Dom said. Spend all this time fighting over shit you think matters but really doesn't. I don't know.*

DEEP BASS: *So he leaves us two million in property and we're going to vote for something he'd have fought us on.*

YOUNG MAN: *You gotta do what you think is right. It's time to sell the acres. Let the city have its new hotels for the ballpark, get some payback for financing the Padres. Two million? We could use two million. Pete would have agreed, sooner or later.*

DEEP BASS: *But part of me still sides with him, you know? That's the last of our ground, last of what we used to be. That was ours since, what was it— 'thirty-two or 'three? We can lobby the Congress and make trade deals all over the world, but it still isn't going to bring our fleet back home or make jobs around here. We still have thirty-one big beautiful*

*super-seiners off of American Samoa. Fifteen-
thousand-ton boats, most of 'em built right here.
What a waste. So why give up the last of it? I can
see Pete's thinking, I really can.*

YOUNG MAN: *Well, you know, Dom, we're a dying
breed.*

DEEP BASS: *But there's different kinds of dying,
Teddy. You looked at Pete the last few months it was
like he was eighteen again, falling in love. Damned
nurse of all things. I'm thinking maybe Pete was
younger than all of us, not older.*

YOUNG MAN: *Cryin' shame. Really. Raegan's brother
got the case.*

DEEP BASS: *Dance on old Pete's grave, probably.*

Victor Braga tapped his foot and looked at McMichael blankly as the detective walked up to him at
the Waterfront bar. He was alone at an outside table,
wearing a pea coat against the January chill. Tall like
his father had been, with thinning gray hair and a
remarkably unlined complexion. His eyes were light
brown and gentle. Earphone wires trailed down to a
disc player that sat on the table beside a glass of what
could have been anything from apple juice to scotch.

"I'm Detective Tom McMichael."

"I can't hear you."

McMichael pointed to his own ears. Victor lifted
one of the speaker pads and said, "It's too loud."

"Then turn the music down."

"Okay."

Victor slipped off the headset and put it on the
table, then concentrated on the player and punched
a button.

"I'm Detective McMichael. I'm investigating the murder of your father."

Victor's eyes widened and his lips hung apart. *"McMichael?"*

"I'm afraid so."

"Holy crap."

"Can I sit down?"

"You're the one that beat me up?"

"My father, allegedly. But that was never proven, Victor. He says he didn't."

"Oh," said Victor good-naturedly, as if considering this possibility with hopefulness. "You can sit down if you want."

"What are you listening to?" McMichael asked, settling into a chair. He saw the bartender looking at him through the crowd, talking on the phone.

"Bing Crosby."

"I like the Raspberries."

"Me too, with chocolate."

McMichael smiled and nodded. "I'd like to ask you about your father."

"You're a policeman?"

"In charge of the case, yes."

Victor's eyes lowered and his brows sagged into heavy crescents and his chin trembled. "I hope they get the electric chair."

"So do I. You going to be okay, Victor? You have plenty of people to do the things you need?"

Victor wiped a tear with his fist, looked at the knuckle. He sighed. "Well, at the hotel they do all the laundry and make sure I'm okay. They get me on the bus to work and have somebody pick me up off the bus later. After work I've got free time. But

I have to be in by midnight or they call Papa or Pat. They feed me and the food's really good. Pat and Gar come over and take me places like the movies or sometimes the zoo."

"Where do you work?"

"Papa owns a car place. A dealership for Fords. I wash the cars for him. You know, some of them. I make enough for the hotel and all the stuff I need. It's the Horton Grand. The best."

"How long have you been at the Grand, Victor?"

"I don't know. A long time."

McMichael wondered at the living arrangements. It was hard to imagine someone with the capacity of a ten-year-old—just three years older than Johnny— living on his own in a hotel.

The waitress brought Victor another scotch rocks and McMichael a shot of Anejo.

"Was your dad worried about anything?"

Victor stared at him. His gentle brown eyes gave away nothing now, and his chin was still. "I don't think so. He was happy."

"Got along with everyone?"

"No, he hated lots of people, too. Hated McMichaels. Hated Irish people. Hated people who didn't know anything about fishing. He hated the cops because they wouldn't let him drive his own car. I think he hated doctors and the government, but I'm not sure."

"Anyone in particular?"

Victor eyed him with undisguised suspicion. "Now, the one who beat me up was your papa, right?"

"Pete believed that."

"Then him. Papa hated him for sure. *Gabriel.* It happened right behind this building."

McMichael waited for Victor to fully comprehend that he was talking to the enemy, but no emotion registered in his light brown eyes.

"Maybe your papa killed him," Victor said optimistically.

"He was drinking that night at Spellacy's."

"Me too. But here."

"Anybody else your dad was mad at?"

"Me."

"How come?"

"It really made him mad when the cars weren't clean by nine."

"Nine in the morning, before the dealership opened?"

"Uh-huh. Especially the dark ones."

McMichael saw the tremble of his chin. Victor looked at him and McMichael waited for him to cut his embarrassed glance away, but Victor stared straight back as the tears ran down his face. He thought of Johnny and how a child could cry without shame.

"Nobody's perfect, Victor."

"Usually by nine-thirty I could do it."

Distract him, McMichael thought, ask him a question like he would ask Johnny after he'd fallen and scraped a knee. "Use a pressure hose or a regular one?"

"Just a regular one," said Victor. "With a good chamois. The chamois's the secret. But they only soak up water when they're wet, not when they're dry. You'd never think of that, but they do."

McMichael sipped his liquor while Victor sighed, wiped his eyes with his fist again, then took two gulps of scotch.

A Jaguar U-turned out front and double-parked. Garland Hansen bounded out, his white hair catching the streetlights and his coattails flapping as he rounded the coupe.

He cleared a gutter puddle in one long stride and bent over the low wall, grabbing the tabletop. "You loser," he said to McMichael. "What do you think you're doing?"

"This is Victor Braga," said McMichael. "We're talking."

"Come with me, Vic."

"Okay, Gar."

"Drink up."

"I am, I am."

"A city full of shitbags and you have to hassle Victor?" Hansen asked. His thumbs were tight on the rim of the table.

The bartender was looking their way again. "We had a drink, talked Fords," said McMichael.

"Maybe the chief would like to know how you spend your time."

"Tell him Victor had scotch and I had tequila. And don't even think about trying to toss this table."

Victor drank down his scotch, burped, then stood. He was taller than McMichael had thought, thicker, too. "Can we get some ice cream, Gar?"

"We'll talk about that in the car."

"Get him some ice cream," said McMichael.

"See you, Detective," said Victor.

"Take care of yourself, Victor. When I make an arrest, you'll be the first to know."

Hansen pushed away from the table with a strenuous Nordic smile and turned back toward his car.

Back home McMichael poured another tequila and called Sally Rainwater. She was up to her shoulders in a molecular biology text but glad to hear from him. She said the peptones were interesting. McMichael, sitting in the dark and looking out a window past the swaying palm fronds, pictured Pete's painting and the director's chair and the dinette where she studied. He told her a little about Kyle Zisch and Patricia and Victor, feeling just exactly how he'd felt whenever he talked to Steffy about work—vague and controlled and editing as he went. No wonder they lose interest, he thought. Who wouldn't?

"Patricia Hansen said she wasn't happy about Pete giving you those things. Said she made some threats," he said.

"We both knew she couldn't do anything. Pete liked me and she couldn't change that. She called me some ripe names, though."

"She's got a foul mouth sometimes."

"Pete said she was a fisherman trapped in a woman's body."

"Might be some truth to that."

"And he told me about this guy she started to like back when she was twelve. A *McMichael*. How this guy's father had beaten up Victor, ruined him. But Patricia didn't listen, didn't care. She liked this guy. So Pete and her father stashed her on one of Pete's big tuna boats and hired a tutor and kept her out at sea—off and on—for almost a year."

McMichael smiled at the memory. And at how Patricia had returned home, bigger, more beautiful, and pointedly uninterested in him. How he'd suffered and dreamed and died a thousand heroic deaths for her. How he'd known it was wrong but loved her anyway. How Gabriel had caught him trying to call her and beat him; caught him trying to mail her a letter and beat him again. Most of all, he smiled at the memory of Patricia circling back at him a few years later, hormonally charged and wildly vindictive toward her family. He'd thought it was love.

"When you came to Pete's house that night I didn't put it together," she said. "Until later. I wondered if you were that McMichael."

"I am."

"Nothing's simple as it seems, is it? Not even a damned peptone. So, did you and Patricia get back together when she came off the boat?"

"It took a while, but yeah."

"Then what happened?"

"She dumped me."

"Because of the family feud?"

"Just because I was me."

"You don't want a fisherman in drag anyway."

"I married a woman named Stephanie and I have a son, John Gabriel. He's seven."

"Then you're a lucky man."

"He's really something."

A pause then, while McMichael wondered what

Johnny would make of Sally Rainwater. It was a year since the separation, only six months since the divorce. McMichael had never tried such a thing. Maybe there was a book about how to do it.

"I know you're not a walk-in clinic," he said. "But invite me over. Right now."

"No. I'm free tomorrow night."

McMichael decided quickly between Sally Rainwater and his son.

"Can't do that," he said. "How about lunch? It would be Johnny and me."

"There's a good place down here called Mario's, right on Seacoast. Great pizza. Noon okay?"

12

Johnny sat sullenly until the pizza arrived. Then he ate with the manners of a pig and pushed a drink into Sally Rainwater's lap.

McMichael guided Johnny out of the booth by his ear, then to the counter to get some towels to wipe up.

"Apologize, son," he said on the way back. "You don't do that."

"Sorry," Johnny mumbled at Sally.

By then she was standing, her back to the booth, wiping herself down with a towel supplied by a busboy. The busboy now hovered nearby, uncertain how to help.

"Don't worry," she said. "Jeans won't hurt that soda."

Johnny walked past her and threw himself into the far side of the booth.

Angry, but feeling as if he'd somehow betrayed his son by his interest in this woman, McMichael got another towel from the counter girl.

When he came back Sally was still dabbing at her pants and his son was gone and the busboy was looking out the window, where McMichael saw an enormous black utility vehicle hunch into a shrieking skid and plow toward Johnny.

McMichael slammed through the door and into a white billow of tire smoke. Another scream of tires to his left and he broke through to see Johnny frozen in the far lane—arms out and eyes wide—as a pickup truck braked and tried to swerve away. The boy looked at his father questioningly. The back end of the truck came around in a cloud of smoke as McMichael hurtled in front of it, tackled Johnny and landed hard. He rolled once and came to rest on his back, clamping his son against him, looking up at a grille and a headlight.

He carried his son to the sidewalk, holding him tight. Johnny was crying now and McMichael felt the tears and the ferocious strength of Johnny's skinny little seven-year-old arms around his neck.

"Are you okay, Johnny? Are you okay?"

Then the pickup driver: *You all right? Should I call nine-one-one? I never saw him! Didn't see him 'til he jumped out!*

"Don't put me down, Dad."

McMichael was swaying with him the way he did when Johnny was a baby. His heart pounded hard and fast and his eyes burned. "Are you sure you're okay? Let me look at you."

That was crazy, kid. Absolutely crazy.

Johnny held on to him even harder. "I'm okay, Dad, just don't put me down."

* * *

Johnny allowed himself to be taken to Sally Rainwater's house. He had an abrasion on his cheek, but that was it. McMichael tended to him in the small bathroom, with Johnny sitting on the counter while his father dabbed the cheek with a warm washcloth. In the mirror McMichael could see his own bloodied and gravel-pitted elbows, the shredded knuckles of his left hand, the round red asphalt burn high on his forehead.

"You got it worse than me, Dad."

"Hardly even feel it. That was the wrong thing to do, Johnny. We're going to talk about it later."

"Let's go to your place."

McMichael made Johnny sit right there on the counter while Sally dressed his wounds. The boy seemed interested in her techniques and tools—the long tweezers to get out the gravel and debris, the foaming antiseptic, the round-ended tape scissors, the quick economy with which she wrapped each knuckle in gauze and tape.

"Are you a doctor, or what?" he asked.

"I will be, someday. One more year of college, then three of med school."

"Oh."

A while later she walked them to the car. McMichael held the door open for Johnny and shut it behind him. Then he turned to Sally Rainwater. "That was really enjoyable. Thanks."

"You don't have to be sarcastic."

He looked at her and could tell she meant it. He sighed and felt the adrenaline butterflies settling, felt tiredness and disappointment coming on. "Maybe some other time."

"That's up to you. Call me."

He offered his bandaged hand and she shook it carefully. In the hard winter sunlight she looked different. The squint lines at the edges of her eyes were new to him and the way she stood with her shoulders back and her head high revealed new facets of what McMichael believed were grace and character.

She struck him as utterly alien, cut from some template he had never seen before, could not recognize or easily understand. He had never seen a woman this way, certainly not Steffy, who had seemed familiar and comprehensible from the first moment they met.

He could see the Phoenix taking off just behind the collar of Sally Rainwater's blouse.

He and Johnny walked Balboa Park, saw the latest IMAX movie, stopped by one of the fountains. Johnny left his father to circle the water, toss in a few coins. McMichael watched him every second. Johnny had never run before, never done anything like what he'd done today. Perilous. So the boy was angry at him, that was understandable. Felt threatened by the new woman. That was understandable, too. But you run into traffic and you have to figure on getting hurt. He's seven, McMichael thought. He should know better. God, he's only seven. Please help me look after this perfect boy.

He called Steffy on his cell phone and told her what had happened. She said, "Oh my God," then went silent as McMichael explained how Johnny had run off into the street.

After a long silence she spoke. "You couldn't stop him?"

"I couldn't imagine it, Steff. I wasn't even looking at him when he took off."

"You should have seen it coming."

"I didn't."

"You should have introduced him to your new friend in some better way."

"If you can think of a better way than over pizza on a Saturday, tell me about it."

He hung up on her. Of all the people he'd ever known she was the best at making him furious.

McMichael and his son walked to the car side by side, but not close. Johnny let his eyes and attention wander everywhere but to his father. McMichael looked at the people around them and saw again what he'd never noticed until the divorce—all the other fathers and children without mothers. Hundreds of them, right here in this one park. Like a convention, he thought. Like us, trying to squeeze real lives out of weekend visitations, maybe alternate Wednesdays and half of Christmas day. What a lousy fucking deal for everybody.

You get what you get.

McMichael thought of a favorite biblical passage, one that summed up the bitter inequities of life on Earth as he knew it: *For to him who has will more be given, and he will have abundance; but from him who has not, even what he has will be taken away.*

Quite a showstopper, he thought. It wasn't one of those passages that Father Shea spent much time on. McMichael thought of Franklin. He thought of Steffy and the oral surgeon and their mountain of booty, topped by the ultimate jewel—his son.

Are you in love with her?"

"I don't know her very well."

"She looks younger than you."

"She is, by ten years."

"That's a lot."

"Burgers or spaghetti, John?"

"I don't like that tattoo on her neck. I think it's to cover something up."

"It covers up a bullet hole. A man shot her."

"Shot her! Why?"

"He was a bad man and a coward."

"Maybe she did something to him. Then she would deserve it."

"Nobody deserves that. Unless they're hurting someone really badly. Bring the buns over here, would you?"

"I wonder what she did to that guy who shot her."

"I honestly don't know."

"You've never shot anyone."

"No. Hey, these burgers are okay tonight."

"Do you want to shoot someone?"

"No. But I would, if I had to."

"I'd like to shoot Clay."

"Don't say that, son."

"But I think it."

"He's not hurting you, is he?"

"He looks right past me. And sometimes I'd like to shoot Mom, too."

"I said don't talk like that."

"Mom divorced you. I know it was her fault."

"No, Johnny, that's where you're wrong. We both agreed it was the best thing to do. For all of us."

McMichael's throat suddenly got thick and painful. Almost gagging on the lie. A lie you tell the person you love most on Earth, to explain why you can't even live in the same house with him anymore. The lie you tell to make it all okay. To grease the gears. So everybody can just get along.

"I hate this video."

"We'll get a different one next time."

"What are the chances of you and Mom ever getting back together?"

"Very small."

"What would have to happen?"

"I can't imagine it, son. I don't know what could bring your mother and me back together."

"Maybe you could just live with us. There's a lot of room and the beach is right outside. It's a better house than the lady's got."

"That probably wouldn't work out very well."

"Why not, because Clay and Mom need their privacy?"

"Exactly."

"Man, that's what they always tell me."

* * *

"Son, don't ever run off like that again. Ever. I want a promise."

"I promise I won't. Don't run away from me, either. You have to promise, too."

"I never will. I promise. I love you, Johnny. I can't explain how much. But it's a lot and it will last forever."

"I love you, too."

"Good night. Sweet dreams, son."

"You too, Dad. Sweet dreams."

On Sunday they went to a pet store to get grit for Johnny's parakeet. McMichael's bullshitting of Kyle Zisch contained elements of truth: Johnny loved birds of prey but Sarge the parakeet was a more sensible household pet.

Just inside the store they were ambushed by the puppy display. There was a litter of black Labs, two cairn terriers and two beagles. Signs encouraged you to touch.

McMichael watched his son lean over and give his hand to a chunky Labrador that took a finger and wagged his tail, growling. Johnny looked back at his father, really smiling for the first time in almost two days. It was like sunrise after a storm.

"Can we get him?"

Johnny had wanted a dog for a year now, and McMichael believed him to be ready to have one. Johnny was a patient and focused boy. He could feed and water a dog, exercise it, clean up after it. But Dr. Clay Blass was allergic to dogs, and that was that.

"When I buy my own place, John."

"Oh."

When he could buy again. Rentals were tough in San Diego, rentals that allowed dogs even tougher. McMichael ignored the fact that he was gone so much, that a puppy can't be left alone for long. And the food and the housebreaking and the expensive shots. He'd cross those bridges later. He watched his boy and the black Lab and another little bit of his heart crumbled away.

Then something else started to bother him.

"When's that going to be, Dad?"

"End of the year, I hope."

"That's forever."

"No. It's eleven months."

The brain thorn from the *Cabrillo Star*, he thought: Patricia's story about the missing twenty grand. *What was it?*

Missing cash. But Pete said it wasn't the gardener because he'd have split to Mexico with it.

And it wasn't Sally because he was giving her things.

And it wasn't the rats because they were busy with the dog food. *The dog food.*

Dog food but no dog. A dog at Pete's six months ago but no dog there the night he died.

He used his cell, pleased to know the number by heart. Sally picked up on the third ring. She told him that Pete had had a dog until a couple of weeks ago. It was a Jack Russell terrier, a feisty little thing, strong and playful and much loved by Pete.

"His name was Zeke."

"Well, what happened to him?"

"He died. Pete woke up New Year's morning and the dog was dead in its bed."

"What did Pete do with him?"

"Well, uh, he broke the law probably, is what he did."

Exactly what Pete would do, McMichael thought. A captain, running his ship, working with what he had. Burial at sea; burial at home. "Where?"

"In his yard. In the sand, just inside the wall. What's going on?"

"Someone plans a robbery or a murder, they have to deal with the dog. Can you show me where the grave is?"

"There's a headstone and everything. Do you really think someone would think that far ahead?"

"It's just something you look into. That's all. It's probably nothing."

Johnny held the black puppy. While its tongue worked Johnny's cheek the boy stared at his father, eyes filled with confusion and anger. McMichael clicked off and smiled. Johnny set the dog back in its pen and led the way to the bird grit.

They asked the clerk about owl parrots, but she had never heard of such a thing. She recommended cockatiels as a logical upgrade from the parakeet.

Johnny walked ahead of his father to the check-out stand, McMichael taking long strides to stay close.

13

The Holy Trinity, thought McMichael: a man's wallet, his calendar and his address book. You want to know the man, believe in these.

He sat with his back to the window in Pete Braga's office, second floor, Monday morning, nine o'clock.

Downstairs, Hector and Barbara were deconstructing the garage in search of cigar boxes that might or might not contain twenty thousand in cash. McMichael could hear Harley and Erik outside, yakking away while they dug for the dog.

Braga's office was a large room, with six oak file cabinets, an old desk and chair, a typewriter and a banker's lamp. No computer. There was a shortwave radio setup, a Grundig weather radio, fax and answering machines—no messages other than the two that Barbara Givens had heard on the night of the murder.

Framed photographs of Pete's tuna boats graced one wall: *Cabrillo Star, Princess Anna, Lisbon Queen.* The centerpiece was a poster-sized black-and-white picture that showed a wiry young man fighting a big tuna with a bamboo pole, muscling an animal twice his weight into the air while the black ocean around him boiled with leaping fish. His back was arched and his arms were bulging but there was a calm focus, almost a serenity, in the unmistakable Braga face.

Other photographs showed two men with two poles working a single line and a single fish. In others, three and even four fishermen pulled together to haul aboard their enormous and valuable treasures. That was before Franklin's time, McMichael thought, back when they broke their backs on the fish rather than on the nets.

Another wall was dedicated to Pete the car man and Pete the politician. There were photos of him standing next to outlandish Ford concept cars, gleaming Mustangs, Ford formula racers and funny cars. Shots of Pete and Anna with a trail of governors, and Tony Gwynn, and Dennis Connor and a Chargers quarterback McMichael didn't recognize. A picture of Pete and Anna with President Kennedy. And Nixon, Ford, Carter, Reagan, Bush, Clinton and Bush again.

Well, McMichael thought, looking at the Kennedy shot: there was at least one Irish-American that Pete didn't hate.

Pete's address book was an old leather-bound spiral volume with his name embossed in gold on the cover.

Using Henry Grothke Jr.'s list of heirs and the disinherited, McMichael found that they were all listed here, except for the estranged son, Carl. He looked to see if Raegan's *Libertad* was listed, but it wasn't. He wrote down Victor's address and room number at the Horton Grand Hotel. Grothke, Steiner & Grothke, of course. Sally Rainwater. He put a last name to deep-voice Dom from *Libertad*—da Rocha. He noted numbers for the mayor, the city councilmen and women, the county supervisors, the Democratic Party chairman, the chief of police and three of the assistant chiefs—Almanza, Bland and Dodge. The port commissioners. And the San Diego diocese, the bishop. Pete had come a long way, McMichael thought, from fisherman to friend of the bishop.

The calendar was a plastic-clad book, very similar to McMichael's own.

He turned to Wednesday, January 8, the day Pete had died: *Dom 8 breakf/plumber 10*

Dom, of the Tunaboat Foundation? McMichael made a note to call him.

And Tuesday, January 7: *call Camlin 9:30/MRI 12*

Monday, January 6: *Grothke noon*

Sunday, January 5: *Grothke noon*

McMichael wondered why you'd meet your lawyer at noon on a Sunday. Golf? Something social? Old Grothke or Junior?

He found a number for Myron Camlin in Pete's address book and dialed. A receptionist told him he'd reached the law office of Myron D. Camlin. McMichael told her who he was and she put him through. He asked the lawyer why Pete Braga had called.

"He was unhappy with Grothke, Steiner and Grothke," said Camlin. "He wanted to talk to me about managing his estate and probate matters. Keep that between us if you will."

"Unhappy why?"

"Apparently they'd lost some documents," said the lawyer. "Pete didn't say what. He was very angry. We set up an appointment for this Friday, so he could tell me exactly what was going on."

McMichael wondered if Pete's Sunday visit to Grothke was to give him one last chance to come up with what was missing. He found the date and time of the Camlin appointment on the calendar. "He didn't say anything more specific about what was lost?"

"No. He said 'documents pertaining to my estate,' or something very close to that. I figured some hard drive crashed and Grothke hadn't backed it up."

"Do you know when these documents went missing?"

"He didn't say."

"Did you and Pete talk about anything else?"

"Nothing. We weren't friends, just acquaintances. I met him at his dealership. Bought some cars from him over the years, kicked a little money into his war chest when he was running for mayor. That was a while back. Do you have a suspect?"

"We're looking at all the leads. Let me give you my number, in case you think of anything that might help."

After hanging up, McMichael searched Pete Braga's office for last year's calendar. He finally found it in a folder labeled "Taxes 2002."

Working forward from last January, he looked for signs of when the documents might have been lost by Grothke, Steiner & Grothke. Pete had met with "Grothke" on November 15, 16, 17. Again on December 20, 21 and 22. Two of the meetings were on Sundays.

McMichael found Pete's phone bills in the tax file, and checked both his home and cell phone calls to Grothke, Steiner & Grothke.

Pete had made a flurry of short calls the day before each meeting. Asking where the docs were? Yelling at somebody to find them? Making appointments to come down and harangue them face-to-face? McMichael wondered if Pete's calendar dates were real appointments, or if they were simply reminders to go downtown to the law offices and raise a little unannounced hell.

Maybe young Grothke would explain it. Something told McMichael that he wouldn't. But if Grothke wasn't forthcoming, he could always sick Patricia on him.

McMichael heard voices from the yard below. He looked out the window to see Harley and Erik, both wearing masks, staring down at a sandy wet clump of what looked like bedsheet. Erik poked at it with a shovel and said something McMichael couldn't make out. Harley slid a body bag next to the clump and unzipped it. Erik looked up and gave McMichael a victory sign.

Pete's wallet was thick and bent from years of use. Two hundred and forty-five dollars—all twenties plus the five. One credit card, an ATM card, a long-distance calling card, proof of car insurance that had expired six months ago, a California fishing license. There were four pictures in the little plastic windows: one of Anna Braga on her wedding day, one of her and Pete, arm in arm maybe ten years later, a mug of Victor and a slightly unfocused snapshot of Sally Rainwater holding a Jack Russell terrier in her arms.

Down in one of the credit card slots McMichael found a small replica of a tuna fish. His scraped knuckles burst into flame as he worked it out. It was flat and made of steel. The detail was good and true: the big eye, the sickle tail, the bumps between the dorsal and tail fins. The words "Lord Protect Us" were etched on the back, and below them "*Cabrillo Star*—August 1952." It had the same gentle bend as the wallet. Fifty years, thought McMichael, fingering the object, wondering how many voyages the *Cabrillo Star* made in 1952, and if this August trip had been Franklin McMichael's fateful journey.

He worked the talisman back into its place. In the slot just behind it McMichael found a FedEx airbill for an envelope sent by Pete Braga for overnight delivery to Henry Grothke Jr. on November 11 of last year, and a U.S. Postal Service Registered Mail receipt for a letter from Pete to Grothke Jr., received December 17. Checking the calendar again, McMichael saw that the letters were sent just prior to Pete's repeated calls and visits to the law firm.

So, he thought: the lost documents were *letters*.

Letters important enough to register with the post office, or to send overnight with a private carrier.

Important enough for follow-up calls, follow-up visits.

Important enough to make Pete Braga want to take his business to another firm. After doing business with Henry Grothke for what, fifty or sixty years?

McMichael put them back, then checked the calendar to see what Pete was doing on the night his dog suddenly died.

December 31: *guests arrive* 7

Throwing a party, thought McMichael. Maybe one of the guests tossed Zeke a bone and it choked him. Everybody drunk and loud, maybe nobody noticed.

He closed the calendar and booked the Holy Trinity as evidence.

Next he looked through Pete Braga's phone bills, bank statements and tax records. Pete Braga Ford had been a moneymaker for the last ten years, so far as McMichael could tell, and probably for many years before that. The accounting and depreciation schedules were dizzyingly complex, the way each new car was ordered and priced according to dealer incentives and buyer rebates and general demand, then began dropping in price as taxes and floor space took their tolls. McMichael wondered why the dealership documents weren't at the dealership, in the business manager's office. Because Pete ran a tight ship, he thought. Because Pete would rather do the work himself than trust someone else to do it.

And Pete had apparently managed to keep all his balls in the air, year after year, hauling down three or four hundred thousand dollars of after-tax income each and paying out close to two million to his employees. So far as McMichael could tell, Pete had never been audited by the IRS. He'd contributed $75,000 to the San Diego diocese each of the last five years.

McMichael found five fat folders containing statements from Pete's stockbroker, Herrold, Teller & Co. of San Diego. Just as Grothke had said, most of Pete's holdings were in blue chips—Ford, of course, Schlumberger, Boeing, Merck, RJR Reynolds. McMichael saw that Braga had not invested since 2000, with the exception of one company—Pacific Transfer—in which he purchased five thousand shares in 2000 at ten dollars per share. In 2001, five thousand more at almost eleven; and in 2002, five thousand at almost thirteen dollars a share. According to the last statement from Herrold, Teller & Co., the stock was valued at $10.45 a share at the end of November. McMichael had never heard of it. He wrote the company name in his notebook and circled it twice.

He found another folder containing Sally Rainwater's professional references. There were four letters, dating back seven years. *We have found Sally to be a terrific person, a wonderful nursing aid, and an important part of our lives.* He booked them.

Hector and Barbara had pulled dozens of boxes into the driveway in front of Pete's garage. McMichael looked down into them at the ancient Christmas ornaments, maternity clothes, toys and rain boots and fishing tackle. No cigar boxes.

McMichael used one of Pete's ladders to get to more boxes up on the rafters. They were arranged on thick plywood, high enough to be difficult to open and almost impossible to see down into. He wrestled them down to Hector one at a time, his knuckles and elbows screaming under the bandages.

He looked at the gauze on his fingers: no blood.

"Accident on a mountain bike, huh?" asked Hector.

Barbara cocked an ear in McMichael's direction. Hector and Barbara both knew he was lying about his injuries and they both knew he'd come clean with them when he wanted to.

"It was either put it down or hit the cactus," McMichael said lamely.

Two hours later they'd gone through every box, every shelf, every corner of Pete Braga's garage.

"Twenty grand," said Hector. "Just stuck in a box. Whoever took it probably knew where to look, Tom. One of those good-for-nothing great-grandchildren. They took the money and the cigar boxes, too. But you know—it was six months ago. It might have had something to do with Pete last week, or it might not have."

"My gut says it did," said McMichael.

"Mine says it didn't," said Hector.

"Mine says take me to lunch," said Barbara. "Come on, let's get this stuff put away."

Erik walked past with the body bag on his way to the CSI van, whistling "How Much Is that Doggie in the Window?"

*   *   *

McMichael passed on lunch. Instead, he wandered the Braga household, trying to figure why someone had killed Pete but not bothered to take the cash from his wallet or the watch off his nightstand or the jewelry from the box in Anna's dresser.

They killed him because he'd done something.
They killed him because he hadn't.
They killed him to keep him from doing something.
They killed him for the fun of it.

In the sun-splashed kitchen he played the messages on the answering machine again. Health insurance for seniors, offered by a recorded voice. Victor, announcing himself and waiting for the answer, then finally hanging up.

He walked the crime scene twice, trying to reconstruct the events based on Sally Rainwater's account and the physical evidence. He noted that the sliding glass door had not one but two locks on it, as well as a partial broom handle down in the track. This made it difficult to get out the door. Unless, of course, you knew about them in advance.

He sat in the chair next to the one that Pete had died in. He imagined being Sally Rainwater and having Pete next to him and what they would talk about. Cars? Peptones? The storm, maybe. *Sally, can you go get us some firewood?* Had Pete heard the footsteps coming up behind him a few minutes later? With the wind outside, maybe not. And the guy comes in and takes the murder weapon off the wall. *Knows it's there? Sure. You don't show up for a murder without having a weapon. The guy's been inside before. Knows the place, knows Pete?* McMichael wondered if it was someone Pete knew well. Well enough for an argument to escalate. That could explain why the club was used, instead of something easier and more efficient, and it could explain why Pete was sitting instead of fighting. McMichael pictured the old man, back turned to his assailant while he chewed him out or pretended to ignore what was being said.

He looked out the window at the dazzling day, then into the black maw of the big fireplace. He looked again at the cutesy plastic sconce that housed the surveillance camera. Too bad on that, he thought: he and Barbara had looked at hours of the surveillance video she had discovered in the library, and found nothing substantial. Pete with dealership employees, Pete with one of the city council members, Pete with the Padres' hitting coach, Pete with Malcolm Case—his ally on the Port Commission. Present with Case was a very large man whom Barbara had identified as Alex Dejano—a casino manager who'd done time for manslaughter. On the tape, Pete, Case and Dejano had talked fishing and football.

McMichael walked through the bedroom and bath again, then out to the deck where he'd made love to Patricia twenty years ago. He toed the platform where the mattress had rested in summer and fall. It impressed him that two decades could rush by so fast. You'd figure a decade would be big and lumbering and slow. A lot had happened, sure, but twenty *years?* He was glad now that she had broken his wild little heart back then. If not, he would never have known Stephanie and there wouldn't have been a Johnny. He'd never stopped wishing Patricia well, or thinking about her. Never really wanted back that piece of him that she'd taken and not returned. Like that silly poem. He shook his head and went back inside.

Standing in one of the first-floor bedrooms, he realized it was Victor's. The bedspread had pictures of sporting equipment on it—balls and bats and baseball gloves and tennis racquets. The wallpaper had sailing boats. In one corner sat an old wooden crate filled with deflated balls, vintage kites and ancient skateboards as well as a new pair of inline skates and a folding scooter and a lunchbox with Luke Skywalker on it. There were tattered posters of Superman and Mickey Mouse and Roadrunner, and newer ones of Batman and the Power Rangers and Digimon. Caught forever in a ten-year-old's mind, thought McMichael, decade after decade, for an entire life. Up in the closet he found a plastic bag of porno magazines that confirmed the age of Victor's body.

McMichael pulled out a scrap of yellow paper from the bottom of the sack. A phone number. The handwriting was childlike and the number was familiar.

He stepped into the hallway and dialed.

"Hi, this is Jimmy Thigpen with the San Diego Police Department. Please leave a message."

"McMichael calling."

He heard the line click alive.

"Hello, Sergeant. This is Sergeant Robb, Internal Affairs."

"I found this number with Victor Braga's collection of naughty magazines."

"Interesting," she said.

"I thought so."

"Maybe you can explain it, McMichael."

"I can talk to Thigpen."

"Good luck," said Robb. "He's not cooperating."

"You weren't Metro/Vice."

14

Thigpen was housed in the protective custody unit of the San Diego County Jail. McMichael walked in from the cool sunshine of Front Street, signed in at the Professional Visits Window and got a gun locker key. Escorted by a deputy to the fourth-floor sally port, he locked his gun away, glancing at the video monitors—one for each cell in case of attempted suicide or suspicious activity.

Thigpen's unit mates were child molesters and aggressive homosexuals, transvestites, a former DA prosecutor on trial for grand theft, a rapist who'd tried to kill himself. The sheriff's lieutenant eyed McMichael with a hard interest, which is what he figured most PD people got when they came to see their wayward little friend.

McMichael and his deputy escort walked past the cells until they came to Jimmy Thigpen. The deputy signaled to the command booth, then the door to Jimmy's cell slid open about a foot and a half.

"We'll be watching on the camera," said the deputy.

"Enjoy the show," said McMichael.

He shook hands with Jimmy. Thigpen was already pale from lack of sunlight and heavier from the confinement and the food. Blue pants and top shirt, white T-shirt, brown rubber shower sandals. To McMichael he still looked about eighteen—hardly any beard, pimples on his chin and cheeks, thick pink lips—though twenty-three was more like it.

"You look kind of lousy," said McMichael.

"Thirty-five nights. Three squares and a bed. Hell is boredom, and this is pure hell."

"Yeah, I'll bet. Hector says hello. Steffy, too."

"How is she?"

"House on the beach. An extra-pretty smile."

"I always liked her."

"Me too. Still do."

"And Johnny?"

"Plain old perfect."

Thigpen smiled. It was a clean and open smile and had always made McMichael think of a yearbook picture. Thigpen was unmarried and had never talked of a regular woman. He was always interested in Johnny. "What's up, Mick?" he asked.

"Pete Braga."

Thigpen nodded, looking up at the camera high in one corner of his cell. "It's got audio, too. How are your writing skills?"

"I got B's in English."

McMichael took out his notebook and pen. His

knuckles barked when he squeezed the pen and wrote:

Your number in Victor Braga's dirty mag bag. What gives?

Thigpen took pad and pen, wrote something that took a while, then handed it back to McMichael: *Popped him for soliciting three times in three months— same girl, same place. After you were gone. Cut him loose first two, felt sorry for him. Booked him for number three. He called me sometimes, thought I was his friend for going easy.*

McMichael: *When was the pop?*

Thigpen: *Mid-November.*

McMichael: *Pete know about all this?*

Thigpen: *Sure.*

McMichael: *Tangible thanks?*

Thigpen: *Offered five grand. I said no.*

McMichael: *V upset?*

Thigpen: *P upset. V cried a lot.*

McMichael: *Court together?*

Thigpen: *Yes. Judge Brooks OR'd him because of P and me.*

McMichael: *Did P punish him?*

Thigpen: *No idea. P's a hothead. V's dumb and strong as a horse.*

McMichael: *V get violent with the girl?*

Thigpen sighed and looked back up at the camera. He waved, then wrote: *No. It was Courtney Gonzalez, the Fifth St. junkie with the dimples, cute? Calls herself Angel.*

McMichael: *You moonlighting for P?*

Thigpen: *Got together with the V thing. Just trailering new cars down to TJ for leather, then back. P had some stolen from him once, wanted someone capable. Overpaid me as thanks for V.*

McMichael: *$300K worth?*

Thigpen: *Don't ask.*

"I'm goddamned asking, Jimmy," said McMichael.

Thigpen looked up at the camera and sighed, then fixed McMichael with a cool stare.

McMichael took back the notebook and wrote: *How often to TJ?*

Thigpen: *Wednesday nights.*

McMichael: *You and V?*

Thigpen frowned slightly, took the pen and wrote: *V once or twice.*

McMichael: *Who's doing it now?*

Thigpen shrugged.

McMichael: *Who was pissed at P, and vice versa?*

Thigpen smiled as he wrote: *P obnoxious. Loud, in your face. Like that old wop Partaglia in Property—remember him?*

McMichael nodded: *Any idea who killed P?*

Thigpen: *None at all. Employee maybe?*

McMichael read the sentence, glanced up at the camera then back to Thigpen. The ex–vice cop had that wide-eyed boy's expression that was such foolproof bait to the working girls. An expression that said, yes ma'am, no ma'am—I'm just here to help.

McMichael wrote again: *Thanks. Tell me what happened to you, Jimmy.*

Thigpen: *I just got careless.*

McMichael: *IAD's afraid you're going to take some guys down with you.*

Thigpen: *Afraid's their job.*

McMichael: *You could make a case—too young, not enough training and supervision.*

Thigpen shrugged.

McMichael: *Are you covering for other cops, Jimmy?*

Something dark registered in Thigpen's eyes. Then he smiled his eighteen-year-old's smile, took the notebook and stood. He ripped out the last several pages, tore the little sheets in half, then quarters, then dumped them into his toilet and flushed it.

The escort deputy appeared and the cell door opened. "The lieutenant wants to see you," he said to McMichael.

"Later, Jimmy."

"Later, Mick."

McMichael followed him to the protective custody command booth, where the lieutenant stood, arms crossed, shaking his head. "I'd like to know what went on in there."

"We just passed kites back and forth, then flushed them."

"Yeah, I saw that. Like a couple of gangbangers. Whose side are you on anyway?"

"I'm with the good guys."

"I'll need a written statement of everything that was communicated," said the lieutenant. "We've got a full legal right to that, according to the California Penal Code."

"What I have is evidence in a murder investigation, so you get nothing. That's in the code, too."

"I can make this uncomfortable for you at Fourteenth Street."

"It's already uncomfortable. But thanks for offering, Lieutenant. I'll take my gun."

The lieutenant hesitated, then nodded to one of the deputies.

McMichael checked his weapon, bolstered it and walked out. The deputies made him wait a long time at each door before buzzing him through. He could see them from the guard booths, smiling at him. But he finally made it out of the jail, steel doors slamming closed behind him.

Assistant Chief Jerry Bland sat heavily at his desk, staring at McMichael. He chewed then didn't. Behind him, the entire wall was taken up with bowling trophies and police awards.

"So is he covering for other guys or isn't he?" asked Bland.

"He's not saying."

Bland shook his head and looked at McMichael without goodwill. Then he stood and went to one of the windows. "I always liked Jimmy Thigpen. Most people did. But I really don't give one shit about a cop who propositions a whore *and* an undercover deputy, takes them to a hotel room full of dope. And happens to have three hundred unexplained grand in the trunk of his car. And won't talk to us. You really think he's just one bad cop, McMichael? Or did he have some help from the other guys on Metro/Vice?"

"I asked him straight out if he was covering, but he didn't answer."

"Great."

"Maybe it is great. Maybe Jimmy's just a messed-up cop who saw some easy action and took it. Solo."

Bland continued to stare at McMichael. "Wouldn't that be nice? Yeah. Maybe Jimmy's the long and short of it, like you said. Maybe I've been worrying about problems we don't have."

Henry Grothke Jr. tapped his fingers on the desktop as McMichael displayed and explained the registered mail and FedEx receipts, each secured in a clear plastic bag.

The lawyer sighed and shook his head. "I can't talk to you about these. It's a blatant breach of confidentiality."

"Pete's dead," said Hector. "So it's not going to bother him. Why's it bother you?"

McMichael tried to look patient. He liked having Hector along to play the bull.

"No," said the attorney. "I won't do it without a subpoena."

"What if you get permission from Patricia?" asked McMichael. "As executor."

Grothke hit him with a sharp little glance, then threw up his hands as if there were no limits to McMichael's depravity. "Go ahead."

McMichael got her on his cell. The connection was bad. She told him she had no idea what her grandfather might have sent to Grothke, Steiner & Grothke, but she didn't care if Henry discussed it. She'd expect a full report from McMichael. He gave Junior the cell and watched his face harden and redden.

Grothke handed him back the phone like it had Ebola virus on it. He looked at Hector, then McMichael, then walked past them and shut the door. When he sat back down his composure was back.

He buzzed the receptionist and told her to hold his calls.

"Pete was thinking about removing the diocese from his will," he said. "He sent us two letters to that effect—November and December of last year."

"How come you didn't tell us before?" asked Mc-Michael.

Grothke looked at him with affronted pride. "It was a matter between a man and his god. You don't consider God a suspect, do you?"

"That's a dumb thing to ask," said Hector.

"Remove the diocese why?" asked McMichael.

Grothke sighed and cleared his throat. "Mr. Braga was unhappy with their decision on naming the new parish out in Poway. Mr. Braga suggested St. Peter's, in consideration of his generous gifting to the diocese for the last four decades. Pete knew, of course, that the name would only be coincidental to his own. Unfortunately, there is already a large parish in a nearby community, Fallbrook, named St. Peter's. The diocese had to decline."

Grothke waited.

"But Pete wouldn't take no for an answer," said McMichael.

"Not Mr. Braga," said Grothke, with a hint of contempt. "He then argued that it be called St. An-na's in memory of his wife. But there *is* no St. Anna in the Catholic religion. So Pete insisted on St. Vic-tor's, but he's not a saint, either. Rumor had it that the diocese decided to go with its original choice, which was Saint *Gabriel's*."

"Ouch," said McMichael.

"No shit?" asked Hector with a big smile.

"None whatsoever."

"Well," said McMichael, "Pete wanted a vanity church and he got shot down. He wanted to cut the diocese out of his will. Why the stonewall and the closed office door?"

Grothke folded his hands on the desk and cleared his throat. "He wrote us two letters to that effect. And we *lost* them."

"How exactly do you lose a letter?" asked Hector. "They got here—the receipts prove that."

"Right," said Grothke quietly. "And then they actually vanished from my desk. The first time it happened I was out of town, though my secretary assured me that a FedEx letter from Mr. Braga had been placed on my desk. I never saw it. I thought, well, all right, there must be some explanation for it. I apologized to Mr. Braga and asked him to send a copy. He ranted and raved because he'd typewritten the letter. He had no computer, nor, apparently, any carbon paper. He procrastinated and probably fumed mightily before he got us a second set of general amendment requests one month later. I read that letter and filed it immediately to protect it from office clutter and prying eyes and careless janitorial people. Three days after I filed it, it was gone, too. Mr. Braga was even more furious. He threatened to take his business somewhere else."

"What happened to the letters?" asked McMichael.

Grothke shook his head and looked down. "I don't know. My secretary has been an employee for eighteen years and has never lost anything, to my knowledge. My father's secretary has been with us for four decades. She's terrific. Our receptionist is intelligent and thorough. There are three partners here, and three other associates. Six paralegals, two secretaries and occasionally an intern. These are top-notch people. They would have no reason to come into my office when I'm not here and take a piece of mail. The janitorial people come and go— they're part of a service contracted by the building management company. Why would a janitor want a valueless letter? Our offices have never been broken into. After-hours security is good. So, all I can conclude is that some visitor to the firm managed somehow to walk out of here with them."

"Which one?" asked Hector.

"If I had a suspect, I'd turn him over," said Grothke. He chuckled quietly.

McMichael and Hector went quiet, let the silence sink in.

"What?" asked Grothke.

Hector offered a meaningless grunt. McMichael stood and went to the window. "Did Pete come here, try to find those letters?"

"Well, he came here to vocalize his concern. He didn't physically look for the letters."

"There were two Sunday meetings with you on his calendar," said McMichael. "They took place just after the letters had been mailed and apparently lost. Did you meet with him here or somewhere else?"

"At the Sea Market Restaurant, there in Tuna Harbor. After mass at St. Agnes."

Hector shook his head. "So, Pete can't buy his name on a church, but he still attends?"

"Of course. He was devout."

"What did you tell him about cutting the diocese out of his will?" asked McMichael.

"Well, nothing really. It was up to Pete."

"Did you tell the bishop?" asked Hector, smiling.

"Gentlemen," said Grothke, "absolutely not."

"Who did you tell?" asked McMichael. "Think before you answer."

Grothke frowned and looked at his desktop. "I discussed it with no one. We practice family law here, Detectives. We're all sensitive to privacy and confidentiality issues. At some point, I would have talked with my father and whichever associate we asked to draft the amendment. But it was too early for that."

"So none of the secretaries or paralegals or other lawyers here could have known that Pete was going to cut out the church?"

"It's possible, but I doubt it," said Grothke.

"Unless they saw the letter," said McMichael.

"Correct."

"Sharona," said Hector. "Before she puts mail on your desk, does she open it?"

"Opens but does not read."

"Saves you lawyers from paper cuts."

McMichael looked down at Grothke's in-box—an old three-tier tray with the mail neatly sorted.

"I heard that your father went on a document-shredding expedition last month," he said.

Grothke blushed and glanced at him unhappily. "I'm surprised Patricia would tell you."

"But he could have shredded those letters?" asked Hector.

"No. They had been . . . misplaced, before the incident."

"Maybe there was another incident," said Hector.

"Yes," said Grothke. "Maybe he lets himself in on a nightly basis and selectively destroys documents. That is possible. Gentlemen? I've been as helpful to you as I can. I'm tired of you and I have a practice. Would you please leave?"

Old Grothke sat in his wheelchair near the window and turned to watch the detectives as they walked by. The red blanket across his lap matched his red vest, worn smartly with a brown tweed suit. McMichael saw the light of recognition in his bright blue eyes and the old man nodded, then looked away.

Sharona Saddler looked without warmth at Hector.

"So," he said. "You and your fiancé that got you the earrings—when's the date?"

"June."

"Going to do it over at St. Agnes?"

"We're Lutherans," she said. "I doubt it."

"I don't think the Lutheran tipped off the bishop," Hector said when they got outside. "More like old Grothke shredded those letters, or maybe thought they were toast and ate them for breakfast."

"I was thinking along those lines, too."

"Maybe talk to him somewhere else, away from Junior and earrings. See what he has to say."

"You don't think Junior's the fiancé, do you?" asked McMichael. "He doesn't wear a ring. I never heard of him being married. Sharona has her nice big diamond."

Hector frowned. "He's sixty and she looks thirty. Junior's about as cute as a stool sample."

The cold east wind nudged McMichael and Hector down Broadway under a blackening winter sky. Workers spilled from the buildings onto the sidewalks, hands at the collars of their coats, leaning homeward. McMichael felt the chill in his legs.

By the time they got to the car he had told Hector about the pizza lunch with Johnny and Sally Rainwater.

"Man," said Hector. "Johnny okay?"

"He's more rattled by Sally than by almost getting killed."

"He's at a sensitive age, Mick."

Hector, a childless bachelor, never seemed to tire of giving McMichael child-rearing tips. "And you ought to stay about a hundred miles away from that woman. Until this case is wrapped."

"She can help us."

"Don't tell me that's why you're making dates."

"Only part of it."

"About *this* big a part, Mick." Hector pinched his fingers together and smiled. "Yeah, okay, sure. I can see why. I can definitely see why. You figure out if she was in bed with him or not?"

"Haven't asked."

"I'd want to get clear on that. If that's what she was doing to keep those gifts coming in, I won't let you get mixed up with her. Even if I have to tie you down."

"I think she's straight up, Heck."

Hector blew a faint plume of breath into the air, dug his car keys from his jeans. "Want a ride?"

"I'll walk it."

"I'm gonna make some calls on Hank Jr. I think it's kind of weird he keeps losing things. So I'll see you tomorrow. And Mick? Nobody with bullet holes in her neck is straight up."

15

McMichael found Dom da Rocha in the American Tunaboat Foundation building on the waterfront. The short, stout da Rocha was locking up the file cabinet in a back office when McMichael knocked on the door frame.

"Can I help ya?" Da Rocha had thin black hair, jug ears, a wide nose and thick black-framed glasses. McMichael guessed mid-seventies. Same deep, clear voice he'd overheard so easily from the attic at *Libertad*.

"Detective Tom McMichael. I'm in charge of Pete's case."

"Ain't that ironic?"

"I need your help."

"I'm sick of this office."

"Let's walk."

"I don't walk so good anymore. I can still drink."

"Name your place."

McMichael followed him across the parking lot to the Sea Market. Da Rocha walked with a limp, his belly larger below the belt than above, but he moved forward with a determined momentum. McMichael wondered what it would be like to feel the cost of every step. The old fisherman was breathing hard by the time they sat down in the restaurant bar.

Da Rocha got a double vodka rocks, McMichael got a shot of tequila and a beer.

"What are your leads?" asked da Rocha.

McMichael stuck to generalities: it probably wasn't a robbery, it looked planned out, it might have been someone familiar with Pete or at least his house, most likely one guy.

"What I'm interested in," said McMichael, "is who profited from it. Pete was wealthy. A lot of people are going to get a lot of stuff."

"Yeah," said da Rocha. "The foundation, we get about two million dollars' worth of fancy houses. But I don't think any of us did it, to tell you the truth."

"No?"

Da Rocha smiled like a man with a razor in his boot. The lines were deep in his dark, weather-beaten face. "We're like a family, the foundation. We argue and fight all the time and nobody agrees on nothing. But when it comes time to get something done, we manage to get along. With Pete gone, we'll vote to sell the land you're sitting on right now. Yeah, this place and the foundation office where you found me, and this little harbor—we own the ground. Got it cheap back in 'thirty-three. Now it's worth about five, maybe seven million. Pete, he was against selling it."

"Wrong price?"

"He said he wanted to drive the price up, but that was bullshit. What Pete wanted was to build a new cannery and bring the tuna fleet back to San Diego. Which is a really dumb idea."

"How come?"

"Because the things that ran us out of business haven't gotten any better. You bring the fleet back here and open a cannery where we're sitting, you'd have to charge ten bucks a can of albacore. Labor costs here? Out of sight. Marine Mammal Protection Act and the damned porpoises? Nobody else plays by that stupid rule. And every country with a coast has got a two-hundred-mile limit now—we can't fish where we used to, soldiers board our ships and run us out at gunpoint. Foreign competition? Damned Japs undersell everybody because their government subsidizes their fleet, and that's after *we* subsidized it after the war. Damned Spaniards run circles around us. You tried to go back into the tuna business in San Diego, you'd get crucified."

McMichael pictured Pete Braga, seated in his trophy room, surrounded by fortune and the artifacts of a life gone by, trying to hatch a way to bring it all back home.

"Did he really believe he could do it?"

"How do you know what a man really believes? Pete, he hired this nurse. You know, mostly just to cook, keep him company. Well, he fell in love with her. Don't ask me about any details because I don't know any. But the last six months or so, Pete's hopping around like a goat, out of his head for this girl. He believes he loves her, so he loves her. He believes he can bring a dead business back to San Diego, so he tries."

McMichael sipped his tequila and looked across the harbor toward Coronado. "The foundation didn't like Pete's stand on its land here. The other port commissioners didn't like him rolling over for the new Airport Authority. Pete was surrounded by unhappy associates."

"That's right," said da Rocha. "The Port Commission, though, that's a whole different level. We're small-time here. We're a bunch of old fishermen with a good lobbyist. We own a little ground, we think about the old days too much. But the Port Commission, they got the whole waterfront. Most powerful seven people in the city. They're the big-time landlord—they got the harbor, the airport, fourteen hotels, fifty-something restaurants and businesses. They got thirty-three miles of water-front. *Miles*, Detective. Every time a dollar changes hands, they get five, six percent of it. Hotel rents a room, Port Commission gets paid. Restaurant sells a drink, Port Commission gets paid. Airport, rental cars, everything—Port Commission gets paid off the top. Millions of dollars, pouring in. They got a building up on Coast Highway, hardly any windows in it. The meetings ain't open to nobody. They make a deal, it's a secret, too. They want to do something, you find out about it after it's done. You make enemies on the Port Commission like Pete did, look out."

"And Pete wanted to give away control over Lindbergh," said McMichael.

Da Rocha smiled. "Pete never gave anything away in his life."

"What would he get out of it?"

"How would I know? He didn't talk to me about stuff like that. Us foundation guys, we were small-time to Pete. I think we just reminded him of who he used to be."

Da Rocha drank, frowned. "See, Pete kind of sold us out."

McMichael studied Dom da Rocha's sun-toughened face, saw the dreamy backwash of memory come into his eyes.

"Pete was a captain by the time the war broke out—only twenty-three years old, but he knew fish and he knew clippers. That was back when they were using bamboo poles and barbless hooks. The hard part was finding the fish. No sonar or spotter planes or anything like that. So you'd cruise the ocean for weeks or months sometimes, looking for birds or a bait-fish boil or the best was a log or a little piece of driftwood. Because on the driftwood there'd be a few little crabs, and just under the crabs would be some anchovies or sardines trying to eat them, and under the bait-fish you'd have a school of mackerel or smelt and under that you'd have the bonito and un-der them you'd have the skipjack and the tuna. It was like a big triangle reaching down into the water, with the driftwood being the point at the top and the big tuna way down at the bottom. You found a log, ev-erybody started gearing up to hit the racks. You could chum through with live bait, get the mackerel hopping and the bonito working, get them into a real frenzy until the tuna came up, the whole bottom of the triangle, and they'd go crazy, hitting hooks with no bait on 'em. Pretty soon you got thirty-pounders coming up, then hundred-pounders. Then the cows would come screaming up out of the depths and you'd have three, four, maybe five guys on one pole with a swivel and you'd have to get a rhythm or you'd break them off, you'd lose them if you weren't working as a team. And you'd pole this three- or four-hundred-pound tuna fish out of the water and into the boat behind you. Just about break your back, and if the fish hit you it would break your arms and your ribs, maybe your skull. Young Danny Hudson got his brains scrambled forever by a three-hundred-pound fish, didn't duck in time. Those cows would jump into the sky and come screamin' past your head and I don't know if you've ever touched a live tuna fish but they're one of the hardest things God ever made, just pure muscle with something like electricity running through them, the scientists spent years trying to figure out what made a tuna fish the strongest living thing and they still don't know. They're like rocks with lightning running through them, they can do fifty miles an hour underwater, think about that a second, you ever get a chance to catch one you'll know exactly what I mean. And all the way down the boat, you got teams of guys down in the rack, hauling up tons and tons of big fish. Four, eight, ten hours straight. You had a good trip, your boat sat lower in the water. Took you forever to get home. There was nothing like it."

Da Rocha was breathing hard, but he smiled at the waitress who brought him his drinks. "How are you, Marilyn?"

"I'm good, Mr. da Rocha. How about you?"

"Old, fat, blind and crippled. But I answer to the name of Lucky."

"If I look as good as you at seventy-nine, I'm going to be a happy lady."

"Flattery." He laughed. "I love it."

"Guys want some dinner?"

"Bring me the usual," said da Rocha. "Bring him the usual, too."

Da Rocha watched her walk away. "I'd like to do it all over again."

McMichael couldn't think of anything to say to that.

"What I would try to do," said da Rocha, "is slow down and love more things. I only loved maybe a few things—fishing, Madeline, my kids and grandkids. But you look at all the things around you, I mean, look at this salt shaker. . . ."

He touched the ordinary wooden shaker, then drank a slug of the fresh vodka. "The war hurt us. The navy needed our refrigerated boats to move food to the Pacific. Pretty much just took them—crews and all. When Italy declared war on us, the Italian boats all got grounded and the men weren't allowed to work, even on the waterfront. The Jap boats got confiscated, and the families got sent away to Manzanar. All the rest of us were moving supplies instead of fishing. Canneries didn't have nothing to can. Those guys with families didn't do so good. So after it was over, we were glad to be back to work. By 'forty-seven Pete was an owner-captain, three boats, good crews, making good money. But he saw things ahead of time, like smart people do. He saw that the purse seiners were going to catch more fish than the pole-and-line teams. He saw that the big boats were going to do away with the clippers and the owner-captains like him. Because one guy couldn't buy a two-hundred-and-eighty-foot super-seiner unless he had about twenty million bucks. It cost five-hundred grand just for the net. The net! And they had spotter planes and helicopters and electronics and gas freezers you wouldn't believe. One boat could carry two thousand *tons* of frozen tuna. Then, when the Santiago Declaration got signed in 'fifty-two—that kept us from fishing off of Chile and Central America—Pete figured that our whole industry was in trouble. That's when he started making his exit."

'Fifty-two, thought McMichael: Franklin's fateful year. Pete seeing the writing on the wall and a thirty-three-year-old quarter-sharer demanding his money. "Fords?"

"That came later, but by 'fifty-three or 'four, Pete was getting out of fishing. He sold his clippers for shares in one of the seiners, but he put most of his money into land in San Diego. I found this all out later. He didn't tell nobody. Pete always had this secret side. He never told us what he was doing or said to us—hey, you guys better figure out a better way to make money, because this industry is going to collapse in the next twenty years. By the time the fleet was all super-seiners, we were the crews and we worked for shares, but it wasn't our business anymore. The owners, they didn't sail with you. You were just a hired hand. The catch got smaller. We had all those problems with the porpoise and the government. Everybody was canning cheaper than we were. We had to go farther and farther for less and less. Last San Diego cannery closed in 'eighty-four. By then, Pete was selling cars, getting his picture taken with politicians and baseball stars, all that."

The waitress brought the dinner: tuna steaks still red in the middle, mashed potatoes, a goofy-looking salad.

Da Rocha examined the fish, thoughtfully cut off a piece. "This ain't frozen. It's probably off a Mexican boat, maybe American. The fresh boat guys, they fly them to market in a helicopter. You get a good one—big and perfect meat—you can get big money from the Japs. The record is forty grand, last I heard. Forty grand for *one fish*. You could trade it straight across for a fuckin' Lexus. For sushi, you know?"

"I didn't know."

"Yeah, well, thank Dom da Rocha for opening your eyes."

"Thanks, Dom."

"How about some port after this?"

McMichael signaled for Marilyn. "Do you think Pete wanting to bring back the fishing was his way of setting things straight with you guys? Even though it would never work?"

"Part of it. The other part was, he just missed the old days. Like everybody. Maybe when he fell in love with the nurse he started thinking he was young again. Love makes you dumb. You know how it is. Hell, maybe you don't."

After dinner the waitress brought the glasses of

port. McMichael drank the sweet wine, thought it hit the spot after rare tuna and tequila and beer. He felt relaxed but alert. "Who on the Port Commission was lined up against Pete?"

"Beats me. I don't even know who's on it. Down here on the waterfront, they call the Port Commission the Brotherhood. Imagine that. A goddamned Brotherhood of politicians and businessmen and scammers all working together like Santa's elves. I just know they were pissed at Pete. From the newspapers and TV."

"Pissed enough to have him killed?"

Da Rocha shrugged. "Why not? You get to be my age you realize that everything's true."

"Except the stuff that isn't."

Da Rocha shrugged. "Things have a way of changing around."

When he had finished his port, Da Rocha stared at McMichael through his thick glasses.

"I was on the *Cabrillo Star* back in 'fifty-two with Frank McMichael," said da Rocha. "We'd gone to nets on the *Star* by then—good, strong nylons ones, but hard to handle and expensive. This was before the Puretic Power Block to haul 'em in. It was a lousy trip. So we blamed it on the new guy—Franklin. Fishermen are like that, superstitious and always looking to blame somebody. He was nice enough. He was friendly to a point, quick with a story or a joke. And not bad for a quarter-sharer—he worked hard. But you get on a trip like that, three or four months out, hardly any fish, you're burning up fuel and patience every hour, it gets bad. Like there's a black cloud hanging over you, and you can't find fish.

Then you finally do and every set you make turns to shit and you finally get desperate and make too big a set and you can't get the fish in fast enough to keep them from gettin' crushed in the net so you end up with a fifty-percent loss, maybe higher. We had some crew fights. Pete, he stayed up in his quarters, we hardly saw him. He was probably thinking of ways to get out of the business. Like I should have been. I remember seeing Frank at the Waterfront the night we came in, already drunk and complaining about not getting paid any. Pete should have paid him something. I mean, he didn't have to. What he did was standard procedure, you don't pay the quarter share on a bad trip, you take the gas and food out of it and subtract that from the share and guess what? On a bad trip the quarter shares don't get a thing. But we all knew Frank was hurting. He had the pub that went under and the family and even a full quarter share isn't much for a guy with debts and a family. Pete could have helped him. He didn't have to make him beg. I don't know what happened later that night on the boat, but it was too damned bad. Pete, man, I didn't see Pete for weeks after that. Nobody did. He sent out the *Star* with another captain, late November. The word was, he just stayed in his room and stared out the window. Then Victor got beaten up behind the bar. Pete loved Victor more than anything. More than money, more than his wife. The boy was only thirteen, big and strong and smart. Doctors said ruined forever, wouldn't develop right. So Pete went kind of sideways after that. I mean actually sideways. His mouth wasn't the same and one ear—I swear to God—it got lower somehow."

McMichael looked into the deep red depths of his port.

"I'm not sayin' Gabriel did it," said da Rocha. "But whoever did, really got Pete where it hurt."

"No," said McMichael. "He says he didn't and I believe him."

"Yeah. Everything's true. Another glass of port?"

"Enough for me."

McMichael paid, then headed up Harbor toward the Santa Fe station and easy taxis. The wind came off the water with a smell that he had always loved. He ducked into one of the harbor cafes and called Sally Rainwater.

"I just wanted to say hello."

"Come over."

She let him inside, took his face in both hands and kissed him. He could smell perfume and see the top of her ear and the darker roots of her hair and the black shoulder of a satin robe, blurred, and beyond them the dinette and the Chinese vase and an open textbook. Her bedroom was cool. She turned off the little Tiffany lamp and in the near dark he watched her arms spread and her robe fall and her body curl then lengthen into the bed. He undressed without a wasted motion, wondering what she would think of him in the light, and how he'd do. Didn't feel his knuckles and elbows. He thought of Johnny and Stephanie, hoped they'd understand. The sheets smelled of laundry soap. Her arms were strong around his neck as she levered him up top, her feet startlingly cold against his. He kissed her mouth and her neck and the bullet hole. She shivered. He entered her and pushed himself up to see her face. All he could really make out was the glimmer in her dark eyes, and the plane of her jawline where it caught the faint light from the living room. She set up a rhythm and he followed, concentrating first on Sally Rainwater's mysterious wet universe, then on the Puretic Power Block, then the Super Bowl coming up, then he squeezed the end of his tongue between his teeth. Sally got a foil square into his palm. A while later, drenched in the unpleasant but affirming smell of latex, he quaked home a chaos of hope and thanks and pure animal pleasure. He barked once. Sally was shaking when he was done so he held still but firmly in place, propping up on his elbows so she could breathe and shake all she wanted. After that, wrapped close together, he listened as her breathing slowed. Nearly the same rate as his own. He thought that he could do this, be right here, a million times, and it would always be a journey into a world that wasn't there until they made it.

Half an hour later McMichael's phone rang. We're up next, he thought. He unclipped the cell from his pants, covered himself with them and sat down naked on the bed. How many times had he done pretty much exactly this?

It was the lieutenant, to say that Team Two had just taken a Clairemont strip-club shooting, so McMichael's people were next on the rotation.

"Someone shot the bouncer dead in the parking lot," the lieutenant said.

"Didn't the same thing happen two years ago?"

"Same club, different bouncer. Just a heads-up,

Tom. I'll make the calls—probably catch Hector in bed with his latest meaningful relationship."

"Yeah," said McMichael. "Thank you, sir."

He hung up and told Sally.

"Same as being a doctor," she said. "At least you never have a chance to get bored."

"True, though some things are hard to interrupt."

"We already got away with one."

"Press our luck?"

She rolled over and sat up and ran her tongue down his spine. Reached both arms around him and brushed away his pants.

McMichael listened to the waves breaking and the wind rattling through the louvered windows of Sally's little house. He ran a finger through the hair above her temple.

"Who did it?" she asked.

"I don't know yet."

"Do you know why?"

"I think it had to do with money, but not the kind of money you find in someone's wallet or safe."

"Did they poison Zeke?"

"I don't know that, either."

McMichael told her about Pete's disagreement with the Tuna Foundation board over their five acres of waterfront. And about the struggle between the Port Commission and the Airport Authority, and the tremendous amounts of money and influence that Pete Braga had been dealing with for four decades.

"According to Pete, he only had one friend left on that Port Commission," she said. "The young one, the real estate developer—Malcolm Case. He came to the house maybe four times. Good-looking, great clothes. He flirted with me when his wife was out of earshot, propositioned me once when a bunch of us went for a sail around the bay. The last time I saw him was New Year's Eve, at the party."

McMichael's brain skipped like a flat rock on water, from the trophy room to the sconce to the security video. "Have you met the casino manager?"

"That's Alex Dejano, a Rio Verde Indian. He beat a man to death in a bar and has no sense of humor. Now he's a Christian. I remember him at the party—late, after midnight—giving Zeke shrimp and mushrooms off his plate."

McMichael made mental notes to watch the surveillance video again, and to talk to both Case and Dejano. Maybe Case, an alleged friend, could name Pete's alleged enemies.

"I have to ask you, Sally."

"What your partner asked me that night?"

"I want to know."

"It wasn't your business then, but I guess it is now. No. We didn't sleep together."

"How was Pete with that?"

"Unhappy at first, then okay with it. The subject came up just once. He had a girlfriend anyway—a professional girlfriend."

"She'd come to his place?"

"Yes. They'd go upstairs for a few hours, then she'd leave and he'd sleep."

"Describe her."

"She used the name Angel. Probably twenty-one or -two, Latina. Attractive in a whore's way—heavy makeup, naughty smile, hard eyes. I could throw her farther than I would trust her. I think she was smacked up most of the time. Pretty sad, it comes to that for a twenty-one-year-old."

"Victor ever come by his father's house when Angel was there?"

"Months ago. He thought Angel actually was an angel."

Victor gets a crush on Dad's girl, thought McMichael. Motive to moon after her? Motive to murder Dad?

"When was the last time you saw Angel?"

Sally was quiet for a while. "The Friday before New Year's Day. Red leather miniskirt and a faux fur coat. Let me get my calendar."

She slipped from under the covers and wrapped the Chinese robe around herself. He watched her vanish down the short hallway, then come back a minute later with a brown leather planner in one hand. Her hair was a mess and her lipstick and makeup had rubbed off and McMichael thought she was the most beautiful woman he'd ever seen and he couldn't believe the good fortune that had come of bad fortune, the luck that had brought him here.

"December twenty-seven," she said.

He looked down at Sally Rainwater's calendar and her small, neat printing. Then he told her about Victor Braga and the three solicitations and Jimmy Thigpen's story about trying to help him out.

"Jimmy Thigpen had been there with her before,"

said Sally. "He said his name was Rex, but I recognized him from the papers when he got busted."

Pete and Jimmy socializing, thought McMichael, if that's what you'd call lining up a girl. "What if Angel wasn't available?"

"A girl who called herself Penny came a couple of times. Wore a copper-colored wig—Penny, get it?"

McMichael remembered Penny from Metro/Vice the same way he remembered Angel—young and hard and somehow cheated, and working themselves into early graves.

"How many times did you see Jimmy at Pete's?" he asked.

"Three or four. The last time was the night before he got busted—back in early December. Pete and the cop had a loud argument in the trophy room. Lots of yelling. I'm sorry—I couldn't make out anything they said. It was a closed-door session. I was trying to read a molecular biology text."

Moonlighting for Pete, thought McMichael. New cars, cheap leather, runs across the border and back.

Now, trying for balance, McMichael hopped to the nearest rock visible in this dark fast river. "Did you see other cops at Pete's? Or hear him talk about any?"

Sally threw an arm over him and rested her head on his chest. "Jerry somebody. On the phone. I got the impression that Pete was asking Jerry for help. Later, Pete said the guy was a good friend but a lousy cop."

"Pete ever mention business in Tijuana?"

"No."

McMichael listened to the wind again, felt the heaviness of Sally Rainwater's head.

"Your witness is going fuzzy," she said. "Maybe you could turn the interrogation lights back on in the morning."

"Sure."

She took a deep breath and let it out. He could feel the warmth of it on his skin.

"I've dreamed about it every night," she said quietly. "I walk into the trophy room with two bundles of firewood and see him in that chair. And always, in the dream, the blood on the floor is moving and boiling, like there are little fish in it. And Pete looks at me. And you know what he says?"

"Tell me."

"*This is your fault.*"

"And what do you say back?"

"I don't say anything. I just walk past the blood boiling with little fish and I kneel down in front of the fireplace and I try to build a fire but it won't start."

"You tried to save his life."

"I think the dream is telling me there was nothing I could do."

"It wasn't your fault."

"But what if it was? Just a minute sooner home. A green light on Rosecrans instead of a red—five miles per hour might have made the difference. If I'd have used the less-than-ten-items line at the market, but this checker told me once never to use those if they've got more than—"

"It wasn't your fault, Sally."

"*More than four customers* because that takes longer

than just one person with a whole cart full of things because that's only one trans—"

"No. You see, it wasn't your fault. You tried to save his life."

"He was my friend. He was my responsibility. They hired me to take care of him, not let him get murdered."

"You did what you could."

"Once, when I was hardly more than a girl, a man died and I could have prevented it."

McMichael felt her heart beating against his chest. "Tell me about it."

"Not now."

"Some other time, then."

"That would be up to me."

He felt the warm pool of tears on his skin, then the cool slap of air as she threw back the covers, walked into the bathroom and slammed the door.

16

It was Tuesday evening by the time McMichael and Paz were granted an audience with Malcolm Case. The port commissioner didn't live in San Diego at all, but in an expensive village northeast of the city.

Case's secretary, Allen, had been apologizing over the phone for the last six hours and sketchily tracing his boss's whereabouts for McMichael: *he travels by helicopter to save time, Detective, he's got a ten o'clock in Newport Beach, then lunch in Beverly Hills with state senator Rothrock, then up the mountain to Big Bear at four. Now, he's eager to meet with you and he proposes a six P.M. meeting at his winter home. He has one hour and will have to excuse himself for dinner at seven sharp. Does six work for you?*

It did work, in giving McMichael time with Barbara Givens and Hector, who'd done some digging into the dizzyingly prosperous life of Malcolm Case. And into the dramatically poignant life of his large sidekick, Alex Dejano.

But it didn't work, in that his time with Johnny—moved from Wednesday to Tuesday this week by Stephanie—would be short.

McMichael sat on Case's backyard patio and watched the twenty-something Allen build fires in two huge, beautifully tiled *chimineas*. Allen chattered away about how beautiful Case's property was, how it was within the covenant of Rancho Santa Fe, but still bordered wild and undevelopable land, how it was just an occasional winter home for Mr. Case because port commissioners had to reside in either Imperial Beach, Chula Vista, National City, Coronado or San Diego.

A brindle Staffordshire terrier sat next to McMichael, nosing her enormous head under his hand every time he stopped petting her. Her name was Gidget.

Beyond McMichael a stand of palms divided the sunshine and shadow upon a deep green lawn. The eastern hills lay still in clean orange light. Hector sat across from him, sullen all day, clipping his nails with a Swiss army knife.

The helicopter landed at three minutes after six. Case ducked and trotted through the gale of the blades, overcoat lifting, tie flapping back across his shoulder, black shoes aglimmer in the softening evening light. He plopped a stainless steel Halliburton case onto the blue tile patio table and gave his dog a big hug and a kiss on the back of her head before offering a hand to McMichael.

"Sorry it took so long," he said. His handshake was strong and his smile welcoming. Dark-haired, compact, thirty years old but looked twenty-five.

"I just closed an eighteen-million dollar ski resort deal in Big Bear. It'll be the jewel of the mountain. I think the thirty inches of new snow convinced them."

"That and your shoeshine," said Hector.

"*Finally*, a smartass," said Case. "I could use a little humor after dealing with those hayseeds in the mountains. Drinks, please, Allen. And tell Christine to come out and say hello."

Allen got their orders and went inside.

"Sit, gentlemen." Case tossed his overcoat over the stainless case, then pulled one of the steer-hide chairs closer to the *chiminea*. "What can you tell me about Pete?"

"What can you tell us?" asked Hector.

"Anything you want," said Case. "Aim me, men. I need a place to start."

"You and Pete and a new airport," said McMichael.

"Excellent. Five of the seven port commissioners wanted to keep Lindbergh Field operating and under Port Commission control because it's a moneymaker and it's fun. We're one of the only port commissions in the world that gets its own airport. Every time we need more money, we slap a rental car surcharge or a runway fee. It's easy. But Pete and I thought differently. We saw ahead. We figured San Diego needs a new airport because Lindbergh is small and dangerous. We figured San Diego also needs a sea cargo terminal. Do you gentlemen know that San Diego Harbor isn't even *rated* as a cargo terminal? So, we proposed to the commission to support a new airport in return for certain concessions from the new Airport Authority. Simple. Well, nobody liked the idea at first—trading a cash cow for a greasy cargo port. But you know, when nobody likes your ideas, that's when things get interesting."

"You want Pacific Transfer to build a cargo terminal on the Lindbergh site, after it closes," said McMichael.

"Yes, I do," said Case.

"And you own Pacific Transfer," said Hector.

"I own fifty-five percent of it. It's public. Pete bought in for fifteen thousand shares. The stock hasn't done squat since I formed the company and took it public three years ago. But when we get the commission to see our wisdom, it's going to go through the roof."

"That's a conflict of interest," said McMichael.

Case shrugged. "We'll float a bid. So will ten other dredging outfits. It's up to the commission to decide."

"Upon which you sit," said McMichael.

"Yep. Commissioners are encouraged to excuse themselves from votes concerning issues in which they have an interest."

"How often you do that?" asked Hector.

Case laughed. "Whenever even a *whiff* of conflict arises, Mr. Paz. Of course, our votes are not public so you don't have any idea what I really do. It's possible that I've *never* abstained due to conflict of interest. It's possible that I can abstain without worry, knowing that my fellow commissioners will do the right thing and vote my way. What are friends for? That's one of the beauties of the commission. That's why, when one of our esteemed brethren resigned from the commission last year, thirty applicants were standing in line the next morning for a job that doesn't pay any salary at all. Commissioners have a way of doing whatever they want. There wasn't even an ethical standards section in our charter, until late last year. And mind you, those are just, well, *guidelines*."

"I liked the way Pete Braga Ford got the leases and sales for Port Commission vehicles," said Hector.

"Me too," said Case. "But he never overcharged—not that I know of. In fact, Pete always made them a very good deal. That's what makes the commission go 'round, gentlemen. That's what makes Western capitalist democracies go 'round, in case you haven't noticed."

"Nice little gravy train," said McMichael.

"Isn't little," said Case. He rose, tossed some more logs into the *chimineas*, then knelt and petted Gidget. "Pete was a good man. Last week we talked about the terminal, tomorrow I'm going to his funeral. That's life, I guess. But what's it got to do with murder?"

"You answer the questions," said Hector.

"Or we'll go downtown and do this," said Case. "Come on, guys. I've never broken a law in my life. I've never had a speeding ticket. I donated one hundred thousand dollars to the Police Fund last year and I'll do it again this year. I'm trying to help you out because Pete was my friend and I think killers should get death."

The fires in the *chimineas* roared and threw fresh orange heat onto the patio. Gidget groaned and stretched in the warmth. Case smiled at the dog, his face a jack-o'-lantern of light and shadow.

Allen arrived with two beers and a dramatically large martini with a twist. McMichael could smell the gin from across the table.

"She'll be right out," said Allen.

"Is she making dinner?"

Allen nodded and Case rolled his eyes. "Give her a hand, *please*."

The secretary walked back into the house with an air of helplessness. A distant pack of coyotes suddenly burst into a yipping chorus and McMichael saw Case look in the direction of the sound.

"What were you and Pete doing to sway two more commissioners your way?" asked McMichael.

"Nothing," said Case. "We already had them. We just hadn't voted yet, made it official."

"How?" asked Hector. "Cut them in on Pacific Transfer?"

"That and more. In fact, you two might consider an investment. It's going to be big, and we'll lock up similar contracts with the Port of Ensenada by June. And better profit down there, because of the labor pool."

Case raised his glass by the stem and sipped. "Wow," he said. "I got the recipe from a bartender in the Clift up in San Francisco. First one of his I ever drank just about knocked me off my stool. There's almost five shots of gin in here."

"How did you bring the other votes your way?" asked McMichael.

"With Pete's railroad idea." Case smiled, sipped again. "Don't know about it? That's okay, nobody really does. It's the other condition of having a cargo terminal instead of an airport. It completes the value. Maybe you didn't know that we have a San Diego inland railroad already in place. Come on, admit you didn't."

"I didn't," said McMichael.

Hector stared into the darkness.

Case smiled proudly. "That's right, gentlemen— one hundred and forty-six beautiful miles of track from the city all the way to the rich cropland of the Imperial Valley. It was built by Adolph Spreckels in nineteen nineteen. And guess what? Nobody uses it. Why? Because it dips down into Mexico—another huge plus from my point of view—and the chicken-shit Feds were afraid the cartels would go wild with it. So the tracks sit, gorgeous and gleaming and empty. Actually, they need a little work. But Pete found a way to get it done."

Case sipped again, took a deep breath and let it out slowly. "The local politicians' best friend," he said. "*Redistricting.* It's where political parties trade pieces of property, like in a Monopoly game. The railroad used to be in one congressional district, overseen by a man of low vision and high gutlessness. The demographics were changing in a way that did not favor his party. We couldn't move the railroad, so we all got together and moved the district. The new representative is all-systems-go to get the railroad up and running. That's *thousands of tons* of cotton and other crops coming into port from the east, *thousands of tons* of cars and raw materials and electronics unloaded in our new cargo terminal, bound by rail for points east. Perfect, or what?"

McMichael heard a door slide shut, saw Case look toward the sprawling home. "Talk about perfect, here's Christine."

She was a petite blonde, very pretty, her hair all bouncy cornsilk curls. She wore black velvet trousers and a matching waistcoat buttoned halfway up. A black lacy blouse. She set down a tray of appetizers. Up closer, McMichael saw that her mouth and nose were small and graceful, her eyes blue and large.

He stood and shook her hand, as did Hector. Her eyes went to the Band-Aids on his fingers but she said nothing. Case made the introductions, then turned the appetizer plate his way. "What we got here, honey?"

"Mushrooms stuffed with crab, inside some wontons," she said, smiling. Her voice was sweet. "Brushed a little olive oil and garlic on them. Enjoy, gentlemen."

She popped one into her mouth with a wink at her husband, then walked back inside.

"Not the best cook in the world," said Case absently, hoisting a wonton and examining it. "You ever see her?"

"Chrissy Barns," said Hector. "One time we got a tip that her production company was shooting out in El Cajon without a business permit. Turned out to be some other smut outfit."

"Good for you, Sergeant Paz," said Case. "A lot of guys, they've seen everything she ever made and they act like they never heard of her. She was actually raised on a farm—so they went with Barns for a screen name. She had that almost wholesome look that married couples went for. The directors liked to do her up barefoot with cutoff jeans and blouses tied across her tummy. Not that they stayed on very long. Anyway, she shot in Woodland Hills and Van Nuys, the usual Valley stuff. Did three B science fictions and a horror, but you can't go from that to straight pictures. No way."

"Pretty woman," said McMichael. He also thought the mushroom wonton was good.

"Once I got her off the dope, she was perfect. Except for the cooking, which she insists on doing. So I suffer, but I do it valiantly."

"You're real impressive," said Hector.

Case smiled and shrugged. "Okay, so I'm a thankless, smart-mouth, near-billionaire punk married to a former adult-content actress. Doesn't mean I don't want to help you with Pete."

McMichael heard the coyotes yapping in the near distance, out beyond the helipad. Case cocked his head in that direction and listened intently. Gidget growled softly but didn't move.

"How did the proposed railroad sway the port commissioners to endorse the new airport?" asked McMichael.

"Not proposed," said Case. "*Actual.* They realized they'd have total control over a cargo port and a railway. Fewer Fed regulations than Lindbergh and a lot less visibility. *Visibility*—don't want that. Then, you know, some individually tailored incentives— food and beverage concessions to Ray's brother's company, permitting and fee schedules per Charlie's aggressive desires, Longshoreman for Ed because he's on their pension board—things like that. Those names are fictitious, by the way, but names aren't the point here."

"The usual side deals and insider trading," said McMichael.

"Call it what you want," said Case. "But all of it—as I explained earlier—is one hundred percent legal. And expected."

"You commission guys think you're pretty smart, don't you?" asked Hector.

Case thought about this. "Smart, no. But we're not afraid to think for ourselves. Pete did. I do. That's why we're appointed. To get things *done*. With all respect, gentlemen, you police aren't in that position. You can't be, or the law would mean nothing. You're the guardians. You enforce. You're given guns and taught to kill. That's why you went into your line of work, isn't it, the power you get? Don't get me wrong, I'm happy to have you on my side."

"I'm not on your side," said Hector, cheerfully.

"No," said Case. "Not personal sides. But in the big scheme of things, I need you and you need me."

"What do I need you for?" asked Hector.

"I'm your employer. I'm a citizen. That's all I mean."

"What about Pete's new cannery," asked McMichael, "where the Tunaboat Foundation is now?"

Case shook his head and smiled. "The foundation guys were bright enough to realize the tuna industry isn't coming back to San Diego. Pete was dreaming. Pete tended to get overly romantic at times. Although, if you think about it, a cannery, a fleet, a commercial cargo harbor *and* a railroad would produce hundreds of millions of dollars over the years. Literally tons of money for jobs, families, civic improvements—the whole socioeconomic structure."

The coyotes burst into a frenzy of snarls and howls and high-pitched whines. It sounded to McMichael like there were fifty of them, just a couple of hundred yards away. Gidget lifted her head, but that was all.

"I hate those things," said Case. "Animals with no natural enemies get out of hand. Parasites. Animals *need* enemies. Keeps them in check."

"Same with people," said Hector.

"Exactly my point," said Case. "Listen, I've got a fenced pasture down there because Chrissy wants a horse. Beyond the pasture there are thirty-two buildable lots of two acres each, and three hundred acres of water district land that will never be developed. It's wild, unimproved scrub. I bought every lot, and I'll sell them someday and make tangible money for doing nothing but paying a little tax. Anyway, the pasture's got wildflowers and the rabbits love flowers, so they dug under the fence. They're all over the pasture around dusk, scores of them. Then the coyotes figured it out. Let me tell you about the coyotes. There are hundreds, thousands of them out there past the fences. This whole city is overrun with them. You can't shoot them. They have no natural enemies. They're everywhere. The fruit falls off all these trees and the rabbits and ground squirrels get fat, and guess what? In come the coyotes and they clean up. Biggest, heaviest coyotes you'll ever see. They'll look at you like you're in their way. They're living off the fat of the land, right here in the covenant."

"Covenant or not," said Hector, "they have to make a living."

"And that they do, Sergeant Paz. They dug the rabbit holes bigger and started coming under the fence at night. You wouldn't believe the sound of coyotes killing rabbits. It sounds exactly like the massacre that it is—wild and crazy and without any restraint. Well, I got sick of looking at the mess the next morning because a coyote will kill six or eight rabbits, take one and leave. Just leave the corpses behind. I wonder if they kill them for the fun of it."

Hector shrugged.

"So one night," Case said, "after the coyotes crawled in and started their slaughter, I walked down and rolled some rocks into the opening. Then I let Gidget here through the gate to see what would happen. That's sixty-five pounds of Staffordshire terrier, if you know the breed. It's the main ingredient of the pit bull. Her and four coyotes—big ones."

At the mention of her name Gidget lifted her bowling-ball head, then clunked it back to the patio.

Case sipped again. "I turned on the pasture floods and watched. Gidget trotted out there and took one look at those animals, then looked back at me. You should understand, Gidget's the sweetest, most easygoing animal I've ever seen. She's like she is now, all the time. But she took off after them, with this whole new *posture*. It was as if a thousand years ago her ancestors had learned something and she still remembered the instructions. Like she'd been waiting her whole life to show me what she could do. I figured, well, four on one ought to be interesting. But the coyotes didn't think so. They scrambled back to the hole under the fence but there was no hole. They split four different ways as fast as they could. Like *they'd* remembered some ancient bit of wisdom. But Gidget's fast, too, and she caught the fattest one by the leg, dragged it down, got it by the throat and did that pit bull thing. Their whole body shakes back and forth and their jaws wrench the opposite way so there's this awesome torque at the end of each shake, and she killed that coyote in less than ten seconds. Had a big slab of something in her mouth when she came up. Dropped it and took off after the next one. Five minutes later she'd killed them all. When I called her back she sat there with blood all over her, panting and wagging her tail at me. That taught me something."

The screen door opened again and McMichael saw Christine and Allen coming toward them, each with a tray.

"What did it teach you?" asked McMichael.

Case frowned and sighed. "To watch out for people who do what they're trained to do. Nothing scarier in the world."

"Like us?" asked Hector.

Case shrugged. "You two guys come to my home and ask if any of my business associates might have beat an old man to death. Fine—I can keep from laughing and try to help. But the commission, we're not the watchdogs. We don't take orders. We don't murder people. We make things happen for the

good of San Diego first, and the good of ourselves
second."

"I think you're more like the coyotes," said Mc-
Michael.

Case nodded amicably. "There's a better chance
that one of your guys killed Pete than one of mine.
That's my opinion. Do what you want with it. Now,
will you excuse me and my wife to dinner? It won't
be any good, but dessert is like nothing you've ever
had."

Johnny pulled open the tremendous wooden door
of his La Jolla mansion at quarter to eight. He
was sweet from his bath and wearing his pajamas,
dwarfed by the entryway behind him. McMichael
stepped inside and picked him up and swung him
gently around, then set him down and checked his
cheek.

"Healing up well," he said.

"Mom put goop and a bandage on it."

"How are things?"

Johnny shrugged. "Okay. I got a piano. Come
see it."

McMichael smelled the cooking and his dinner-
less stomach gurgled. He looked down the long
entryway. It had an arched ceiling and rough white
plaster with inset tile. The chandelier was a brawny
wrought-iron design that looked very old but ran
on electricity. The rug runner was Persian, he
had learned. Stephanie had described the home as
"Moroccan modern." It looked to McMichael like
a hotel he couldn't afford a night in.

Stephanie walked toward him with her no-

nonsense tilt of head. Her dark brown hair was short now. She wore white jeans and a black knit tank, socks. She was back in her pre-Johnny shape, curvy and inviting.

"Hi, Stephanie," he said.

"Hey, Miker. When you're done with John, I'd like to talk to you. How about a drink?"

"I'm fine," he said.

McMichael beheld his son's new piano. It was placed, naturally, in the music room, amidst Dr. Clay Blass's guitar collection. The guitars stood up in their stands like the museum pieces they were, each signed—Johnny had shown him early on—by the pop musician who had once played it.

McMichael stepped between the Jimi Hendrix and the Tom Petty and ran his hand over the dark rich wood of the baby grand.

"It's for my birthday but I got it early," said Johnny. He sat at the instrument and lifted the fallboard. He tapped a few keys without apparent purpose or interest. "Got lessons, too."

"That's a nice gift. Your grandmother could play a little."

"Yeah," Johnny said, flipping down the door and sliding off the bench. "Want to see my room?"

"Absolutely."

Johnny's spacious room had its own bath and deck overlooking the Pacific. The rich red curtains were drawn. His bed was made up and turned down. It was amazing to McMichael how little remained of the possessions Johnny'd had just a year ago, when they broke up their household: a few wooden boxes from *Libertad*, a trunk of balls and gloves, a Batman poster, a little bookshelf CD player, a basketball trophy and a soccer team picture. They looked smaller here. McMichael thought of Victor Braga's quarters in the Horton Grand, of what it would be like to stay ten years old—or seven—forever.

"Mom almost killed me when I told her what happened."

"I knew she would."

McMichael had delivered his wounded and unhappy son to Dr. Blass on Sunday evening while Steffy was in the shower.

"I got this crystal radio kit but I can't figure it out. Will you help me?"

Half an hour later McMichael was finally finished winding the wire. It was exacting and slow but Johnny held the spool on a pencil and watched every turn, correcting his father when a loop was loose or crooked or kinked. They talked about school: handball, when to fight and when to walk, how hard cursive writing was going to be. McMichael saw the blood coming through the holes of his knuckle dressings.

They were about to attach the crystal when Stephanie came in and said it was time for bed.

"Quarter to *nine*," she said with a weak smile. "Go to bed now, John. I'll come back and tuck you in."

"Dad's going to."

"After that, I mean."

Later Stephanie guided McMichael to the family library and sat him in front of a panoramic view of the black Pacific. Clay Blass came in to say hello and offer him a drink, which McMichael declined.

Blass was fiftyish, trim and tan, with curly gray hair and a thoughtful face. He wore round, wire-rimmed glasses. His fingers were surgeon's fingers—long, slender and somehow intelligent. He labored through some small talk, then excused himself, pecked his wife on the cheek, and shut the door quietly behind him.

"That was a stupid thing to do, Tom—just throw a new woman at him like that."

"I didn't throw her, Steffy. We had lunch."

"And Johnny almost got killed."

"He's never done anything like that."

"Neither have you," said Stephanie. "This is all new to him. That's the point. Tom, I'm all for you dating, I am totally for that. But you've got your son to consider. You had to know his reaction was going to be strong."

"I had no idea that would happen."

"You should have talked to me about it first," she said. "I could have told you how I introduced Clay into—"

"It's none of your business how I introduce my son to my friends."

She looked at him hard. "How could you let him into the street?"

"He ran into the street when I wasn't looking at him. You cannot watch a person every second of the day, waiting for them to run into the street. You might think *you* could, but you can't. So get off your high horse. You look wrong on it."

"I'm on the high horse? You can't even admit you made a mistake that almost killed your son. I'd have never let that happen."

McMichael couldn't see the logic in her argument and he couldn't muster himself for a fight. In the twelve years he'd known Stephanie he'd never actually won one.

She shook her head in disbelief at McMichael's negligence, then put her hands on her hips, straightened her back and sighed. Her dismissals had always hurt and infuriated him, but he did his best to ignore it. At this moment he was extremely pleased not to be married to her.

"I know you didn't mean to hurt him, Tom."

"You've got that right."

"Just remember you have a son to consider."

"That would be hard to forget," said McMichael.

"Sarcastic as ever, I see."

"Good night."

He turned to go but she stepped in front of him. *"Bullet holes?"*

"Someone shot her. It was eight years ago."

"Okay. I know that's none of my business. But keep in mind, Tom, that you're not just looking for a good time. You're looking for a stepmother for John."

"I'm not looking for either."

"Maybe you should be. How old is she?"

"Twenty-eight."

"And no children?"

McMichael shook his head.

"Where did you meet her?"

"At work."

"Well, good luck. And next Wednesday is bad for you and Johnny," she said.

McMichael had become amazed at the new decisiveness with which his ex-wife organized his life.

"Clay has a function," she said. "He wants all of us there. Sorry. I know that makes two weeks in a row."

"Saturday, then," he said. "Don't break that one on me."

"No. I promise."

She walked him to the front door. "You look different," she said.

"Same old guy."

"Your son loves you more than anything in the world," said Stephanie. "You're the hero. You can do no wrong. Somehow he's got it in his head that I wanted you out, and he resents me for it."

"You did want me out."

"I wanted a husband who liked me as much as his job. *And we both agreed it was best.*"

"You know the truth, Steffy. So do I and so does Johnny. Good night."

McMichael cruised the Gaslamp Quarter looking for working girls, spotted one of his old Metro/Vice ladies crossing Fourth at J Street. Ellie, the surfer girl from Ocean Beach. She'd changed her hair from blond to red. He pulled over and waved. She made the plainwrap immediately, went the other way.

He got out and trotted after her. "Ellie! Tom McMichael here. We have to talk."

She turned a corner. When McMichael rounded it a moment later she had one black boot resting against the bricks, one on the sidewalk and the rest of herself wrapped in a pea coat. She was lighting a smoke.

"Haven't seen you in a while," she said.

"I'm on Homicide now."

"Big leagues. No more hassling the girls."

"Seen Angel around?"

"Not for a while. That creep retard was stalking her."

"So I hear."

She looked him over. "What do you want Angel for?"

"Conversation."

"She's gone. It's too bad."

"What's wrong with being gone?"

"No whore ever disappeared because something good happened to her."

McMichael nodded. "When was the last time you saw her?"

She puffed and watched the smoke hang in the cold air. "Couple weeks."

He waited while Ellie took another puff. "Must have been a Monday. Yeah, Monday I saw her at the Cooler. It's two-for-one night."

"What's the word on her, then—gone two weeks? People must be talking."

She dropped the cigarette and ground it out with her boot. "There's no word. She had the old retard after her and she disappeared. The girls see Victor coming, we just clear out."

"Has he been around much?"

"He's around too much. Walks more than we do."

"Ever date his old man?" asked McMichael.

"He was Angel's."

"Penny still working out of the Palms?"

Ellie shrugged.

It took him half an hour to find Penny. Her john came from the Palms lobby first, looked furtively in both directions before crossing the street and ducking into a Mexican restaurant. He looked like a man running through rain but it wasn't raining.

Five minutes later Penny came strolling out in a faux python miniskirt with matching boots, and a long leather coat with a fur collar. She was tall, with a toothy smile and pretty eyes. The wig shined vehemently in the streetlights.

"I'm clean, not holding and not working," she said.

"I believe all that."

"Come on, McMan."

"I want to talk."

"Not here."

They walked to a parking lot on Sixth. She led him to the back where nobody would see them.

"All right," she said. "I could sure use forty bucks for the collection plate on Sunday."

McMichael gave her twenty. "I heard you and Pete Braga were dating."

"Yeah," she said quietly. "Once or twice."

"When was the last time?"

"A few days before he died. I think it was a Sunday. His place out on the point."

"See anybody there?"

"Just him. Alone."

"Pete worried, say anything to get you thinking?"

She thought a moment, popped a breath mint. "He said they were going to name a church after him. Which was weird, considering what we were doing."

"You lift anything?"

She screwed her face into an attempted mask of innocence. "Shit, McMan, what do you think I am?"

"What did you lift, Penny?"

"Scout's honor, nothing," she said. "Pete tipped me a hundred on a hundred, got the taxi both ways, everything. Had some nurse hanging around, watched me coming and going. Made me nervous. Why would I steal from him?"

"What did you make of the nurse?"

Penny shook her head, pulled the coat tighter around her chin. "Looked like she'd seen it all."

"Explain that."

"It's just a look. We understood each other, you know what I'm saying? I wondered why she wasn't doing him for two hundred and no travel. It's hard work, though, a guy who's eighty-something."

"You know Victor?"

"Everybody knows Victor. I stay away from him. Always have."

"Why's that?"

"Look what happened to Angel."

"What did happen to Angel?"

"Gone for two weeks? No word to anyone? Nothing good, I can tell you that much."

"You see anything else interesting?"

"Possibly."

McMichael gave her another twenty.

"Actually, I saw Angel the last night she was on

the street. Day after New Year's. Thursday. Angel was there on Broadway, down from the Grant about a block. Car pulls up and Angel gets in."

"Tell me about that car."

"One of those big SUVs that all look the same. The color of wine. Red wine."

"What time?"

"About midnight."

"Get a look at the driver?"

"No. Wrong angle, too dark. But the SUV had Pete Braga Ford plates on it—brand-new. Went down Broadway toward Harbor Drive with Angel inside. That's gotta be worth something."

"See you in church," he said.

"Remember not to stare."

She snatched another bill and disappeared into the alley behind the lot.

17

Victor was hosing off a new Explorer when McMichael walked across the lot of Pete Braga Ford the next morning. McMichael waved and Victor looked at him while the water bounced off a door and onto his boots. He turned off the hose and stood there with the posture of a kid sizing up a questionable adult.

McMichael, dressed in his funeral and wedding suit, had brought a bag of doughnuts. "Hello, Victor!"

"McMichael."

"Beautiful day."

Victor looked up.

"Doughnut? I got chocolate and maple bars."

"Maybe both?"

Victor dropped the hose and McMichael gave him two doughnuts, then helped himself to a chocolate. "I got milk, too."

"That would be good."

"I was wondering if you could tell me about Jimmy Thigpen and you guys going to Mexico."

"Jimmy went to jail. So now it's just two of us."

"Who's the other guy?"

Victor frowned and shrugged. Tentatively, he picked some frosting off the maple bar, then took a big bite. Then a bite of the chocolate one.

McMichael continued to fish: "So, you guys load up one of those big transport trailers and truck down the new cars for leather?"

Victor nodded. "Once a week, or something like that."

"Where do you take them?"

"The upholstery place. I can't remember the name, but Mason knows where it is."

McMichael offered him some milk. Victor set his maple bar on a dry swatch of concrete. Then he locked the carton between his doughnut arm and his stomach and went to work on it with his free hand.

"So it's just you and Mason now."

"Yeah. These cartons are hard to get sometimes."

"I like the plastic bottles better," said McMichael. "But these were all they had at Seven-Eleven. Hey, you know Mason? Now, does he work here at the dealership with you, or does he have another job, like Jimmy did?"

The carton popped open and some milk spilled onto his hand. Victor licked it off, raising his eyebrows at the taste. "Mace works down in Imperial Beach for the police. He's got a gun like Jimmy's."

"Oh, right—Mace is an Imperial Beach cop."

"Yeah."

"That's interesting, Victor."

"I guess."

McMichael finished off the doughnut and opened his milk. "How did you meet Jimmy?"

Victor traded the milk for the maple bar, spent a lot of time picking at the frosting. "I don't know."

"He told me it was to do with Angel."

"Yeah."

"Why don't you tell me about her, too?"

"I gotta wash the cars."

"Finish your breakfast. I'll rinse."

McMichael took up the hose and sprayed the suds off the vehicle. He worked his way around, then back to Victor.

"You missed a spot," said Victor. He smiled and pointed and McMichael sprayed again.

"Angel was your friend," said McMichael.

"I had some dates with her."

"And Jimmy caught you."

"Yeah. The first time I didn't know it was illegal. The second time I forgot. The third time he took me to jail and Dad had to come get me out."

McMichael turned off the hose. "How'd that go?"

"Dad was real mad," said Victor. "Jimmy apologized but said he had to do his job."

"Angel was your dad's friend, right? You met her at his house?"

"Yeah. Then I saw her around. She was always downtown. In the Gaslamp sometimes."

"So it was kind of like you and your dad had the same girlfriend?"

"We did," said Victor. "Then she moved."

"Where?"

"I don't know."

"Then how do you know she moved?"

"I know she's been gone a long time. That's what I meant."

"When was the last time you saw her, Victor?"

He frowned and took another bite. "Either . . . a month or a week. A week is . . ."

"That's seven days."

"Yeah, it would be a week, then. Or maybe more than that. I talked to her down on Grape Street I think it was. I just said hello and asked how she was doing, that's all. Dad and Jimmy and everybody told me to leave her alone. I think she was scared of me. I didn't mean to scare her."

"Did you hurt her?"

Victor finished off the doughnut and wiped his fingers on his pants. "No. I wouldn't do that."

"Did you two ever kiss or touch or have sex?"

Victor colored and looked up at the Pete Braga Ford sign. "No. Every time I talked to her she'd call the cops. The more I tried to explain the more afraid she'd get."

"Explain what, Victor?"

He looked down, then at the Ford. "Just that I . . . you know."

"No, what?"

"I just . . . come on, you know what I mean."

"Tell me."

"I *liked* her. *Okay?*"

Blushing deeply, Victor pushed the rest of his maple bar into his mouth, then pulled up a stool and went to work on the roof of the car with a chamois.

"You ever drive, Victor?" asked McMichael. "Just borrow a vehicle, maybe, go for a spin, bring it back later?"

Victor didn't look back at him. His jaws worked and he finally swallowed. "I don't have a license."

"All these new cars, be nice to drive one."

"I don't want to talk anymore. I just want to do my job."

McMichael found the general manager in his office, dressed in black, laughing it up with one of the saleswomen. He was an amiable man named Charley Farrell, who shooed out his employee and shut the door when McMichael introduced himself. He expressed grief at the death of his boss and offered to help however he could.

The dealership was "going gangbusters," according to Farrell: unit sales up—they were now eighth biggest volume dealer in the nation. Profit up also. Pete Braga Ford has top-dealer status with Detroit, he told McMichael, which means you can get the units you want when you want them, and you get fewer dogs. They'd tested the certified, pre-owned market with some success.

"The new Birds are still moving fast, but our markup isn't twenty grand like it used to be. And vans," he said, "solid. The new Windstar is tearing up Japan, too."

Farrell said morale was good, but on-the-floor turnover was as high as ever. "You know salesmen," he said. "They come and go. But management is solid here. We've all been with Pete for at least fifteen, twenty years. I started here on the floor in nineteen seventy. I was thirty-three, wrecked marriage, had a boy with health problems. My firewood and hauling business was going under—got sued when a tree fell into a house and my insurance wouldn't cover. Pete picked me up, put me to work. Or like the bookkeeper, she's been here forty-five years. Solid."

McMichael asked what some of the standing disagreements were, but Farrell said there weren't any. Fishing, McMichael asked if everyone agreed on the direction of the dealership.

Farrell laughed. "Around here you either agreed with Pete or you walked. His granddaughter, Patricia, had some ideas about this place a few years back and *wham*—he shut her down. With Pete, you couldn't have a better friend or a worse enemy. Right now, we're still in shock. Pat's been down here talking to us, telling us things will go on like they were before. You can pass a franchise down to your children or grandchildren, long as Detroit approves it. I really don't know how it'll shake down. I think I'll hang it up next year. I'm sixty-six. I'm ready."

He told McMichael that the upholstery runs to Mexico were being handled by the same company that always handled them—Auto Leather International. He tapped his computer keyboard and printed a phone number and address for Mason Axelgaard, Vice President. The prefix and P.O. box were Imperial Beach. McMichael folded the sheet and put it in his pocket.

"We have seven cars going down tonight, and six coming back," he said.

"Mace will be here then, what?"

"Around seven, every Wednesday." Farrell pursed his lips, tapped his desktop with a pen. "Jimmy Thigpen used to work for him. I guess you know Jimmy."

"We all know Jimmy."

"Bad thing. You had to like him. I got the impression he needed the extra money. To be working with the cars, I mean."

"How come they take Victor down for that?"

"I think just to be nice. Victor likes it. Pete never minded. You know, he's supposed to wash the cars, but he only gets a few done and the windows are usually pretty streaked."

McMichael gave the GM one of his business cards. "Can I ask you a favor?"

"Sure," said Charley Farrell.

"Tell me if you guys sold a wine-colored SUV recently. And if so, to whom."

"Escape, Explorer, Expedition or Excursion?"

"Any and all."

"We move a lot of SUVs these days. Give me a day, will you?"

The flagship for Pete Braga's burial at sea was a one-hundred-and-fifty-foot motor yacht owned and named by Garland Hansen's failing beach products company, *Shred!* McMichael wondered if using the boat was a promotional stunt arranged by Garland—getting a little exposure during this time of anguish and grief.

McMichael and Hector stood near the Tuna Harbor dock and watched the mourners board. There were reporters and cameras set up near the bottom of the ramp. McMichael recognized the local TV reporter, and one of the *Union-Tribune* guys who covered the cop house.

"You weren't hoping for an invitation, were you?" asked Hector, fingering McMichael's suit coat.

"Not really."

"Just paying respects?"

"That's all."

"Or maybe Rainwater likes you in basic black."

"You're annoying, Hector. Is that how you get all those confessions?"

Paz smiled. "Just looking out for my partner. You still hot for her?"

"The other night we got together. I like her."

Hector said nothing for a while. "She tell you about getting shot?"

"No. We tried to keep it light."

"Hard to get heavy when you're ripping someone's clothes off."

"True. We talked about Pete a lot. No, she wasn't doing him."

"Oh, yeah?"

"Unless she flat-out lied."

"Naw, she wouldn't do that."

"Hector, what do you have on her?"

He shrugged. "I didn't trust her that night and I still don't. Maybe she didn't conk him, but I think she had something to do with it. She doesn't sit right with me, Tom."

McMichael tried to revisit his old suspicions of her, but he couldn't. When he thought of Sally

Rainwater he thought of beauty and brains and enough guts to try to save the old man's life. Thought of her tongue going down his back.

"Hey," said Hector, "there's Patricia. Umm-hmm."

Patricia came down the boarding ramp, arm in arm with Garland. She was wearing a trim black skirt and jacket, and a veiled hat. McMichael could tell by the cant of her head that she saw him, but that was all. Garland's hair was bright white in the winter sun. Victor shuffled along behind her. His suit pants were too big at the waist so he had to keep hoisting them up. He examined his zipper. Next to him was a stocky balding man with a mustache and cool sunglasses.

"One of Pete's guys on the TJ runs is an Imperial Beach cop," said McMichael. "I think that's him with Victor."

Hector was quiet while Victor and possibly Mason Axelgaard stepped aboard. "Doesn't sound right. Two cops and a sixty-three-year-old boy, running cars back and forth to TJ. How much money did Jimmy say he made?"

"He didn't. Just said Pete overpaid him. Round-about thanks for watching out for Victor."

"Why use cops for a trucker's job?"

"Jimmy said Pete wanted some security for his cars."

"Cops shouldn't moonlight," said Hector.

"Maybe they ought to pay us more."

"Pay what it's worth, at least. You risk your life for these citizens, and they try to lowball you. They're lowballing themselves, but they don't realize it.

Maybe we should ask Malcolm Case for a raise, since he employs us."

"I felt like kicking his ass."

"I felt like stealing his wife."

"Remember she can't cook," said McMichael.

"Except I don't think she wants to be stolen," said Hector. "A guy like that, though? He'll step in it someday. You'll see. I wonder if he watches his wife's movies."

McMichael watched as Assistant Chiefs Jerry Bland and Ed Almanza arrived together in dark suits and sunglasses. Barbara Givens walked between them.

Then Henry Grothke Jr., walking slightly ahead of his wheel-chaired father, who was pushed by a black man heavy with muscles.

"I did some work on Junior," said Hector. "Couldn't nail anything. Clean with the bar, no complaints. No record with us. But he's got no wife, either. Never has, and he's fifty-two years old. I asked around with some of my fag friends but they didn't know anything about him. It bugs me that he lost those letters."

"It bugs me, too," said McMichael. He watched Patricia and Garland disappear into the crowd. "Maybe Patricia knows something."

A while later, *Shred!* eased off her moorings and started out across the harbor. Half a dozen ancillary ships followed respectfully in her wake, five heavily filled with mourners, one bristling with cameras and mikes and windswept reporters.

18

At seven o'clock they were parked in the darkness across from Pete Braga Ford, watching Victor as he sat on the curb outside the showroom, eating a bag of chips. Victor's earphones were clamped to his head and a CD player rested in his lap.

The new cars sat in orderly rows, orange windshield letters proclaiming today-only discounts. The evening salespeople loitered at the various doorways, eyes on the lot. The floodlights made an island of brightness in the winter dark. McMichael noticed that the wind had changed to the west. The weather station said a new storm was headed in tomorrow.

"Amazing you can be a full-sized adult and have the mind of a ten-year-old," said Hector. "I have a nephew like that, but he writes kids' TV shows, makes tons of money."

"Maybe Victor's smarter than we think he is," said McMichael.

"Look at the way he studies each chip before he eats it."

Ten minutes later a new black SUV pulled into the service area and Victor's companion from the funeral got out. Thirty, McMichael figured—thick and strong but light on his feet. He nodded at the sales force, then walked over to Victor and clapped a hand on his shoulder. Victor offered him some chips. Mason Axelgaard helped himself, then walked into the wide driveway between the showroom and the service department.

A few minutes later a big red Mack came rumbling onto the drive, Axelgaard perched in the cab. The dealership floodlamps threw light at the truck and the shiny red paint threw it back. Smoke shot up from the gleaming chrome exhaust pipe. Victor collected his chips and player, climbed in.

As the tractor made the slow, lumbering turn onto the street, McMichael read the writing on the door: *Pete Braga Ford/Let the Captain Take Care of You.* The trailer carried three vans, two pickups and two Mustangs.

"Nice rig," said Hector. "Run you what, a hundred and twenty grand?"

"Pete was doing okay for himself."

McMichael drove, staying four, sometimes five or six cars back. Easy, tracking a red Mack loaded with new Fords. He fell back another few car lengths when they hit Interstate 5 south.

Through National City and Chula Vista, past Imperial Beach, then down into the border town of San Ysidro. By the time they hit Camino de la Plaza the retail signs were in English and Spanish—car insurance and currency exchange and parking. The houses and retail buildings were crowded together and even in the darkness McMichael could see their bright colors. The big Mack turned right on Virginia.

"He's going to the commercial gate," said Hector. "They'll stop everybody. U.S. might play ball with us, but the Mexican side is going to be tough."

McMichael looked out at the flashing yellow lights and the brightly lit U.S. Customs building, the zebra-striped barriers and orange pylons and the wall of concrete K-rails trailing off into Mexico. Two men in uniform stood in the door of the building. Four Customs and two San Ysidro Police cruisers waited along a chain-link fence topped with concertina wire. There were two southbound lanes open. McMichael watched Axelgaard and Victor take the right, so he took the left. Up ahead he saw a United States Customs agent reach up and take a clipboard from Axelgaard.

The big truck was still there when McMichael pulled forward. He shifted his body to the left, resting his right hand on the wheel, trying to look casual and keep his face and profile turned away from Victor, sitting up high, just a few yards away. He handed his badge holder to the inspector, who looked at him, then Hector. The Customs man handed back the holder and took Hector's. His nameplate said J. Alvarez.

"Business or pleasure?" he said.

"Business. We're working a burglary ring. Some Mexican nationals involved, maybe."

"Are you armed?"

"Service weapons, yes."

"You're supposed to have a warrant."

"We're not that far yet. This ought to go real smooth. We're just watching." McMichael patted the binoculars on the seat between him and Hector.

The inspector looked over at the truck again, then leaned in and gave Hector his badge and holder.

"Stay cool," he said. "And use the passenger vehicle lanes next time. I don't want to see you here again without some paper."

"Thanks. Cool it is."

The Mack rolled forward with a guttural snarl and a belch of white smoke and McMichael steered the Crown Victoria toward the Mexican Customs booth.

It was larger and busier than the U.S. version, three lanes leading into a low pavilion with clusters of floodlights bathing the street white. The Mexican flag lifted slightly, then fell in the cool air, Quetzalcoatl and the snake locked in a slow-motion struggle. *Federales* with machine guns stood in groups of four—they looked like Indians from the provinces, hard-eyed sixteen-year-olds, lean and watchful.

The Customs officials were working in teams—two for the interview and two to circle the vehicle. One of each team had a mirror on wheels with a long handle. Both carried carbines on straps over their shoulders.

"Guns," said Hector. "The only thing they don't want in this country is guns."

The timing got iffy. Axelgaard and Victor made the checkpoint faster than McMichael had hoped.

He had just pulled into the inspection zone when he heard the Mack engine accelerate. He figured a hundred-yard lead into TJ and they'd loose them.

"*Buenos noches,*" he said, offering his badge. "*Policia de Ciudad San Diego.*"

They were here on business, McMichael explained in his passable Spanish.

The inspector said nothing. Didn't take the badge holder. The inspector behind him glared past McMichael at Hector. Another pushed his mirror under the front end and frowned into the reflection.

The first inspector looked over at the red truck, then took McMichael's badge. "Open the trunk."

McMichael pulled the latch, saw the trunk rise in the rearview. He could hear the wheels of the mirror as they rolled along Hector's side of the Ford. Voices, then the sound of his detective's case being set on the ground.

The inspector asked him if he was carrying weapons. McMichael told him they each had a sidearm, department-issue Smith & Wesson nine millimeters, no backups, no riot shotguns, no sniper rifles.

Ahead, he saw the red Mack pause into another gear, a puff of smoke rise from the light into the dark. The trunk slammed shut.

The inspector handed back McMichael's badge holder. He asked if they were working narcotics and McMichael said no, they were working a murder, a *gringo* in San Diego, a U.S. citizen, nothing to do with Mexico at all.

"Everything in Mexico has to do with Mexico," said the inspector.

He stepped away from the car and waved it forward.

Tijuana: cramped and loud, busses and trucks and ancient cars belching from red light to red light, cars fitted with rooftop loudspeakers blaring out advertisements, shop windows filled with shoes, windows of dresses, windows of meat and televisions and jewelry and perfume, the smell of smog and burning trash, of septic water and *carnitas* and diesel; traffic lights timed for congestion and frustration, hell-bent drivers with legal right-of-way, pedestrians sprinting for the curbs and jumping oily pools of rainwater thrown into sudden roostertail fans by the fabled Tijuana taxis.

"This place scares me to death," said Hector.

"That's why I drove."

McMichael, who had negotiated Tijuana as a southbound surfer during his high school and college years, had long ago learned to contribute to the chaos instead of trying to improve on it. He chirped the Crown Vic tires through a watery intersection to make a green, hooking a left turn just ahead of an oncoming city bus.

Eight minutes later he had double-parked on a crowded street off of Avenida Revolución. He watched Axelgaard wrestle a series of tiny three-point turns to get the Mack and the cars through a chain-link gate manned by three young men. Two Doberman pinschers stood behind the gate in a pool of light, ears pointed skyward. The gate was the only opening in an eight-foot brick wall that ran the entire length of the block, then turned and disappeared into the darkness at the far side. It was topped with broken bottles, a thousand jagged edges in the dull city light. A billboard that stood behind the wall announced in English:

DIAZ LEATHER ARTISTS
FACTORY & WHOLESALE
UPHOLSTERY WELCOME

When the back end of the trailer moved through, the men pushed the gate closed and locked three large chains. The dogs followed them from the light into the darkness.

An hour later the men opened the gates again and McMichael could see the big red tractor moving toward him in the darkness. Again, Axelgaard made three-point turns to get the long trailer past the walls. Once the rig was on Revolución, McMichael kept well behind, following his way back to the commercial crossing.

This time he chose the same Customs lane as Axelgaard, but stayed three vehicles back. He wanted to see how it went for two *gringos* and a trailer load of new Fords. There were only six cars on the return trip, he noted: two minivans, three SUVs and a Mustang.

The Mack grumbled up to the check station. The inspector talked to Axelgaard, then waved them through.

"Wow," said Hector. "Smooth as silk. I'll bet the Americans won't be."

McMichael rolled down the window and held out his badge again. It was a different inspector, with the same placidly suspicious expression on his face. No mirrors this time through.

Hector chatted him up in Spanish while McMichael watched Axelgaard pull up to the U.S. Customs booth.

"*Gracias,*" said Hector, pointing McMichael forward.

He had just pulled into the American zone when a U.S. Customs dog handler worked his dogs up one side of the trailer and down the other. Then the lift lowered and both dogs and handler rode up. The dogs put their noses to the new cars. They showed no interest that McMichael could see.

The dogs and handler rode the lift back down and the red Mack was waved through.

"Unbelievable," said Hector. "It took thirty seconds."

It took the detectives—badges, guns and an SDPD law enforcement vehicle—close to twenty minutes.

This time, a curly-haired U.S. Customs officer—not the cooperative one from before—took one look at McMichael's badge and made them pull into the inspection area. They looked under the hood, in the trunk, removed the inside door panels and spent several minutes manipulating the headrests. They checked the glove box, the map compartments, the toolbox, McMichael's detective kit—a cheapish mock-leather briefcase he'd bought at Kmart—as well as the spare tire space and the wheelwells. One dog got the interior, one the exterior. Two officers used two mirrors, overlapping and repeating each other's work.

"Okay," said Goldilocks. "Next time, get warrants or stay home. It's all different since nine eleven. Everybody waits."

"Some people get through pretty quick," said Hector.

"I see some guys two, three times a day," said the officer. "You're new. I don't like new. What are you working?"

McMichael noted the name on his badge: M. Axelgaard. He shot Hector his shut-the-fuck-up look, then turned back to the Customs man.

"Armed robbery out in El Cajon," said McMichael. "Witness was an illegal, got scared and came back home. We got an address from his sister."

"Any luck?"

"All bad."

"That's TJ. Later, boys."

They outran the Mack to the dealership and slipped into a dark parking lot across the street. Eleven o'clock now, Pete Braga Ford closed for the day. McMichael carried the night-vision glasses as they crossed the street. They stayed clear of the outdoor service department lights, which were left on for the much-advertised Braga Ford 24-hour Service Drop-off. McMichael tried the chain-link gate but it was locked.

"You first," said Hector.

McMichael slid the binoculars under, then they climbed the gate one at a time, the other spread-eagled against the mesh, trying to hold it quiet.

They found an open pickup back in the repair lot, across from Axelgaard's shiny SUV, with a good line of sight to the gate and the service bays. McMichael got in and ran his hands along the column until he found the tilt steering lever.

"I'm on the roof," said Hector. "If something goes froggy, meet me at the car."

"Here, Heck." McMichael gave him the binoculars, then watched Hector's bullish, small-footed body trot across the driveway and vanish behind the service bay. In that moment McMichael thought of Hector as his best friend, and he loved him, especially for the ways they were different.

When the Mack's headlights crept across the asphalt in front of him, McMichael slid down and watched between the dash and the upper arc of the steering wheel, like a short person driving.

The service area was big enough for Axelgaard to turn around with only four three-points. Victor climbed out and offered somewhat vague hand signals. Then Axelgaard backed the rig against the far wall, gunned the engine once, killed it and got out.

Axelgaard walked into the light and clapped a hand on Victor's shoulder and handed him what looked like money. Victor nodded obediently, dug into his pocket for something, and walked to the waiting room door.

The lights came on inside and McMichael saw him standing in front of the vending machines.

Axelgaard looked at Victor, too, then hustled back to the trailer, climbed up and keyed open the trunk of the Mustang. He pulled out a large duffel, closed the trunk quietly with an elbow, then hopped down and carefully set the bag into the back of his SUV.

Victor was still deciding what to buy.

Axelgaard trotted back to the trailer, jumped up and removed another duffel from the back of one of the minivans. Stashed that in his vehicle, too. Got another from one of the SUVs. The duffels didn't seem particularly heavy and McMichael noted the way that Axelgaard held them at both ends, as if something inside could shift or break.

By the time Victor came out with candy bars, Axelgaard had pulled his vehicle around to pick him up.

It was an easy tail downtown to the Horton Grand, where Axelgaard dropped off Victor out front. Victor waved to the valet and walked inside.

After that McMichael couldn't keep the SUV in sight without making a spectacle of himself, so he fell back and let Axelgaard lead the way down Silver Strand. By the time they reached Imperial Beach the traffic was thin and McMichael fell back more.

"This is touchy," he said.

"I'm still on him," said Hector.

Axelgaard took Palm to Calla, and parked along the oceanfront. McMichael turned into a driveway and cut the lights and engine, hoping the home-owner wouldn't come out and make a scene. He thought of Sally Rainwater in her drafty little house on the sand, just a mile or so south. He looked down the block at the rough Pacific moving in moonlight.

Axelgaard's SUV went dark and the driver's door opened. The muscled cop swung out, shut the door quietly and went to the back of the vehicle. He checked his watch, and so did McMichael: 11:55. Then Axelgaard swung out the back doors and carried the duffels, one at a time, out to the sand. He set them down carefully.

"Like there's something fragile in them," whispered Hector.

"The dogs didn't even wag their tails."

"Maybe it isn't dope."

"What, then?"

At midnight a white helicopter lowered from the black sky. It circled lazily and touched down in a blizzard of sand. A Bell Executive, noted McMichael. He got out his notebook to write down the numbers, but there weren't any.

"Heavy shit," said Hector. "These are cartel guys."

The pilot trotted from under the blades, joining Axelgaard at the duffels. They didn't say a word. They each took a duffel and the cop followed the pilot back to the chopper. Then Axelgaard came back for the third package while the pilot disappeared back into the cockpit. By the time Axelgaard had cleared the prop, the engine gunned louder and the sand lifted again and the helo pulled up into the dark sky.

"Two minutes," said Hector.

"Slick," said McMichael.

They watched Axelgaard guide the SUV into a three-point turn and head back the way he had come.

"Bye for now," said Hector. "Put this together with Pete."

Silence then as McMichael headed up Palm, bound for Silver Strand. He felt a brain thorn forming, way back in his mind, too far back to get to right now.

"All right," he said finally. "Thigpen and Pete met when Thigpen kept running across Victor and Angel. Thigpen felt sorry for Victor, this brain-damaged man-boy chasing after his dad's hooker. Thigpen tried to go light on him. The old man offered Jimmy an easy job and overpaid him, as thanks for helping out his son."

"Okay."

"The Axelgaard boys already had their border thing in place, but they didn't have a safe way of moving that much product. Maybe they didn't have the guts to *try* moving that much product. But all of a sudden, Thigpen's got legit business on both sides of the border, and a tractor trailer loaded with new Fords. He goes to work for Pete, and for the Axelgaards, too. Pete finds out. But he doesn't go to the cops because he's still a captain at heart, he's used to taking care of his own problems. And because he's let his own son get mixed up in it. And who knows, maybe Pete thought *he'd* be suspected. It sure wouldn't look good for Pete Braga Ford."

"All right."

"So he calls Jimmy on it. A big argument at Pete's home, early December—I've got a witness to it. Thigpen and Axelgaard realize that Pete's not only trying to take away the biggest fortune they'll ever make, he could always change his mind and just turn them in. So they think proactive and take him out. With Pete gone, it's business as usual. Thigpen was in jail by then, but the Axelgaards weren't."

Hector said nothing as they sped along Silver Strand, the black ocean stretching all the way to the stars.

"Why did they start taking Victor along? Why risk letting him see what he sees?"

"He's a hostage, but he doesn't know it," said McMichael. "With Victor along, the TJ people saw security, because Pete Braga's son is in on it. And stateside, Pete's less likely to make trouble if his own helpless boy is part of it."

Hector went quiet again until they were almost to the Coronado Bridge. "Why didn't Pete come to us when he found out what Thigpen was doing?"

"Because he's a do-it-yourselfer."

"No," said Hector. "I don't think so. Pete was smart. Pete could find fish and sell cars and play politics. He was smart enough not to crash a drug operation on his own. They're messing with his son, and he's playing boat captain? Naw. He'd come to us."

"Maybe he did," said McMichael. "Maybe Narco is working these guys."

"They'd have told us after the murder," said Hector.

McMichael thought it through. The brain thorn brought him back to the way that Axelgaard had handled the duffels.

"Pete had phone numbers for three assistant chiefs," said McMichael. "Almanza, Dodge and Bland Jerry."

"I'll see what I can find out," said Hector. "If someone's protecting the department by snuffing the truth about Jimmy, that makes him a goddamned narco runner with a badge."

"And maybe a shot caller."

"No shit," said Hector. "One of the team could have staked the place out and waited until the nurse took off to get something. Could have been one of the brothers. Could have been one of *us*. But either way, his prints would have been in the law enforcement register. Unless they used some clean cheap labor from TJ."

"But you'd have to figure a hired guy would help himself to Pete's wallet or watch because they were right out in the open," said McMichael. "And a hired guy, how's he going to know about the big diamond earrings and that hummingbird with all the jewels?"

"True," said Hector. "And why would a pro hit Pete so many times?"

They were back on the mainland by the time Hector spoke again. "Maybe the argument between Jimmy and Pete was about something else. Maybe Pete never knew what Jimmy was up to. Maybe nobody we saw tonight had anything to do with Pete."

"I thought of that, too," said McMichael.

"A Fed and a cop, running drugs from Mexico. We gotta tell Rawlings."

"First I want to talk to Jimmy one more time."

"Do it quick or we look bad."

They made headquarters at one-thirteen in the morning. Hector yawned and got out, banged his knuckles on the Crown Vic's hood as he headed for his car.

19

"Pete's dog died from poisoning," said Barbara Givens. "He had a large amount of undigested strychnine in his stomach, and enough in his blood to kill him."

It was nine in the morning, a stiff wind coming off the water and a dark wall of clouds advancing from far north. McMichael stood in the Team Three pen, his leather jacket still zipped against the cold, and took Arnold Stiles's toxicology report from Givens.

"Steak," she said. "That was in his stomach, too. It looked like some of the strychnine had been put in capsules for a slow dissolve, some left loose to do the job quick. The guy used an oral tranq, too, so the animal wouldn't make too much noise while he died—meperidine, active ingredient of Demerol."

The tox report put the time of ingestion and death somewhere between December 30 and January 2.

"Rainwater saw the dog alive on New Year's Eve," said McMichael. "Pete had a party."

"Like to see that guest list," said Barbara.

"I can get it." McMichael called Patricia's number and told her what he needed. Then he called Jimmy Thigpen's lawyer. The lawyer said absolutely no visits from law enforcement, until McMichael told him—in slightly more than general terms—why he needed to see Jimmy somewhere they could talk without being heard.

"I'll arrange it," said the attorney.

McMichael was escorted into the protective custody exercise yard at eleven-fifteen.

Thigpen looked plump and pale, his hair a mess, his blue jail pants rolled into thick cuffs but still too long. He squinted in the true sunlight of the yard, looking up at the cold white sky. The yard was a hundred feet square with walls on four sides and a chain-link roof. There was a backboard and hoop. Near the west wall a timid rhombus of sunlight angled onto the concrete. The yard was empty now, with a deputy on the other side of a Plexiglas observation window looking at them while he drank his coffee.

They walked counterclockwise, McMichael on the inside.

"I got a look at your part-time job," said McMichael. "TJ."

Thigpen didn't look at him. "The upholstery? How did you manage that?"

"Victor and Axelgaard One to Diaz Leather Artists to Axelgaard Two. New cars, easy passage, three duffels. Axelgaard—brothers or cousins or what?"

Thigpen peered at McMichael. "Funny, walking

in a circle like this," said Thigpen. "Makes me feel like a lab rat."

McMichael didn't answer.

"Look, Mick," said Thigpen. "I don't know what you're talking about. I have to say that. You know how it works. My lawyer's trying to work a deal with the DA. There's no profit in me talking to you."

"That's not quite true."

"Then what's your offer?"

"I'm after Pete's killer. Not you."

"That's not much of a help to me," said Thigpen.

"Heck and I are the only ones who know what Auto Leather International is all about. I can keep you out of my version for right now. I can tell Narco that we stumbled onto the Axelgaards through Victor. It would be almost the truth, because I didn't see you do squat."

Thigpen said nothing.

"Internal Affairs knows you were moonlighting for Pete Braga Ford," said McMichael. "That's all they know, so far as I can tell—they think it was legit. I can leave it to them to connect you up to it or not, until the Axelgaard boys go down. When that happens, they'll blow you wide open. I'm just offering you a little head start."

Thigpen nodded forlornly, looking down at his rubber shower sandals. "You'd do that for me?"

"No. I'd do it for Pete."

They walked into a turn. McMichael saw the deputy behind the Plexiglas, elbows on the table and coffee cup poised.

"They're brothers," said Thigpen.

"Coke, smack or weed?"

"Whatever."

"Pete know?"

Thigpen shrugged. "He had us tailed—worried about Victor. He screamed at me one night at his house. But we had Victor up to his eyes in it, said we'd throw him to the cartel. So Pete backed off."

"You sure he didn't go to the cops, Feds maybe?"

Thigpen shook his head.

"Did the Axelgaard brothers take him out?"

"No. They talked about it but nobody was up to doing something like that. They're not killers, Mc-Michael. Anyway, we had Pete good with Victor and with the girl."

"Angel."

"Got her to run a hidden video from her purse during one of their business transactions. Cute little gadget—I rigged it up myself with a lens hole in the fabric. As an old Metro/Vice guy, you'd have loved it. Anyway, we had the old buzzard cold, and he knew it. I mean, he didn't have many people left to save face for, but he did have a business to run. And all his commissions and committees and shit. He figured the best thing he could do was keep his mouth shut, make sure his son didn't get tossed to the cartel sharks."

"You know where Angel went?"

Thigpen stared down at the lines. "No idea. You know how the working girls are."

"Ever meet Malcolm Case and Alex Dejano?"

"I met them and that was it. Out of my league. I think Dejano's got casino money to burn."

"Do you know what it was that Pete kept sending over to his attorneys and they kept losing?"

Thigpen grinned. "No, sorry."

"Did you talk to him after you got popped?"

"Not once."

"Did you ever meet the Hansens?"

Thigpen shrugged. "Met them. She's a beauty and not very nice. Garland's one of those losers who acts like he's somebody and gets away with it. I get the feeling she leads him around by the nose."

"What about the other grandchildren?"

"Never met any of them. It's not like we socialized, Mick. I tried to help Victor, Pete tried to pay me back. That was about the size of it."

"You don't know anything about who killed him?"

Thigpen shook his head. They did a lap in silence. The guard behind the glass smirked, crossed his arms and sat back.

"I was stupid, Mick. Everything in the world going for me except potloads of money. So what do I do? Sell it all out for the money—job, my brother and sister, friends. I'm not even that greedy a guy. First thing I realized when I held my first tax-free, off-the-books hundred grand was, what do I do with this? Buy a car. Buy some women. Buy some furniture, a couple trips to places I didn't even like. Just about as stupid as a guy could get."

"You fell for the green, Jimmy."

"You ever tempted?"

"Naw. I'm simpleminded."

They walked along under the Plexiglas window, then back into the small slant of sunshine near the west wall.

"The money fucks you up," said Thigpen. "One day I'm helping Victor because I feel sorry for him being in love with a whore. A few weeks later I'm telling his old man we'll kill his son if he rats on us."

Thigpen's brow was furrowed heavily, his mouth tight. "But then, I could never figure who the hell I really was. So I acted like whoever I was with, right? I invented myself minute by minute. When I'd try to look at myself in the mirror, really have a serious talk with myself about things getting out of hand, there *was* no me. Just this twenty-three-year-old guy with pimples and all this easy money, and a puzzled look on his stupid fucking face."

Once again into the cold shade, wispy clouds sliding by overhead and a dust devil trapped in the northeast corner of the yard.

"I learned something from my father," said Mc-Michael. "He showed me what happens if you cross the line and can't get back over. It wrecked him. He broke my mother's heart. He sucked the money and the love and the life right out of her. He's drunk himself stupid every night since I've known him— that's pushing forty years. It scared the shit out of me. I *had* to become a cop. I needed to know exactly where that line was, all the time. I see the line, man, I jump back from it. I don't even dream about crossing over. So, I'm a tight-ass mick cop with sixteen years in, and when I hit my twenty-five and a full pension, I'm gone. I stick up for my friends. I try to do what's right. But I'm not going to end up like him. I'm not crossing. That's what he taught me about being a man."

"That's a good lesson."

"He's a good father. Even passed out in his own puke I never doubted he loved me."

Thigpen looked at him thoughtfully. That expression again, thought McMichael—the eighteen-year-old at graduation, the Eagle Scout, the team captain. Then it vanished. "That's a lot of love if you can feel it through puke," he said.

"His heart is huge."

"My old man was good, too. I miss him."

They walked around again, McMichael watching as the swatch of sunshine faded away, listening to the scuffing of Jimmy Thigpen's cuffs on the concrete.

Patricia had given him a Park Towers address and a one o'clock arrival time. McMichael heard the first drops of the new storm smack the awning overhead as he ducked into the lobby. He called her on one of the house phones and she rang him into the elevator bank. Twenty-two stories up he stepped off into a vestibule with a black marble floor and a gigantic arrangement of fresh tropical flowers.

She let him into a big apartment with picture windows facing west, black clouds marching toward them at eye level, the Pacific stretching away in a plate of metallic gray. Light hardwood floors, white walls with big floral paintings on them, hanging metal lamps.

"Hey, McMike," she said. "Give me that jacket."

"All yours," he said, shrugging out of it.

She kissed him on the cheek before taking the jacket and tossing it onto a red leather sofa. Her perfume was rich and light and drilled a hole to the exact center of McMichael's brain. She was wearing a short brown sleeveless dress and heels with ankle straps. Hair up, a little black zigzag falling down over her forehead.

"What do you think?"

"Of what?"

"My place."

"What's wrong with home?"

She shook her head. "I left Garland. Long story. How about a nice drink?"

"Whatever you're having."

McMichael saw the wind blast the trees in the park below them, then heard the swoosh of raindrops on the window.

"Come sit down," she said. "Don't be a furnishing."

He walked into the kitchen and sat across the island counter while she made her former favorite drink: gimlets.

"Tell me about Garland," he said.

"Five years of baby-sitting. You get tired of your guy crying himself to sleep in your arms. I mean, enough's enough."

"I didn't know he was a tortured soul."

"He hates himself. Sooner or later, you start to agree with his judgment. Wears a girl out."

She handed him a drink. They raised their glasses very slightly, then sipped.

"I don't mean to be hard," she said. "When Pete died, something inside me just gave up. Garland and I hadn't shared a bed in a year. I bought this place months ago because I knew I'd need it someday. And I thought, what's keeping you? You're thirty-eight, you feel like a dried-up old bag, you've got a little money coming through inheritance. You don't have a child to consider. Grandpa doesn't need you any-more. So get out. Break Garland's heart once—good and clean—and let him move on. He's good-looking. He can put on a good show. He works hard. He'll land somewhere better. I filed last week."

"Should I be sorry or happy?"

She smiled, teeth white and lips red in her smooth, olive Portuguese face. "I'm happy. You can feel what-ever you want. I love this apartment. I'm not really moved in yet, but the basics are here. Come on, I'll show you."

There was a small dining alcove right up by the window, views of the city and the harbor. Her din-ing table was a big rectangle of beveled-edge glass balanced on four clear acrylic cylinders. Set for two.

The master bedroom was big and somewhat di-sheveled in a manner that McMichael remembered: clothes tossed on a chair, the *Union-Tribune* spread over an unmade bed, a tennis racquet, tennis shoes, a can of balls and a warm-up jacket piled in one cor-ner, bathroom counter cluttered with bottles and tubes and brushes.

"I guess I'm a lousy housekeeper," she said thoughtfully. "But at least this time I'm doing it all myself. No cleaning lady. No cook. It's my ship and I'll run it how I want."

"You sound like Pete."

"I know." She giggled softly.

The guest room was small and almost empty, just a twin bed and a chest of drawers with a mirror above it, one painting and one potted king palm.

"Let's eat while I tell you about New Year's Eve." She served a bouillabaisse with sourdough rolls and a Caesar salad with plenty of sardines and dressing. McMichael remembered that Patricia was a good cook and a world-class eater who failed to gain weight.

"There were fifteen guests at Grandpa's house for New Year's," she said. "Seventeen total, counting Pete and the nurse. Me, Garland, Malcolm Case and his porn-star wife, a casino guy named Alex Dejano and his girlfriend, Charley Farrell from the dealership and his wife, the Silvas, the Bezes and Victor. Some terrifically boring cop and his miniature wife came by for a few minutes early on— Blank or Blanda or something like that."

"Jerry Bland. We call him Bland Jerry."

"Bland is right."

McMichael wasn't surprised, but he was. Bland wasn't the only cop in Pete's little black book, but he was the only cop at the party.

"Was Zeke inside the whole time, or did he go in and out?"

"The dog? In and out, I guess. Grandpa told me he died that night."

McMichael told her about the autopsy and the strychnine.

Patricia's face lost its radiance as she listened. She spooned some broth, the black zigzag of hair aimed down at the bowl. "Why, so they could come back and kill him without the dog barking?"

"That's a good assumption."

"You're talking about one cold-blooded piece of work, McMichael."

"Exactly."

"What a rotten job you have."

"It's an honest buck."

"So much for my cheery little lunch."

They ate without talking, spoons clinking in the bowls, rain driving against the windows. McMichael saw a web of white lightning break out over the ocean, then heard a moan of distant thunder.

"The nurse told me she saw Dejano feeding the dog," said McMichael.

"I didn't. But we left early."

"Why?"

"Grandpa was a boring drunk. I didn't like being around him when he was like that. And you get Charley Farrell and Pete together, it's just Fords, Fords, Fords. I get a new demo from the dealership every six months, but I don't want to talk about the damned things."

"Garland and Pete get along?"

"Garland thought Pete was a savage and Pete thought Garland was a poofter. That was one uptight dud of a New Year's Eve party—for us, anyway. But you go out of loyalty, you know? And they used to be fun. Used to be a hundred people or more. But Pete, he just seemed to be turning on everyone. Hardly had any family, hardly any friends. Malcolm Case a friend? Or that nurse? Pete was bottom feeding."

McMichael thought about Sally Rainwater trying to resuscitate Pete, her hands on his bloody pulp of a head, her mouth on his, all the panic and terror she went through.

"What are you going to do with the dealership?" he asked.

"Sell it and divide by five." She looked at him, a hint of apology in her dark eyes. "It's easy and clean.

Detroit said we can keep it, but I never wanted to sell cars."

"Charley told me you had some ideas for the dealership."

"Boy, did I. Radical concepts like more Web exposure and more local TV. Grandpa didn't care for them."

"What does the rest of the family want?"

"Just the money. My brother James made noises about keeping the franchise, but he's in Dallas and wants to stay in Dallas. That's not going to work."

"Did you help Pete out with the business?"

"Some. It kind of runs itself. He had me look at the books, make sure everything was on the up-and-up. Grandpa wasn't the most trusting of men."

"What did you find?"

"Nothing. He was concerned that his old bookkeeper was losing her mind, but she wasn't. She wasn't exactly computer literate, but her numbers added up. Imagine keeping the books on a multimillion-dollar business with paper and pencil. Detroit told me that any new owners would have to switch to a computer system."

Patricia took their bowls into the kitchen and came back with seconds. She put a hand on McMichael's shoulder as she set the bowl in front of him.

"What's your opinion of Grothke Junior?" he asked.

She said nothing until she was seated again. "One of those oddball bachelors you wonder about."

"How about his legal skills?"

"Adequate. Why?"

"He lost those letters that Pete sent him. About getting a church named for himself or Anna or Victor."

"Just lost them? How do you lose letters?"

McMichael didn't answer. Maybe Junior was just absentminded, he thought. No way to open an investigation of him just because his office lost some correspondence. They could press him, but Junior seemed pretty fed up with answering questions.

McMichael finished his seconds and sipped his drink.

"Thank you," he said.

"Always so polite, McMike."

"That was Mom's answer to chaos. Now it's mine."

"It's a nice quality. Thanks for paying your long-distance respects at the service. I couldn't invite you."

"I know."

"Nice to see the chief there. Grandpa liked people who were in charge."

They ate and watched the rain fall past the window.

"How's Gabriel?"

"He's the same." McMichael drank the rest of his gimlet and watched another bolt of lightning crack through the black sky.

"And how are you, Tommy? I mean really. I'd like to know."

He looked at her, marveling that the years could leave Patricia untouched.

"I'm good," he said. "I like the job. I love Johnny. The divorce was rotten but you heal up."

"Sounds like there's something missing. Or maybe you're holding out on me." She smiled and drank.

"I've got a little something going."

"Who?"

"You don't know her."

"Then tell me who she is. Someone at work?"

He nodded.

"Cops always end up with cops. At least on TV."

"We eat doughnuts and drink coffee together. Talk in Penal Code."

Patricia laughed. Her arms were dark and smooth, pale underneath when she raised them to fiddle with her hair.

"I wrote you a letter when I heard about you and your wife," she said. "Never mailed it. Wrote you another one a few weeks later, but didn't mail that one, either."

"Went through some stamps."

She smiled, set the zigzag back and it fell down again. "I never stopped thinking about you. I never stopped dreaming about you. We had something good, Thomas."

"We did."

"Still think about me?" she asked.

"I stopped."

"Do you dream?"

"Couldn't stop those."

"I couldn't, either," she said. "I enjoyed them."

"Don't go back, Patricia."

"Too painful for little McMikey?"

"Just unnecessary."

"What if I want to go forward? What I tried to say in the letters was I wished we could spend some time together. It's probably insane. I can't explain why I wrecked us, Tom. But I had to. I felt like history was making me do it. That the McMichaels and the Bragas were making me do it. Pete and Victor and Gabriel and Franklin. You know what I wish? I wish I could take a fire hose and blast it all away. Just cream it off the face of the earth. And see what's left standing. See if it's us."

"Wow."

"And all you wanted was a party list and lunch."

He looked at her across the table and the twenty years, saw the girl he'd loved and the woman she'd become. She stood and came over to him, put her arms around his shoulders and rested her head against his face. McMichael felt like he was being sucked down a big smooth tunnel, straight backward in time, body spinning in the rifled groove of the years.

He stood.

"McMike, did you *completely* stop thinking about me?"

"No." McMichael smiled and pulled on his jacket.

"Do me a favor? Forgive me for being eighteen once in my life?"

"I did that a long time ago."

"Then reconsider me. And don't be a stranger."

He tried to see her as a beautiful woman in a brown dress in a warm room in the rain. It was easy.

"Okay."

She closed the door behind him but he didn't hear it lock.

20

McMichael and Hector walked into Homicide Captain Don Rawlings's office at three that afternoon. McMichael closed the door without asking permission, then sat down and watched the black clouds blowing into the window.

Rawlings was sixty, tall and soft-spoken, though his temper was feared. McMichael liked him and trusted him and wanted to have his job someday, many years from now, when he was good enough to do it.

Rawlings listened to his tale of Victor Braga, new Fords, TJ and two law enforcement men running narcotics into the country.

Rawlings listened, back straight, eyes expressionless, hands folded on the desk. "So you never saw what was in the bags?"

"Wasn't tamales," said Hector.

"No," said the captain. "What's your guess on weight?"

"Fifty pounds each," said Hector. "Times three."

"Axelgaard Two didn't think it was suspicious when you two guys came through right behind his brother and Victor Braga?"

"McMichael made up a quick tale about a robbery and a witness with a Tijuana address," said Hector. "I think he bought it."

Rawlings nodded. "Wasn't Jimmy Thigpen working for Pete Braga?"

So much for Jimmy's head start, thought McMichael. "Yes," he said.

"The same thing, right, allegedly transporting cars down to Mexico for leather upholstery?"

McMichael nodded.

"Was Jimmy in on this?" asked the captain.

"Neck deep," said McMichael.

"You talked to him four hours ago. What did he say?"

"He said he made a big mistake."

"He said he was 'just about as stupid as a guy could get,'" said Rawlings.

"Exactly," said McMichael. "I didn't know the yard was miked."

"It isn't," said the captain.

McMichael squared himself in the chair.

"Internal Affairs knew Jimmy was moonlighting," said Rawlings. "But they didn't know he was running drugs. Who else was in on this with him—who else from San Diego PD?"

"I don't think anyone was," said McMichael.

"That was a little risky, offering Thigpen a deal," said Rawlings.

It's like he was fucking *there*, thought McMichael. "I thought it was worth the trade, for information on Pete."

Rawlings offered a very minor nod. "Keep this to yourselves, gentlemen. Absolutely to yourselves. I'm unhappy with it, and heads will roll. Basically, good job."

"Yes, sir."

"Yes, sir."

"McMichael, that line you said you'd never cross—you tiptoed right up to it with Thigpen."

"I know."

"I've nudged it myself, once or twice."

"Then I feel a little bit less like an ass, sir."

"Has your old man really been drunk for forty years?"

"Longer, I think."

"The deputy reads lips. A few of them do. They bring them in for special visits like yours."

Just after five they were standing in the lobby of Grothke, Steiner & Grothke, explaining to Sharona Saddler that they wanted to talk to Henry Grothke Sr.

"Impossible," she said. "He's not seeing anyone at the current time."

"He's sitting in there looking at us," said Hector. "He can see us just fine."

"You're not clients."

Old Grothke gazed at them through the glass wall of his office, then smiled and waved.

Henry Jr. came flapping down the hallway, sleeves rolled up, frowning, a pencil in his hand.

"The pestilential detectives are back. *Now* what do you want?"

"We want to talk to your father," said Hector.

"I've absolutely had it," said Junior. "I will not allow you to disrupt our business anymore. I've gone out of my way to help you. And you barge in here with no warning and no appointment and make even more demands on our time? I demand that you leave immediately."

"We just want a few minutes," said McMichael.

"Sharona, call security."

Sharona already had the phone to her ear and her fingers on the keypad.

"We're going," said McMichael.

"Plan B," said Hector, as they got into the elevator.

They stood under an awning on State Street and watched the rain pour down. Old Grothke's van and driver—as cased by Hector on Monday evening—pulled up at five-thirty. The driver parked in the loading zone and flipped the handicapped placard onto the dash. He ran around the van and into the Bay Towers entrance.

Eight minutes later the driver pushed Old Grothke out onto the sidewalk under the awning, using the big wheels to prod McMichael and Hector out of the way.

"Handicap, man—you blind?"

"We can see fine," said Hector.

"Don't you go nowhere, Hankie Baby. Derek'll be right back."

Grothke looked up at McMichael with burdened blue eyes that showed no sign of recognition.

Derek set the wheelchair brake and hunched through the rain to the driver's seat of the van. Once inside he slammed the door shut. A moment later McMichael saw the back door of the van roll up, then a ramp slide out and lower to the street.

"Derek is disrespectful," said Grothke to no one in particular. "But a helluva good driver."

Derek hustled back, kicked up the wheelchair brake and raced Old Grothke through the raindrops to the ramp. While he got the chair locked into place Hector climbed into the driver's seat.

The driver had just activated the ramp when McMichael jumped onto it and badged him.

"McMichael, Homicide," he said. "Get back up front and sit in the passenger side."

"What the—"

"Am I going to have a problem with you?"

A big shake of his head, a big smile. "I don't ever have trouble with the police."

"Then get on it."

Derek jumped to the pavement and scrambled around the van. When the ramp clunked into place, McMichael hit a blue button to retract it. As the ramp groaned backward Old Grothke's head jiggled and raindrops rolled down his thin white face.

The interior had seats along both sides but none in the middle. The floor carpet had been replaced with plywood to accommodate wheelchairs. A moment later the back door rolled down.

"Is this a robbery?" asked Grothke, eyes wide.

"Relax, sir," said McMichael. "We're the cops you talked to last week. Remember? Vultures in the ice cream?"

Grothke's face locked into seriousness. McMichael saw the battle going on behind his eyes. Then, illumination, like sunlight through clouds. "Detective McMichael! Of course I remember."

McMichael poked his head into the driver's cab. Derek was in the passenger seat, saying something to Hector about applying to SDPD back in 'ninety-two but his back was bad and he had this one thing on his record.

"Go stand outside," said Hector. "Distribute your weight on both feet equally. Save that back."

"It's raining out there, man."

"Then go inside, dumbass."

When Hector had locked the driver out he climbed back and sat down across from Grothke.

"That driver's kind of rude," he said.

Grothke nodded slowly. "No respect."

"Thanks for meeting with us," said McMichael. He handed the old man a clean folded handkerchief. "We won't take up much of your time. We just wanted to know about those letters that Pete Braga mailed to your firm. He sent you one in November and another one in December, but both of them just disappeared after they got to your office."

"Oh," said Grothke, nodding. "Those."

"Did you see them?"

"See what?" asked Grothke.

Hector shot McMichael a look.

"The letters from Pete Braga, sir," said McMichael.

"Of course."

"They were about Pete changing his will," said

McMichael. "He wanted to remove the Catholic Church as a beneficiary."

Old Grothke studied McMichael with a kind of freshness in his bright blue eyes, as if seeing McMichael for the first time. "No," he said. "They weren't about the Church."

McMichael and Hector looked at each other.

"They pertain to the weather," said Grothke. "A change in the weather. And I'll correctly handle the matter, as I have for fifty years."

"The letters were about weather?" asked McMichael.

"Yes."

"The ones that Pete Braga mailed to your firm, then were lost or misplaced?"

"Nothing has been lost, I can assure you."

"Then where are they?" asked Hector. "Pete came to your firm six times at the end of last year, trying to find those things."

Grothke smiled at Hector, then McMichael. He dabbed at his forehead with the handkerchief. "I assume full responsibility for them. They are in my possession."

"Would you mind if we just looked at them, sir?" asked McMichael. "Pete was murdered last week, as I'm sure you know."

Grothke's face went blank and his pale blue eyes seemed to freeze. "He sold me a Country Squire station wagon in nineteen sixty-two. Red. A material that suggested wood on each side. Very convincing."

"What did you do with the letters, sir?" asked McMichael. "The ones pertaining to a change in the weather."

The rain roared against the roof of the van. Through the side window McMichael could see the driver smoking a cigarette under the awning of the Bay Towers entrance, irate workers crowded under with him, waiting for taxis and buses or for a good time to run to the next overhang.

Grothke was staring straight ahead now, his eyes seemingly focused on something close but puzzling. He breathed deeply in and deeply out. "Sometimes, I stand on the edge of a memory and look in. I see nothing clearly. It's like water in a pool after a rock is thrown in. Then, if I look long enough, the water gets smoother and smoother and the ripples vanish and I can see again."

"That's beautiful, Mr. Grothke," said Hector. "It really is."

McMichael heard no sarcasm in Hector's voice.

Grothke looked at Hector, then to McMichael. "I'm not sure where I put them," he said. "But I will correctly handle the matter, as I have for the last fifty years. And I promise you now, on my good name, that I will locate and deliver to you these missing letters."

"Did you shred them?" asked McMichael.

Grothke eyed him suspiciously. "I don't think so."

"Put them in your briefcase?" asked Hector.

"It has been searched."

"Take them home?" asked Hector.

"I looked there. We all did."

Another downpour bellowed against the top of the van.

"They had to do with weather like this," said

Grothke, looking up at the roof somewhat dreamily. "I remember. A change."

"You mean rain?" asked Hector.

"Yes."

"Rainwater?" asked McMichael.

"*Yes! Rainwater.* It's a name."

"What about her?" asked McMichael, looking not at Grothke but at Hector.

"Pete wanted his will changed for Rainwater."

21

"I told him not to," said Sally Rainwater. "He said he was going to do it anyway. Pure Pete. I assumed he was kidding me because he kidded me about a lot of things."

"Apparently not this."

"What did he want to do, exactly?"

"Nobody can find the letters."

It was eight that night and the rain had stopped. McMichael and Sally walked south down the shoreline of Imperial Beach. The sand was cold and the stars bright and the pier lights made pools of silver on the rough black sea.

"You should have told me," said McMichael.

"It seemed insane," she said. "And totally for show, so I didn't tell you. *He was going to change his will for me.* It's got an ugly ring to it and it implies ugly things about me. If I had known that he had done it—I would have told you. I apologize if I screwed up your investigation, but I don't think like a cop."

"You still should have told me."

"You should have asked."

"I need to know everything."

"Then that's going to be an awful long talk," said Sally. "I worked for him for eight months. Forty hours a week is one hell of a lot of time. Ask me anything and I'll tell you, but I can't read your mind. Come on."

They walked down the pier, past the place where Hector had parked just a week ago to watch the monstrous waves roll past.

"I don't see how a law firm can just lose letters," she said. "What's going on there?"

"The old man is forgetful and confused. But I think it's more than that. His son says the letters were about the Church. Not you."

Sally laughed quietly and shook her head. "Pete was pissed at the Catholics, I know that. I think he wanted a new church named after himself."

"So says Grothke Junior."

"Will you hold my hand, or am I a suspect again?"

"No. Sorry."

Taking her hand McMichael felt angry and stupid and he knew he could either kick Sally Rainwater or himself or just let it go. It was not in his nature to let things go.

"Cheer up," she said. "You need wine and dinner."

They got a booth in a little steakhouse near the pier. There was a good fire in the fireplace and hardly any customers. McMichael drank a glass of red wine, felt better. He looked at Sally and was glad to be here with her, anger and stupidity aside. She wore light makeup and she'd brushed her straw-colored hair out long and loose. A black turtleneck sweater and jeans and the same kind of low-heeled boots she'd worn at Pete's that night. Pearls in her ears. In the warm orange light of the table candle she seemed singular and exotic.

She told him a story about Pete and her trying to hook up a new VCR, how Pete got so mad he ended up throwing it out a window, then tried to return it to the store and told them it was like that when he took it out of the box. She told him about cruising Point Loma for hours some nights, her driving and Pete yapping about the old days and the Portuguese, about the uncle who drowned when a line caught around his foot and a big fish pulled him overboard and swam down with him, the cousin who lost her hand at the Westgate Cannery, Mary's triplets and Frank's polio and Crazy Eva who had her heart broken and shot the guy twice but didn't kill him and when he got out of the hospital she ran over him with a car, which did. Sally said whenever they'd cruise Point Loma they'd stop at St. Agnes's and say prayers and sometimes Pete would leave the place with tears on his cheeks and sometimes he'd have that twinkle in his eye and she figured he'd prayed for God to fix his enemies. And the nights with Victor—lots of nights just hanging around with Victor—hit a restaurant or burger place then the Waterfront while father and son talked and argued and remembered the old days.

"I'm trying to tell you everything," she said. "How do I know what's important and what's not?"

"Keep going. I'm interested in enemies."

"He had a lot of them. He thought people were after him, after his things. He didn't trust most people. Didn't even trust his granddaughter, Patricia."

McMichael looked at her over his menu. "Tell me about that."

"He said if she ever asked me for a house key the answer was no. I asked him why and Pete said it was none of my business. Then that Pete smile—the one where you couldn't tell if he was wicked or just amused. I dropped it, because I figured it really *wasn't* any of my business, but I think she'd disappointed or hurt him in some way. Could have been years ago, for all I know."

The waitress took their orders and brought more wine.

"So," said McMichael. "Did Patricia ever ask you for a key?"

"No. Never."

McMichael leaned back and let the warmth from the fireplace seep into him. He watched Sally Rainwater stare into the flames.

"Pete talked a lot about Anna," said Sally. "She's only been gone three years. They got married when they were seventeen. Pete quit school at fourteen to fish. He got his first boat at fifteen, to work the market trade. But he said the Italians had the markets cornered and the fish were getting thin, so he needed a bigger boat for longer runs. Anna's family didn't have much money, but Pete convinced them to loan him six hundred dollars for a bigger boat. He paid them back in two years. Ten years later he bought them a two-story house off of Rosecrans."

"Sounds like Pete talked more about Pete," said McMichael.

"Always! He really was an arrogant old man. But he was sweet, too. He told me the only regret he had was all the worry he caused Anna. He wished he'd have been gentler with her, because life was just as hard for a woman left onshore as it was for a man who went to sea. Three, four months sometimes. Pete said all the money and gifts in the world didn't make up for the days and nights they'd never get to spend with each other. He really, genuinely missed her. He wanted that lost time back, now that he couldn't get it. Don't we all?"

He saw how Pete Braga could have fallen for Sally. It wasn't only youth and beauty and character. It was something simpler, too. She was there to receive what Pete never gave Anna enough of—his hours.

"What did he say about his will?"

Sally sipped her wine. "He told me once that he was going to make sure I got the house when he died. The first time he said that I think I ignored him. The second time I told him I didn't want his stinking house. He liked that. He laughed at that. He said it did stink—it stunk like tuna fish. That was all he ever said about the topic."

With a cool little wobble of nerves, McMichael remembered Hector's words: *Maybe she wants the really cool stuff. Like a house at the beach.*

"Why didn't you want it?"

She looked at him steadily. It struck McMichael

that she was weighing something in him rather than in herself.

"It didn't seem right," she said. "I did accept gifts from Pete—you saw some of them. I told you about the ten grand for the car. I thought about those gifts before I took them. I thought a lot about what was right and what wasn't. I guessed at his fortune to understand what these things were costing him. And I came to believe it was good for me to take them. But his home? Where he'd lived with his wife and raised a family? No, that had a completely different meaning to me."

"What did he want in return?"

"Nothing."

"You believed that?"

"I did and still do. He ordered me to his bed the second week I was there. I told him I wouldn't, and if he brought it up again I'd have to quit. He didn't, and that was that."

McMichael said nothing, thinking of Pete and Angel and Victor.

"It surprised me, Tom. I was ready for that second pass. I was ready to go find another job. But what he wanted was my time and my company. Though he understood all along that for me it was work. He understood that I gave my time for his money."

"Maybe he was going to rewrite his will for you anyway."

"I guess Pete was capable of that."

"Old Grothke said so."

"Pete also loved to needle and tease and taunt and shock," she said. "When he gave somebody something, he wanted credit for it. He wanted to be thanked and lauded and praised. So I think if he'd made that change, he'd have told me."

McMichael told her about Pete's calls and visits to the firm, his meetings with Grothke Jr. at the Sea Market Restaurant after mass at St. Agnes's. "He kept the mailing receipts in his wallet, that's how important those letters were. By early January Pete was ready to change law firms. He was talking to Myron Camlin about taking over his legal affairs. A few days later he was dead."

She studied the fire for a long while. "He didn't say one word about any of that to me."

They had another glass of wine after dinner. They talked about Johnny and autographed guitars and Sally's life at the age of seven: dirt poor in the town of Hagville, Kentucky—a place she said she would never go back to so long as she lived. McMichael saw the darkness pass over her face as she said this, realized it was no joke at all. *Once . . . when I was hardly more than a girl, a man died and I could have prevented it. . . .*

"I got a job," she said. "Elderly woman out on Coronado. Very nice. I'll be with her five nights a week from five until eleven. You can get me there on the cell, anytime."

"I'll call," he said.

She smiled and brushed his hand lightly.

Behind Sally's little house they stopped under a streetlight and kissed. He wondered idly if they looked like a movie. Her hands were cold underneath his jacket. McMichael surrendered to the taste of her, his vision focusing south to the great blackness of the borderland and Tijuana, where the faint lights dotted the hills. He felt strong and protective and tender. She led him by the hand from the sidewalk to her room, letting go only long enough to fish the keys from her purse.

22

Hector met him outside the headquarters employee entrance at seven-thirty the next morning. His face was dark and humorless and he looked like he'd barely slept.

"We gotta talk but we can't do it here," he said.

They walked over to Spider's, next to the boxing club on Fourteenth Street. The Internet-and-coffee room was empty as Hector grimly led the way through a blue door in the back. The bar was empty, too—billiards tables brushed and balls racked for play, the big televisions all turned to a Super Bowl preview featuring four ex–pro quarterbacks.

McMichael and Hector took a corner booth and the bartender brought them coffee, then turned up the TV volume to give them a little privacy.

Hector leaned up close. "First of all, Rainwater isn't her real name. It's Gaglosta. Second, she killed a guy with a meat cleaver when she was seventeen. She was his *caretaker.*"

McMichael said nothing to the hostile pity in his partner's eyes.

"Dade County Juvenile Court judge ruled self-defense, sealed the record because she was so young," said Hector. "She legally changed her name when she was eighteen. Didn't get a Social Security number until then. That's why Rainwater didn't pop when we ran the records and warrants check that night."

"Let's take a walk, Heck."

Hector dropped some bills on the table and they walked back out. The fierce morning sun and turquoise blue sky did nothing to brighten McMichael's oddly tunneled and unfocused eyesight.

"A *meat cleaver?*"

"Uh-huh."

"What happened?"

"She was in the guy's house. Working, late morning. She said the guy started groping her, wouldn't stop. She said he was going to rape her if she didn't do something. They were in the kitchen and the meat cleaver was handy. Dade County prosecutors wanted to charge her, but the juvenile court petitioned and the state kicked it down to them."

"How many times she hit him?"

"Once."

"How old was the guy, what condition?"

"Thirty-five and brain damaged from a motorcycle wreck. No priors, no incidents, clean. He worked in a bank, taught Sunday school to fourth-graders before the accident. His friends and neighbors weren't happy with Sally Gaglosta and the state court."

McMichael tried to process the information but his mind had gone dim, like a dying lightbulb. "Brain damage doesn't preclude violence. It can *cause* it. Can't it?"

Hector looked at him hard. "In Gaglosta's possible defense, she was from Hagville, Kentucky, foot of the Appalachians and the Alleghenies. She had one brother in prison for bank robbery, another in prison for growing dope in the hollows. One sister that just vanished. Her mom lived with a boyfriend to keep the welfare checks coming. Six kids, three fathers. Sally split when she was fifteen, moved in with an older sister in Miami."

They headed up Fourteenth and dropped back down onto Broadway, circled headquarters once, then started a second lap.

"She didn't sit right with me," Hector said quietly. "Not from the first second I saw her that night. It took me a couple of days to track all that down. I thought it was my obligation, Tom, as a partner and a friend."

"You're good at both, Hector."

Silence then, as they walked toward the headquarters doors. "Maybe it *was* self-defense," said Hector, unconvinced.

"Damn right," said McMichael.

More silence.

"Hey, I met a couple of flight attendants at *Libertad* last night. They're up for a foursome sometime but I get the blonde. I made you sound like a cross between Ricky Martin and the guy in *Gladiator*."

"That's me."

"Yesterday evening," said Hector, "Bland asked

me about you and the nurse. Asked if you two were an item. I said beats me but the nurse isn't a suspect anyway, so who cares? I didn't say jack about anything else, and I won't unless he pulls me onto his IAD carpet. Who knows, maybe I'd still tell him to shove it."

"Don't sink for me, Hector."

"I can take care of myself. I hope you can."

"Close the door," said Bland. "Have a seat."

McMichael had barely made it into the Team Three pen when the assistant chief called him into his office.

"The spooks caught you," said Bland. He handed McMichael a large white envelope with the City of San Diego seal and address in one corner.

McMichael's heart ducked and dove, the spooks being Professional Standards Unit—the foot soldiers for IAD, cops who spy on other cops, nameless and faceless, guys you'd never make for the law, didn't even work out of the Fourteenth St. headquarters. They had more power over their fellow SDPD officers than the Constitution of the United States.

McMichael slid out the black-and-white photographs: he and Sally Rainwater standing outside Mario's with glowering Johnny, he and Sally Rainwater walking the pier hand in hand, going into the steakhouse, making out under the streetlamp and on her porch. The killers were the close-ups, apparently taken through the louvered windows of her bedroom, a truly humiliating series that ended in a picture of McMichael with his head thrown back in a grimace of pleasure. He looked like a baboon with a haircut.

"What's the idea here?" he asked.

"I don't see any ideas here at all. No rational thought, no professional standards. Explain yourself."

"I like her and we're spending time."

"You sure are. The blood was hardly dry on Pete Braga's floor when you're banging the suspect." Bland's thick bovine face cracked into something like a smile.

"She's not a suspect."

"Oh, no? The only witness, covered in blood, pointing a finger at the door? She's not a suspect?"

"We've got prints on the weapon—not hers. We've got prints on the sliding glass door—not hers. She didn't kill him."

"And she's got no idea who did?"

"That's correct."

"Who *is* a suspect?"

"We've got some leads but no suspect."

"Leads, fingerprints, but no suspect."

McMichael said nothing. He remembered Sally's refusal to talk about what had happened, and how she might have prevented a man's death. He remembered her sadness. But he wasn't sure what this implied. Shame? Guilt? Pain? He held Bland's stare for a beat, then looked away.

"How old are you, McMichael?"

"I'm thirty-eight."

Bland shook his head. "You're acting more like eighteen. In fact, I've got a nephew eighteen who has more sense than you. Maybe you don't want to button down this case. Maybe you like the idea that Pete Braga got his, just like he gave it to Frank McMichael back in the dark ages."

"It was nineteen fifty-two."

Bland sat back, fingers locked behind his head. "I've got some options here, McMichael. I can throw this to IAD. I can throw it to Captain Rawlings and let him deal with you. I could just punt to the chief and let him get the ulcers."

McMichael nodded. "You could stand behind a fellow officer and trust his judgment."

"That option scares me. Because if this blows up—say the nurse set the old man up, say she was in on it with one of her *other* boy toys—my ass blows up with it. Why would I take that risk for you?"

"No," McMichael said evenly, "you wouldn't."

Bland lifted one heavy brow. "McMichael, say I was willing. Say you're right about the nurse, and she's God's gift to the human race. This still *looks* bad. Appearances are part of my job. One of the many things I'm paid for is to make sure we appear proper and competent and professional. This makes you—us—appear to be the opposite. Now, do you agree with that or not?"

McMichael tried to look at it from the outside, as if he were Bland or Hector or Rawlings. It wasn't difficult. "It looks bad. And I realize I could have made a mistake."

"And what if you did?"

"I'll fire me myself."

Bland chuckled without levity. "Now we're getting somewhere. I'm going to talk to Rawlings about this. I don't know. In the meantime, try a little harder not to fuck up."

"Yes, sir."

"We're all on a team, Detective. When you stink, I stink."

"I won't make you stink, sir. I've got to do what I think is right."

"You looked pretty right in that last picture."

McMichael didn't answer for a while. "Why did you do this?"

"Not me," said Bland. "IAD got wind of it and decided to check it out. You did the rest."

"Got wind of it how?"

Bland shook his head. "The PSU guys were tracking you because of Jimmy. Why's he talking to you but nobody else? How come you two are passing kites back and forth like a couple of gangsters? So they followed you to the pizza place, saw you and the nurse. Now you're hanging out with a *near* suspect in a high-profile homicide, plus this shit with Jimmy. That's weird, McMichael, no matter what you think. IAD told the spooks to run with it, see what you were doing. Guess what? You were doing *her*. IAD came to me with the frank photos."

"Great people to work with."

"What else could they do?"

Bland regarded McMichael with his small, unmerciful eyes. "Tell me, is she really that special, really worth all this?"

"I think so."

Special enough to take a meat cleaver to a brain-damaged patient, he thought. Bland's placid face seemed to be staring at him from the end of a long narrow tunnel.

The assistant chief sat back again, sighing. "I don't get you, McMichael. You've had a clean record here for sixteen years. Good years. Some nice citations, no complaints. Climbing the ladder. Homicide at thirty-seven. Captain Rawlings went all out for you because he thought you'd fit into Team Three. All of a sudden you're Jimmy Thigpen's soul mate and you're humping the only witness/suspect in a murder case. Just yesterday I got a complaint from Henry Grothke, saying you were harassing him at his office. Then I get another one from some ambulance driver, says you commandeered his vehicle, made him stand out in the rain. What gives with you? You bored? Tired?"

"Jimmy and I just happened to work Metro/Vice, sir. I don't think he has anyone else to talk to. So far as Sally Rainwater goes, my ass is on the line and I know it. Grothke's father has managed to misplace something material to the Braga case, I just have to figure out where it went. The driver, I made him wait outside while we interviewed Old Grothke. He was under an awning, not in the rain."

"Tell me about these lawyers."

McMichael filled him in, just enough details to justify the alleged harassment.

A note of dour amusement crept into Bland's face. "What did Thigpen have to say when you saw him yesterday?"

"He said he blew it. He regrets what he did."

"Which was what, exactly, to have three-hundred-plus grand lying around at his attempted two-hooker party?"

"He offered no details, sir."

"That's all he said?"

"Not much else."

"Rawlings has got his lip-reading buddies over there at the jail, and that's all they could come up with for him? You and Thigpen talked for what, ten minutes?"

"We mostly just walked around, sir."

"Yeah, right. McMichael, get out of here."

McMichael sat at his desk with Sally Rainwater's references. He read the letters and the names of the writers, realizing how easily you could fake the damn things with a decent printer, a few different kinds of paper and a little practice on the signatures. Rainwater wasn't even her real name. Legal, but not real.

I have nothing but the highest praise for Miss Rainwater, who helped my husband back to health at a time when my own cancer had disabled me as a caretaker . . . thoughtful, courteous and good humored . . . endlessly patient and very understanding of our special needs . . . Sincerely, Alma Beasley. He read all five of them—believing every one of them, not believing any.

When he was finished he dug out Raegan's customer list from *Libertad* and read down the names. Then he looked away for a moment and read the names again, having failed to register a single one. He could feel Hector's eyes burning into his back, even though Hector was upstairs in Bland's office.

He could feel Barbara's eyes on him, too, even though he was pretty sure she hadn't yet been told what a total dumbshit he was. Staring at the list he wished he could make himself small enough to crawl into the "O" of *maduro*—just slither right through the paper into another dimension where he would be competent and unrecognized.

He called Charley Farrell at the dealership and asked about selling a wine-colored Escape, Explorer, Expedition or Excursion.

"Sergeant McMichael," he said. "I completely forgot. Give me a few more hours, will you?"

Arthur Flagler, the crime lab director, called at ten-twelve.

"You ought to drop by when you get a minute," he said. "Like right now."

McMichael rode the elevator up, wished it would just keep going.

Flagler welcomed him to his office with a wicked smile.

"We came up with something else from Pete Braga's," he said. "The wine samples we took from those glasses by the fireplace? Well, somehow they got put aside—in the refrigerator, of course—and we overlooked them. I was looking for a set of fingers in the freezer, figured maybe someone had put them in the refrigerator instead. They hadn't, but I found the wine. Ran some basic tox tests yesterday. The nurse was drinking with him that night, right?"

McMichael nodded.

"Well, her wine probably tasted just fine. But Pete's—from the glass closest to his chair? Loaded with meperidine, which is a strong tranquilizer."

"Same thing his dog ate on New Year's Eve," said McMichael.

"Correct."

"Pete's prints on one glass and Rainwater's on the other?"

Flagler smiled and nodded. "Hers on the glass without the meperidene, mind you."

"But Pete didn't have meperidine in his system?"

"Oddly enough, he did not."

"Thanks, Arthur."

McMichael left the headquarters building, walked the eight blocks west to Kettner, rode the trolley up past the airport then back down again, wandered around the Gaslamp, snuck past *Libertad* with his face hidden from Raegan, spent some time in an import store featuring African tribal crafts, among them a gigantic black mask, six feet high and three across, carved from dark brown wood and festooned with brass rings and ivory and animal claws, tufts of savannah grass and crude twine, the eyes furious and bloody, the mouth a gaping snarl, the war paint stacked in scintillating bars of blue and yellow and red.

He walked Fourth and Fifth Avenues, Island and Market, bought a paper on Second and threw it away on Third. He tried to think rationally.

In defense of Sally Rainwater he came up with justifiable homicide, terrible childhood, taking care of herself, trying to help others, friend of the sick, coincidence, bad timing, bad luck. He tried to delete any personal feelings or opinions about her, except for his gut call that she *wouldn't*. These still counted, didn't they—belief, judgment, faith in someone? Strongest of all was what wasn't there: a reason to kill Pete Braga.

Against her he came up with means, opportunity and prior action. She'd killed someone with a blow to the head before. Self-defense or not, she had the physical and mental ability to attack with violence and take a life. This was a fact. It seemed clear to him that she could not have killed Pete Braga alone—the fingerprints on the club told him that, almost certainly—but she could have organized the entry and the attack. All she needed was to leave the door open behind her when she left. Simple to poison Zeke on New Year's Eve. Simple to spike Pete's wine that night. She was *there*. Maybe she'd switched out the club when she was finished, thrown the used one in the bay and set the new one—with the sales clerk's prints on it—in the blood. *It's a gift for my brother. What's the best way to hold it? Oh, wow, just like that?*

But again, why? He was giving her gifts. He might have been trying to cut her into his will but hadn't yet. Why kill the old man?

He could get a search warrant for her home—controlled substances and stolen property. The meperidine could be small enough to hide anywhere, which would neatly justify a detailed and thorough search. Maybe they'd find her motive, too, something he hadn't thought of, something precious and attainable only with Pete dead. A search could reveal nothing, too.

Logical.

He could talk to her first, hear her explanations. And risk letting her destroy evidence?

Idiotic.

He could step aside, let Hector and the rest of Team Three serve the warrant and search the house, not have to look at Sally Rainwater.

Gutless.

He could wait until she'd gone to work and look around inside her house himself, test the waters. And let the PSU get a few more good shots of him conducting an illegal search?

Beyond dumb.

They could surveil her, see if she's really attending her classes. Maybe she's meeting a fence, her partner, the guy who used the fish billy. Let her lead them to the real pay dirt.

Expensive and iffy.

He found himself at the Santa Fe station, looking across the tracks toward the bay. Then he was outside headquarters, considering the odd blue-and-white paint.

When in doubt, he thought, you go with the evidence. You go with what you know. With what you've been taught.

McMichael went up to Homicide and told Rawlings he wanted a warrant to search for controlled substances and stolen property in Sally Rainwater's home in Imperial Beach.

"Who's going to search the place?" asked Rawlings.

"All of us."

"Make sure Barbara's there."

Two hours later he had it.

*   *   *

She opened the door and her face went white and blank. Her dark eyes went from McMichael to Hector and Barbara, then back to McMichael. He couldn't tell what filled them—fury or disappointment or just surprise.

"Sorry," he said. "We need to have a look around."

"For what?"

"Meperidine, strychnine and stolen property from Pete Braga's home," he said, holding up the document. "It's all right here, under scope of search. We ask you to stay and help us."

"*Help* you?" She looked past him to the two uniforms standing out in the sand. She was wearing sweats and athletic shoes and her old denim jacket over a sweater.

She threw the door closed but McMichael had his toe in and the door bounced off and slowly shuddered open. She had stepped back into the kitchen, and the stare with which she met him as he came into her house was like nothing McMichael had ever seen before. He had seen anger, but never so focused, never so personal. The uniforms barged in behind him.

"Stay with her," said McMichael.

"Yes, sir."

Sally Rainwater turned her back to them, stood in front of her kitchen sink, put her hands on the counter for support and stared out her drafty louvered window toward Tijuana.

Down inside the radiator vent in the second bedroom, Barbara found a *Libertad* pyramids box containing a pair of almost comically large diamond earrings hidden in a pair of men's socks.

In the attic, among a collection of old paint cans and solvents and stains, Hector found an aspirin bottle containing eight capsules of what appeared to be Demerol.

In the top of the crowded hallway closet Mc-Michael found two Dunhill cigar boxes containing what looked like about twenty thousand cash. And a small wadded paper bag containing Anna's hummingbird, once described by Sally as the most beautiful man-made thing she'd ever seen.

Sally Rainwater stared down at the collection, arranged by McMichael on the coffee table in her living room.

"I've never seen those things before," she said.

"What, they crawled in here and hid themselves?" asked Hector.

"I need a lawyer," she said.

"Lawyers are for people charged with crimes," said Barbara, the standard cop line for getting someone to talk without one. "You're not charged. Can you explain these things?"

Sally continued to stare at the evidence against her. The angle of her head suggested puzzlement, her tears suggested grief. But, as McMichael saw when she looked at him, her eyes were fury.

"*I trusted you.*"

"Everyone's got a sad story," said Hector, while the uniform cuffed her hands. Hector Mirandized her, reading off the card to get it right.

23

McMichael and his son walked into Spellacy's at six, collected Gabriel off his stool and got a booth. The place was already busy, Friday night—darts and billiards in the back, the bar three deep and loud, waitresses squeezing through the crowds with serving trays while Celtic-rock-fusion music whinnied through the loudspeakers. Hugh wasn't tending the bar tonight, McMichael noticed, but his brother Clancy seemed to be handling things just fine.

McMichael sat across from his father and son and was momentarily lifted from his dark mood by the sight of them together. With Johnny, Gabriel was far lighter than McMichael ever remembered him. His father listened, which was nearly absent from McMichael's memories of boyhood. The two talked and joked and Gabriel gave Johnny liberties that McMichael rarely did—indulging some pretty bad manners, rolling with Johnny's puerile insults, encouraging Johnny's jokes: *Under the Toilet Seat* by

Seymor Butts! *Yellow River* by I. P. Freeley! *Brown Trail* by Squat and Leavitt!

Another little boy came over and challenged Johnny to darts. McMichael watched them hustle to the bar to get darts from Clancy Spellacy, then edge through the crowd to an open board.

Gabriel waved a waitress over for another shot and a Guinness. McMichael stuck with his barely touched half-pint.

"We arrested the nurse," he said. "We're not sure exactly how she figures in, but somehow."

Gabriel blinked his clear blue eyes. "His caretaker, Tommy! Lots of that in the news these days—the younger generation preying on the older."

"Yeah."

"Drink up. You've got a whole weekend to forget about it and be with your boy. What you shouldn't forget is that Pete was shown the same mercy he showed your grandfather."

"I'll remember, Pop."

"Who was trying to feed a family."

"I know."

Gabriel eyed him with slightly drunken affection.

Tim Keller pulled up a chair while they ate dinner, tried to enlist McMichael in a Sons of Ireland pancake breakfast on Sunday after church. He said Irish cops always made the best breakfast chefs—Rourke and O'Grady from the sheriff's would be there. He studied McMichael with his cheerful, delinquent eyes.

After dinner McMichael and his son walked down to the waterfront, then south toward Broadway.

They stopped in the Harbor Cruise coffeeshop for hot chocolate then fell in with the light foot traffic on the boardwalk.

Victor Braga shuffled along a hundred feet ahead of them, headphones on, carrying a heavy plastic bag in each hand.

"There's Victor Braga," said Johnny. "But Grandpa didn't do it."

The story—with Gabriel as the guilty attacker—had found Johnny's ears on his first-grade playground one day. Johnny had come home, excited that his grandfather was the star of a legend. McMichael and Stephanie had told him their agreed-upon version: Johnny's great-grandfather Franklin had been cheated out of money by a boat captain, and the captain had killed him. Someone—*no one knows who*—had beaten up the captain's son a little while later. Victor, the son, was never the same after the beating. Some people blamed the beating on Grandpa Gabriel. Others said he didn't do it. Tim Keller said he was with Grandpa that night and Grandpa didn't do it. Grandpa always said he was innocent, *and we believe him*. In this country you are innocent until proven guilty.

"How retarded is he?" asked Johnny, spooning the whipped cream into his mouth.

"Keep your voice down. Age ten, I heard."

"What grade is that?" whispered Johnny.

"Fifth, say."

"Fifth-graders get to walk around at night?"

"Not usually."

"How old is he, really?"

"Grandpa's age—sixty-three or so."

"How old is that in dog years?"

"About nine."

"I wish I had a dog."

"We'll get you one someday. That's a promise, John."

They turned up Broadway to the car, Johnny slopping the hot chocolate on his jacket while McMichael watched Victor trudge patiently southward toward Tuna Harbor.

After Johnny went to bed, McMichael poured an illogically large glass of tequila, added some ice and sank down into his couch. He turned on the local news, volume low. The tequila did nothing to clarify his thoughts so he drank more. All it really did was make him want to go back to the night he'd driven to Sally Rainwater's house to tell her that her prints weren't on the fish club and that her story checked and that she was, what, *beautiful* and he just wanted to look at her?—to go back to that drive down Silver Strand Boulevard, turn the damned Crown Vic around and drive it home. He leaned his head against the sofa, shaking it slowly. Too late. Too late for that. Too late for everything. Too late for him and Steffy. Too late for Gabe and Victor and Patricia and Garland. Too late for everybody, like we're all gears notched just wrong into the gears next to us—one giant clock, always off, too late, too late, too late.

In local news today, an Imperial Beach woman was detained in connection with the bludgeon murder of car dealer and former San Diego mayor Pete Braga. Sally Rainwater, twenty-eight, was taken into custody early this afternoon at her waterfront home. Police captain Don Rawlings said only that the woman—who was employed as a caretaker in the home of Braga—was arrested at her home and later charged with possession of stolen property. Braga, a former commercial tuna boat captain and a longtime fixture on San Diego's political scene, was found savagely beaten in his Point Loma home last Wednesday night. Police still have no motive for the killing. Braga was eighty-four. In other news . . .

McMichael still didn't know exactly what the district attorney would charge her with. They would take the weekend to decide. He was pleased that there was no mention of the caretaker's romantic involvement with the lead detective on the case. Yet. Just wait until her lawyer hears about that one, he thought. Bad cop. Bad arrest. Bad case.

He took another drink, clicked off the TV. He washed his face in the bathroom sink, looking at himself while he dried. He noted the red-brown curly hair, the dull blue eyes, the thick County Cork ears. He wondered how he could look like a regular mick on the outside, but on the inside feel like the African mask he'd seen earlier. Feel like hell.

It took him a long time to fall asleep. He lay there feeling that he'd sinned in doing his job. That he'd betrayed innocence. He couldn't fully believe that Sally Rainwater had been involved in Pete's death, though he thought it was possible. It was absolutely possible. Wasn't it?

The physical evidence was there, concealed in her house. They were lucky to have it. You base your decisions on the evidence. The evidence leads you to form opinions, not the other way around. A frame was possible, sure, but so were visitors from other galaxies and Bigfoot.

Get a grip, he thought. The evidence was pointing at her. Live with it. She's going to have to.

They spent part of Saturday in bird stores. McMichael had included Johnny in basic detective work before, and Johnny enjoyed it. He told his son about the yellow feather at the crime scene, making him promise to tell no one about it. Johnny listened intently and nodded gravely. McMichael had noticed very early on that Johnny could keep a secret. He had bought him a small notebook—same black cover as his own—and a decent pen.

At Urban Rainforest they were told that owl parrots were available by special order only. It could take up to two months and the cost would be five hundred dollars per bird. The store manager did not recommend them as pets because they were large and noisy at night. No, he could not remember selling one recently. The last one was maybe six months ago or more. He was kind enough to consult his computer and come up with the buyer's name— Peggy Harvey, who lived at 624 Conejo in El Cajon. He had sold a pair back in February of last year to Gary Deetz of San Diego. McMichael wrote down the information, as did Johnny.

Some fathers surf with their sons, he thought. Some interview witnesses.

The girl at Bird Brains told them much the same thing, but her price was three hundred and fifty dollars, delivery time two weeks, maybe less. She had a stainless steel stud implanted along one eyebrow, and a ring in the other, which made McMichael wince.

"God bless America!" squawked a green parrot who was loose in the store and was now walking up and down the sales counter.

"That's Ernie," said the girl. She smiled at Johnny. "Why do you want an owlie?"

"I don't. Dad's a detective and we're working a case."

"Cool. What are you, a sergeant?"

"Just a kid," he said shyly.

"Ever caught a bad guy?"

"No," he said, looking down.

"I'm a ladies' man!" shrieked Ernie.

She told them that she sold a pair of owlies about six months ago to a collector in San Diego. She was willing to dig through her receipts in the back if Johnny could watch the store. She winked at McMichael, who smiled and winced inwardly again as the stud winked, too.

McMichael and Johnny looked at the macaws and cockatoos, the cockatiels and Amazons, the mynahs and toucans and finches and doves. When Johnny approached Ernie, who now sat atop the cash register, the bird cocked his head with exaggerated curiosity.

"Show me the money!" he called out.

Johnny wrote in his notebook while the bird continued to eye him.

"Carry on. Carry on."

Johnny laughed and wrote and for a moment McMichael's heart felt light and free and he wanted to stay in this moment for hours.

Ten minutes later the girl came out, shaking her head. "Sorry, he paid cash, so I've got no check or card number or anything."

"Describe him."

"Whew, that was a while back. A guy. White guy. Middle-aged, maybe fifty. Good-looking, kind of athletic. Tall and fit . . . you know, slender. Short hair, blond I think."

"Glasses?"

"I can't remember."

"What was he wearing?"

"I can't remember that either."

"Did he say anything that stuck in your head?"

"No worries. No worries," said Ernie.

"I'm sorry," she said. "He just seemed like a regular guy who wanted a couple of owl parrots. Oh, I remember something. When I told him that the owl parrots stay up all night he said that wouldn't bother him, because his aviary was outside. He used the word 'aviary.' When a customer says that word, I always picture a big collection, with lights and screens and heat lamps and tropical plants and all. A real jungle."

"Got that, son?"

Johnny nodded, finishing up his entry in the black notebook. They both thanked her and headed to the door.

"Ya'll come back now, hear? Hear? Hear?"

At Birds of a Feather, a tall, storklike Englishman told them that he'd sold "perhaps a dozen" owl parrots since he opened three years ago. "Most of them go to collectors, you know? The serious fanciers."

"Any recent sales?"

"Yes. A woman purchased a pair—male and female—sometime last autumn. October, I believe."

He described the buyer as thirtyish, white, with blonde hair. Medium height. "If I remember right, she said it was a gift. Her husband was a fancier of the parrot in all its many forms, and he wanted this rather difficult bird for his collection."

"Do you have a way to look up her name?"

The man smiled and shook his head. "I don't keep track of that kind of information. Privacy, you know."

On Sunday they stopped by the Sons of Ireland Pancake Breakfast in Mission Bay. The syrup and salt air smelled good together and Johnny had a lightness about him that McMichael hadn't seen in months.

McMichael donated twenty dollars to the scholarship fund but told Hugh Spellacy he couldn't stay to help out with the cooking.

"My two days with Johnny," he said.

"It's okay, Tom," said Spellacy. "We've got things under control here. But Tom, can I have a word with you?"

McMichael followed Hugh down a walkway toward the bay, Hugh wiping his hands on the apron tied to his waist. They stopped and Hugh shook out a smoke and lit it, arching the match into a trash can. "Just about that gag the other night—I don't know where it was going."

"The gag?"

"Gabe and Tim and that game about them being in my pub the night before. They weren't. I figured you knew that, but given that Pete was killed and Gabriel's got this history . . ."

"What did he tell you to say?"

"He said to cover for him is what he said. Same with Tim. I mean, it's none of my business, Tom. But a man did die that night."

McMichael nodded but said nothing, suddenly angry at his father. Then the anger turned to something heavier as he seriously pondered the possibility of Gabriel and Tim being mixed up in the murder of Pete Braga. He looked back to find Johnny eyeing him, paper plate raised almost to his face.

"Tim and Gabe, you know," said Hugh Spellacy. "They've missed a few Wednesdays. They blame it on the meat pie special, but I don't think that's the truth of it."

"Thanks, Hugh."

An hour later they walked into the table tennis room at the Balboa Activity Center. They'd stumbled upon the games a year ago, and had been back almost every week since.

McMichael played a few games with Johnny, then retired to let the boy find some real competition. Johnny was already a mid-level seven-year-old but he easily cleaned McMichael's clock. There were twenty tables set up on Sundays, and players from all over the county.

McMichael stood back and watched Johnny square off with a young Chinese-American boy. He saw the focus come into his son's face, saw the way his concentration took him out of himself and into the game. McMichael loved the wide-eyed innocence with which Johnny tracked the rapid flight of the balls, loved his determination and his nascent grace, loved the sound of the paddles and the rhythm of the rallies, loved Johnny's smile when he'd made a good shot or had one made against him. What a feeling, to watch your son lose a close one and still shake hands when it was over.

He pictured Sally Rainwater, sitting in her cell in the women's jail. What could he have done differently in the beginning, except to ignore the voice that told him she was rare and good? What do you do with that voice, just say go away, I can't trust you?

Then he imagined Stephanie, sitting on the deck of her home, maybe reading a novel or talking with her new husband. Difficult to imagine her without all the ugliness that they became, and even more difficult now, with her body toned and her weight gone and a glow about her that he hadn't seen in years.

Strange, he thought, that the product of so much desire and heartache and disappointment could be the skinny little boy with the big eyes now rapping forehands back at his opponent with such an uncluttered, casual joy.

24

"We've got criminal negligence for leaving Pete Braga alone and defenseless," said Assistant District Attorney Gerald Dale. "Grand theft and illegal possession of controlled substances—pending the lab work on the pills. Right now I think we can get her for six, maybe eight years. But murder is the hard one. If we go with conspiracy we need her coconspirator. Otherwise we've got exculpatory prints on the gloves. Attempted murder with the drug in the wine? Dicey. We're still missing some large pieces if we want a good homicide case. But if we can do it right, prove conspiracy, come up with the partner and prove it was done in commission of a felony— guess what? That's capital. We can ask for death."

It was Monday morning, just after ten. The meeting was in Rawlings's office—Team Three, the prosecutor and Assistant Chief Jerry Bland.

"But she's killed before," said Hector. "Practically the same way."

"I might not even be able to get that into evidence," said Dale. "A sealed juvenile case? Self-defense? No, Hector—you guys want murder, you've got some work to do. You have to put that Fish Whack'r in someone's hands."

"What about the old boyfriend?" asked Rawlings.

"Dylan Feder," said McMichael. "He skipped on his parole officer last month and hasn't been seen since. But the prints on the weapon aren't his and we've got no evidence that he's here, or contacted her. Her phone records are due here this morning and we've got her address book. We'll be talking to people out at the university. That's one area we haven't looked into."

"A university student trying to become a doctor," said Rawlings. "This will make some news."

"Yes, sir," said McMichael. He stood and went to the window. Another clear cool day, one huge white cloud in front of the sun.

"What?" asked Rawlings.

"I don't like this case as much as I should," said McMichael. "The hummingbird. The cash. Those things are nothing compared to getting a piece of Pete Braga's estate. Pete was trying to write her into his will. He *told* her he was thinking about doing it. Why kill him if he was trying to cut her in? What's her motive?"

"A bird in the hand," said Bland. "A little jeweled bird. And you don't know what Pete was doing with his will. All you've got is lost letters and an old man's faulty memory. For all you know, he told the nurse to bugger off and find another sugar daddy. That's motive."

"I still don't like it as much as I should."

Over the weekend, he'd learned, Bland had talked to Rawlings and the chief about the PSU photographs and McMichael's relationship with Sally Rainwater. Ditto the rest of Team Three and, undoubtedly, Gerald Dale. McMichael had gotten over his initial shame. Now it was all out in the open and he felt like a man with a big scarlet "A" for asshole sewn on his shirt. By nine that morning he'd already gotten three messages from *Union-Tribune* reporters, two from the San Diego *Times*. Had they gotten onto him and Sally, or were they just calling because they still thought he was lead detective on the case?

"The search turned up some pretty convincing evidence," said Rawlings. "Do you think it was planted?"

"I believe it's possible."

Hector looked at him.

"By whom?" asked Rawlings.

"I have no idea," said McMichael.

"Oh, Christ," said Bland. "Your relationship with the suspect is affecting your judgment."

"It is," said McMichael.

"That doesn't make him wrong," Barbara said sharply. She glanced at McMichael, all cheer gone from her clear blue eyes. Then she turned back to Bland. "We've got to look at all the possibilities here. We're talking about a murder and a woman's life."

"Maybe you two should hire out to the defense," said Bland. He appeared to chew on something.

Rawlings raised his hands in a gesture of placation. "I put Hector in charge of the team," he said.

"That won't be enough if it gets to the media," said Bland. "Gerald, do you think she'll use this hanky-panky with McMichael?"

"Gene Goldman took the case on contingency from what I've heard," said Dale. "Wrongful arrest is what he's looking for, how he's going to get paid. So he'll damn well use it, if the charges are dropped or she's acquitted. But that's still ahead of us. We haven't charged her with anything but the stolen property. Yet."

"When you going to write them up, Gerald?" asked Hector.

"It's written and ready. I just wanted you guys clear on it—I can't file a murder or conspiracy charge with what I've got."

"We can add those later," said Rawlings. "Hector, it's your call now."

Hector glanced at McMichael, then his captain. "File what we've got. We'll come in with murder when we're ready."

"Done," said the prosecutor.

25

At noon McMichael and Hector drove onto the Rio Verde Reservation in north San Diego County. The village of Rio Verde greeted them with its poor face—rust-riddled cars in the dusty yards, washing machines on the porches and sun-faded sofas under towering, leafless sycamores. A little boy with a soft drink in his hand stared at them as they drove past.

But directly across the highway stood the new casino—seven restaurants, an entertainment complex, three hundred slot machines and sixty blackjack tables all housed in an immense and elegant brick-and-glass structure. The parking garage was three stories high.

Alex Dejano, tribal elder and operations manager for the Rio Verde Casino & Resort, welcomed them into his third-floor suite with crushing handshakes.

McMichael guessed him at six five or six, right at three hundred. Dark skin and eyes, a black ponytail, knife scars on his face and forehead, a sullen face that broke into an engaging smile when Dejano introduced himself.

Dejano explained that he'd been introduced to Pete Braga by Malcolm Case. Case was an old acquaintance who knew that Dejano—the Rio Verde tribe of Indians, to be more accurate—had some money that needed to be put to work.

"Casino money," said McMichael.

"The casino has turned out to be profitable," said Dejano. His voice was soft and high-pitched for such a big man, McMichael thought. He noted the scars and pits on Dejano's big, padded hands.

Dejano said that Pete Braga and Malcom Case had an idea to open a cargo terminal when the old airport closed, then link it up with the old Spreckels railroad that runs out to Imperial Valley.

"And Case's company, Pacific Transfer, would build the terminal," said McMichael.

Dejano nodded. "Rio Verde bought two million in Pacific Transfer stock," he said. "It looked like a good investment. But the rest of Pete's idea looked foolish to us. He wanted to build a fish cannery at Tuna Harbor, where the restaurant and Tunaboat Foundation is. Load up the railroad cars with his product and get richer."

"Not likely," said McMichael.

"Impossible is more like it," said Dejano. "You're talking ten, fifteen million to build a cannery like he wanted. Then you've got all the problems with the fleet and the licensing and the fishing regulations that keep changing, the porpoise and the competition and the high labor here in the States. All the same things that ran Pete's business out of here twenty years ago."

"Hasn't really changed," said McMichael.

"Not really. One thing you understand by now if you're an Indian—don't exploit the animals and the land around you. Exploit people. There's an endless supply of people. But you can only kill so many bison or deer or tuna before the supply dries up. You want to kill something, fine, but eat it. Don't sell it. I don't think Pete learned that. He was naive. Arrogant, too."

"Arrogant like how?" asked Hector.

"For instance, he wanted me to buy the right-of-way on Indian land for any new railroad track that would have to be built north of the border. See, the Congress and state legislature weren't happy about a railroad dipping down into Mexico—jurisdiction, narcotics, illegals—all sorts of problems. Pete's idea was to build some new track in East County and skip Mexico altogether. He assumed the native tribes who own that desert would give me a sweet deal for the rights because I'm a native, too. Because redskins are just one big happy savage family. And I'd sell them to him cheap. That's not how it works."

"So you decided not to buy into the cargo terminal, just into Case's company, which would do the construction," said Hector.

Dejano nodded his big head. "When Pete got killed we figured we'd back off. No telling what the Port Commission or the Tunaboat Foundation might do without Pete on them. Sink the whole project, if they felt like it. And just between you and me, I don't always trust Malcolm Case to do what's best for the Rio Verde people. Or anybody else, for that matter."

McMichael wrote quickly, trying to get his exact words. "Tell us about New Year's Eve," he said.

Dejano looked at him with unconcealed suspicion. "What about it?"

"We're interested in the nurse," said Hector.

Dejano stared placidly at them, dark eyes lost in the huge dark face. "She bash him?"

"We're thinking she may have been involved," said McMichael. "She might have known it was coming."

"Shit," said Dejano. "Pete loved her."

"Tell us about that," said Hector.

"You should have seen the gleam in that old man's eye when she walked into the room. Or when he talked to her. Or about her. I met Pete two years ago. Before the nurse, he was just an old fart who wouldn't admit his days were getting short. But after he hired her, he could laugh at himself some. He could see he wasn't right all the time. So if she set him up to get whacked . . . man, I don't know what to say."

McMichael noted the difference between Dejano's version of Pete and Patricia's version. Patricia saw him meaner; Dejano saw him happier.

"Pete ever say anything to you about changing his will?" asked Hector.

Dejano frowned and nodded. "That night, New Year's Eve. He was watching her make drinks and toss popcorn to Pete's dog. Me and Pete were over in the corner talking. He said he liked her so much he'd leave her the house if he could. I asked him why he couldn't. He just winked."

"That's all he said about it?" asked McMichael.

"Yeah, I took it as a joke, you know? We're all drunk. You're talking shit just to hear yourself say it."

McMichael wondered how Pete's comments would go over with his granddaughter. "Was Patricia there?"

"She and her husband were gone by then," said Dejano.

"Did Case and the nurse have a thing?" asked Hector, glancing at McMichael.

"Case is always talking up the pretty ones. It didn't look like he was getting very far."

"What about you and the nurse?" asked McMichael. Some inner wire twinged inside him. He felt it vibrate then go still.

The big man peered at McMichael, face darkening, thick fingers tapping his desktop. "I made a pass. Maybe two. I said if I ever met the guy who did her neck like that, I'd squeeze the brains out of his head."

"Get far with that line?" asked Hector.

"No."

"How'd your date like it?" asked McMichael.

"Put it this way. It was a New Year's, but it wasn't happy for me and my lady."

"The nurse and Victor get along?" asked Hector.

"They seemed to like each other."

"How about the nurse and Angel?"

Dejano shook his head. "Didn't meet any Angel."

"She was Pete's professional company," said Mc-Michael. "A prostitute."

"Never met her."

"How about Penny? She's a prostitute, too."

Dejano smiled. "Pete still had it in him, eh?"

"Until someone bashed it out," said Hector.

Dejano studied them in silence.

"I don't have any ideas about that," he finally said. "But I don't think the guy who did it was at the party. It was a holiday. That's friends and family."

"What about the nurse and Patricia?" asked Mc-Michael.

Dejano shrugged. "I don't remember them talking or doing anything together."

"They might not have much to say," said Hector, "if Patricia thought he wanted to give the house away."

"But Patricia wasn't there for that," said Dejano. "And I still think Pete was joking."

"Jokes are always true," said Hector.

And if this one was true and Patricia knew, thought McMichael, she had motive to kill her grandfather. He thought of how angry Patricia had been about the gifts to Sally Rainwater. *Common prostitute.* True, Patricia had known nothing about Pete's letters to Grothke, Steiner & Grothke—she'd asked McMichael to tell *her* what they were about. But she could have learned about Pete's plans some other way. Could she bludgeon him? Probably not. But what about someone else? Someone she could trust. Someone who'd stand to profit along with her? What about Garland? Or Victor? Something for Sally Rainwater meant less for them.

McMichael looked out the window to the pretty green hills of the reservation land, the little lake they'd built off to one side of the casino, the cloudless blue sky. He felt a shadow float over his soul. Motive and opportunity, he thought. Patricia might have had both.

"You see anybody feeding the dog, besides Sally Rainwater?" asked Hector.

"I gave him some mushrooms, I think. What's that got to do with anything?"

"He died that night of strychnine poisoning," said Hector. "We figure someone at the party did it."

"What the hell for?"

"Maybe get him out of the way."

"That's ugly, man. I didn't see anybody feed the dog except for me and Sally. Last I saw of the dog, Pete had him in his arms, dancing with him. Come to think of it, the dog didn't look too good. He was panting a lot, tongue hanging out."

McMichael pictured a drunken Pete waltzing with his poisoned dog. "How were Patricia and Pete with each other that night?" he asked.

Dejano shrugged again, big shoulders stretching the fabric of his shirt. "Old man kind of ignored her. Patricia, she gets along with people. In control of herself, you know? She brought a big bunch of flowers in a nice glass vase. Pete clipped one of them off with his pocketknife, stuck it in his lapel."

Driving back through Rio Verde, McMichael looked out at the poverty and neglect, wondered how much gambling money was coming back to the people.

What did they need with two million dollars of stock in Pacific Transfer when their own school bus stood broken down by the side of the road, tires flat and windows broken? What would it take to fix it—one hour's worth of casino profit?

"I didn't see Patricia or Garland as possible suspects," said McMichael.

"Me neither," said Hector. "But if Old Grothke's telling us the straight story, then the nurse's cut has to come out of someone else's."

"It doesn't read right to me," said McMichael. He thought of Garland Hansen's heated reaction to seeing him with Victor that night at the Waterfront. He'd assumed that Garland was just eager to lay the blame for Pete on the most obvious person—Sally Rainwater. But laying the blame on Sally could be part of a show.

"That would be funny, wouldn't it?"

"What's that, Heck?"

"Us putting the wrong person in jail."

Back at his desk, McMichael had two more phone messages from newspaper reporters and one from a local television news station. He couldn't believe they were onto him and Sally Rainwater so fast, but what else could it be? Was Sally's lawyer behind it, lighting the fires? He screwed up his courage and called them back, grateful to get two answering machines and only one live body, who told him that the television news reporter was in makeup and not available.

He got through to Charley Farrell, who had sold three wine-colored SUVs in the last three months.

McMichael took down the names, addresses and phone numbers of the proud new owners: Andre Proulx of San Diego, Dawn Bigley of Carlsbad and Eqbar Quatrah of La Jolla.

Then he logged on to VICAP for an update on Dylan Feder. Thirty-four days into his parole skip and he still had not been seen.

McMichael talked to Feder's Dade County parole officer, a rough-voiced man named Norm Briggs. Briggs said he had thought Feder was going to play it straight, because he'd checked out of prison and into his designated Miami motel, contacted his P.O., went out and got a job selling advertising space in an adult newspaper. He'd found a girlfriend, passed four drug tests, seemed to be turning things around.

"Then he cut out," said Briggs. "Now he's looking at eighteen more months in lockup, just for skipping out on a job and a girl and me. Stupid. Another year he'd have been free and clear."

"Any idea where he went?"

"I got a maybe from Dallas PD, and I got a maybe from Tucson PD."

"Coming west."

"Sally still in San Diego?"

"We just arrested her in connection with a robbery-homicide."

McMichael explained the basics.

"That surprises me," said Briggs. "I had her for a pretty good lady with bad judgment when it comes to men."

"Probably so," said McMichael.

"Feder's terms don't let him within fifty miles of

her. That's good for the rest of his life. He never said one word to me about her. But hey, a hundred bucks to a PI and he's got an address and phone."

"Where's he likely to show up?"

"He's a ladies' man. Clubs, bars. Anywhere there's women to prey on. He was selling space in one of those dating tabloids here in Miami. Doing pretty well for himself. You might look into the local skin rags."

"Are the VICAP mugs good?"

"He changes his facial hair a lot—mustache and a little Vandyke—there one day and gone the next. He's a body guy, too, always in the gym. Big muscles, tight clothes. You know the type."

"No aka's?"

"None he's used before. But you can bet he's got at least one now."

It took McMichael just two calls to get Dade County Juvenile Court judge Paul Ramos on the line. He remembered Sally Gaglosta and was also surprised to hear of her arrest.

"How good was her self-defense story?" McMichael asked.

"It was her against him. She was lucid and specific and credible. He was dim and contradictory. She told me she hit him with the dull side of that cleaver so she wouldn't hurt him too bad. I believed her, and thought it was a remarkable thing to be thinking, under the circumstances. Trouble is, the dull side's the heavy side and she hit him where the skull was weak from the motorcycle crash. Now, he'd been a pillar before the accident—degree from the University of Florida, worked in a local bank, churchgoer. Sally, she came from bad circumstances in Pike County, Kentucky. I talked to her mother, one of her sisters. Sad, troubled lives. I thought it was to Sally's credit that she'd risen above those circumstances as far as she had."

McMichael thought a moment. "Did you have any evidence that she was working it somehow—stealing, or manipulating him?"

"The investigators turned everything upside down at least once and didn't come up with anything. Not long after, her boyfriend tried to kill her. To be honest with you, I wasn't surprised."

"How so?"

"Sally Gaglosta has bad luck. Pure and simple. Just being born into that family was bad enough. Then the attack, then this boyfriend shooting her. I'm not saying she's a bad person at all. She's not, in my opinion. Just, some people, they're lightning rods for trouble. She's one of them. Miami's no place to be with luck like hers."

While McMichael thought about this thing called luck, he ran records checks on Proulx, Bigley and Quatrah. Bigley and Quatrah came back clean.

But Proulx popped with convictions for assault and soliciting prostitution.

Boom, thought McMichael. The other kind of luck.

McMichael looked through Sally Rainwater's phone records. Most of her calls for November, December and early January were local. With the help of a reverse directory and the security departments of both the cell and landline phone companies, he put names to all of them.

An hour later he'd run warrant and records checks, finding all but one of them clean. There were calls to the school friend she'd talked to from Ye Olde Plank on the night of the murder. Two sisters back East. She'd called Dr. Jonathan Bailes of the University of California at La Jolla twice in November. She had called her mother in Hagville, Kentucky, just once, at noon PST on Christmas day. And her brother—the convicted pot farmer—in Pikeville a few minutes later.

Nothing seemed unusual and nothing caught McMichael's eye. He talked briefly to the girlfriend and the professor, and they seemed concerned, willing to talk, and straight up. The other brother was still in prison. The sisters were out of state. She hadn't called a soul in Florida.

Where was her accomplice? And how was she talking to him or her or them? Pay phones, he thought. Or maybe he was calling her. Or maybe there wasn't one.

The desk officer called him at two-thirty to say that McMichael had a visitor in the lobby. "Lance Wood," said the desk cop. "He says he wants to talk to you about Pete Braga."

"Can we go outside?" asked Lance Wood. He looked at McMichael with steady blue eyes, then turned to look behind him. He looked early twenties, tall and tanned, with a thatch of straw-blond hair. He was wearing a hooded sweatshirt, shorts and thongs despite the cool January afternoon. McMichael noted the edge of a plastic shopping bag visible in the sweatshirt pocket.

"How come?" asked McMichael.

"Because this is a police station."

"Let's go outside."

They sat on a planter wall, well away from the headquarters entrance. McMichael looked out at the old gray buildings, humbled against the intense blue sky.

"I got your name from the paper," said Wood.

"Okay."

"I scavenge the harbor a couple times a week in my kayak, hit the good spots for finds. After a storm I go out for sure, because the high tides wash up all sorts of good stuff. I was down off of Point Loma a couple of days after that Braga guy got killed, but I didn't know it."

"Didn't know about Pete?"

"Yeah, I don't read the news or watch TV, so I just heard about it two days ago from one of the guys out surfing at Ralph's. He said the old man got beat to death with a fish club right in his own house. The wood and glass one down at Poinsettia Street."

"That's what happened."

Lance Wood reached into the front pocket of his sweatshirt and pulled out a plastic bag with something in it. "I found this down the beach from that house. Friday, after he got killed."

Wood slid a fish bat from the bag. It looked identical to the one lying in Pete's blood in the trophy room.

"Set it on the wall here," said McMichael.

"I've touched it a bunch."

"That's okay."

"When I heard about the old guy, I looked hard at this thing. Thought maybe it was important."

McMichael looked down at the bat. Exactly like the one they'd gotten at Braga's, so far as he could see. "I'm going to have to take this," said McMichael.

"That's why I brought it."

McMichael wrote down his address and phone, talked a little about kayaking and scavenging the bay, found out that Lance had gone to the same high school he did, knew a few of the same families.

"Sorry it took so long," Wood said. "I keep stuff. I hung it on a nail in the garage, figured I might find a use for it someday."

"Don't be. Will you show me where you found it?"

"About a hundred yards south of the house."

"I mean exactly," said McMichael.

"I can do that."

"I'll drive."

"You'll have to. I walked here."

McMichael carried the bat back into the building, took it upstairs, asked Hector to book it into evidence ASAP, get it to Arthur Flagler in the lab and run an NCIC check on Lance Wood. He wrote down Wood's phone and address and hustled back downstairs.

When he came back down Wood was still sitting on the wall. McMichael led the way to his car. "How come you don't like the cop house?" he asked.

"I got busted for pot when I was nineteen. One joint. Cop shoved me and my girlfriend around more than he had to. A lot more. So I shoved back, and got the living shit beat out of me, right in front of her."

"That's rough."

"You're telling me."

Lance Wood had found the club on the beach, one hundred and eight McMichael steps from the south corner of the wall in front of Pete Braga's house.

"It was here," said Wood. "About fifty feet above the waterline, but the tide was low by then. It could have washed up, or it could have been dropped. Buried, maybe."

They stood on a pretty little beach, a spit of sand that swept gracefully into the bay. The remnant of an old seawall angled from the sand down into the water. A bright white gull stood on the wall and eyed them antisocially. To the south McMichael saw the boatyard cranes rising into the pale blue sky, a Coast Guard cutter on patrol, the barren tip of Coronado Island. A silver passenger jet lowered over the hills toward Lindbergh Field.

"Think it's the murder weapon?" asked Lance.

"We'll have to look at it," said McMichael.

He drove Wood to his Pacific Beach apartment, getting a message from Hector on the way: Wood had come up as a convicted drug offender on NCIC—possession of marijuana, nineteen ninety-eight, clean since.

McMichael asked him about it.

"I was just young and got caught," said Wood. "Everybody smoked grass. I guess you guys can find out anything about anybody."

"Just the bad stuff," said McMichael. "The computer won't tell anybody that you helped a cop. So, thank you."

Wood nodded, frowning. "No problem."

McMichael stepped into Pete Braga's trophy room. Again he pictured the silver-haired old man there, oblivious to the intruder as the wind kicked at the window glass. He pictured the man in the dark jogging suit, creeping straight toward the fireplace with the club he'd use on Pete. He pictured the club coming up in the gloved hand, and he heard the first shattering, pressurized concussion of aluminum on bone. He saw Pete's body vibrating as it slumped, the blood flying off the club every time it was raised, the roostertail of liquid splattering against the lights. Again and again. Sixteen times, at least.

You're tired and you're breathing hard, but you think you're smart, don't you? You see the tear in your glove, but you've planned for this—you know the wall club is clean and will stay clean, if you're just careful. And you are. You set down your weapon near Pete, go to the trophy wall and lift the Fish Whack'r off the nail between the dorado and the barracuda, gently, by the leather strap, and you rest it in the bloody pool next to Pete, then let it drop. This way, the cops will have the wrong one to work with from the start. This way, the murder weapon can go into the storm that will wipe it clean.

Yes, McMichael thought: you knew about the club on the wall and you got one just like it. To cover and confuse. To make things harder on us. You gave us the *wrong* murder weapon.

And you knew exactly when the nurse was gone. Because you watched her from your car, parked in the darkness on the street, figuring she'd have to leave him alone one of these nights? Because you'd seen her do it before? Or because she told you?

And you knew Zeke wouldn't be a problem because you took care of the little terrier once and for all on New Year's Eve. Eat, eat. Dance, dance. Pant, pant.

Maybe you fed him the poison from outside that night. Maybe you snuck up to the wall and tossed him a treat. Maybe.

Or maybe you were invited to the party. Because you are friend, or family, or an acquaintance valuable in business.

You thought you were smart and careful and clever, but you weren't smart enough to know your fingerprints would be inside the gloves. Or that your club would wash up on shore.

McMichael walked to the sliding glass door and unlocked all three locks. He pulled it open to a fresh blast of air, trotted across the sand, hopped the wall and headed south toward Aster Street. For a moment he stood there and looked back to where the street hit the beach—concrete steps with a rust-pitted handrail, steel warning stanchions with reflectors, a large Norfolk Island pine casting the end of the cul-de-sac into shade. Entirely possible, he thought, that the neighbors just didn't see the car.

He imagined the basher, breathing hard as he grabbed a handful of sand and ran it up and down the handle of the Fish Whack'r, then hurled it into the bay. Too dark to see it land. Too windy to hear it.

Then the gloves—jamming them into the wet sand to clean them, peeling them off from the back, stuffing them down into the warm-up jacket, then deep into the trash can. You can't be stopped or seen with the gloves on. You can't be stopped or seen with the bloody jacket.

Now he's running for the car. He knows he just has to drive away, and he'll never be caught. The storm makes him think everything's going to be covered, changed, erased. He doesn't know that the storm will trick him, wash his weapon onto the shore. He doesn't know that his prints are on the latex.

McMichael's cell phone vibrated against his side and Captain Don Rawlings's voice yanked him back to reality.

"We found Courtney Gonzalez down in the desert," he said. "Shallow grave, the coyotes got some of her. Had two hundred dollars and a CDL in her coat pocket."

"Angel," said McMichael.

"She is now," said Rawlings. "Rattlesnake Gorge Road. Two miles north of Highway Eight. Sheriffs are there."

26

Hector drove east, fast, a gumball on top to clear the traffic and the windows cracked for the good cool air. McMichael tossed aside the map book and watched San Diego turn into La Mesa, El Cajon, Alpine, Japutul, Pine Valley. They climbed into the huge rock formations of the San Vicente Mountains, tremendous tan boulders piled precariously skyward as if dumped there by a god with leftover material.

Rattlesnake Gorge Road looped north into Anza-Borrego State Park. McMichael could see a helicopter hovering above a glint of metal far out in the desert. Hector turned onto a dirt road, breaking the tires loose with a satisfied grin, rocks popping off the undercarriage of the Crown Vic as he gunned it to outrun the dust.

There were two INS trucks, three sheriff's cruisers and an evidence van parked in a line along the right side of the road. Hector slowed well in advance and rolled in behind the van. The helicopter was fixed in the sky as if painted on.

They trudged abreast through the rocky terrain. McMichael picked his way around the cholla cacti, their needles blond and brilliant in the raw desert sun. Tan sand. Tan boulders rising against the sky. Two vultures circling high as if this was old news to them, which, McMichael realized, it was.

They stood with the other men outside a rectangle of crime scene ribbon wrapped around a spindly ocotillo and three cholla. Before them a young woman lay facedown in a shallow hole. Black hair, dark skin, black remnants of clothing stuck to her swollen body, a black leather jacket caught on one wrist but otherwise pulled completely off and inverted. One hand had been chewed off. Her left boot lay ten yards away with part of her leg still in it. Large green flies droned above her without marked enthusiasm, strangely audible within the broader sound of the chopper.

"Fuck," said Hector.

"That's eloquent," said one of the INS agents.

"Fuck *you*," McMichael said quietly. "How's that?"

"We're the ones who found her," said the agent. "Following some illegals through the hills."

"And we found some money and her driver's license snapped in one of the jacket pockets," said a deputy. "My watch commander is tight with Captain Rawlings, so we got the word to you fast."

McMichael looked back to the road. It was only eighty feet away and both the INS and San Diego sheriff's vehicles were parked well short of where the dumper's vehicle would likely have been parked. But the recent storm would have made it this far east, he knew, destroying any tire tracks, footprints or drag marks. Looking down at the ground around him McMichael saw no marks at all, just desert soil, cleaned by rain and baked hard again by the sun. Even the animal tracks had been washed away.

Two hours later Bob Harley and Erik Fiore had put what was left of Courtney Gonzalez into a body bag and the body bag into an SDPD Field Evidence Team van. Harley said it looked to him like the body had been there for at least two weeks, but Stiles would be able to tell better when he got her on the table. Hector had told Barbara to stay with Flagler while he worked the second fish bat— nothing to do out in the desert but watch the crime scene guys scoop up a girl who didn't deserve to die.

The INS and sheriffs were gone, leaving just McMichael and Hector standing near the shallow grave as the evidence van wobbled away down the dirt road.

"Victor?" asked McMichael. "Kill the thing you love but can't have?"

Hector shook his head. "But he can't even drive. Not supposed to drive, anyway."

"Then you try," said McMichael.

Hector walked around the grave, toed a rock, looked up at the mountains of boulders surrounding them. "There's the brothers, not willing to take a chance on Victor blabbing company secrets to the girl of his dreams. And Angel blabbing those secrets to customers, or us."

"I can buy that," said McMichael. "Or maybe she already talked. Maybe this was just payback from Auto Leather International. Basic damage control."

Hector thought about this, kicked a rock. "There's lots of creeps who prey on the working girls. Maybe Angel just got unlucky."

McMichael nodded, squinting in the ferocious sunlight. "I don't think it's a coincidence, Heck."

"No such thing," said Hector.

"Let's see what Mr. Assault and Solicitation was up to that night."

Andre Proulx was tall, lean and handsome. He was thirty-one, with an assault conviction on a prostitute in New Orleans in 1994 and a soliciting conviction in Los Angeles in '96. He was the lead chef and one-third partner in a Gaslamp restaurant called Provençal, which is where McMichael and Hector found him at three o'clock that afternoon.

He stood at a counter in his kitchen whites with a knife in one hand and a bunch of carrots in the other.

"It is not always good to see the police," he said with a wry smile. His voice was deep and clear and accented.

"It's never good to see creeps like you," said Hector, sliding his badge back into his pocket. "Put that knife down and come over here."

Proulx set the knife on the counter and tossed the carrots beside it. He was goateed and sharp-nosed, with a shaved head and a gold stud in his left ear. His face was compact and well proportioned.

"How can I help you?" he asked.

"Tell us about January second," said McMichael. "Thursday night."

"May I go to my calendar? It is in the office, over here."

Hector held out his hand and Proulx ambled through the kitchen, past the stoves and freezers, to a storage corner piled with white plastic tubs. He moved with a lanky ease, something casually superior in his walk. At the far wall he swung open a door.

The office was small and cluttered, with a steel desk and folding metal chairs, two telephones, a computer and printer. The walls had posters of the French countryside and American dragsters taped at careless angles.

Proulx went behind the desk and sat, then tapped the keyboard and stared at the monitor.

"I was working, of course," he said. "It was one of my kitchen nights. Bad weather. We served forty dinners. The scallops did not arrive and we disappointed several customers."

"When was your last seating?" asked McMichael.

"Approximately ten."

"When did they leave?" asked Hector.

Proulx looked up at them. "I think eleven-thirty."

"Then what?" asked McMichael.

"I walked over to *Libertad* to smoke and relax. I let the manager and crew do the scrubbing and cleaning that night. I was in the kitchen from morning on. Very tired."

McMichael and Hector traded glances, and it hit McMichael.

I met a nice guy last week. Local restaurateur. Very French. Very handsome, very mysterious.

"Why do you need a computer to tell that?" asked Hector.

Proulx smiled. It was a happy, uneven grin. "It just helps me remember. These winter nights? They all seem very similar."

"Tell me about *Libertad*," said McMichael.

"I stayed there for maybe one hour. I talked to the owner. At twelve-thirty I walked back here to my apartment. It is over us, on floor four."

"Then what?" asked Hector.

"I drank two glasses of Bordeaux and showered. I was in the bed by one or one-thirty."

"Alone?" asked McMichael.

Proulx looked down with an air of reluctance, rolled his shoulders. "I was with a woman."

"Raegan," said McMichael. He stared at Proulx, but saw Hector glance his way.

Proulx smiled his sunny smile but the rest of his face was dark. "Yes. Do you know her?"

"She's my sister."

Proulx looked at McMichael as if he'd been caught at something but wasn't quite sure what. "What am I being asked to do?"

"To answer simple questions," said Hector.

"Am I not to date a policeman's sister?"

"You're not to beat women or solicit prostitutes in my city," said McMichael. "I'm not so sure you should even *be* in my city."

"Yes, I am," said Proulx. "I have resident status. I am documented. All of that trouble is the past."

Hector leaned across the desk and looked at

Proulx like he was something in a zoo. "This guy doesn't get it, Tom."

"Not fully."

"What do you got inside that skull of yours, Andre—onions?"

"Shallots, of course."

Hector pushed back from the desk, shaking his head. "Let's just deport him."

"You can't," said Proulx. "I have resident sta—"

"You tell Raegan about your criminal record?" McMichael asked.

Proulx's face hardened into a look of dinged pride. "No."

"You jerk-wad cowards never do," said Hector.

Proulx stared at him. "It's the past. I'm trying to forget it and be a better man."

"Take it easy," said Hector. "I'll tell Raegan for you."

"Please don't. I like her very much."

"But you beat the shit out of women you *don't* like quite so much?" asked McMichael.

"Never again," said Proulx. "Look, I was very young. And foolish. The assault was a slap, when my money was stolen. The solicitation was when I was drunk and unhappy. Never again. I have a business now, and we're doing well here. I have no time for these things."

"Any time for Angel Gonzalez?" asked McMichael.

He watched Proulx's face closely but saw no deceit in it, which meant nothing.

"I don't know Angel Gonzalez."

"Sure you do," said Hector. "She's the working

girl with the pretty face and the dimples. Been up and down the sidewalk out there about a million times."

"No. I haven't seen her."

"Well, some people saw you," said McMichael. "Thursday, January two. You were in your pretty new SUV, picked up Angel Gonzalez on Broadway, drove toward the harbor."

Proulx frowned and shook his head. McMichael saw the first signs of worry in his face. "Impossible. Ask Raegan."

"If her story is any different than yours," said Hector, "I'm going to throw you back in jail."

"That's okay," said Proulx.

"What is?" asked McMichael.

"She will drop me. Raegan will drop me, but that's okay."

"My heart's breaking," said Hector.

Proulx shot a look at him, and in it McMichael saw anger and control.

"I will tell her myself," he said.

"Too late for that," said McMichael.

They sat across the street at Bombay, drinking coffee outside and waiting for Andre to come hustling out, bound for *Libertad* and a scene with Raegan. McMichael called her on his cell phone and confirmed that Andre Proulx had indeed been in her company on the night in question. Raegan was unhappy to learn of Andre's past but did a cavalier job of hiding it. She had always fought pain with good humor.

Proulx came outside Provençal just once, to write

the specials on the sidewalk menu in bright pink chalk. Squatting in front of the stand, he traced a line down the back of the hostess's calf and she bapped him with a handful of menus, giggling.

"Creep," said Hector. "See, that's what I was saying about women. Why they put up with guys like that while it takes me two, three *nights* of yapping to come up with a phone number. I don't get it."

"I guess Andre does."

"Hire them for sex, beat them, lie to them. And Raegan? She's smart. She's been around, knows the score."

McMichael didn't get it, either.

Just before five o'clock, a disheveled Arthur Flagler came into the Team Three pen to announce that he'd found microscopic bone fragments on Fish Whack'r #2, and that Bob Harley had coaxed fingerprints and a "respectable partial palm print" from the handle using the bench laser.

"Unfortunately, there aren't many palm prints in the fingerprint registers," he said. "Give me three days for a DNA comparison on the bone frags. I did a visual comparison of Lance Wood's prints and the prints on the inside of the gloves. No match."

McMichael smiled. "You're amazing, Arthur."

"I know."

San Diego *Times* reporter Rob Skelton called a little after six.

"Can you help me round out a suspect profile on Sally Rainwater?" he asked.

McMichael told him he couldn't discuss an active

case or ongoing investigation—department policy. Public Information might be able to help him.

"I really don't enjoy being nosy, but were you involved with her?" asked Skelton.

"I can't discuss an active case or ongoing investigation," McMichael said again, his heart plummeting toward the lobby four floors below.

"I'm going with what I have, then," said the reporter.

McMichael hung up. Gene Goldman, he thought—Sally's lawyer—loading the cannons for battle.

He called the women's jail out in Santee.

McMichael walked into the jail at seven-thirty and said he was there to see inmate Sally Rainwater. A few minutes later the amused deputy said that he would be allowed a contact visit, not the standard phoner between the glass. He was told there would be no touching of any kind—no hugging or shaking hands—nothing.

McMichael surrendered his weapon and was pat searched before being led into a glass-walled room.

Sally came in wearing the jail suit—blue, too big, the same plastic shower sandals Jimmy Thigpen had. Her hair was pulled back in a tight ponytail and her face looked caved and haunted.

They sat across a table from each other.

"You've got the wrong person," she said.

"Were you set up?"

"All the way."

"Do you know who?"

"I've got no idea."

"I'm doing what I can. Things aren't lining up just right."

"For you or for me?"

He nodded. "For anybody. Look, the press is onto us. I figure Goldman is trying to make the PD look bad. I thought we'd both be better off without bringing that in. What I'm saying is, we don't have to talk about it."

She shook her head. "I haven't told him."

McMichael saw a female deputy stroll by on the other side of the glass wall, trying to look disinterested.

"I haven't told anyone," she said. "So it had to come from your side."

McMichael felt cool pricks of sweat on his scalp. Bland. Rawlings. Barbara and Sergeant Hatter. IAD and their foot soldiers, the Professional Standards Unit. Right on down to Rob Skelton at the *Times*.

"Then I've got a problem," he said.

"It's going to be mine, too. Though Gene might not see it that way. I guess we could be a large embarrassment to the department."

McMichael looked straight into her dark brown eyes, saw exhaustion. "You should have told me about Florida," he said.

Sally shook her head. "It was an ugly thing and it made me ashamed, even though I had to do what I did. You know what it's like to carry around a memory like that? When I think of it, it all comes back. I can feel his body and smell his breath. I wasn't ready to go there. Not in front of you."

"It looks bad, the circumstances being similar."

"They weren't similar at all. That man in Florida came at me fast and hard. Stronger than hell. He was going to do it. He was going to rape me right there in the kitchen. It wasn't part of my job to get raped. Did you come to threaten me with that?"

"No, please. I didn't. I'm not."

"Why did you come?"

"I wanted to make sure you were okay."

"I'm fine. You're pathetic."

McMichael nodded and went to the door.

"You don't know quality when you see it," said Sally.

He waited while the deputy moved toward the door to let him out.

"Anna's hummingbird," she said. "The one you found at my place? That wasn't from Pete's. Pete's was genuine. The one they planted in my home was fake. It was obvious."

"I'll have it examined."

"You do that."

The deputy let McMichael out. When he looked back through the glass the room was empty.

He sat with Hector in a corner of *Libertad*, lost in the smoke of a Churchill, a tumbler of tequila on the coffee table in front of him. He watched Raegan making her rounds. She looked waiflike as she moved through the crowded room, red hair bouncing and her eyes set like peridots in her fair, thrifty face. A group of pretty young women had taken Teofilo's Room and McMichael could see them through the glass, noting how absolutely they ignored him. A batch of young San Diego firemen occupied Papa's Place, and the Cuba Room was filled with a raucous birthday celebration featuring much howling and a dancer in a thong and silver heels. Through the big windows McMichael could see Fifth Avenue, busy for a post-stormy Monday, pedestrians hustling through the traffic and diners still waiting for tables at nine.

Raegan broke away and sat down with them, setting her martini glass on the table. McMichael knew it was only water, but Raegan floated a twist in it to set a festive tone for her establishment. She looked a little dark in the eyes.

"You handsome brutes behaving yourselves?"

"I'm trying my best," said Hector. "But it doesn't come naturally."

She glanced into Teofilo's. "Tom, I happen to know that one of those young ladies likes the way you look."

McMichael nodded but said nothing. *You don't know quality when you see it.*

"She have a friend?" asked Hector.

"Dozens. You guys look wrung out as I feel. Long day?"

McMichael nodded and sipped his drink. "Sorry about Andre. But his name came up and we had to check him out."

He told her about the sighting of the wine-colored SUV, and the list of new owners given to him by Charley Farrell. She squinted just slightly, McMichael able to trace this look of deliberation back as long as he had known her, held her on his lap, rocked with her, held her hand as she put one miniature shoe in front of the other and learned to walk.

"To tell you the truth," she said, "Andre's sell-by date was already up."

"You can do a lot better than him," said Hector. "And be careful of him. These roosters, when you ruffle their little feathers . . ."

"Thanks, Heck," she said with a weak smile. "Well, back on the chain gang!"

She gulped the water dramatically, messed up Hector's shining black hair, kicked McMichael's leg and edged back into her crowd.

Just after ten the Axelgaard brothers and two other men walked in, all smiles for the ladies in Teofilo's. One of the women held open the door and in walked the four men. The brothers were well muscled and walked with an air of importance. Mason—balding, mustachioed—wore a black leather sport coat and jeans. Golden-haired Martin, the U.S. Customs man, was dressed in a black suit that swayed expensively as he walked. The other two were Mexican and dressed for nightclubbing. Could be anything from DEA to cartel enforcers, thought McMichael; this close to the border, the lines got blurred.

Hector buried his face in a magazine. McMichael headed for the restroom on the other side of the room. He didn't think that Martin remembered him from the border crossing, which suggested arrogance and a low level of attention. McMichael had often found dull people to be the most explosive and, oddly enough, the most successful criminals.

Hector met him in the bathroom. McMichael

leaned against the door and Hector hit the hand dryer. "If we stay, they'll make us," he said.

Hector nodded. "Let's wait outside and tail them."

"I'll get Raegan's keys. We're dead in the Ford."

They sat across the street in Raegan's ride, a little BMW sports car with nifty analog gauges and a red leather interior. An hour later, the brothers came out with two pretty women and got into a black Mercedes four-door parked in a red zone. The men took the front seats, women the back. A moment later the car slid away from the curb with a chirp of tires.

"Maybe the other two guys are looking for people like us," said Hector. "Is there a back way out of Raegan's?"

"Yeah, but she won't let customers use it."

"Smart girl. I wonder where the party is."

It was at the Hyatt, site of Jimmy Thigpen's attempted celebration back in December. The Mercedes pulled into self parking so McMichael did, too, finding a space far enough away to watch. The fab four walked across the lot, each brother coupled up with one of the women. The women both wore high-heeled shoes and their long blonde hair shone in the lot lights.

McMichael and Hector climbed out of the little car and followed at a distance, talking loudly about the Super Bowl—it would come down to defense and special teams if you asked Hector, McMichael braying about the underdogs and five points but sticking with the overs and unders for serious money.

They stopped and backed into the shadow of the big building when the brothers and their dates turned for the lobby.

"I don't think we're invited," said Hector.

They stood in the shadow for a while, watching an occasional car head past them for the parking lot. McMichael looked up at the clear sky and the stars sprinkled in the dark, saw a falling star and wished his son would become a good man.

"I wonder what Jimmy did with his cash," said Hector. "All those border runs. Something tells me he made a lot more than three hundred grand."

"Yeah," said McMichael, "If you're running cartel loads across the line with a Mack track, you're in for some good money."

They had just stepped out of the shadows when a familiar Ford sedan glided down the drive toward the parking lot. Just instinct, then, as McMichael saw the radio antenna on top and pulled Hector back into the darkness.

They waited two minutes to see Jerry Bland come marching toward the lobby, dressed in a gray suit and carrying a leather briefcase. McMichael had to stare at him an extra beat just to believe his own eyes.

Half an hour later Bland strode back across the parking lot and let himself into the sedan as McMichael and Hector watched from the cramped little sports car. Bland swung the briefcase into the back, shut the door quietly and climbed into the driver's seat.

"He was in on it with Thigpen," said Hector. "That's why he's been riding your ass about what

Jimmy knows. So worried about how his department is going to look. Assistant goddamned fucking chief of police."

McMichael just stared. Bland pulled from his space and swung onto the drive. McMichael started Raegan's car and followed a long way back.

"And he had IAD take those pictures of you and the nurse, just to keep you busy with something else," said Hector.

McMichael watched the sedan roll toward the boulevard. He let a Caddy that was leaving the hotel go in front of him, then a Porsche.

Then a clear picture cracked in McMichael's mind, like lightning in a black sky.

Boom.

"What about this, Hector—*Pete went to Bland about Jimmy.* That's why nobody else at San Diego PD ever knew. But Pete wondered why Bland didn't do anything. Pete wanted action. Bland put him off as long as he could, then had him shut up."

"How?"

"He went to the Axelgaards for help—it's their problem, too, right?—and they put him onto a clean cartel boy from south of the border—no prints, no record. Get him up for the job, get him back the same night. Pete got hit on a Wednesday night. That's Tijuana night. Everybody was in place. Clean."

"Bland," muttered Hector. "What's he do to earn his keep with these guys?"

"He's police protection *upstairs, seventh floor,*" said McMichael. "He keeps the department off of Jimmy and the brothers. And what about the distribution

end—they're moving seventy-five kilos of something through the border every week. It's got to
make the streets here. Bland knows what Narcotics
is up to—the assistant chiefs have full access to all
department operations except IAD's. With him on
the inside, the sellers know where the heat's going
to be."

"Oooh," crooned Hector. "This is getting good
in lots of bad ways."

"Why not?"

"I didn't say I didn't like it. Keep going, Mick."

"Let's get particular—Bland took care of Zeke
at the party. He knew about Sally being with Pete
five days a week and figured she was good to hang
a frame on. He set her up with some stolen property. Like you said, I walked into the mess and got
my picture taken. More diversion. More clutter."

"Sure. Okay."

"And I think you were right, back in Rattlesnake
Gorge—these guys took out Angel because Victor
would tell her anything to get a date. Victor's the
liability but Angel paid the price. I like that. It lines
up."

Hector exhaled, shaking his head. "None of them
drives a wine-colored sport ute with Pete Braga
plates."

"I can't explain that yet," said McMichael. "I'm
going to lean on the dealership guy, though."

"How did Bland get the earrings out of Pete's
place?"

"Same way the hitter got in. He just waited until
Sally and Pete went on an errand."

"He wouldn't know the combination to the floor safe," said Hector.

"The earrings weren't in the floor safe. They were in the jewelry box in Anna's old dresser."

Hector looked hard at McMichael. "But why would Bland frame the nurse with a cheap hummingbird instead of the real one?"

"So he could pocket the real thing."

"Who spiked Pete's wine?"

"The hitter, on his way out," said McMichael. "Just like Bland told him to."

"The hitter, not the nurse?"

"No meperedine in Pete's system, right? That's because it was a postmortem spike. The drug wasn't for Pete, it was to implicate Sally. Just like the two fish clubs were for us. That's the beauty of it— Bland knew the layout at Pete's place, right down to the Fish Whack'r. I'm liking this, Hector. You're liking it, too, I know you are."

"Getting the nurse out of jail is what you'd like."

"Sure as hell would."

Hector leaned closer. "How about this, McMichael—you like taking down an assistant chief for dope and murder?"

"Sure," said McMichael. His throat felt thick and his heart was pounding hard. "Why not?"

"I wonder where he does his banking," said Hector.

They followed Bland, safely padded by at least two cars, McMichael vaguely remembering that the assistant chief lived in Kensington. Thirteen minutes later Bland turned onto a residential street of clean little houses. It looked like a street from the thirties, cute porches and rose beds and everybody's lawn happy and neat. McMichael pulled over and cut the lights. The Ford slid into a garage as the door scrolled up to a stop. The welcome-home light was already on. A tiny gray-haired woman in a robe came from the side door and hugged him when he got out of the car.

Twenty minutes later they woke up Captain Rawlings in his home out in Alpine. He answered the door with an unhappy expression on his face and a .357 magnum revolver in his hand.

They sat in his den with the door closed and told him the story. Rawlings sat in the dim lamplight, an aging man in a worn robe.

By the time McMichael was finished telling him what they'd seen, Rawlings seemed to have grown smaller. "When's the next run to Tijuana?" he asked quietly.

"Day after tomorrow," said McMichael. "Wednesday."

"We can arrest the brothers at the border, and serve Bland a search warrant one minute later. I'll go to Judge Abella tomorrow. He can keep a secret for forty-eight hours. Maybe."

"That gives Bland two days to lose the money," said Hector.

Rawlings thought for a moment. "I'll get PSU to surveil him until then. Shouldn't be hard, since he spends ten hours a day at work. He's not going anywhere tonight, right?"

"He's shacked up at home with the luggage and the wife," said Hector.

"Mitzi," said Rawlings. "Christ. This is going to be something. Professional Standards Unit shadowing their own boss."

"Maybe we should use Team Three homicide," said McMichael. "He's not *our* boss."

Rawlings studied him. His eyes were moist black pits in his pale face. "I like that idea. As much as I like anything about this mess. Do it. Don't get caught."

27

McMichael got coffee and the morning San Diego *Times*, took a stool in the back bar of Spider's.

SAN DIEGO DETECTIVE LINKED TO BRAGA MURDER SUSPECT

Defense Lawyer to File Wrongful Arrest

By Rob Skelton

A police detective in the Pete Braga murder case has been romantically linked to the woman arrested in connection with the brutal bludgeon murder.

Detective Thomas McMichael, 38, a sixteen-year veteran of the force, was seen publicly with Sally Rainwater, 28, of Imperial Beach in the days before her arrest.

Neither McMichael nor Rainwater would comment on the relationship.

However, photographs showing the two together at restaurants in Imperial Beach were made available to the San Diego *Times.*

"This is a mockery of law and a betrayal of trust," said defense lawyer Gene Goldman. "My client is a victim of illegal and unprofessional police procedure. She is innocent of the crimes charged. Both she and the alleged evidence against her have been manipulated by the San Diego PD and Detective McMichael in particular."

Goldman went on to say that he was "professionally and personally appalled" by the department's actions.

Earlier today Rainwater was charged with possession of stolen property belonging to Pete Braga, gross negligence for leaving him alone the night of his death, and possession of controlled substances.

Braga, former San Diego mayor, tuna fleet captain and a colorful area businessman, was clubbed to death in his Point Loma home January 8.

Rainwater is a nurse's aid employed by Braga at the time of the killing. She has not been charged with the murder.

She was questioned the night of the killing but remained free until Friday, when a search of her beachfront home netted what a Police Department spokesman described as "substantial evidence."

Detective McMichael visited Rainwater at the women's jail on Monday, according to

Sheriff's Department sources. "They had a brief discussion," said one deputy, who asked to remain nameless.

McMichael read the story, his gut tightening with each paragraph, his eyes hardly blinking at all. He imagined his fist going through Bland's forehead.

The picture beside it showed him and Sally leaving Ye Olde Plank hand in hand, McMichael's face turned toward her with a sucky, solicitous smile.

Rawlings, Bland and Chief Kerr were waiting in Kerr's seventh-floor office. McMichael sat.

"You're off the case," said Kerr.

"I understand."

"Where'd they get the picture?" asked Bland.

McMichael took a deep breath and stared at him. "I have no idea, sir. The only one who had pictures like that was you."

"That *Times* shot wasn't on the PSU roll," Bland said. "It came from somewhere else."

McMichael marveled at Bland's breadth of deception, his bovine calm and perfect execution.

"The damage is done," said Kerr. "Don, I want you to field the press and media on this. They're not going to settle for Public Information."

Rawlings nodded, looking down with the same lightless expression he'd had a few hours earlier in his den at home. "Tom, take the Courtney Gonzalez case. Stay away from Braga and the nurse. A couple thousand miles away would do."

"Yes, sir."

"I still think a leave of absence would be the best thing for this department," said Bland.

"Then take one," said McMichael.

"Can it and beat it," said Kerr. "Take the day off and get out of here. Tom, your ice is thin."

"I want to know who took those pictures," said Bland. "One of the nurse's friends? Maybe your buddy Hector?"

McMichael looked out the window, but saw only Bland's misdirections spinning wider and wider and wider.

"We'll get to the bottom of it, Jerry," said Rawlings. "Don't worry about that."

"It's my job to worry," said Bland. "This man gets the day off and I have to scramble around here cleaning up his messes."

Enjoy the last few days you'll live out of prison, McMichael wanted to say, but he held his tongue. He slammed the door behind him and took the elevator down toward the bright sunshine.

He was about to get into his car when his cell phone rang.

"That was stupid, but she's hell for pretty," said Patricia.

"Gee, thanks."

"I'll bet you could use a little distraction."

"A long trip to a faraway planet would be nice."

"I'll pick you up in half an hour."

"Do that."

"Bring a jacket. And you gotta tell me where you live, McMike."

* * *

She was driving a red Mercedes convertible, a red scarf around her black hair, big sunglasses and a black leather car coat. Under the coat was a polka-dot outfit that reminded him of Marilyn Monroe.

"No Ford?"

"I could never tell Grandpa I bought this. Get in."

They drove to the Shelter Island yacht basin, parked in a spot at the San Diego Yacht Club.

"Provisions in the tiny trunk," she said.

McMichael carried the bag of wine, cheese and bread. Patricia led the way to a fifty-foot tournament-rigged Tiara with twin Cat diesels, new blue canvas and fresh hull paint. *Corrinna Braga.*

"One of Grandpa's toys," said Patricia. "I think I'll end up with it, since I'm the only one who knows how to use it."

Ten minutes later they were taxiing through the harbor, the Cats puttering them along at three knots while the breeze slapped cool against McMichael's face. There were stratus clouds high in the north and the sky was a hard, close blue. When Patricia hit the Pacific she gunned the diesels and aimed west. Standing beside her McMichael felt the power rise up under him, felt the bow lift and the stern auger down, watched a gull glide past for inspection then snap away fast in the wind.

Patricia yanked off her scarf and tossed it below-decks, started talking fast and loud over the engines:

"I love this thing, Tom. I'd have gone with twin Mercs or eight-ninety-twos for more speed but the Cats get me around. Only got sixty hours on them. Pete gave this to

*my mom and dad the year before they died in the wreck.
Named it for my mom. I gave it back to him when Anna
died, seemed like the right thing to do. Pete and Gar and
me, we'd scream over to Catalina and fish for a couple of
days, live right on board, cook up our catch and drink
good port. Hours of that. Gar would vomit and sleep until
noon. God, I miss him. Pete, not Gar."*

"Not Gar."

*"Hey, I'm still a speed demon, Tom, remember that
old Mustang I had back after high school and how we'd
get it going out the Eight toward Yuma, hit a hundred
and float past the sand dunes thinking we could hop
from mirage to mirage? Man, that was great, remember that Ford V-Eight with the air conditioner that blew
cubes and we could get from San Diego to Rosarito on
the toll road in nothing flat? Eat lobsters and drink tequila 'til we rolled to a hotel, get up and have more lobsters for breakfast?"*

"Yeah, I remember."

"So how could you get mixed up with the nurse?"

"Good question."

*"Thing is you can't hit a hundred on water, but fifty
feels just like it, maybe better because you get the up and
down and the yaw. More dimensions of speed. Was it
anything like we used to be, you and that young blonde?"*

"Let's talk about something else."

"You and Stephanie like us?"

"Chrissakes, Pat, just drop that shit, will you?"

"You're right, McMike. I said I'd distract you!"

She eased the boat into a loose port turn, then
tightened her into a dizzying spin that sent McMichael's brain to one side of his skull as the hull dug
into the sea and the spray shot off to starboard and

the engines groaned against the load and the backwash almost bucked them over. Patricia laughed and straightened *Corrinna Braga*, heading east at a less adamant pace.

They came back into the harbor, chugged north past the navy boatyards. McMichael stared at the battleships and destroyers and the floating hospital—majestic gray mountains of steel sitting impossibly high in the water, bristling with ordnance.

Back in the slip at Shelter Island they sat down by the bait tank with their backs to the wind and the wine open between them.

"Who killed him, Tommy?"

"I can't talk about it."

"Are you still on the case?"

"Just the edge of it now."

"Because of the nurse?"

McMichael nodded, drank some wine, said nothing.

"It was the nurse, wasn't it? She suckered you in so you'd lose your bearings."

He shrugged.

"So, I can't talk about your exes and I can't talk about my grandpa. Are we down to odds on the Super Bowl?"

"It was nice of you to rescue me today," he said.

"You're such a square, Tom. You were always such a square. Although, for a few months there, when we were nineteen, I really had you going."

Oh, did you, he thought.

She moved the wine, sat close and put her head on his shoulder. McMichael smelled perfume and salt air. He put his arm around her, felt her shudder. He wondered what it would be like to love her again, after the lifetime that had ended when he and Stephanie broke apart. It wasn't like it was, because Johnny had most of his heart and Steffy maybe some, and even Sally Rainwater had a piece of it. Patricia had her part, too. But there was a big piece that was still his, oddly aloof and calculating and convinced of its own value, though willing to be given.

He felt a slight tapping on his thigh, looked down to see the drops soaking into his jeans.

"Stupid," she said.

"What is?"

"Me. This. I'm unraveling, ever since Pete. Like he held me together. I obsess. I can't turn it off."

She wiped her face, set her hand on his leg by the teardrops. "I think about Garland and who I am and what I'm going to do. And I think about you all the time like some kind of mantra or something. I go back twenty years and start thinking *that* was my life, that was the best it was ever going to be and I was too dumb to know it. I think it's just that I'm older, McMike. I hate getting older. This is the first time I can remember not looking forward to something."

"You're thirty-eight. You're a beauty and you've got a whole life out there."

"Where?"

"Wherever you make it."

"Selling Fords in San Diego?"

"Sounds good to me."

"Yeah. Sure, Tom. We have the best climate in the world."

"And the zoo."

"I can still have a child."

"That would be good."

"Gar shot blanks. My boyfriend before Gar got me pregnant but it didn't take. Twice."

"You've got the time."

"I'm leaving for good."

"You mean that?"

"Going to wrap up the estate, fly away. I'll rent out the fancy condo. I'm thinking Santa Cruz or maybe Newport Beach. Gotta stay near the water."

She sniffed and straightened and ran her fingers under her eyes, looked at the melted makeup. "Sorry."

"Don't be sorry."

"Thanks for hanging. Nice to have a friend. Come on, I'll take you home."

Outside McMichael's apartment Patricia slid the car into park and reached across him to dig into the glove box. She pulled out some sheets of paper, folded lengthwise, opened them and set them in his lap.

"Henry finally came up with these letters from Grandpa," she said. "You guys hadn't presented a subpoena for them and he figured the best thing was to get them to you this way."

McMichael studied the letterhead, the typed text, the aggressive signature of Peter Braga at the bottom. "Where were these?"

"Old Grothke had them in his suit coat pocket."

"Oh, come on. Junior said they'd looked everywhere for them."

"According to Junior, they'd checked his father's

pockets every day since the letters got lost. And his blankets and the Sea World bag on his wheelchair and his briefcase, too. Who knows? Maybe he's got lots of suits."

The letters were addressed to Henry Grothke Sr., at the downtown address.

Dear Henry,

It has come to my attention that I've ponied up almost two million dollars to the San Diego Diocese over my lifetime. In light of that faith and goodwill I proposed that the new church being built in north county be named either St. Peter's, St. Anna's or St. Victor's in tribute to the Braga family. From the Diocese I've received only reasons why this cannot be done. Therefore, I want to remove the Diocese from my will. They will receive nothing upon my death. Please rewrite the will accordingly. I also want you to reverse the charitable remaindered trust we set up to give them the houses in Rancho Santa Fe and Mammoth. Cut them out totally, Henry. I've had enough of their hypocrisy!

Sincerely,
Peter Augustino Braga

The second letter was a shorter, more vehement version of the first, with elaborate scoldings of Grothke, Steiner & Grothke for "losing, throwing away or shredding" the previous directive. There was a threat at the end of it to "swing" Pete's legal business elsewhere if Grothke couldn't "keep track of things" and do as he "was told."

"Take them," said Patricia. "Maybe they'll help."

McMichael thanked her, kissed her cheek and pushed his way out of the convertible.

He shut the door and waved to her but she was staring down at the steering wheel and didn't look up.

Gabriel sat on his usual stool, the usual pint and shot on the bar before him. He saw his son, broke into a dissociated smile.

McMichael sat beside him, ordered up a pint from Hugh.

"You fell for the nurse," said Gabriel.

"It's over and I'm off the case."

"Ah, son, the things life throws at us."

McMichael drank the stout, watched Tim Keller shuffle in from the street, heard the cook slapping the pub grub plates onto the counter under the heat lamps. He caught Hugh in a sideways glance.

"Take a walk with me, Pop."

"But why?"

"Just to walk."

"I do enough of that."

"I don't. Come on."

They headed up Front Street in the fading light, pigeons lifting up to roost in the eaves, the traffic thick on Ash, an ocean breeze tossing Gabriel's thick white hair. McMichael looked behind them to see Tim Keller ambling along, making no attempt to hide his surveillance of Gabe.

"Where were you the night Pete was killed?"

asked McMichael. "Don't tell me Spellacy's because I know you weren't."

"The damned publican, telling stories again."

"It wasn't Hugh. Now come on. Cough it. I'm trying to tie up some loose ends."

"But a man's got a right to his privacy, Tom."

McMichael pulled his father by the arm, not hard, but threw his back up against the bank building. His father's lightness surprised him, and so did his poor balance, and the impact.

"Sorry, Pop. Really."

"I'd have beaten you for that just a few years ago."

"This is now. And I need to know where you were that Wednesday."

Gabriel blinked slowly and turned away, shaking his head. "Tim and I, we bus and hoof to St. Agnes's on Wednesdays."

"What for?"

"That's your business, too? Be careful."

"Why? Why go there?"

"It's not your concern."

"Tell me why."

"There's no reason to—"

"Goddamn it, why go to St. Agnes's? What the hell do you and Tim have to do at St. Agnes's?"

Gabriel started off down the sidewalk again, McMichael keeping pace.

"Why, Pop?"

"For the food, son."

The food. Son.

God, thought McMichael. It hit him hard, brought things he'd never wanted to see right into focus. Gabriel McMichael on the dole at St. Agnes's, shoveling down the free food to make it back to the pub for more drinks.

Gabriel looked back with the same expression that he'd worn for all the years McMichael had known him: shameful pride.

"Come on, Pop," McMichael said quietly. "Slow down. I'm sorry."

They made their way back toward Spellacy's. At the corner of Front and B Gabriel stumbled off the curb and McMichael caught him by his coat sleeve, yanked him away from a car that threw a wave of gutter water that half drenched the old man and McMichael, too, sent them staggering backward while someone yelled *stupidfuckers* from a yellow convertible.

"You all right, Pop?"

"Sonofabitch, Tom."

"You gotta be careful, Pop."

"I saw him, Tommy. Just couldn't get the old bones moving in time."

"You okay?"

"I'm okay, I'm okay. Let go of me."

McMichael and Hector pulled the midnight stake-out shift on Assistant Chief of Police Jerry Bland. They relieved Barbara and Hatter, trading them Hector's Camaro for Barbara's personal car—a conversion van loaded with family vacation gear. There was a luggage rack on top piled with duffels and coolers, a windsurfing board, beach chairs and an umbrella, a portable barbecue with its top lashed tight with bungee cords. Barbara had even thrown handfuls of beach sand against the tinted windows to leave a convincing layer of dust.

Hector parked it in a new spot: three houses down and around a corner from the Bland residence, which gave them a good straight-ahead view. If Bland flushed, they'd follow the radio homer that Hatter—stooping down in the department parking lot to look for the loose change that had somehow jumped out of his pocket—had affixed beneath the bumper of Bland's take-home Ford earlier in the day.

The kitchen light in the Bland residence was on at midnight and still on at two. McMichael reclined the passenger seat just slightly, poured coffee from his thermos. Hector sat behind the wheel, hunched in his leather coat.

"What do you think it takes," asked Hector, "for a guy like Bland to end up doing this kind of crap?"

McMichael sipped his not-very-good coffee. "Just lots of money."

"Yeah, but look at him—he lives in the same house. Probably has the same car in the garage. He's put his kids through school or whatever. If he gets sick he's got insurance. What is he? A sixty-year-old cop with a good pension, could retire any time he wants. Bunch of goddamned cash in his house. Stupid."

"True. At least Jimmy blew his on the obvious."

"It's all that cartel money, so close. It's like a magnet. Guys up in San Francisco, they don't have to live with it, day in and day out. Even L.A. But we get up in the morning, smell the roses and the coke, too. It's right there."

McMichael listened to a night bird chattering in the magnolia tree behind them. "I think about Johnny and that," he said. "All the grass and powder coming up through TJ."

"It goes everywhere," said Hector. "You can't run away from it."

"Idaho would be nice," said McMichael. "Or Oregon."

"Jackson went up to Wyoming and got himself shot."

"Guns everywhere up there, too."

"You'd never see Johnny."

"That's why I won't leave."

"He's a good kid. 'Nother doughnut?"

"Sure."

McMichael's brain thorn kicked in as he thought of the way the duffels were handled, the way the dope dogs ignored the new Fords, the dispatch with which the anonymous helo picked up the goods.

"If it's not dope, what is it?"

"I've been thinking about that," said Hector. "And I haven't come up with anything. What else do they have down there that we want but aren't supposed to buy? I don't think it's bullshit cigarettes and switchblades."

McMichael dozed from four to five. Hector from five to six. McMichael looked out the window at the light in Bland's kitchen, constant as the northern star. He thought about Johnny and wondered when his son would turn on him, lose respect for him, do all the things that adolescents were supposed to do. He thought briefly of Steffy, tried to figure out the primary thing he'd done wrong. But that train of thought went where it always went— straight down the tracks of their past until vanishing in the long black tunnel of moments and decisions, each one important in ways that neither of them had known. He wondered what Sally Rainwater was doing in the women's jail out in Santee. Dreaming about what an asshole he was? He thought about Patricia out on *Corrinna Braga*, the way she cried. He wondered why he couldn't get it back for her, get back the way he used to feel. She was prettier than ever. And open to him. With her, he could come full circle. It looked good on paper, but he couldn't make it true. Maybe it was just fear. Maybe he had too good a memory. *You have it wrong, Tom—I'm not dumping you because you're a McMichael. I'm dumping you because you're you.* Maybe it was just pride. Or revenge. He thought of Gabriel in the St. Agnes's food line. He wondered if his own face was beginning to reveal the same shameful pride as his father's.

A delivery man in a pickup truck chucked a San Diego *Times* onto Bland's lawn at five fifty-five. The lights in Bland's living room came on at six-ten. Hector yawned. At seven-thirty the assistant chief's Crown Victoria backed from the garage onto the street and turned toward them. They sank out of sight below the windows and McMichael listened to the big sedan ease past.

The homer worked like a dream, allowing Hector and McMichael to follow from a safe distance. Bland drove straight to headquarters and pulled into the department parking lot like he'd done every morning for thirty-five years.

At noon, Homicide Team Three met with Rawlings at the Spreckels Organ Pavilion in Balboa Park. High above the studied greenery of the park, scattered clouds admitted a winter sunshine that couldn't warm the shadows. The captain stood with his back to the big empty stage, his soldiers gathered around him while a pack of children romped and cavorted among the empty seats of the amphitheater.

"It's us, Customs, INS, FBI, and Imperial Beach and San Ysidro Police," said Rawlings. "We've got compromised employees in three of the agencies. Everyone's being as silent as they can be, but all we can do is hope this is airtight. If anything leaks to the Axelgaards or to our man next to the chief, we won't see any red truck or any dope tonight."

Rawlings squinted into the cool sunlight. "We'll let the brothers make the run into Tijuana, let them come back out. We'll have four undercover Narcotics people down at Diaz Leather to make sure the pickup looks good. As soon as the Customs brother waves the Mack through, FBI is going to block the road with a transport van, San Ysidro SWAT snipers are going to cover from the overhead catwalks, and we'll make the extraction from the truck. Barbara, Hatter and I will be on the American side in a pickup truck with a camper—detained by Customs in Inspection Area One. When the rig pulls up, keep your faces down and away. If they make us, things could get hot fast. If they make us, draw your weapons, find cover and watch *everybody*. We don't know what kind of manpower they might have on the Mexico side, and we already know that one U.S. Customs agent and one Imperial Beach cop are in the bag. So watch the tourists, watch the *Federales*, watch the damned drug dogs."

McMichael saw the anxiety in Rawlings's old face and the worry deep in his pale blue eyes. Hector looked eager, Barbara cool, Hatter unreadable.

"I want radio wires and full body armor on all of you," said Rawlings. "Wear hats, glasses, whatever you can to change your appearance. Be careful with Victor Braga—he's a hostage even though he doesn't know it. McMichael and Hector, you're on Bland—wherever he goes. Let's hope he stays home. As soon as we've got the brothers I'll radio you to serve the warrant. I'll have backup there by the time you get out of the surveillance van. Don't approach the door until the uniforms are with you. Be careful with the old buzzard. We'll have four helos in the air before midnight over Imperial Beach. They'll force the phantom chopper out of the air or blow it out. Questions?"

"Why do I have to miss the fun?" asked Hector.

"You have to keep your partner out of trouble."

McMichael used the afternoon to play catch-up. He called Charley Farrell out at the dealership, who said he'd check his records again and go further back in his search for wine-colored SUVs sold or leased in the last year. Didn't think he'd find anything he didn't find before.

He checked with Barbara Givens, who had taken Anna's hummingbird to a jeweler she knew. He told her that the "jewels" were just glass, eight dollars' worth max, but the workmanship was very good. He had seen similar decorative hummingbirds for sale but couldn't remember where—possibly at the swap meet in Oceanside.

He talked to Johnny for almost half an hour, getting an earful about this new puppy his mother had bought, a chocolate Labrador retriever that he'd named Brownie. McMichael was happy at the joy in his son's voice, sad that he couldn't be there to see his face. It crushed him in some unsupportable way that he wasn't the man who had gotten his own son a dog. But Johnny was happy and McMichael smiled as he pictured his boy with the new puppy, and Dr. Clay Blass sneezing, breaking out in hives, maybe an aneurysm or sudden heart failure.

"You can see him tonight, Dad!"

"I wish I could. But your mother has plans for you."

"Oh."

McMichael let the silence murder him because he thought he deserved it.

He returned Dr. Arnold Stiles's call and learned that Courtney "Angel" Gonzalez had been killed by two .22 caliber bullets shot into her head. Stiles had found star-shaped flesh tears and unburned gunpowder around the entry wounds, which indicated "extremely close range." One bullet had entered her left temple and exited her right. One had gone in above her left ear, traveled down at a sharp angle and lodged near the cortex. The exit wound on the right temple had some very small fragments of safety glass imbedded around it.

Stiles put the time of death between December twenty-fifth and January fifth, which lined up with Penny's last sighting of Angel on Thursday, January second.

"Sorry I couldn't get more for you," said Stiles. McMichael pictured him in his blood-splattered glasses and washable necktie. "But she had at least two weeks out in that desert, Detective."

"Did she put up a fight?"

"No signs of that, but the flies, beetles, ants,

coyotes and vultures worked her over pretty good. No contusions to the skull, none of her bones or teeth were broken. No ligature marks that I could make out."

"Safety glass around the wound?" asked McMichael. "Shower glass?"

"Maybe," said Stiles. "Or maybe she was sitting in a car, passenger's side. The driver just reaches out and bap, bap. The bullet went through the soft part of her head and through the window. Thus the glass frags. Drive and dump. I doubt you got tire tracks with all the storms."

McMichael imagined the wine-colored SUV. He thanked the ME and hung up.

One contemplative minute later he got a call from Barbara Givens: Dylan Feder had been arrested for public drunkenness in Palm Springs. Palm Springs PD ran a warrant check and when it came up hot, they called Dade County. Feder's P.O. had thought of Feder's connection in San Diego.

One less creep to worry about here, thought McMichael. He thought of Sally Rainwater sitting in jail.

An hour before his shift was to end, he drove down to the waterfront and walked along the Embarcadero, trying to clear his mind of sleeplessness, feelings of having failed Johnny and a steady hum of doubt about the coming night. He'd seen the same doubt in Rawlings's eyes.

He walked past the cafés and tour boats, past the *Berkeley* and the *Star of India*, glancing up at a darkening sky that refused to allow optimism. Another storm front was coming in and McMichael thought he could feel a barometric drop in his own body, this sense that things were about to change.

He checked the postcards in the tour boat shop, wondered who might like a note and a picture of San Diego Harbor. He bought one for Johnny, slid it into his pocket.

At a stand offering ocean-themed T-shirts he looked at the whales and dolphins pictured on the cotton, wondered why artists had to make their faces look human. He pictured the living Angel Gonzalez—a pretty girl of seemingly average intelligence with no meanness in her that he had ever seen.

A jewelry maker had set up a small card table to show off his wares. There were necklaces made of coral and shells, matching bracelets. And jewelry boxes, too, covered with faux gemstones in red and green and amber.

Dangling by monofilament from a small branch of driftwood was a flock of hummingbirds, turning absently in the breeze, their detailed glass feathers catching the last of the afternoon light. McMichael touched one.

"I've got tabletop hummingbirds, too," said the craftsman, bringing up a bag from his side of the table. He was short and gray-haired, with an enormous mustache and hoops in his left ear. "Here."

He pulled a small cardboard box from the bag, opened it and set the bird on the table.

"Anna's hummingbird," said McMichael.

"I've got some ruby-throats and some hybrids, too."

The bird on the table looked, to McMichael,

almost identical to the one they'd found in Sally Rainwater's house.

You don't know quality when you see it.

"May I?"

"Go for it."

He picked it up and set it in his palm. Just like Pete's, he thought: head up, tail fanned, little wings extended. The crown was a shroud of pale violet made of tiny glass drops. The eyes were black and the body a metallic silver. And when you set it on a flat surface, which he did, it balanced just barely on two small, flattened feet.

"Sell a lot of these?"

"A lot."

"Recently?"

"It's been a few days. Last month I'd say ten. Stocking stuffers. They're only thirty-five dollars."

The most beautiful man-made thing I've ever seen.

"Where'd you get the idea?"

"Friend of my dad, old tuna boat skipper. He had one from Panama, only with real jewels. I was just a kid but I never forgot it. He got murdered two weeks ago."

"Been making them long?"

"Off and on, thirty years. The public changes. One year it's birds. Next it's flowers. Then angels. After nine eleven it was all flags but that's tapered off."

"I'll take this one," said McMichael.

"She's a beauty."

29

Bland came home at six thirty-seven that evening. He parked in his garage then came out to the driveway, holding a small bouquet of flowers. He examined the moths swirling around the streetlamp. He wore the same gray suit and brown shoes that never seemed to change, the same placid, thorough expression that had gotten him through almost four decades of police work. He looked at the surveillance van for a while, tapping the flowers against his leg, and McMichael wondered if he was going to come over to check it out.

"Don't even dream about it," said Hector.

Bland turned and went back into the garage. McMichael saw the garage door lurch downward and the house door swing open to a rectangle of domestic light.

At seven-thirty they ate cooling take-out tacos and drank more coffee. At nine-thirty the lights in the Bland house went off. Almost an hour later McMichael saw the garage door rise and Bland's take-home Crown Victoria back into the street and turn in their direction.

They slumped down below dashboard level and McMichael watched the Crown Vic's headlights move across the headliner front to back, then heard the big Ford swoosh past fast.

The homer led them south. They picked up Bland on Adams and tailed him three cars back to Interstate 15 southbound. Bland made the light and they didn't, and by the time they got the big van moving on the freeway the Crown Victoria was nowhere in sight. But the homer beeped faster and louder when McMichael hit ninety in the fast lane, just in time to follow Bland onto the 805 south.

"He's in a goddamned hurry," said Hector.

"Maybe he wants to see his shipment arrive," said McMichael.

"If he makes our guys, we're dead."

McMichael had long ago noted that when the situation got tight, Hector's voice rose and he seemed to fret more.

"No," said McMichael. "Once that Mack gets in line, there's no turning around. Even if Bland sees one of us, it's going to be too late."

"That's him in lane two, man. Slow *down*."

McMichael coasted and Hector called Rawlings. He told the captain the score, said yessir twice, punched off.

"He said the same thing you did. Said they got good disguises. Whatever that means."

They tailed, comfortably back, to the South Bay Parkway. Then onto Interstate 5, headed for the border.

"Yeah," said Hector. "He wants to *watch*. I still don't like this, Mick. I don't like Bland close enough to recognize our guys, then calling the brothers. Goddamned costumes or not. If they know they're blown, man, anything could happen."

McMichael veered off on San Ysidro Boulevard, took the side streets toward the commercial vehicle gate.

They parked behind a liquor store, grabbed the binoculars and hustled into the shadows. When the traffic got thin they ran across Virginia Avenue and ducked around the corner of a closed *carneceria*. Looking around the building McMichael could see the commercial gate and the big floodlights up on the scaffolding, the INS and Customs vehicles parked in apparent disarray, the uniformed agents moving in and out of the booths, one line of trucks southbound and another coming back north into the bright lights of America.

McMichael watched as the vehicle exhaust roiled up into the lights then dissipated into the darkness. The walls of the Customs building threw sharp shadows across the tableau. The gunmen on the catwalks looked down with lazy alertness and McMichael had the unwelcome, illogical premonition that they were Axelgaard people, not theirs.

Bland's white Ford emerged from the darkness, glided alongside a chain-link fence topped with concertina wire, stopped forty yards in front of them and thirty yards to the left, directly between the detectives and the border crossing.

"Perfect," whispered Hector, retreating behind the corner.

"Plenty damned close," McMichael whispered back.

They giggled dryly and leaned around the wall again, McMichael standing and Hector kneeling, two half faces peering around the plane of the building like cartoon characters. McMichael saw that Bland had gotten out to lean against the Crown Vic, his elbows propped on the roof and a pair of binoculars snug to his face.

McMichael stepped away from the building just far enough to get his own binoculars up and focused. He could see the breeze moving the hair on Bland's head. Beyond Bland, McMichael barely recognized Rawlings, a black cowboy hat pulled low, a gray corduroy jacket with a yoked back, and scuffed black cowboy boots. He stood with his fists on his hips, watching the drug dogs sniff his pickup truck in the inspection area. The truck had a magnetic sign on the door that said BOB MCGUANE CUTTING HORSES—TEMECULA, CA, and a bed filled with alfalfa bales. McMichael spotted Hatter slouching on a bench, wrapped to his ears in a serape, looking dirty and disconsolate. Bent next to him, similarly dressed against the January chill, her face charcoaled to a black mask of neglect, was Barbara Givens. McMichael noted that her disguise failed to hide her hopeful blue eyes.

Hector pulled him back behind the corner. "You see Barbara and the captain?" he whispered excitedly. "Where the hell is Hatter?"

"Right next to her," said McMichael.

"Oh, too good."

Hector smiled and peered around the corner

again. McMichael checked his watch, made sure—
for the third time—that his cell phone was on vibrate
and not ring, then leaned back out over Hector.

He focused his glasses on the northbound Mexican Customs lane and saw the big red Mack idling
three vehicles back. Mason Axelgaard of the Imperial Beach Police was at the helm, and Victor Braga
sat next to him, headphones over his ears, gazing
out the window and bobbing his head. McMichael
lowered the binoculars just slightly, picking up
Bland's backside and noting the cell phone now lying on the roof of the Ford, just inches from Bland's
right elbow. *Too late*, he thought. *Even if he spots one
of them, it's too late now.*

But Bland gave no air of recognition or worry.
He set his binoculars down on the roof and let his
arms drop to his sides, shaking his hands to get
the circulation going. He swung around slowly and
McMichael stepped behind the wall of the butcher
shop, pulling Hector with him.

For the next twenty minutes they took turns at
the corner. At eleven-forty the Auto Leather International rig, laden with new Fords, lumbered forward through the hovering exhaust and onto United
States asphalt.

McMichael checked Bland: still on point, leaning against his car, field glasses up and aimed. Then
the rest of Homicide Team Three—Rawlings looking puzzled as a U.S. Customs agent showed him a
clipboard, Hatter and Barbara still on the bench,
huddled in their serapes. He could see the gunmen
high on the catwalks and the INS patrolmen loitering outside the Customs booth.

A moment later, curly-haired Martin Axelgaard walked from the booth and into the ferocious white light, giving the Mack a hard, accusatory look. He went to the driver's side and said something up to his brother. Mason handed down a slip of paper. Victor leaned over and pulled a headphone away from one ear. Two more Customs men came from the booth, one moving along the trailer and looking up at the new cars. The other came around the front, looked at the license plate and entered something on a handheld device. The dog handlers walked their animals up one side of the trailer and down the other, but didn't bother to get up near the cars.

Martin Axelgaard handed the slip back up to his brother and waved him through.

McMichael thought: *here we go.*

Rawlings sauntered toward the Mack. Hatter and Barbara stood, loosened the serapes and fell in behind him, heads down.

The Mack's engine groaned and a blast of fresh exhaust spilled from the pipe and into the air. A white panel van moved away from the inspection area and cut a slow angle across the asphalt, stopping a few yards in front of the Mack. Mason Axelgaard hit the horn. The van didn't move and nobody got out of it. He hit the horn again—a nerve-rattling airhorn that made McMichael flinch even this far away. The gunmen on the catwalk unshouldered their carbines.

Golden-haired Martin Axelgaard strode from the Customs booth toward the panel van while

Rawlings rounded the front of the Mack, headed for the driver's side.

The back of the van flew open and three FBI men spilled out, sidearms drawn at Mason Axelgaard in the truck. Rawlings drew from under his corduroy jacket and backed off, holding his badge up high with one hand and his automatic at his side with the other, yelling something up at Mason as Barbara and Hatter shed their serapes, drew their weapons and ran to the front of the rig.

Bland's head quickly vanished from the bottom of McMichael's round, binocular view. He was in the Crown Vic and rolling. McMichael stepped away from the building as the Ford sped down the street, Bland's cell phone bouncing to the pavement, and when he got the glasses back up McMichael saw Mason step down from the cab with his hands submissively behind his head while Rawlings shouted something up at Victor.

Out on the driveway Martin raised his hands as the FBI men swarmed him.

Victor tumbled down out of the Mack, trying to keep hold of his CD player. Mason looked back sharply at him, then turned again to Rawlings, and at the same time his hands came together in front of him and a comet of orange flame flashed from his weapon a full second before McMichael even heard it.

Rawlings went down hard, his badge holder suspended for a split second in midair before it dropped to the ground beside him.

Hatter and Barbara, the cab blocking their view,

flew around the front. Victor stumbled between Mason and the Bureau men.

McMichael ran into the street and pointlessly yelled *"NO!"* He was almost to the first fence when Hector blew past him on his short, thick legs.

McMichael saw Hatter round the truck ahead of Barbara.

Axelgaard shot him, too.

Barbara dropped, rolled and got off three, but Axelgaard climbed back into the truck just as an ear-splitting alarm went off and a bank of emergency lights flashed on. The truck lurched forward.

McMichael caught up with Hector at the line of vehicles waiting to leave the country, sprinted along while he dug out his badge and his nine millimeter. They held their badges high as they ran into the inspection area, McMichael half expecting a bullet to find him.

The INS vans screamed uselessly past them, and one of the catwalk gunmen fired down, but another one shot him off the scaffolding and he tumbled down through the lights and shadows and hit the asphalt with a smack. Victor dove away from the rig and the FBI men opened up. McMichael watched the overhead gunman pitch headfirst into the trailer of new cars, his automatic chattering away as he fell.

Martin Axelgaard broke away and sprinted for the Mexico-side fence but the Bureau men cut him down before he got close.

McMichael ran hard, wondering why he couldn't go fast enough to help anybody. He saw the Mack accelerating toward the panel van as Barbara and a staggering Mark Hatter pulled Rawlings to the

Customs booth. Victor was crawling in the same direction, head low and butt high. The Bureau agents dove away from the truck and fired, and McMichael saw one of the SWAT snipers place three quick shots in a tight group through the windshield. The Mack slowed and Mason staggered out, wheeling and shooting wildly as McMichael and Hector and Hatter and the FBI men and the SWAT snipers up in the catwalk took him down in a brief, horrendous fusillade of small arms fire. One of the FBI men swung into the truck and killed the engine.

Gunsmoke lingered and slowly rose to join the exhaust and the lights and the darkness. The alarm screamed but for a moment no one moved—thankful prayers or just shock.

The calamity had taken thirty seconds.

McMichael trotted over to Rawlings, who was unconscious and bleeding hard from his ears and mouth while Barbara sat astride him and tried to pound his heart back into action. His cowboy hat lay a few feet away, up on its crown.

"You hang in there, Captain. You're hanging in, Captain. Don, Don? Hang in there with me now!"

She pounded and grunted and looked up at McMichael with hopeless eyes as the blood, sweat and tears ran down her charcoal-smudged face.

"Bland," said McMichael, taking Hector by the arm.

Silence in the family van as McMichael hit the emergency flashers and tried to gun it onto the freeway and Hector called ahead for the backup.

Taillights came toward them at a steadily accelerating rate and McMichael laid on the horn to clear the fast lane.

"He got it in the head," said Hector. "All that armor and he gets it in the head. *Fucking Axelgaards. Fucking Bland. Fucking Jimmy.*"

"Hatter's armor saved him."

"Rawlings looked bad. Oh, man."

McMichael sailed on, hands jittery and his eyeballs strangely heavy in his face, the weight of his own heart beginning to register through the dimming rush of adrenaline.

The lights were on in the back rooms of Bland's house. Two black-and-whites were waiting at the nearest corner and they fell in behind the van.

Four uniforms jangled up the walk behind the detectives, two of them carrying riot guns with the ten-shell magazines. McMichael felt alert again, light on his feet and ready. He thought he smelled something burning, wondered if it was the gunpowder from the border still alive in his nose.

He held the search warrant in one hand and his automatic in the other. Hector took the right side of the door and knocked sharply.

The porch light came on and Jerry Bland, dressed in a plaid bathrobe and slippers, opened the door. "What?"

"We've got a warrant, Bland," said McMichael. "This is it."

Bland's face looked ancient in the porch light. He stared past McMichael at the uniforms. "For my home?"

"Here," said McMichael, handing Bland the warrant book. "You can sign off or not. We're coming in."

"What are you looking for?"

"Read the damned thing, Bland. You like watching Rawlings get it tonight?" McMichael held up Bland's cell phone, then slid it back into his pocket.

Bland's mouth opened and his small eyes registered comprehension. "Come in."

McMichael pushed through, followed by Hector and the uniforms. One of them greeted Bland with a "good evening, sir. Sorry to bother you."

"You are not sorry," said Hector with a sharp glance. He shook his head in disgust and patted down the assistant chief, who raised his arms compliantly. Hector then cuffed him, hands behind his back. "You guys are not sorry. Stay with him. Don't let him out of your sight, not for one second."

Bland looked helpless with his robe and slippers and the stunned expression on his face. "I can help you guys find whatever it is you're looking for."

"Cash in a leather briefcase," said McMichael. He smelled smoke again.

"I've got one of those. But there's no cash in it."

Mitzi came into the room from the hallway. "Jerry, what's this?"

"Just a department thing, hon."

Bland padded across the floor and bent so she could hug him. She was a slight woman, short gray hair and a round, pleasant face. Wrapped in a heavy terry robe, she peered at McMichael over her husband's shoulder. She didn't look like she'd been sleeping.

"Can I get anyone coffee?"

"What's burning?" asked McMichael as the answer dawned on him.

"Probably charcoal from the barbecue," said Bland. "We had pork tenderloin to—"

"Money," said Hector.

"Watch them."

McMichael hustled down the hallway, the old hardwood creaking under him, through what appeared to be the master bedroom, then outside through a set of French doors.

Hector barged past him to the smoking barbecue, kicked it over onto the patio and danced through the sparks and embers and smoke, spreading out the half-consumed stacks of bills. The outer layers of cash were curled and rimmed with orange.

McMichael dragged over the garden hose and sprayed it all down while Hector scuffed his boot bottoms across the lawn. He returned from a darkened corner of the backyard with a leather briefcase, raised it in one hand and let the lid drop open.

"What a dumbshit," he said.

They found Jerry and Mitzi sitting together on the couch in the living room. Bland's face was white. He looked like he was chewing something, then not. The four uniforms stood back, watching them with uncomfortable looks on their faces.

"We're going downtown," said McMichael.

Bland took a deep breath, rose and sighed. Mitzi stood and hugged him. Bland bent again, hands still cuffed behind him, settling his face into her hair.

"I love you, Mitz."

"I love you, Jerry." She was sobbing and trembling hard. "I did what you told me to, hon."

"You're the best gal ever."

Bland turned from his wife and kind of backed up against her. For one baffling moment McMichael thought he was groping her. Bland looked at him without interest. Then he bent over at the waist and a terrific explosion concussed the room. Mitzi collapsed. Bland straightened and arched his back and a second shot roared into the walls. A red hole opened on the stomach of his robe and his head flew back. McMichael ducked and cleared leather just as Bland's knees hit the floor. Then his face. The snub-nosed detective special was still locked in his cuffed hands.

30

McMichael remembered a time when he was six and asked his parents for a dog. His mother was against it because dogs were dirty and she was a fastidious homemaker and she had her hands full with baby Raegan.

Their little two-bedroom in Logan Heights shone like a jewel under Margaret's determined care. McMichael could remember the smell of lemon oil on the Sears Early American dining room set, of vinegar on the window glass and pine disinfectant on the linoleum floors. Once, his father, dramatizing some point about Margaret's domestic obsessions, had eaten a fried egg off the floor, rising with a victorious smile.

They didn't get the dog. Gabriel seemed to take this harder than his son. Though the specifics were no longer clear to him, McMichael recalled that Gabriel was around the house even less, and more than usually short-tempered.

But McMichael clearly remembered Gabriel showing up one Saturday afternoon around Christmas with a Shetland pony borrowed from a friend. He'd watched his father lead the shaggy animal up the walk of their house, push open the front door and slap the animal through with a hearty "*Eeee-hahhh!*" A theatrical fight had followed, with Margaret screaming both Gabriel and the pony back out of the house, Raegan wailing and the neighbors all gathered outside to see the show. Gabriel had led the horse around the block for hours after, every kid in the 'hood getting a ride. McMichael didn't see his father around the house again until midsummer.

McMichael thought of all this as he sat with Raegan next to his father's hospital bed early Thursday morning, three short hours after the catastrophe at the border and Jerry Bland's attempted murder-suicide.

Raegan's message had greeted McMichael when he finally got home that morning, well after two o'clock, his mind strangely disengaged and his guts just starting to unknot from the shock.

Tom, Dad's had an accident. He's okay, Tom, but some bones are broken. We're at General.

Captain Don Rawlings was dead.

As were Mason and Martin Axelgaard, and two of the gunmen on the catwalk.

And Jerry Bland.

Mitzi was critical.

Hatter had a bruise the size of a soccer ball on his chest: Mason Axelgaard's .38 soft-tip had almost—but not quite—made it through the vest.

McMichael let go of his father's hand when Tim Keller walked in, reeking of alcohol.

"Ah, Tommy. Like I told Raegan, we were on our way back from St. Agnes's—spaghetti night—and Gabe just walked into the street. The car wasn't going fast but it knocked him up on the windshield. Two broken legs, as you can see. And a concussion, too."

"I do see, Tim. Excuse us, please."

"I'm sticking with a friend, Tom. And don't be blaming me."

"Go."

"I'm stick—"

McMichael rose and guided Tim out by the collar of his jacket, slammed the door. He sat there with Raegan until the sun came up and Gabe finally opened his eyes, just barely visible beneath the gauze turban that covered his head.

Gabriel's eyes moved left to right, then back again. Then up and down. They found his daughter, then his son, and settled. His eye sockets were black and the whites were a bloody red.

"Tommy. Rae," he whispered.

"You're okay, Pop," said McMichael. "You're going to be just—"

"I love you, Dad," said Raegan.

"I never saw a thing."

"You don't have to talk," said Raegan.

"My head feels like they've got it in a vise."

He sipped some water that Raegan held up for him. A nurse bustled in and shot something into the IV drip, bustled out.

Gabriel's eyes closed and he slept.

* * *

McMichael lay on the floor beside the bed, a blanket under his head, his jacket zipped to his chin and his feet freezing cold. He dreamed of red waves breaking on black sand—wave after wave, set after set, endless red waves stacked all the way to the horizon.

He woke at first light to a nurse with a cup of coffee for him.

"Where's Rae?"

"She went home, Dad. Up all night."

"Good."

"Why is that good?"

"Hold my hand, Tom."

McMichael held the rough old hand, thought about the feel of that hand on his face back when he was seven and had stumbled into a glass coffee table. The glass had shattered and cut his cheek deeply, but McMichael had feared repercussions and had hidden in a closet. Gabe heard the sound and followed the blood trail. Gabe found him and helped him out and held his son's blood-and-tear-covered face in his big hands. The roughness is what McMichael remembered now, and the soothing, lighthearted way that Gabe got him into the bathroom and then to the emergency room for shots and stitches.

"Over the years, there's been a lot of talk about what happened to Victor Braga behind the Waterfront."

"Sure has, Pop."

"I think you should know the real truth of it, son."

"Yes."

"I did it."

"I know."

"How?"

"It lined up."

"I was angry. I was furious. I was looking for trouble. Your grandfather Franklin was a good and gentle man."

"It's okay, Pop."

"I didn't want to go to jail."

"No one does."

"So there it is. The policeman's old man damn near beat a boy to death and never paid for it."

"I think you paid."

"There's some truth in that, Tom. I don't know what to tell Rae."

"Tell her what you told me."

"Don't know if I can. Maybe you could."

"It would mean more from you."

"Same story, either way."

"Not really."

Gabriel was quiet for a long while. "Tommy, could you find me a cup of coffee like that, maybe put a nip in it? I feel a little off. There's a bottle in my coat, in that closet there. I remember checking it in the ambulance. Never broke! And they try to tell you there's no God."

McMichael walked down Market Street in the early morning light, the collar of his bomber's jacket up, a Padres cap low. The storm clouds were black in the north, as if it were still night in that direction. He resolved to do something about his father, though he wasn't sure what. Move him in, maybe. Get Gabe on a monthly allowance so he wouldn't be busing and walking five miles for a handout on Wednesday nights. Check him into a detox program, but McMichael guessed that it would end up like the other two times: Gabriel would only stay sober under lock and key. Maybe he and Raegan could come up with something workable.

He tried to think of some way to help Victor, too. While McMichael had always suspected his father's guilt, to have it confirmed brought to him a fuller sense of his own responsibilities. He realized again that a truth can heal but a lie is an open sore, year after year, generation after generation.

The rain started hard and fast and McMichael felt his cell phone shake against his hip.

"Tom, Hector here. You got to see this. We're in the Property Room."

Hector met him at the door. In a brightly lit back storage room, Barbara and Hatter, the chief, Arthur Flagler and Assistant District Attorney Gerald Dale all stood around three large rectangular aluminum crates. A faint vapor rose slowly from them. A big man in a welder's suit stood like an executioner off to the side, his torch and bottle and helmet hung on a stand by the wall, his gloves still in his hand.

Lying near the crates were three gray duffels that McMichael saw were similar to those from last week's Tijuana run—same size and color.

"Here's our dope," said Hector. "It took us half the night to convince the Feds that this was our case and our evidence."

McMichael knelt and looked into one of the boxes. Four small coolers were arranged tightly inside; around them were blocks of dry ice. The coolers had been fitted with what looked like very small refrigerator racks. On the top rack rested a row of thick, nearly identical, organic items. Six, each sealed in a plastic bag filled with a clear fluid.

Staring down through the rack, McMichael saw another row.

"Kidneys," said Flagler. "Human. One hundred and forty-six of them."

McMichael stood. He felt a little dizzy. Scores of chaotic murder scenes had not prepared him for the neat mutilation before him now. "We need to talk to Jimmy."

"I'm prepared to offer him a deal," said Dale. "You can present it to him. You're the only one he'll talk to."

31

Module E, Professional Visits Room Five, had two seats for cops and lawyers on one side of a molded plastic table and one on the other side for the inmate. Four blank walls. It was smaller than a two-bunk jail cell. McMichael stood with his back to the windowed door. Jimmy Thigpen, down on hands and knees to inspect the table bottom, rose with a grunt and a shy smile.

"We're secure," he said. "Unless they've got a mike in the heater vent."

"They can't use anything you say here in court, Jimmy. You know that."

"They can use it a few other places, though."

"I've got a deal for you, straight from Gerald Dale's office. Simple, straightforward, a good one for you."

"Oh?"

"Everything you know about the organs—the Axelgaards, Bland, the people at the Mexico end and the people stateside. Everything you know about Pete Braga. You give me the basics right now and fill in the details later in sworn depositions, Jimmy. Dale will give you immunity, if he likes what he hears."

Thigpen looked at him matter-of-factly. "But you can't file on me in any of that border stuff. Everybody's dead, and you never saw me do a thing."

"Victor did."

Worry crossed Thigpen's face as he tried to guess the weight of Victor's testimony. "What about my money?"

"Asset forfeiture. You lose it."

Thigpen smiled his boy's smile. McMichael noted that he had put on even more jailhouse weight. His shirt was tight on him around the middle.

"Drop the grass and the solicitation?"

"No."

In fact, Dale had given McMichael the solicitation charge to bargain with.

"I've been in here for forty-five days, Tom."

"It all goes toward your time."

"Naw," said Jimmy. "I'll talk to walk."

"I want everything about those runs."

"Drop the women and dope, Mick."

McMichael nodded. "The women, okay. But you're stuck on the dope, Jimmy. It's our way of saving a little face. And making sure you don't get back into law enforcement."

"What's my guarantee?"

"You don't get one."

Thigpen studied McMichael, then nodded, his smile coming back faintly. He sat on one of the small benches. "I came into it late, when I got the job from Pete. Before, they were using a van. But if something went wrong with the schedules the van would be easy to search."

"In case you didn't get Martin Axelgaard as the inspector."

"Right."

"How'd you get started?"

"I got talking to Mason one night. We knew each other from the cop golf league. When I told him about taking the new cars down to TJ for budget leather, well . . . one thing led to another. Pete didn't care that I brought Mason along. To Pete, he was just another tough cop keeping the cars secure."

"Where did the organs come from?"

"Just from poor people. Mexico, Guatemala, El Salvador. Places like that."

"How much were they worth?"

"We paid three hundred and fifty each. Only marked them up to a grand to undercut the Indian suppliers. That made us about a hundred thousand profit if we got twelve coolers' worth. The first five or six runs, it was less. The first time, we only had twenty-four and half of them went bad. Then we got the hang of it. The trick is this packing solution they invented at the University of Wisconsin. Viaspan. They had to be perfect organs—you couldn't sell a bad one. Young teenagers have the best."

"What was Bland's job?"

Thigpen shook his head. "He was just shaking us down. Pete ratted to Bland when Victor said something that made him curious. Pete hired a private eye, who followed us down and back. Stupid. They all figured drugs. Bland had us cold. I had to do something so I offered to cut him in. Said he'd think about it. I was surprised he took the deal. But it was a lot of money for doing nothing."

"How much?"

"Twenty thousand a week. He didn't actually do anything except bullshit Pete for as long as he could. He got Pete to believe they were working an inter-agency sting. And the sting was taking time."

"When Bland couldn't stall him any longer, what did he do?"

Thigpen shrugged. "The second I heard about Pete, I figured Bland for it."

"He never said anything about that?"

"Not to me, but I was in here, Tom. Maybe to the brothers."

McMichael thought of Sally Rainwater, sitting in the women's jail out in Santee. "Do you have any evidence at all that he killed Pete?"

"No. But I heard his wife might make it. She might know some things."

McMichael imagined questioning Mitzi Bland as to her husband's role in the murder of Pete Braga. Barbara Givens's early questions—asked as the doctors were shooing her out of the ICU—had led Barbara to believe that Mitzi knew something about her husband's second career. McMichael wondered what Mitzi had thought about putting the revolver in her robe pocket. *I did what you told me to, hon.* McMichael didn't look forward to interviewing Mitzi Bland. Another task of low order, he thought, another homicide shitpile to dig through.

"Who's this Dr. Morese?"

Jimmy's mouth hung open. "You got him, too?"

"Our helos forced him down on Imperial Beach."

Thigpen looked crushed, as if Morese were somehow infallible or superhuman.

"French Canadian," Thigpen said. "A medical doctor but didn't like medicine. Went into funeral homes, selling off parts mail order, but now he's got contacts at the hospitals and universities all over the world. Most of the things went over to the Middle East, is what I heard. We were competing with the Indian suppliers, like I said. Ours were cheaper and hardly any HIV or hepatitis. Better stuff."

Stuff, thought McMichael. Parts. Units. Items. Merchandise. Product. "How did you get the people at Diaz Leather into the loop?"

"Money, Tom. How do you think?"

McMichael could feel his anger rising. "Did Bland kill Courtney Gonzalez?"

"I don't know for sure, but it makes sense. Victor—well, you know Victor. No telling what he'd say. He's just a boy."

"Then why didn't Bland kill him, too?"

"Beats me. Maybe he had a soft spot for Victor, like I did."

It made no sense to McMichael that Bland would silence Angel but not Victor, soft spot or not.

"But why did you keep taking Victor down to TJ with you?"

"At first it was to implicate him, keep Pete off our backs. After Pete got it, though, they wanted Victor close. No reason to leave him out, maybe making him mad, and him getting Charley Farrell or Patricia involved. They figured that as long as he was happy he wouldn't be telling any tales."

"Charley know?"

Thigpen shook his head. "Just us, and for a while, Pete."

"Patricia?"

"No."

"Garland?"

Thigpen shook his head again, this time with an air of annoyance. McMichael looked hard into Jimmy's eyes, saw no contrition at all.

"Jimmy, you picked on people so poor and desperate they'd sell parts of their bodies for three hundred bucks?"

"Three fifty. That's a lot of money in some places."

"You ever meet one of them?"

Thigpen looked puzzled. "No. Why?"

"How could you do that?"

"Nobody made them sell. It was their choice. I heard the facilities were real clean, it was easy."

"What facilities?"

"Mobile unit. Drove around village to village, like a bookmobile."

McMichael pictured it: some broken-down paramedic van limping down a dusty village road, leaving a wake of dazed and wounded villagers a few hundred dollars richer. The post-op care was probably fantastic.

"I'd send you down for all of it, if it was up to me."

Thigpen looked surprised. "At least you get to hang Bland. Even though he's dead."

"I'd rather hang you."

Thigpen shrugged and looked away. "Yeah. I let a lot of people down."

"You got Rawlings killed."

"I just drove the damned truck, Mick."

"And Bland and the brothers and two San Ysidro cops. And Mitzi, with her insides torn apart, maybe paralyzed, maybe won't even make it."

"I do feel bad," he said sincerely.

"And you cut open all those people for *parts*."

"They made money. And look at all the good people we saved. Kidneys, man—God gave us two so we could help each other out. It's not all bad, and I just drove. I wasn't out there with the damned scalpel."

McMichael pushed off the wall and backhanded Jimmy hard in the face. Jimmy looked back at him with wet eyes and a red cheek and McMichael hooked him in the side and put him down. Thigpen curled into a ball, gasping. Then he made a breathless shriek that didn't sound fully human.

"Kidney shot," said McMichael. "But don't worry, you've got two of them."

Charley Farrell called just before noon to say he had found no additional wine-colored SUV's sold or leased in the last year. "Sorry," he said.

"Thanks for trying."

"That was one heck of a shoot-out at the border, according to the news."

"It was grim."

"How many died?"

"Five."

"And that captain."

"Rawlings, yes."

A moment of respect.

"Well. Detective, I don't know if this helps, but Garland Hansen—that's Patricia's husband—he checked out an Expedition a few months back, drove it a while, then turned it back in, early January. It was Bordeaux red—Detroit's idea for a paint name. Those dealer demos don't show up on the lease or sale books. So, maybe talk to him."

"He turned it in when?"

"See here . . . January the fourth. Saturday."

"Why so soon?"

"He picked up a rock or something, shattered out the window. Said he didn't want the car back because the seats weren't comfortable and the mileage was lousy."

Or maybe she was sitting in a car, passenger side. The driver just reached out and bap, bap.

"Which window?"

"Right side, front."

Garland, thought McMichael—anxious husband of Patricia, soon to lose half of the community property in a divorce, and *all* of what might come to him and Patricia after Pete's death. Garland—unhappy in life, seeing his company failing and his wife packing her bags. Garland—alleged protector of Victor, but protecting him from what? A dangerous woman?

"Give me the VIN on that car, Charley. And the date Garland took it home."

He called Patricia next, under the pretense of clarifying some of the probate terms of her grandfather's will. He asked if she was going ahead with the divorce proceeding, which she was. In fact, she was moving some things out of her and Garland's house this morning, while her husband was up in San Francisco on business.

"Need a hand with the heavy stuff?" McMichael asked.

"I could use that," she said. She gave him the address, told him she'd be there in an hour, offered to buy lunch. "I'm really sorry to hear about your captain and all that bloody business at the border. And really thankful it wasn't you who caught a bullet, Tom."

McMichael told Hector he was going to help Patricia move some things, then signed out of the Homicide/Robbery/Special Investigations Unit. He walked past Captain Don Rawlings's closed door, which was completely covered in sheets of black construction paper. Rawlings's nameplate showed through a box cut from the paper. On the floor was a flower arrangement—orchids wrapped around a gnarled branch, black rocks in a black ceramic bowl, some tufts of greenery showing through the rocks.

Look what thirty-four years gets you, thought McMichael. He touched the paper with his palm.

32

The Hansen home was out on Point Loma, less than a mile from Pete's place but a few blocks up from the water. McMichael parked on a steep short street, pushed down hard on the parking brake. He walked toward the house smelling the cool Pacific just a few hundred yards away. The Hansen driveway was gated so he used the intercom. Patricia buzzed him in.

The house was set far back from the curb, beneath three towering pines. It was white plaster with a brown tile roof and Castilian wrought iron over the windows. McMichael felt a chill as he walked from the cool winter sunlight into the eternal shade of the trees. Patricia's red Mercedes with a small rental trailer attached was parked in front of the garage. The door knocker was an iron ring with a black cast hummingbird flying inside it but he couldn't tell if it was Anna's.

McMichael stood in the kitchen while Patricia placed wineglasses in a partitioned box. She wore old jeans, new athletic shoes and a Henley shirt with the sleeves pushed to her elbows. Hair up, the black zigzag bouncing off her forehead.

"Fifty bucks a pop for these," she said. "Have to take care of them. Gar, hell, he'll drink an Opus One from a coffee mug if it saves him half a step to the cupboard."

She glanced at the double sink, one side filled with dirty mugs and tumblers and flatware.

"I should quit ragging on him," she said. "This makes me sad, packing up. Nine years with that guy, and they weren't all bad."

"I did this, too," he said. "A top-fiver of rotten days."

She looked at him, nodded, went back to the wineglasses. This was exactly the kind of place that would have set them off twenty years ago, a place forbidden and irresistible. Her and her husband's bed, just a room away. McMichael's mind wandered pleasantly back to an evening on Pete's deck, then rushed forward to Rawlings on the ground at the border.

"There's boxes by the door you could load in," she said. "Books and papers."

McMichael carried a heavy box outside to the trailer, pushed it along the steel floor to one corner. He wondered if his old love poem based on "Trees" was in there. Three more heavy boxes. He stood in the shade of the pine for a moment and watched a jet from Lindbergh rise west over the ocean. He heard a shrill squawking sound from somewhere behind the Hansen home, wondered if there were monkeys in the eucalyptus.

She passed him on the walkway with a box and a smile. McMichael carried out the last box, then helped her with some things from the garage— golf clubs, skis, exercise contraptions. He heard the monkeys in the tree again.

"What's that?" he asked.

"Gar's friends." She led him down the walkway to the backyard.

The monkeys weren't monkeys at all, but birds. The aviary took up almost half of the big shaded yard. There were high poles with green mesh strung over the top and sides, but he could hardly see it against the foliage. What he did see were the canaries and finches flitting around their feeders, the parrots and macaws sidling and squawking, the peacocks dragging their elaborate robes of color across the gravel-and-poop-strewn ground. Two flamingos stood by a gurgling pool and looked at McMichael as if he were common.

"Got any owl parrots?" he asked.

"They're those big drowsy ones right there," she said, pointing. "Sleep all day, squawk all night. Gar bought them half a year ago. Are you interested in birds?"

"Some of them."

McMichael remembered the girl in Bird Brains describing the buyer of two owl parrots six months ago, thought of Johnny writing notes in his black notebook. *White guy. Maybe fifty. Athletic. Goodlooking. Short blond hair.*

"There are wild parrots here on the point," she said. "Came up from Mexico and stayed."

"So," said McMichael, "Garland goes in there once a day to feed them, maybe check the water?"

She looked at him with suspicion, nodding. "What's up, Tom?"

"Johnny's got a parakeet. Wants a walk-in aviary someday, like this one."

"The birds have to be compatible. Talk to Garland. He'll tell you all about it."

"Maybe I'll do that."

He helped her carry a cedar chest into the trailer, climbing inside to get it up against one side. When he was finished he wiped his brow and sat back on his haunches. "Got something to drink, Pat?"

In the kitchen she offered to spike the soft drink with rum or vodka but McMichael declined.

"Did I freak you out with all my nostalgia talk on the boat?" she asked.

He shook his head. He was trying to calculate the chances of an owl parrot feather attaching to Garland's black running suit, then falling off during a beating. Pretty decent, was what he came up with.

"I'm sorry if I did. I want to keep you close, Tom."

"I value you," he said.

"But not enough to get to know me again? I've actually changed in some good ways."

"I believe you. Did you and Garland drive a lot of demo vehicles from the dealership?"

She looked at him hard. "You came over here to question me?"

"And to help with the heavy stuff."

She smiled without enthusiasm. "Sure, we drove demo cars. Mostly Gar. Who cares?"

"The last time anybody saw Courtney Gonzalez alive, she was getting into a wine-colored SUV with Pete Braga plates. That was Thursday, January second."

McMichael watched a darkness come to Patricia's face. "Who's Courtney Gonzalez?"

"One of Pete's girlfriends. A professional girlfriend. She got murdered and dumped."

Patricia shook her head with finality. "I never met one of them. I heard he had them. There are some things you don't want to know about your grandfather."

"Garland drove a wine-colored SUV for a month or so, didn't he?"

"Yep."

The doorbell rang and she sighed, then went to answer it. A minute later Patricia came back with a FedEx envelope and tossed it on a stool.

"Tom," she said, "you want to know about Gar, talk to Gar. He's all yours."

"When will he be back?"

"This evening, sometime—United from San Francisco. You're not really serious about him killing anybody are you?"

"Not really," he said, shaking his head as he lied. "I'm still just fishing."

"He's the supreme coward."

"People can surprise you."

"Garland as a killer," she said flatly. "I don't know whether to laugh or shudder."

"When did you tell him you were divorcing him? Was it before or after Pete died?"

"After. But he had to know before. I can't fake things."

"How did he react?"

"He threw a bottle of vodka through the sliding glass door. Then cried. Went to his room and locked the door. We had separate rooms by then."

He nodded. "No sense in telling him I was asking these things, Pat."

"No. You want to go get some lunch?"

"I've got some things to do. Rain check?"

"Whatever, Tom. I'll walk you out."

McMichael delivered to Arthur Flagler the table knife and fork he'd swiped from Garland Hansen's sink and pocketed while Patricia was collecting the FedEx envelope. He spilled them from a paper towel onto one of Flagler's light tables.

"Compare the prints on these to the prints inside the gloves," McMichael said.

"Whose expensive but tasteless silverware do we have the honor of dusting here?"

"It doesn't matter."

"No case number? No chain of custody? Those things matter in what we quaintly refer to as courts of law."

"I need these fast, Arthur."

"You'll get them when I'm done, Sergeant."

From his desk McMichael called United Airlines and confirmed the scheduled arrival of United Express flight 687 from San Francisco at six-twenty.

Then he called Hector and told him they had a special passenger to meet at Lindbergh in a few hours. McMichael told him about the SUV, the owl parrots, the divorce, and Garland Hansen's imperiled stake in Pete Braga's estate.

He read his notes from Bird Brains. It was a good description of Garland, and the girl with the stainless steel stud in her eyebrow seemed sharp enough to pull Hansen out of a lineup. McMichael smiled to himself, looking forward to telling Johnny that their notes had paid off.

McMichael was sitting in Gabriel's room at San Diego General Hospital, listening to his father tell stories about his mother and watching the darkness fall, when his cell phone rang.

"I found something extremely upsetting in my garage," said Patricia. "I think you need to see them."

"What are they?"

"They can't be described."

McMichael called Hector but got the machine.

33

Point Loma was dark against the sky as McMichael headed up North Harbor Drive. The evening was crisp already, the last of sunset just a fading pale stripe in the western sky. A stiff breeze rocked the yachts at Spanish Landing.

The Hansen driveway gate was open. When he pulled in he saw Patricia's red Mercedes parked in a flood of white light coming from the garage. It was tucked up close to the open door, the rental trailer still attached. In the rearview he saw the gate roll closed.

They can't be described.

Patricia was leaning against the car door, hunched against the chill in a leather jacket, a wool watch cap pulled down to cover her ears. She looked away as he cut the lights and parked behind her.

He got out and shut his door quietly.

"Thanks for coming," she said. She was wearing black gloves and her face looked flushed and some-how eager.

"You're welcome. What is it, Pat?"

She shook her head and pushed away from the car. As he walked into the fluorescent light of the garage McMichael noted the box springs and mattress leaning up against one wall, two tireless bicycles hanging along another, a workbench, the Peg-Board wall hung with various tools. There was a lawnmower, a leaf blower, a chainsaw and a boat trailer. And four towers of boxes stacked and leaning, apparently on their way to the trailer. A cobweb swayed in the breeze. A lamp had been set up on an old chest of drawers, the naked bulb glowing over a big stainless steel tub.

McMichael stepped to it and looked down.

"I had to put a sheet over them," she said.

He reached down to lift it and heard the terrible crack of impact. Felt it. Then another. The sheet turned red. So did the metal tub, into which he felt himself falling, the sides reeling up past him as it swallowed him into the shiny red tunnel.

The last thing he heard was Patricia's voice.

"Do it again."

McMichael opened his eyes to two of everything: glove boxes, dashboard vents, outside temperature readouts of 51 degrees, tach and speed dials, two overlapping circles of steering wheels held at ten and two o'clock by four gloved hands. His head felt open on top, an air-dried pain over a throbbing ache inside. It felt wet and sticky. He couldn't raise it straight back, just to the left a little as his twin visions multiplied and diminished.

He looked down at his hands, bloody and cinched

at the wrists by a plastic tie. He noted that his knees were spread but his feet were held together by something heavy and tight. With significant anguish he turned his head down to see his bloody shirt, then let it loll to the left again.

"Welcome back, McMichael."

The voice was high-pitched and anxious. He cocked an eye to confirm Patricia as the speaker and driver.

"How's the head?" asked someone behind him.

From some suspecting cranny of his brain McMichael processed the sound, managed to connect it to one he'd heard before. Gar. McMichael felt something hard and inhuman jab into his head from behind, three times.

"More where that came from, so don't get any giant ideas," said Garland. "Watch the goddamned road, Pat."

McMichael lolled his head to the right, felt the stickiness of blood on his neck, saw the market where Sally Rainwater had bought firewood. He let his eyes fall to the sideview mirror, wondering if Hector was by some miracle behind them. But all he could see was the flank of the vehicle he was riding in and the lights shooting back along it. By pressing the inside of his upper left arm against his side he confirmed that his weapon was gone. With the inside of his right elbow against his other side he knew his phone was gone, too.

He coughed, felt the top of his head open to the stars. He swallowed a mouthful of shaved metal and gave one experimental, cutting tug on his wrist ties.

"Too bad you drew the case," said Patricia. "I

knew the chances were one in four, but I could never win a hand at blackjack, either."

McMichael squinted at the buildings along Rosecrans. Triplicate now. His head felt volcanic, but he was oddly outside himself, too, detached and objective, like he was watching himself go through this. He tried to focus his vision out beyond the rearview, but all he got was blur.

"We're all going for a sail," Patricia said brightly. "In case you were wondering. Aboard *Christina* and this little skiff Gar never registered. But the skiff is going to blow up accidentally with only you on it. Which, on the plus side, is why Gar hasn't already shot you."

McMichael tried to digest the details of his own death, but they seemed distant and inapplicable. "Why kill Pete?" he managed.

"Tom, that's a long and very personal story. I wasn't appreciated."

Garland chuckled from the back.

"And Tom, you know nothing in the world pisses me off like not being appreciated."

"Rainwater?"

"Born to fall and very convenient. You were a minus and she was a plus and you canceled each other out. I'm good at math, remember? Gar, he's good at sneaking in and out of places, leaving things for cops to find."

"He doesn't need the details," said Garland.

"I was just showing off," said Patricia. "But my hands are shaking I'm so nervous."

"Watch the road, goddamn it."

"Don't yell, Gar."

"Watch the *road, Patricia*."

"I see the road."

"Good. Pat's the micromanager," said Garland, stabbing at McMichael's head again. "I'm the big-picture guy. You want an executive summary, McMikey? Here goes. The old man tried to cut us out, so he could cut the nurse in. But we were the ones putting up with his endless shit, year after year. His petty little games, his foul mouth, his whores and his tantrums. What was his wedding present to us? He threatened to disinherit Pat if we went through with it. Pat managed to talk him out of it. Stuff like that builds up, man, it fucking *builds up*. Pretty soon, it blows."

"It takes you over," said Patricia.

McMichael let his head loll right again, tried to pick up some sign of Hector. He'd left his destination on Hector's machine. But Hector was keyed to meeting Garland Hansen's plane at the airport. McMichael figured that by the time things went froggy at Lindbergh Field, he'd be ten fathoms down. When Patricia changed lanes he saw a white Crown Victoria two cars back, but the picture changed when she straightened out.

"Bland and the TJ thing?" His voice was little more than a whisper.

"Blandon the TJ thing?" asked Patricia. "Gar must have hit you harder than I thought."

"What the hell are you talking about?" Garland asked, rapping the back of McMichael's head with something hard. "Blandon who?"

McMichael checked the sideview mirror for the Crown Vic, saw nothing but the lights flickering down the side panel. He had figured by now that they were in some kind of SUV—probably a big Ford, an Excursion or Explosion or whatever they called them. He found the power window control down to his right, and the power door lock, both conveniently illuminated. He thought of Johnny in La Jolla and his father at General and his mother in the ground and Raegan at *Libertad* and Sally Rainwater in the Santee women's jail. Where was Hector?

"Why Angel?" McMichael heard himself ask.

"I took control of some of Grandma's possessions after she died. You know, it takes a woman to appreciate certain things. But the hooker caught me switching out Grandma's hummingbird for a fake. She said maybe I could take care of her, and Grandpa would never know. So I took care of her. We'd put in too much planning to have a whore mess it up. After her, Pete wasn't that hard. You just do what you have to do. And you? You'll be easy, McMichael. You always were."

He sat with his head bowed, smelling his blood, watching the lights do freakish things on the windshield.

"Like my divorce story?" asked Patricia. "The apartment and the boxes at our place? We're going to rent out the apartment. And tomorrow we move the boxed stuff to Pete's house. Me and Gar are going to kind of squat there, possession being nine-tenths of—"

Suddenly, flashes of red and blue lights shot through the interior. Garland cursed and Patricia's gloved hands tightened on the wheel. McMichael managed to turn his head to the right, very slowly, and from the corner of his eye he saw two Crown Victorias with two gum-balls on the top, two faint faces of Hector as he drove the cars under a streetlamp.

"Goddamn it!" yelled Garland.

"You're dead," McMichael muttered.

"Bull*shit*," said Patricia. She slowed for a red light, then gunned the big vehicle through it as brakes screeched and horns blared from both sides. Chrome and paint flashed past McMichael's eyes. He forced his head around again, to see Hector trapped in the intersection behind them. Ahead, an SDPD cruiser bumped from a parking lot onto the boulevard with full lights and sound. Then another right behind it.

"Can't outrun a radio," said McMichael.

Garland reached past the headrest and whacked the side of McMichael's face, up on the cheekbone. McMichael wrenched right and tried to get a finger onto the lock control but Garland yanked him back, McMichael's head slapping back against the rest.

Patricia gunned it south on Harbor Drive, a high-velocity shot past Spanish Landing and the airport. Two PD cruisers slid into the intersection at Grape but Patricia charged over the curb and onto the sidewalk. A young man, eyes wide in the headlights, pushed a woman and child to the ground and McMichael saw his legs and feet vanish under the hood. No thump. From the corner of his eye he saw a splayed tangle of family as the SUV roared by. Patricia caught greens at Ash and Broadway, but ran a red light at Pacific Coast Highway with the heel of one hand on the horn and—to McMichael's breathless stupefaction—both of her eyes closed. Garland yelled and pulled McMichael back hard by the collar of his jacket. McMichael wheeled left and brought up his cuffed hands, landing flush on Garland's jaw, which got McMichael's head a ferocious jolt back to the rest, Garland yanking him by his hair. Ahead McMichael could see two more PD cars blocking the boulevard, officers with their sidearms braced on the hoods, a cop who looked about twenty years old aiming a riot gun at the windshield as Patricia swerved to the right, crashed into the back end of one unit that moved slowly out of the way as the big SUV screeched under throttle and cops seemed to fall from the sky. She bullied past and free. Green lights at Fifth and Eighth, patrol cars howling into line behind them. McMichael's vision doubled his estimate of catastrophe as Patricia barged along at sixty miles an hour toward Crosby Street.

"Get back on the freeway," yelled Garland. "They can't block it."

"The Five? Where's the Five, Gar?"

"Straight ahead, left on Crosby, babe, you've driven it a million times!"

Patricia made the turn but two SDPD cars were waiting for them and she swerved right on National, then hooked another quick right to miss an oncoming city bus.

"Nooo!" bellowed Garland, but it was too late as the SUV groaned onto the ramp and the great stanchions of the Coronado Bridge rose in the darkness beyond the windshield.

"There's no exits!" shouted Garland. "It's a fucking *bridge*, Pat."

"Look, a carpool lane!"

McMichael felt the vehicle gently climb, then saw before him the lights that traced the graceful rise and fall of the bridge all the way to Coronado. The water below was black and silver and the navy battleships were black shapes without light. As the SUV climbed out over the dark water McMichael's stomach took a sickening drop.

"Pull over and stop," he said.

"Shut the—" said Garland.

"Pat, you'll kill us all."

She accelerated. The bridge lights came faster and the oncoming headlights blurred. As they topped the span and began the long way down onto the island he saw the flashing lights of the roadblock up ahead. McMichael felt an odd clarity sweep over him. To his left the oncoming traffic suddenly was gone—stopped upstream by the police. Ahead of them two rows of cruisers blocked the road from median to railing, headlights on high and warning lights flashing. To the right was black air and a long fall into the water and McMichael knew what Patricia would do.

"Hold on, men," she said.

Then the deafening sound of metal shearing on concrete. The right side of the SUV caught and buckled under, but its motion was suddenly and horrifically overridden when the back end flipped up and over the rail and fell into the night.

McMichael's world reversed.

He looked through the window at the bridge

lights receding above him. He slammed his weight against the door and fumbled for the lock control, pressed the up button. Punched the shoulder strap loose. Yanked the door handle. Shoved off the transmission hump with both feet. Put shoulder and head and arm and soul into it. The door blasted open and flung McMichael into space. The next thing he knew he was upside down, falling through darkness and a dazzling consortium of lights and all he could think to do was tighten himself into a ball and hope that he would hit water and not a battleship and that his major bones wouldn't break and the SUV wouldn't land on top of him. *God*, he thought: *I believe in you*.

34

"San Diego Police detective Thomas McMichael is in stable condition tonight at General Hospital, one day after his *dramatic* fall from the Coronado Bridge. Channel Eight's Manny Alonzo has the story. . . ."

McMichael viewed the television screen with the grateful disbelief of anyone who has given himself up for dead. Manny was standing on the bridge, where the SUV had flipped over. The rain poured down around the edge of his umbrella and the lights of Coronado twinkled in the background.

"Don't turn it off," said Hector. "I want to see the good part again."

McMichael watched through a Vicodin haze, his left leg in a half cast for a broken tibia, his left shoulder relocated, his head shaved and wrapped in gauze and bearing twenty-six staples, his wrists lacerated by the plastic ties and needing fourteen stitches to close. He felt like Frankenstein. His concussion was relatively mild, according to Dr. Miles

Fellon, who used this as a basis for jokes about the hardness of McMichael's head.

". . . and it was here, on the Coronado Bridge, where the tragic high-speed chase finally ended," said Alonzo. "The sport utility vehicle driven by Patricia Hansen literally *flipped* over this railing right here, plummeting almost two *hundred* feet into the icy waters of Glorietta Bay. Hansen, granddaughter of former San Diego mayor Pete Braga, was killed in the fall. Her husband—*Shred!* executive Garland Hansen—who was a passenger in the car with Detective McMichael, is missing and presumed dead. Now, San Diego Police are *still* trying to piece together last night's bizarre events. . . ."

McMichael half closed his eyes, half listened to the report.

Gabriel, legs splayed by casts, sat in his wheelchair on one side of the bed. He'd been infernally chatty, jabbering all afternoon how a broken calf bone was nothing compared to the two thighbones that he had to deal with. He said the pain made him feel closer to God but frankly questioned if that was a good thing, nipping regularly from a dark pint bottle he kept under his butt.

Hector sat on the other side of McMichael's bed, leaning forward on his thick forearms to catch himself on the tube again.

"Yeah, look, Mick—here it is."

McMichael drowsily watched the footage from last night: a pale and silent Hector pulling his partner from the black water of the bay. McMichael, bound and barely conscious, looked dead. Hector looked fine. He'd jumped off the bridge when he saw the SUV go over, pausing just long enough to toss his gun, shoes and wallet into the car. He told McMichael later that landing in the bay was like having your balls walloped against a frozen sidewalk.

". . . Police are still not saying how—or even *if*—these events are connected to the brutal murder of Pete Braga just over two weeks ago in his Point Loma home. Many questions here. Manny Alonzo on the Coronado Bridge in the Coronado rain—back to you, Julie."

McMichael watched the pretty anchorwoman lock her blue eyes on the TelePrompTer and frown very slightly.

"I never got to talk to her," Hector noted gravely.

"In a related—"

"I could relate," said Hector.

"Sally Rainwater, the twenty-eight-year-old premed student at—"

"And total babe," said Hector.

"She's the one, son? She looks just like your mother did!"

"—was released from the women's jail in Santee late this afternoon. All charges against her have been dropped—charges that stemmed from the still-unsolved murder of San Diego's Pete Braga. As if this case could get any *more* complex, Ms. Rainwater and Detective McMichael are believed to have been romantically involved during the early days of the investigation. Ms. Rainwater stayed inside her beachfront Imperial Beach home, and did not speak to reporters."

Gabriel fixed McMichael with a wickedly complicitous smile as he leaned over and worked his bottle back out.

"Send her some flowers, Mick," said Hector. "Tell her you spent the whole morning with lawyers, just for her. Tell her you're sorry. Tell her your whole body hurts and you need a nurse."

McMichael aimed the remote at Hector and turned him off. Then his father. He picked up the phone, sat it on his belly, and called Victor again.

Johnny and Stephanie came later that evening. McMichael could smell the puppy on his boy when he hugged him and he thought it was a wonderful smell. Johnny brought him a picture of the little chocolate Lab, not much bigger than a football, pointed out his good features, stated that Brownie was almost housebroken. Stephanie rolled her eyes and smiled at McMichael with a full-body wince.

They stayed almost an hour. During that time McMichael drifted in and out of pretending that they were a family again. It was so easy: these moments connected directly back with other moments, and the time between them was banished. He remembered coming home after day shift in the summers years ago, cracking a beer and sitting in the little living room with the view of the harbor and the freeway, with Johnny climbing on and off his lap, yapping about the events of the day; remembered Stephanie in her simple sundresses, hair up for the heat, how fresh and content she seemed; he could smell her, even—this bulk-sized body lotion that to McMichael was better than any perfume; he remembered the neighbor's radio and the jets lowering toward Lindbergh and the bedroom where their nights ended and their days began.

"We have to go, Johnny," said Steffy. She reached her face toward McMichael hesitantly, like a pecking bird, kissed him on the third try, then backed away with tears in her eyes. Johnny looked at her with an uncomprehending expression.

Then the chief, ADA Gerald Dale again, Barbara Givens and Mark Hatter, a couple of the old Metro/Vice faces, even Andrea Robb from Internal Affairs. Then Hector, on his way to the Gaslamp to "cash in" on his fifteen minutes.

Dr. Fellon came by just after dinner and told McMichael he wanted to keep him overnight "to be on the safe side." If the swelling in McMichael's head went down and he was feeling capable, he could go home in the morning.

"Turned out to be Patricia's prints on the gloves," Hector said, lowering McMichael into the passenger seat and sliding the crutches into the back.

It was Saturday morning and the rain had turned to showers. McMichael watched Hector roll the wheelchair back to the hospital entrance and tried to digest what he had just been told, tried to imagine Patricia swinging the bloody club, over and over, again and again. What possible unappreciation could account for that?

Hector plunked into the driver's seat.

"That doesn't make sense to me," McMichael said.

"And they found Garland half an hour ago, washed up dead on the navy beach."

"That does."

They made it halfway to McMichael's apartment without talking.

"Mitzi Bland is going to make it," said Hector. "That's what the doctor said. See? Good news. I'm trying to cheer you up."

McMichael spent a few hours on the phone, then hobbled around his apartment on crutches, getting the hang of them. For the first time in his life he was glad his place was small. The worst part was the throbbing down in his left calf, the deep-down ache of broken bone. And his wrists hurt, too, with the pressure of his weight and the cuts of the plastic fasteners that had sliced into him. A little blood had seeped up through the dressings. But even with all this nagging him, he couldn't get Patricia out of his mind. Like a brain thorn, only bigger, he thought. A brain tree. A brain forest.

Raegan came for lunch and stayed almost all afternoon. She brought food and flowers and one of her best cigars, which McMichael fingered and smelled but didn't light. She straightened and dusted and sorted the mail and talked about this guy she'd met at *Libertad* a couple of nights back: funny and good-looking and she liked his eyes and the way he talked. He was from Wichita Falls, Texas, just brought up by the Padres from AAA, a ninety-two-mile-an-hour fastball. McMichael told her to step out of the box if she needed more time. She wasn't sure of the baseball metaphor but left him with a big pot of stew on the stove and a vivid lipstick smudge, he saw later, on his cheek.

When Raegan was gone he finally mustered the courage to call Sally Rainwater. No longer in service and no new number.

He spent the evening and early night in his bed, head and cast resting on pillows. The rain had slowed to light showers and the wind was slapping the palm fronds against the windows.

He kept thinking about Patricia's penchant for destruction. There was the thrill of it. For as far back as he could remember Patricia had been the one to flaunt the rules. Openly. Proudly. Happily. Maybe it was like any other exciting thing: you needed more and more to get the same feeling. Drinkers. Dopers. Speed freaks. Adrenaline junkies. Thrill seekers. *It takes you over.* There was always something of the show-off in it, too: look at me, me, me. She had always thought of herself as larger than life, better than the rest. In some ways she really was. He wondered if the bottom of it was self-hatred. If the destruction of things was just a long warm-up for destroying herself. But maybe it was simpler. Maybe she wanted to go out like her mom and dad had, join them somehow. Or maybe there was just a kink in her wiring, some faulty relay that might have shown up on a PET scan as a small red ember where there should have been an ocean of cool blue. Maybe you had to put all the conjecture together and stir it to know why a bright and beautiful woman would do what she had done. Maybe you could never know.

Many years ago he saw in Patricia what he thought was lacking in himself: spirit and passion and the courage to take a chance. Gabriel had proved to him long before how one mistake can ruin you and those you love. What a towering lesson that was. So McMichael had pulled for Patricia to prove the opposite: that you can turn mistakes to your advantage, outrun the consequences if you have to, do what you want and let the world sort it out. Even as roadkill he still wanted her to pull it off. It worked for her, for a while. It worked a while for most of the guys he sent to prison, too.

He closed his eyes and listened to the wind and fell asleep with the image of Patricia's smiling face still luminous in his mind.

35

Super Bowl Sunday afternoon was clear and cool as McMichael worked himself into the driver's seat of his take-home Ford. He leaned the crutches against the seat beside him, used both hands to get his left leg and cast into the car. It hurt like a sonofabitch but he wouldn't risk pain pills and driving. Thank God for automatic transmissions, he thought.

Traffic was heavy—a city abuzz with the big game. He listened briefly to the pregame radio. When he climbed onto the Coronado Bridge a lavishly illustrated dread hit him and he remembered every second of that ride, right down to the strange wild smell that had filled the cab as Patricia gunned the SUV toward the roadblock. The smell of terror. But he guided the Crown Vic up the span and down toward Coronado, noting the scraped and bent railing where they'd gone over. There wasn't really much to it. The other drivers didn't even slow down for a better look. Bigger things on their minds—point spreads and kegs and traffic into Qualcomm Stadium. McMichael wondered if short memories were, in the long run, a good thing.

He dropped down onto Silver Strand Boulevard and headed south. The wind was up and he could see little puffs of sand swirling off to his right. The ocean was brightly beveled and even McMichael's good sunglasses couldn't keep him from squinting. He wore a Padres cap very loosely on his head to keep himself and the world from having to look at his bandages.

Sally Rainwater's place looked different, even from a distance. The potted plants on the porch were gone, and a man that McMichael had never seen before was touching up the paint on the front door.

McMichael noted the FOR RENT sign propped against the railing as he labored onto the porch. A radio had the pregame show on.

The man stopped painting and looked at him. "You're the cop," he said.

"I take it she moved."

"Gone by Friday evening."

To McMichael, Friday seemed like two years ago, not two days ago. So, she'd gotten out of jail, packed up and split. Didn't waste a second. He admired her resolve and efficiency.

He looked through the open front door, at the wall where one of Pete Braga's paintings had hung. The sailing scene—a man and his boat against a raw and violent ocean. A sea without blue. He could see the nail hole. "Do you have a number for her?"

"Didn't leave me one," said the landlord. "Paid up cash and that was that."

"Did she say where she was going?"

The landlord shook his head and set down the paint can. "She never did say very much. Kept the place clean, though. I gave her the deposit back. The news vans smashed up some ice plant over by the street, but that's about it."

"Can I go in?"

The landlord stared at McMichael. "Sure."

McMichael stood in the living room, looked at the small, sun-blasted kitchen. He walked down the hallway where they'd scared Sally Rainwater half to death, past the closet where they'd found the evidence hidden by Patricia and Garland, then into the bedroom. The louvered windows were open, the two faulty panes replaced by new ones with the stickers still on them. He tried to picture what the room had looked like with the bed there and Sally in it. It was easy.

On his way out the landlord told him the rent was fifteen hundred but he'd knock off a hundred if a cop wanted it. McMichael said he'd ask around.

He found Victor in his room at the Horton Grand, watching cartoons on TV. Victor told him he could come in, took a bag of potato chips off a chair so McMichael could sit.

"Have you seen *SpongeBob SquarePants*?" Victor asked.

"A couple of times."

"I like the way the bubbles come up. But I think if fish talked, there'd be more bubbles."

"Me too. How are you, Victor?"

Victor shrugged. "I miss Pat and Gar. Were you the other guy in the car?"

"Yeah, that was me."

"Pat always drove way too fast. Gar would yell at her."

"I remember that about her, too. Do you need anything, Victor?"

Victor looked at him blankly, then back at the screen. "Like what?"

"Help with paperwork, or someone to drive you somewhere, maybe?"

"No, thanks. They found Angel."

"I know."

"I don't get why someone would kill her. She was really nice."

McMichael said nothing to that. He could see no reason to tell Victor who had killed the angel in his life, or why. For a hummingbird made of jewels.

"I guess you'll have a lot of money coming your way soon," said McMichael. "When they get the estate straightened out."

"Yeah," said Victor. "And I still got my job. Charley's a good guy."

"I'm going to leave one of my cards here on the table," said McMichael. "You call me if you need anything."

Victor looked at him. "I called the police to find out when they're going to bury Angel. They wouldn't tell me."

"I'll find out. I'll drive you if you want."

"Cool."

"Later, Victor."

*   *   *

Just after the opening kickoff McMichael's home phone rang. It was a desk officer calling from headquarters saying that Henry Grothke Sr. was in the lobby demanding to show something to McMichael.

"He refuses to leave it, or even tell me what it is. But it appears to be a tub of ice cream, sir. Fudge marble."

"I'll be there in fifteen minutes."

McMichael hobbled toward the civilian entrance of police headquarters. He saw Old Grothke's van pulled into a no-parking zone, saw Derek smoking a cigarette as he leaned against the vehicle.

Inside, Old Grothke sat in his wheelchair facing the door, hands clasped over an ice cream carton resting on his red blanket. He wore a blue suit with a gray tie and matching handkerchief. The suit was marked with what appeared to be dried ice cream. *There's always vultures in the ice cream.*

His clear blue eyes locked onto McMichael's face as he approached.

"Detective McMichael," he said.

"Hello, Mr. Grothke."

"Look—proof of my sanity."

McMichael balanced his armpits over the crutches and accepted the ice cream carton. It was wet and warm and left a gooey semicircle on the old man's blanket. It was in fact marble fudge. He pulled off the top and looked inside. It was half full of melted brown sludge. The upper half was packed with letter envelopes locked inside a plastic freezer bag.

"Pete's letters, as promised," said Grothke. "I forgot where I put them."

"Odd place to put business correspondence," said McMichael.

"They searched my whole place and couldn't find them."

"Who searched it?"

"My son. And Pete Braga's granddaughter. Derek even helped them and he's supposed to work for me."

McMichael touched the ice-cream-smeared freezer bag. "I'm going to have to take these somewhere else to open them. You're welcome to come upstairs with me if you want."

Grothke smiled. "I can't explain how happy I was to remember where I'd put these. I didn't just open the freezer and find them. I *remembered perfectly* where they were."

"Let's go read them, Mr. Grothke."

He put the carton back on old Grothke's lap and they took the elevator up. It took McMichael three phone calls from his desk to get the lab open, this being an American high holy day. Finally he reached Arthur Flagler at home, who gave an okay to the watch commander, who ordered one of the desk officers to open up examination room three.

McMichael got one of the Team One detectives to roll Grothke up to an exam table. McMichael set his crutches aside, snapped a length of white paper towels off the roller to one side, and laid the paper on the tabletop. Set the carton at one end, gloved up and sat down.

"I'll need a pair of those, too," said Grothke. "I wanted to be a detective when I was young."

"Sure."

He helped the old man get the latex on. Grothke held up his ephemeral, gloved hands and stared intently at them.

McMichael checked his tape recorder, then turned it on and placed it out of the way to his right. He unlocked the freezer bag and used tweezers to pull out one of the two envelopes. Pete Braga's name and home address were embossed on the back. The front was hand-addressed to Henry Grothke Sr., personal and confidential, at the firm's downtown address. The text appeared to be typed. McMichael stated the time and date, had Grothke identify himself and confirm them, then read the letter out loud.

December 16

Dear Henry,

Since your crew seems incapable of keeping track of correspondence, I'm writing you again with specific instructions on how to change my will. As I explained in last month's letter (November 8), which you have apparently lost, I wish to eliminate that portion of my estate which will go to my granddaughter, Patricia Hansen, and to her pathetic husband, upon my death.

Her and her husband's attempts to get control of Pete Braga Ford were childish. Her secret meddling with my real estate and stocks has become dangerous. (I assume you still have the documents she forged my signature on. I suspect she has faked more than just my signature on others.) She is duplicitous and untrustworthy. She can scream at me all she wants but that garden hose beating hurt for weeks (I assume you have the earlier pictures I sent). Things are missing from the house but every time I change the locks she comes up with new keys. I believe she has discovered the combination to my floor safe. I believe she has poisoned my fiber drinks but I can't prove that, yet. She's trying to turn Victor against me, telling lies, scaring him, playing tricks on his undeveloped mind. I've had enough. Cut her out of the estate.

I want the rest of Patricia's former share to go to Sally Rainwater, my nurse. She's a wonderful girl, wants to be a doctor someday, and could use some opportunity in her life. Beautiful, too.

Tell neither of them anything about this. I don't want to incur any more of the Braga wrath. Living with my own for eighty-four years has been enough. And Sally would fight me on it for sure. She's an old-fashioned girl.

Call me as soon as you have something for me to sign. I'm not in a big hurry, Hank, but I'd appreciate it if you didn't lose this letter, too.

Sincerely,
Pete

McMichael set the letter on the paper towels and looked at Old Grothke. "What happened to the November letter?"

"I read it and it disappeared. Now it's in that bag."

"Explain, Mr. Grothke."

"Well, the first letter disappeared out of my drawer at work. I looked all over for it. Then the second letter came and it disappeared, too. I thought I was losing my mind because, in actuality, I am. I spent hours going through my file cabinets and computer files. I spent hours searching my house and my garage and my mountain cabin out in Julian. I finally found them in my son's office safe."

Old Grothke smiled thinly, eyes merry. "I discovered the combination years ago."

"Henry had taken them," said McMichael. "And he told Patricia about them."

Grothke stared at him. "I suspect that to be the case. He was her attorney and wanted to see to her best interests. He had the hots for her, too, if you know what I mean."

"He got Pete killed."

Grothke nodded. He looked long and hard at the tape recorder but said nothing.

"When you found them in your son's safe, you took them back."

"I put them in the bag and put the bag in the ice cream and forgot. I found my favorite trout flies in the freezer once. Years ago. I'd set each one in its own compartment of the ice cube tray, then filled them with water. They were beautiful cubes."

McMichael read the other letter, then sat back and looked out the window to the weakening afternoon light. "You would have made a good detective, Mr. Grothke. You're a tad slow these days, but you get the job done."

"I'm ninety-two."

"You just cracked your first case."

"Do you offer a reserve or volunteer program?"

"Yes, we do," said McMichael. He had a brief vision of Old Grothke riding along on patrol, red blanket folded over his ancient lap. "I'll get you the information."

But first, McMichael thought, I'm going to talk with your son.

Young Grothke denied ever reading the letters. *Saw* them, yes; *read* them, no. He said he looked everywhere he could think of, trying to help his confused father out of a professional embarrassment, then reasoned that the old man had misplaced them or even destroyed them in a fit of senile dementia. He told Patricia what had happened, because she was part of the family and he thought she might know why they were important. She said that they probably related to Pete Braga's attempted naming of a church after himself or his wife, because Pete had talked several times about this. Pete was in a huff about the diocese, as he was with most things. Just why Patricia had pretended not to know what the letters said was a matter of *her* deception, not his.

Grothke sweated profusely during the interview. He would not allow a tape recording. He finally stopped answering questions by citing Fifth Amendment protections and asked McMichael to get out of his house so he could watch what was left of the game.

"You and Patricia have a little thing going?" McMichael asked.

"An attorney-client relationship is all we ever had," said Grothke.

But his face told another story altogether.

"You tell me the whole truth here, Mr. Grothke, and there's a chance I can help you."

"I'm innocent, Detective."

"Then I'd like to clear up some details. How about ten o'clock tomorrow morning? Downtown, unless you'd rather do it here. You have a right to an attorney, if you think you need one. You'll probably spend some time in the jail before you post bond, if one is granted."

Grothke's face went from red to white as McMichael heaved upward and got the crutches in place.

"You don't understand. I was only trying to help her," he said. His voice trembled.

"Mind if I sit back down, Mr. Grothke?"

"No. Please."

"I'll need to record this."

"I have absolutely nothing to hide."

"I'm sure that's true. We'll just get comfortable and talk. Turn on the game if you'd like, but keep the volume off."

36

By the time he got home it was dark and cold and his head ached and his leg was throbbing. He took a pain pill and poured a short tequila. For a while he watched the moon rise beyond the palm tree outside his window. The drugs made him feel still and uncomplicated.

He wrote Johnny a letter, something he often did when he couldn't be with his son and a phone call just wasn't enough. He kept it informative, trying to describe in matter-of-fact terms how it felt to fall into the black ocean from a bridge two hundred feet high. He tried to give his crutches and stitches a humorous slant. He said to give Brownie a hug for him. When he finally wrote "I love you and miss you" at the end, it felt like the only thing he'd really wanted to say in the first place.

He ate Raegan's stew for dinner. He was leaning against the sink counter when he heard the knock at the door. He got onto the crutches, swung into action.

Sally Rainwater stood in the porch light, wrapped in a long black coat. Hair down, jeans and boots.

"You okay?" she asked.

"I feel great."

"I meant it."

"So did I, Sally. You're the best thing my eyes could have seen."

The expression on her face was not quite a smile. "I've been thinking."

"There's room for that in here."

He pushed open the door with a crutch and tried to stand back but she put her arms around him. He couldn't move and couldn't speak and didn't want to.

Acknowledgments

I sincerely thank Dave Bridgman, San Diego PD Firearms Instructor (retired), for his generous introductions to San Diego law enforcement and to International Practical Shooting Confederation competition. Also, Captain Ron Newman (retired) for his overview of the Robbery/Homicide/Special Investigations Unit of San Diego's fine police force.

Thanks to Lieutenant George Foote, Lieutenant Lisa Miller and Deputy Sean Zdunich of the San Diego Sheriff's Department for getting me into jail and back out.

Many thanks to Chuck Bencik of the San Diego Historical Society, who provided me with much information on the once majestic but now departed tuna fleet. In particular, August Felando's outstanding series of articles published by the Maritime Museum Association of San Diego, which reminded me that history happens quietly, one second at a time.

Researcher Sherry Merryman unearthed some arcane and disturbing facts for me, as she has done before and I hope she will do again.

Thanks to Sal Proetto and Matt Parker for fishing stories.

Thanks also to Meg Eastman for her help on the subjects of creation and evolution.

And thanks to Larry Ragle, retired head of the Orange County Sheriff-Coroner Department crime lab, for still more good advice.

As always, the truth is theirs and the mistakes are mine.

T. Jefferson Parker
Fallbrook, California

Turn the page for a taste of
two-time Edgar® Award-winning author
T. Jefferson Parker's

CALIFORNIA GIRL

Available in paperback from
Harper
An Imprint of HarperCollins*Publishers*

1

HERE AND NOW

I drove past the old SunBlesst packinghouse today. Nothing left of it. Not one stick. Now there's a bedroom store, a pet emporium, and a supermarket. Big and new. Moms and dads and kids everywhere. Pretty people, especially the moms. Young, with time to dream, wake up, and dream again.

I still have a piece of the flooring I tore off the SunBlesst packinghouse back in sixty-eight. When I was young. When I thought that what had happened there shouldn't ever happen anywhere. When I thought it was up to me to put things right.

I'm made of that place—of the old wood and the rusted conveyors and the pigeons in the eaves and the sunlight slanting through the cracks. Of Janelle Vonn. Of everything that went down, there in October, 1968. Even made of the wind that blew that month, dry and hot off the desert, huffing across Orange County to the sea.

I have a piece of the picket fence from the grassy knoll at Dealey Plaza, too. And a piece of rock that came not far from where *Mercury 1* lifted off. And one of Charlie Manson's guitar picks.

But those are different stories.

Later I met my brother Andy at the Fisherman's Restaurant down in San Clemente. Late August. The day was bright as a brushfire, no clouds, sun flashing off the waves and tabletops. Andy looked at me like someone had hit him in the stomach.

"It's about Janelle," he said.

Janelle Vonn in the SunBlesst orange packinghouse in Tustin.

Thirty-six years ago, two brothers who didn't look much alike, staring down at her and across at each other while the pigeons cooed and the wind blew through the old slats.

A different world then, different world now.

Same brothers. Andy stayed thin and wiry. Tough as a boiled owl. Me, I've filled out some, though I can still shiver the heavy bag in the sheriff's gym.

San Clemente, and you have to think Nixon. The western White House, right up the road. I picture him walking down the beach with the Secret Service guys ahead and behind. Too many secrets and nobody but the seagulls to tell them to. Andy's newspaper ran a cartoon of him once, after he'd been chased out of office, and the cartoon showed him walking the beach with a metal detector, looking for coins. Thought that was a funny one. I kind of liked Dick Nixon. Grew up just over the hill from us. He was tight with my old man and his Bircher friends for a while, used to come to the house back in the fifties when he was vice president and in the early sixties when he'd lost for governor. They'd sit around, drink scotch, make plans. Nixon had a way of making you feel important. It's an old pol's trick, I know. I even knew it then. In fifty-six I graduated from the L.A. Sheriff's Academy and Dick Nixon sent me a note. The vice president. Nice handwriting. It's still in my collection of things.

But that's a different story, too.

"You don't look so good, Andy," I said.

Brothers and we still don't look much alike. An old cop and an old reporter. There used to be four of us Becker boys. Raised some hell. Just three now.

I looked at Andy and I could see something different in his face.

"What gives?" I asked.

"Listen to me, Nick. Everything we thought about Janelle Vonn was wrong."

2

1954

"Because the Vonns are direct descendants of murderers, that's why," said David Becker. "One of their relatives got hung in Texas. And I saw Lenny Vonn bust a brick with his bare hands once. One chop. That's exactly what he'll do to Nick's head. The Vonns are crazy."

The Becker brothers. Four of them, walking down Holt Avenue in Tustin for a rumble. June and still light out, the sun stalled high above the groves like it didn't want to come down. Air sweet and clean with the smell of oranges.

Nick was second oldest. He imagined Lenny Vonn's hand crashing into his skull. Wondered how a skull compared to a brick. Nick was sixteen and strong, had played Tustin varsity football as a sophomore, started both ways. Not a talker.

Andy was the baby. Twelve, skinny, buck-toothed. He wasn't officially a part of the rumble but figured there was no way Lenny Vonn could crush Nick's skull. Nick was God.

David, the one who had seen Lenny Vonn break the brick with his hand, was eighteen. He was the oldest and smart but graceless and unformed.

"I'll yank Casey Vonn's head off and piss down his neck." This from Clay, fifteen. He smiled at each of his brothers in turn, a clean, straight-toothed grin that was both knowing and mean.

Clay had gotten them into this. Grabbed dumb Casey Vonn's new baseball cap and tossed it over the fence to the German shepherd that snarled and snapped and threw himself at the chain link every time the school kids came past. Clay laughed while the dog tore it to shreds. Told Casey he'd throw *him* over next time. Casey so dumb he believed it.

The next day at school Casey's big brother Lenny shoved David hard against the lockers and said it was rumble time for what happened to Casey's cap. Lenny was large and chinless, with an enormous Adam's apple and sideburns like Elvis. Brothers, said Lenny, three-on-three, the packinghouse, no weapons. On David's face, breath like coffee and cavities. David asked Lenny to forgive Clay, said he'd pay for a new hat. Lenny spit in David's face.

The Becker brothers angled into one of the grove rows, walking along the irrigation ditch, clods of earth throwing them off-balance and doves whisking through the sky above them. Nick led the way.

"The Vonns got two sisters," said Clay.

"Can they fight?" asked Andy.

"Maybe I'll *make out* with them when we're done beating up their brothers," said Clay.

"They're seven and five," said David. He knew right from wrong and wrong angered him. He was going off to college in September. He stopped and shook out a Lucky Strike and tapped it on the side of his lighter. Nick saw his hands shaking.

"Gimme a cigarette," said Clay.

David gave Clay the pack and lighter. He lit one and put another behind his ear.

"Me, too," said Andy.

"No," said Nick.

"I don't want to do this," said David. He coughed. He'd spent hours the night before praying for courage.

"Fine," said Nick. "It'll be me and Clay."

"I can fight," said Andy.

"No," Nick and David both said.

Clay's cigarette looked good so Nick plucked it out of his mouth and took a puff.

Nick saw by the look on his face that David didn't want his baby brother to see him get his ass kicked.

"Keep your hands high," Nick said. "If we stay back-to-back we'll be all right." Like there was a science to this kind of thing.

The SunBlesst packinghouse sat behind the railroad tracks in the middle of the grove. The tracks marked the city limits but everyone thought of the packinghouse as being in Tustin. It was a big wooden building with a metal roof and twenty-foot-high metal sliding doors that let the conveyors swing out to the freight cars. The wood was black with creosote. On one of the doors was a giant painting of one of the SunBlesst orange box labels. It showed a raven-haired beauty holding out a perfect navel orange and smiling. Behind her were rows of orange trees. The sky above the trees was indigo blue and the words *California Girl* charged out of it in bright yellow letters. Once someone had left a flatcar of labels outside and the Becker boys threw them into a Santa Ana wind that blew them all over town, onto the lawns and streets and school yards, and everywhere he went for a week Nick saw that pretty woman offering him an orange.

The Vonns were waiting for them by the railroad tracks. Lenny had his T-shirt tucked in tight and his cigarettes rolled into his right shirtsleeve, Levi's cuffs rolled into two-inchers, work boots. His brothers more or less the same. Black hair and big round ears. Lenny flicked his smoke into the gravel and stared at Nick.

Nick figured it was him against Lenny, Clay against Casey, and David the oldest against the middle Vonn kid, Ethan. "What do you say, Lenny?" he called out.

"I say fuck you."

"That's all?"

"And your whole ugly family."

Casey Vonn laughed. Then Ethan.

Nick stopped at the bottom of the railroad berm, where the gravel led up to the ties and tracks. David and Clay came up beside him. Sweat rolled down David's cheek. Nick turned to see young Andy hanging back in the orange grove.

"You know, Lenny, we could just apologize to you and not fight."

"It's too late for apologies. The dog ate the hat. It was new."

"Then you apologize to us," said Clay. "How about that?"

"For what?" asked Lenny.

"For being so dumb," said Clay. "Look at you dumb shitheels trying to be cool."

War screams then, and gravel chattering and dust rising as the Vonns hurled themselves down the berm.

Nick figured on a left from Lenny because of where Lenny kept his cigarettes. Lenny flew toward him and Nick stepped away and got him with a left hook. Lenny wheeled and came back at him and Nick drove a straight right into his nose. Felt the crack. Lenny went to one knee, wiped the blood off his face, and looked at it. Pouring like a faucet thrown on.

"Gung fuggin kiw you."

The blood unnerved him and Nick let Lenny stand up. Knew it was a mistake but let him up anyway. He caught Lenny coming in with a big left haymaker that landed high above the ear and sent a bullet of pain up his hand.

Then someone clobbered Nick from behind and he was down before he felt or heard it. Looking back, he saw Clay pummeling Casey, David down and looking his way but no opponent in sight, Andy still watching from the trees. Then a shadow falling above him and Nick understood someone was about to club him again.

This time he heard it. Ethan behind him with something big and heavy. Felt the jolt, then the loud whine in his ears. Lenny kicked him in the face. Kicked him again in the ribs. Nick felt the fight huff out of him.

Clay slugged Casey one more time and climbed off. Saw Ethan Vonn swing the short thick branch at Nick and his brother crumple like something dead and Lenny kicking him hard.

Clay covered the distance fast and jumped Ethan the clubber from behind. They fell onto Nick and rolled off. Clay came up with the club and caught Lenny low. Lenny stumbled back, two disbelieving eyes wide open through the blood as Andy rocketed through the air and knocked him to the ground.

Ethan struggled to his feet, turned, and labored up the berm.

Nick got himself upright as Lenny shrugged off Andy and sidled away, half crawling and half falling after his brother.

Clay kicked at him but missed.

Andy, on hands and knees, breathed fast and hard.

"Yer fuggin dead," said Lenny.

"Yeah, yeah," said Nick.

"Dumb shitheels," said Clay.

Nick picked up the club, then took a knee like they did in football. His head hurt and he felt the vomit stirring inside. He watched two Lennys make the top of the berm, faces and sideburns and shirts soaked in blood. Twin Caseys clambered up next, both blubbering, eyes swollen and lips cut. He felt a hand on his shoulder and he knew without turning it was David.

Nick looked up to see four girls looking down at

him from the tracks. Then just two. The bigger one had brown braids and wore a dirty pink blouse. The younger one was dark-haired and dimpled and had an inquisitive look on her face.

The older one stepped down the berm a few feet toward the Becker brothers and launched a white rock that flew wild. Then another. She scurried back up and ran away.

The younger one followed her sister's footsteps almost exactly. She had a faded blue dress and a red ribbon in her hair and a pair of scuffed brown cowboy boots. An orange in each hand. The SunBlesst girl's baby sister, thought Nick. Looked about five.

"I am Janelle Vonn and those are my brothers," she said.

She dropped the oranges and scrambled back up the gravel and out of sight.

3

That night Max and Monika Becker loaded their four sons into the Studebaker and drove across town to the Vonns' house. The Studebaker was a green fifty-one Champion with the big conical nose for a front end and an oddly sloping rear. They called it the Submarine. They cruised along Holt Avenue through the groves, Max erect behind the wheel and Monika's straight yellow hair lifting in the window breeze.

Nick sat on the scratchy backseat, felt his knuckles throbbing all the way up into his ears. Still seeing double sometimes, his neck thick with pain and a big lump risen on the back of his head. Didn't say anything to his parents about the vision trouble because he hated doctors.

David sat up front beside his mom, thinking he'd be glad to get to State, out of this stupid small-town stuff, into something more than oranges and fistfights.

Clay sat in the back, pummeling Casey Vonn

again between thoughts of this Dorothy girl in his homeroom. Wished he could smoke like his dad was doing. The Vonns were shitheels.

Between Clay and Nick, young Andy sat with the pride of the new warrior, his heart beating hard and true. He had fought alongside Nick, and they had won. The world outside the windows of the Studebaker now seemed not only larger but more attainable.

The Vonns' house was old but it sat right around the corner from a new tract freshly cut from an orange grove. The house was wood—not stucco like the new ones—and the white paint was peeling and the roof sagged and two of the windows were plywood. The lawn was just dead weeds. The new tract had streetlights but they stopped short of the Vonn place.

"We're staying here, boys," said Monika Becker, turning her pretty face to the backseat.

"I'm not going to apologize," said Clay.

"You'll do exactly what your father told you to."

"I won't mean it."

"That's another topic, Clay. For now, keep a civil tongue in your head and mind your manners."

Nick watched his father flick his cigarette butt into the curb and start up the dark driveway. Khaki trousers and a white shirt tucked in with the sleeves rolled up. Irish Setter boots and a belt the same color. Nick had always liked the old man's walk: loose and casual but his head always up and steady. His father didn't miss much. He could tell what was wrong with an orange grove by looking at one leaf from it, tell a grower how to up the yield without running down the sugars or ruining the soil. Hardly needed his lab over at the SunBlesst corporate building for things like that. He could see his wife's depressions coming days before they hit, would rearrange his work hours to be there for her. Or, if they stood in the corner of an orange grove in early September with their Remington pumps, it was always his father who saw the birds way out in the blue, his father who could tell a dove from a nighthawk through a hundred yards of twilight. And of course he'd knock it down before you were really sure you saw it.

A porch light went on and the door opened. Nick saw a small woman, then a tall man with overalls and no shirt. The woman's hair was dark and pulled back tight. She looked older than his mom, but Nick figured they must be about the same age. Mr. Vonn had long, active muscles that bunched when he shook Nick's father's hand. A dark triangular face, small chin. He looked to Nick like a man from another country.

Nick listened to their voices through the open window of the Studebaker, but he couldn't make out much. His father gestured back to the car, canting his head inquisitively. Then Mr. Vonn disappeared and Mrs. Vonn turned and watched. She brought her hand to her collar. A minute later the three Vonn boys came single file onto the porch—Lenny, then Casey, then Ethan. Casey's eyebrows and cheeks were covered by white tape.

"Oh my gosh, boys—what did you do to that poor Ethan?"

"That's Casey," said Clay.

"Don't confuse the issue, Clay."

"They started it, Mom," he said.

She snapped around and caught his face in her big hand. When she was angry her voice went to a throaty hiss and her lips pulled back around her big straight teeth and Nick thought she was scarier than his dad. *You started it, Clay. You started it with the baseball cap and your arrogant attitude. Don't you lie to me.*

"No, ma'am, no."

"Someday someone's going to rain on your parade in a big way, Clay. That, I guarantee. And when it happens we'll see how tough you are."

Then Max Becker turned to wave them out of the car.

Monika locked eyes with each of them in turn. "Do not disappoint me, boys. Do exactly what we talked about."

They stood behind their father on the porch, spread in the pool of light. The Vonn boys faced them from a few feet away. Nick saw that Casey's face was swollen badly and Lenny's nose was huge and red. Their big ears were backlit pink by the porch light. He saw that Mrs. Vonn's knuckles were big where she held her collar and stared at him with shiny black eyes.

Clay apologized unconvincingly but handed Casey a dollar to cover the baseball cap. Said to give him the change at school.

Max Becker cleared his throat.

David and Andy said they were sorry.

When it was Nick's turn he was looking not at the Vonns but beyond them, into the living room behind the open door, at the peeling walls and sagging brown sofa and the floor lamp with the dented shade and the fraying braided rug and the cheap lighted china hutch with nothing inside it but a few coffee mugs and votive candles and a collector's plate with the face of the Virgin Mary on it displayed upright in the flickering light.

He had never seen such failure before. And he understood in one instant that it could be his someday.

"I'm sorry," he said. He meant it for Lenny but couldn't take his eyes off the room.

The Vonn boys didn't say a word. Nick figured they were thinking revenge.

Just then the Vonn daughters hustled into his vision, the older one still in her dirty pink blouse, holding a cob of corn and glaring at him. Then Janelle Vonn, changed into a white dancer's tutu that hung almost to her knees, clunked across the floor in her cowboy boots with a small guitar slung over one shoulder. She had the same inquisitive look she'd had out in the orange grove, and one eye swollen shut and blackening.

"I'm sorry," Nick said again.

Mrs. Vonn turned back into the house and the girls scattered away like chicks. The door slammed.

His parents said nothing on the drive back home. Nick could tell that a new worry had taken ahold of them. Not the rumble. That was over now. Their dad had locked their shotguns in the gun cabinet and told them there'd be no bird hunting this year. Said that boys who couldn't control their fists couldn't be trusted with firearms. Pretty goddamned simple. Backhanded Clay hard above one ear, sent him spinning. Would have taken a belt to them like the old days, but even Andy was too big for that now.

No, the new worry was Janelle, and how she'd gotten her eye closed. Nick was pretty sure it was connected to him hitting Lenny. And Clay hitting Casey. And Ethan hitting David. Maybe even his father hitting Clay. Each hit causing the next one until there was no one left to hit but a little girl with a tutu and a guitar.